From
SAND
and
ASH

From
SAND
and
ASH

AMY HARMON

LAKE UNION
PUBLISHING

Text copyright © 2016 Amy Sutorius Harmon
All rights reserved.

Published by Lake Union Publishing, Seattle

www.apub.com

Amazon, the Amazon logo, and Lake Union Publishing are trademarks of Amazon.com, Inc., or its affiliates.

ISBN-13: 9781503939325
ISBN-10: 1503939324

Cover design by Laura Klynstra

Printed in the United States of America

To the real Rabbi Nathan Cassuto—
I have no words, only awe

PROLOGUE

24 March, 1944

Angelo must have slept in the damp grass beside the road for a while, but the evening was cold and his cassock was thin, and he awoke, shivering. Even that small movement made him moan, but at least the sharp pain along his right side revived him. It was dark, and his mouth was so dry he licked the dew from the grass near his face. He had to move in order to get warm, and he had to move to find water. He had to move to find Eva.

He struggled to his feet and took a step, then another, telling himself that walking wouldn't hurt as badly as lying down. Each breath felt like fire, and he was pretty sure a few of his ribs were broken. The darkness and his bad leg made each step precarious, but he found the posture that hurt the least and settled into a sort of rhythm, limping along the Via Ardeatina toward Rome. At least he hoped he was going toward Rome. God help him if he was turned around. He could barely see out of his right eye, his left eye was swollen shut, and his nose was broken. No loss there. It had never been his best feature. He was missing three fingernails on his right hand, and the smallest finger on his left was broken. At one point he stumbled and fell, only to catch himself on his oddly bent pinkie. The pain had him retching and seeing stars, fighting to remain conscious. He gingerly pushed himself onto his knees so he could moan a prayer to the Madonna, begging her to help him just a little longer. She did, and he kept moving.

It wasn't that far to the Church of Santa Cecilia in Trastevere— five miles, maybe? But he was moving so slowly it would take him hours to reach it, and he had no idea what time it was. The darkness was welcome, if only to hide him. He was supposed to be dead, and he would be safer if people continued to believe it. He could only imagine how he looked—hair matted with blood and grime, his cassock filthy with gore and stinking of sweat and death. He'd been wearing it for three days. He looked like a messenger from hell instead of a member of God's army.

He knew there was another church along this road—there was a church or five along every road in Rome. He searched his memory for the pastor's name but couldn't produce it. There was a monastery nearby too, and a school. He'd placed a few refugees in each. Children. Jews. But the road was quiet. He hadn't seen a soul since the trucks carrying German soldiers, well-used weapons, and empty cases of cognac had rumbled away, leaving the old quarry and the catacombs behind. There was new death in the catacombs now. Old ghosts would have no more claim to the caves of Ardeatine.

It took him a painful eternity to reach the church, but he picked up his pace when he saw the fountain. He practically fell into it, face-first, choking when he gasped in pain and inhaled a mouthful of water instead of swallowing it. It was brackish and would probably make him sick, but it was the best thing he'd ever tasted. He drank his fill and eased himself up, trying not to cry out as his shredded fingertips grazed the icy surface. He washed as best he could, cleaning the blood and dirt from his hair and his skin. If he didn't make his destination before sunrise, he wanted to make himself as presentable as possible, and the water revived him.

He started in fright when a shadow loomed over him, only to realize it was just a man made of stone. A statue. The statue looked down in frozen compassion, hands extended but unable to help him. Angelo didn't know the name of the saint or the significance of the statue—the name of the church eluded him too—but something about it, the solemnity of expression, the melancholy acceptance in the stance, made him think of Donatello's sculpture of Saint George and the day Angelo had found his calling.

He'd been thirteen when Saint George had spoken to him. Not audibly. Angelo wasn't a fool or a seer. But Saint George had spoken to him, all the same. He'd been on crutches that day, his leg too sore to wear his prosthetic. The school excursion had tired him, and keeping up with the other boys was of little interest to him anyway. Father Sebastiano had brought them to the Palazzo del Bargello, and Angelo hadn't made it much farther than the entrance when he saw the statue.

It was recessed and elevated so he couldn't touch it. But he wanted to. He got as close as he could and stood with his head back, gazing up at the statue as Saint George stared off into an ancient distance with an innocence that belied his armor and a fearlessness that contradicted the concerned slant of his brows. His eyes were wide and clear, his back was straight, and he faced the approaching threat with steadiness, though he barely looked old enough to wield a sword. Angelo could only gape at his face, transfixed. He'd stayed in that same position for a long time, ignoring the famed dome, the frescoes, and the stained glass. The enormity of the museum and all its wonders were reduced to that one sculpture.

Now, more than a dozen years later, he stood peering up at a statue that wasn't Donatello's famed sculpture, yet he beseeched him anyway. "Help me, *San Giorgio*," he said aloud, hoping the heavens were listening. "Help me to face what is to come."

Angelo turned and staggered away from the fountain, back to the road that was as ancient as Rome itself, feeling the eyes of the unknown sculpture on his weary back. Angelo's thoughts returned to his champion, to the long-ago afternoon when things had been made so clear, when immortality seemed like a prize and not terrible torture. He hurt too much to be tempted by immortality now. Death sounded so much more inviting.

That long-ago afternoon, he had eventually been joined in his contemplation of Saint George, but was unaware of it until the man spoke up, telling him the story behind the art.

"George was a Roman soldier, a captain of sorts. He would not renounce his faith in Christ. He was promised gold and power and riches if he would simply worship the gods of the empire. See, the emperor did not want to kill him. He valued young George very much. But George refused."

Angelo had pulled his eyes from Donatello's sculpture. The man beside him was a priest like Father Sebastiano, older than Angelo's father, but younger than his grandfather, Santino. The priest's eyes were bright and his hair neatly groomed. His face was kind and curious, but his hands were clasped behind his back, his very posture bearing solemn witness to his self-denial.

"Did he die?" Angelo had asked.

"Yes, he did," the priest answered gravely.

Angelo had supposed as much, but the truth still wounded him. He had wanted the young hero to be victorious.

"He died, but he defeated the dragon," the priest added gently.

That hadn't made any sense to Angelo, and he wrinkled his nose in confusion as his eyes returned to the sculpture and the huge shield in George's hand. He thought this was a true story, and there was no such thing as a dragon.

"The dragon?" he asked. "He fought a dragon?"

"Evil. Temptation. Fear. The dragon is a symbol of the battle he must have waged within himself to stay true to his God."

Angelo nodded, understanding perfectly. They fell into silence once more, staring at the sculpture of the soldier brought to life by a master's hand.

"What's your name, young man?" the priest had asked him.

"Angelo," he answered. "Angelo Bianco."

"Angelo, Saint George lived more than fifteen hundred years ago. Yet we are still talking about him. I think that makes him immortal . . . don't you?"

The thought had moved Angelo to tears that he tried to blink away. "Yes, Father," he whispered. "I do."

"He risked everything, and he is now immortal."

He risked everything, and he is now immortal.

Angelo groaned, the memory making his stomach twist. Oh, the irony. Oh, the incredible, terrible irony. He too had risked everything, and he may have lost the only thing he would trade his immortality for.

As dawn started to creep into the eastern sky, pale light falling over spires and campaniles onto the Eternal City, Angelo finally reached the gates of Santa Cecilia. The bells of Lauds began to ring, as if to welcome him back, but Angelo could only cling to the iron spires and pray that, by some miracle, Eva waited for him inside.

Mother Francesca discovered him a few minutes later, sitting with his back against the gate as if he'd been propped there by Satan's henchmen. She must have thought he was dead, because she cried out in horror, crossing herself as she ran for assistance. Angelo was too tired to reassure her.

He watched through swollen lids as Mario Sonnino appeared above him, checking his pulse and crying out instructions to several others to carry him inside.

"It's not safe." Angelo struggled to speak. Mario was not safe outside the gate. Mario was not safe *inside* the gate.

"Someone could see you," Angelo tried to warn him, but the words were sloppy on his lips.

"Take him up the stairs to Eva's room!" Mario commanded.

"Where's Eva?" Angelo asked, forcing the words out, needing to know.

No one answered him. They took the stairs quickly, and Angelo cried out as his ribs protested the motion. He was laid carefully on the bed, and Eva's scent rose up around him.

"Eva?" he asked again, louder this time. He peered through the eye that wasn't completely swollen shut, trying to see, but the shapes were blurred and the people were ominously silent.

"We haven't seen her for three days, Angelo," Mario finally answered. "The Germans took her."

24 March, 1944

Via Tasso

*Confession: My name is Batsheva Rosselli, not Eva Bianco,
and I am a Jew. Angelo Bianco is not my brother but a priest
who wanted only to protect me from the very place I now find
myself.*

*The first time I met Angelo, he was a child. Like me. A child with eyes that
had known too much disappointment for someone so young. He didn't speak
for a long time after he arrived in Italy. He just watched. I thought it was
because he was American. I thought it was because he didn't understand.
It makes me laugh a little to think of it now, how I would act things out
and speak so loudly, as if there were something wrong with his ears. I would
dance around him, playing my violin and singing little songs, just to see if
he would smile. When he did, I would hug him and kiss his cheeks. There
was nothing wrong with his ears or his comprehension. He understood me
perfectly. He was just listening. Observing. Learning.*

    *Camillo, my very patient father, would tell me to leave him alone, but
I couldn't. I simply couldn't. I realize now how the pattern never changed.
I danced around him for years, trying to get his attention, wanting only to
see him smile. Wanting only to be near him, wanting only to love him and*

be loved by him. I was rebelling even then, pushing back against the fear, though I didn't recognize it. Rebellion was always my biggest ally, though sometimes I hated her. She looked like me and hurt like me, but she wouldn't let me give up. And when fear took my reasons for fighting, rebellion gave them back.

My father told me once that we are on earth to learn. God wants us to receive everything that life was meant to teach. Then we take what we've learned, and it becomes our offering to God and to mankind. But we have to live in order to learn. And sometimes we have to fight in order to live.

This is my offering. These are the lessons I learned, the tiny acts of rebellion that kept me alive, and the love that fed my hope, when I had nothing but hope itself.

Eva Rosselli

1929

CHAPTER 1
FLORENCE

"Santino has a grandson. Did you know that?" Eva's father asked.

"Nonno has a grandson?" Eva asked.

"Yes, Nonno. Though he isn't really your *nonno*. You know that too, don't you?"

"He *is* my *nonno*, because he loves me so much," Eva reasoned.

"Yes, but he isn't my father, and he wasn't your mamma's father. So he isn't your grandfather," her father explained patiently.

"Yes, Babbo. I know," Eva said crossly, not at all sure why he insisted. "So Fabia isn't really my grandmother." It felt like a lie to say such a thing out loud.

"Yes. Exactly. Santino and Fabia had a son, you see. He left Florence and went to America when he was a young man, because there was more opportunity for him there. He married an American girl, and they had a little boy."

"How old is the boy?"

"Eleven or twelve. He is a couple of years older than you."

"What's his name?"

"His name is Angelo, like his father, I think. But, please, Batsheva, listen for a moment. Stop interrupting." Eva's *babbo* only used her long name when he was growing impatient, so she listened and held her tongue.

"Angelo's mother died," he said sadly.

"Is that why Nonna was crying yesterday when she read her telegram?" Eva had already forgotten that she wasn't supposed to interrupt.

"Yes. Santino and Fabia want their son to bring the boy to Italy. He has had some medical problems, an issue with his leg, apparently. They want him to live here. With us. At least for a while. Santino's older brother is a priest, and they think the boy can go to the seminary here in Florence. He is a little old to start, but he was in a Catholic school in America, so he won't be too far behind. He may even be advanced." Her father said this as if he were thinking out loud, rather than communicating anything Eva actually needed to hear. "And I will help where I can," he mused.

"We will be friends, I think," Eva said. "Because we have both lost our mothers."

"This is true. And he will need a friend, Eva."

Eva couldn't remember her mother. She died of tuberculosis when Eva was little. Eva had a vague memory of her lying very still in bed with her eyes closed. Eva couldn't have been more than four years old, but she could still remember the height of that bed and the elation of success when she pulled herself up and over the side while clutching her tiny violin. She had wanted to play a song for her.

She had crawled to her mother's side and touched her feverish cheek, the high, red color of a consumptive making her look like a rouged doll. Her mother had opened her lids slowly, her eyes glazed and drugged, furthering the comparison. It had frightened Eva, the almost lifeless figure with glassy blue eyes staring up at her. Then Eva's mother had said her daughter's name, and it crackled and broke between her lips like old paper.

"Batsheva," she had whispered, the word followed by a cough that had racked her frame and made her body shake. The way she said the name, the rasping whisper, the way she sighed through the syllables like it was the last word she would ever say, had made Eva hate her name for a very long time. When her father would call her Batsheva after her mother's death, she would cry and cover her ears.

That's when her *babbo* had started to call her Eva.

That was all Eva remembered of her mother's life, of their very short life together, and she had tried to forget it. It wasn't a memory she cherished. She would much rather hold her mother's picture, pretending to remember the lovely woman with the soft brown hair and porcelain skin, holding Eva in her lap, sitting next to a much younger Camillo, no gray in his black hair, his face serious beneath smiling brown eyes.

Eva had tried to remember being the infant in the frame, the tiny girl who sat in her mother's lap and gazed up intently at the woman who held her. But hard as she tried, she couldn't remember that woman. Eva didn't even look like her mother. She just looked like her father, Camillo, with paler skin and rosier lips.

It was hard to love or miss someone you didn't even know.

Eva wondered if Angelo, Santino's grandson, loved his mother. She hoped he didn't love her too much. Loving someone and then losing them would be much worse than not having them at all.

"Why are you so sad?" Eva asked, pulling her knees up under her long nightgown. She'd found Angelo watching the storm in her father's library, the doors opened to the balcony, the rain falling heavily onto the pink flagstones below. She didn't think he would answer. He hadn't answered her yet. He had been living in their villa with his *nonno* and *nonna* for three months, and Eva had done everything in her power to make him her friend. She had played the violin for him. She had danced for him. She had splashed in the fountain in her school uniform and gotten scolded just to make him laugh. He did laugh sometimes. And that kept her trying harder. But he'd never talked to her.

"I miss my mother."

Eva's heart lurched in surprise. He was talking to her. In Italian. Eva knew Angelo understood when he was spoken to, but she had expected him to speak in English, like an American.

"I don't remember my mother. She died when I was four," she said, hoping he would say something else.

"You don't remember anything?" he asked.

"My father has told me some things. My mother was Austrian, not Italian like my *babbo*. Her name was Adele Adler. Beautiful name, isn't it? I write it sometimes in my very best penmanship. Her name sounds like an American film star. She even looked like one a little. My father says it was love at first sight." She was babbling, but Angelo was looking at her with interest, so she didn't stop.

"The first time my *babbo* saw my mamma, he was in Vienna on business, selling his wine bottles. Babbo has a glass company, you know. He sells his bottles to all the wineries. Austria has very good wine. Babbo has let me taste it." She thought Angelo should know how sophisticated she was.

"Did she play the violin too?" Angelo asked hesitantly.

"No. Mamma wasn't musical. But she wanted me to be a great violinist just like my grandfather Adler. He is very famous. Or so Uncle Felix says." She shrugged. "Tell me about your mother."

He was silent for several seconds, and Eva thought he was going to revert to silence once again.

"Her hair was dark like yours," he whispered. He reached out slowly and touched her hair. Eva held her breath as he fingered a long curl and then dropped his hand.

"What color were her eyes?" she asked gently.

"Brown . . . like yours too."

"Was she beautiful like me?" This was asked without guile, for Eva had always been told how beautiful she was and accepted it with a shrug.

The boy tipped his head to the side and reflected on this. "I suppose. To me she was. And she was soft." He said the word in English, and Eva wrinkled her nose at this, not sure she understood. "Soft? *Soffice o grassa?*"

"No. Not *grassa*. Not fat. Everything about her comforted me. She was . . . soft." The answer was so wise, so specific, so old, that she could only stare.

"But . . . your *nonna* is soft too," she offered eventually, trying to find something, anything, to say.

"Not in the same way. Nonna fusses. She tries to make me happy. Nonna wants to give me love. But it isn't the same. Mamma *was* love. And she didn't even have to try. She just . . . was."

They sat watching the rain then, and Eva thought about mothers and lovely, soft things and the lonely way the rain made her feel, even though she wasn't alone.

"Do you want to be my brother, Angelo? I don't have a brother. I would like one very much," she said, her gaze tracing his profile.

"I have a sister," Angelo whispered, not answering her, not looking away from the rain. "She is still in America. She was born . . . and my mamma died. And now she is in America, and I am here."

"Your father is there with her, though."

He shook his head sadly. "He gave her to my aunt. She is my mamma's sister. She wanted a baby."

"She didn't want you?" Eva asked, confused. Angelo shrugged as if it didn't matter.

"What is her name . . . your baby sister?" Eva pressed.

"Papà named her Anna after Mamma."

"You will see her again."

Angelo turned his face toward her, and his eyes were more gray than blue in the shadow of the small lamp on Camillo's desk.

"I don't think I will. Papà said Italy is my home now. I don't want Italy to be my home, Eva. I want my family." His voice broke, and he looked down at his hands like he was ashamed at his weakness. It was the first time he had said her name, and Eva reached for his hand.

"I will be your family, Angelo. I will be a good sister. I promise. You can even call me Anna when we are alone if you want to."

Angelo swallowed, his throat working, and his hand tightened around hers.

"I don't want to call you Anna," he said with a sob in his throat. He looked at Eva again, blinking away tears. "I don't want to call you Anna, but I will be your brother."

"You can be a Rosselli if you want to. Babbo wouldn't mind."

"I will be Angelo Rosselli Bianco." He smiled at that and swiped at his nose.

"And I will be Batsheva Rosselli Bianco."

"Batsheva?" It was Angelo's turn to furrow his brow.

"Yes. It's my name. But everyone just calls me Eva. It's a Hebrew name," she said proudly.

"Hebrew?"

"Yes. We are *ebrei*."

"*Ebrei?*"

"We are Jews."

"What does that mean?"

"I'm not sure, exactly." She shrugged. "I don't go to religious lessons at school. And I'm not Catholic. Most of my friends don't know our prayers, and they don't go to temple. Except my cousins Levi and Claudia. They are Jewish too."

"You aren't Catholic?" Angelo asked, shocked.

"No."

"Do you believe in Jesus?"

"What do you mean, believe in him?"

"That he is God?"

Eva wrinkled her forehead. "No. I don't think so. Jesus is not what we call him."

"You don't go to Mass?"

"No. We go to temple. But not very often," she admitted. "My *babbo* says you don't have to go to a synagogue to talk to God."

"I went to a Catholic school and Mass every Sunday. Mamma and I always went to Mass." Angelo hadn't lost the shocked expression on his face. "I don't know if I can be your brother, Eva."

"Why?" she squeaked, perplexed.

"Because we aren't the same religion."

"Jews and Catholics can't be brothers and sisters?"

Angelo was quiet, contemplative. "I don't know," he admitted finally.

"I think they can," she said firmly. "Babbo and Uncle Augusto are brothers, and they don't agree on very much."

"Well, then. We will agree on everything else," Angelo said gravely. "To make up for it."

Eva nodded, just as solemnly. "Everything else."

"Why are you always arguing with me?" Angelo sighed, throwing his hands in the air.

"I'm not always arguing with you!" Eva argued.

Angelo just rolled his eyes and tried to shake his persistent shadow. She followed him everywhere, and he usually didn't mind, but he'd spent the morning teaching her to play baseball—nobody in Italy played baseball—and now his leg was bothering him. He wanted Eva to go away so he could attend to it.

"So, what exactly is wrong with your leg?" Eva asked, noticing his discomfort. She'd already taught Angelo the basics of soccer, and though Angelo couldn't run very well, he could protect and defend. He was a superb goalie. Still, as much time as they'd spent playing together, he hadn't ever talked about his leg, and she'd been surprisingly patient, waiting for him to reveal the secret. She was tired of waiting.

"There's nothing wrong with it . . . exactly. It just isn't all there."

Eva sucked in her breath in horror. A missing leg was so much worse than she had imagined.

"Can I see?" she begged.

"Why?" Angelo shifted uncomfortably.

"Because I've never seen a missing leg."

"Well, that's the problem. You can't see what isn't there."

Eva sighed in exasperation. "I want to see the part that *is* there."

"I would have to take off my trousers," he challenged, trying to shock her.

"So?" she said saucily, shrugging her shoulders. "I don't care about your smelly underwear."

When he raised his eyebrows in surprise, she pressed sweetly, "Please, Angelo? No one shows me anything interesting. Everyone treats me like a baby."

Everyone did treat Eva like a tiny princess. She was doted on, and Angelo had noticed that she didn't especially enjoy it.

"All right. But you have to show me something too."

"Like what?" She lowered her brows doubtfully. "My legs are just normal. My whole body is normal. What do you want me to show you?"

Angelo seemed to ponder that for a moment. Eva was sure he was going to ask to see her girl parts. Nonno would paddle them, and Nonna would cross herself and get out her black beads and start praying if they were caught, but Eva was curious too and wouldn't mind having her questions about boy parts answered.

"I want you to show me that book you write in. And I want you to read it to me," Angelo said.

Eva was surprised, but it was probably safer than show-and-tell, and she only had to think about it for five seconds.

"All right." Her hand shot out to take his in a brisk handshake. From Angelo's glower, she knew he was worried about the deal he'd made. Her willingness to shake probably had him thinking he was getting the raw end of it. He probably thought she wrote about him. She did. But she didn't care if he knew about it.

Still, he shook her hand and began to pull up his right pant leg. All the other Florentine boys wore short pants almost year-round, but not Angelo. Angelo looked like a little man in his trousers and ugly black boots.

"I thought you had to take off your trousers!" Eva huffed, not liking that she'd already been lied to.

"I just wanted to see what you'd say. You aren't a lady, that's for sure."

"I am too! I'm just not a silly lady who makes a fuss about a boy's baggy underwear."

He stretched his leg out, the adjustable steel columns strapped to his knee and upper leg on one end and attached to a black boot on the other.

Eva touched the adjustable braces with an outstretched hand, fascinated.

"It helps me walk. My *papà* made it for me." His face changed at the mention of his father, the way it always did. Angelo's father was a blacksmith, and he had promised to train Angelo to make things out of metal too. Angelo didn't need two legs to build things with his hands. But that had been before his mother died. His father was in America, Angelo was in Italy, and nobody would be teaching Angelo to work metal.

"Can you take it off?" Eva really wanted to see him in all his legless glory. Angelo unbuckled the straps and moaned a little, as if it were a relief to loosen them.

He pulled the prosthetic free, and Eva stared down at the leg that ended just below his knee, her eyes wide, her lips parted in a soundless *O*.

Angelo looked embarrassed and maybe a little ashamed, as if he'd done something wrong. She reached out and took his hand immediately.

"Does it hurt?" The leather looked soft, and he wore a thick sock to protect his skin from the weight and pull of the contraption. But it wasn't like pulling on a boot, and the oddly shaped lump just below his knee was red and chafed.

"Wearing the metal leg is a little uncomfortable. But I like being able to walk. I used a crutch for a long time. The brace is adjustable, and it will grow with me, at least for a few years. I can still use the crutch when my leg gets tired."

"How did you lose your leg?"

"I never really had it."

"You were born without it?"

"My mother said the doctor thinks the cord in her stomach was wrapped around it early on and it wasn't getting any blood. It didn't grow right and parts of my leg died. They removed the dead parts after I was born." He shrugged. "Mamma said it wasn't a big deal if I didn't allow it to be."

"Some of it grew right." Eva's eyes were on the muscles of his bared thigh, and Angelo blushed and immediately began reattaching his metal leg so he could push his trousers back down. His embarrassment made Eva blush too. She just wanted him to know his leg looked fine to her.

"I do exercises every day. I jump and lunge and squat so that my legs are strong. The doctors told me that the stronger I am, the more I can do. I am very strong," he added shyly, his eyes darting to Eva's face before he looked down again. She was impressed, and she smiled, nodding.

Eva suddenly stood up and left the room. Angelo watched her go, probably wondering if she was done with him, but she was back before he was finished buckling the final strap. She held a book in her hands, and she sat down close to him on his bed. He scooted over immediately, almost falling onto the floor. She wondered if she made him feel shaky inside. She felt like that around him sometimes. But she kind of enjoyed the sensation. He glanced at Eva, and she recognized the look. Babbo looked at her like that when she did something he didn't understand.

"Don't you want to see my book?" she asked.

"I want you to show me," he insisted, not taking it.

"Okay. Well, this is my book of confessions." She opened the soft leather cover and turned through the pages, not letting him get a very good look at any of them.

"You have very nice penmanship, but I don't read Italian very well. Speaking it is one thing, but I've only ever read in English."

Eva nodded, glad that he couldn't easily read her thoughts or her words.

"I thought it was your diary." He sounded disappointed. "Who are you confessing to?" he asked.

"Oh, it's definitely my diary. But I confess things. Very private things." She waggled her eyebrows at him, letting him know that he was hearing very privileged information indeed. Mostly, she just wrote about her day, but she had to make it sound good.

"Read one to me," Angelo insisted.

"I thought you were shy," she said drily. "You aren't. You are quite bossy, actually. I'm glad."

Angelo tapped the book, drawing Eva's attention from him to the pages.

"All right. I will read you the confession I wrote about you when you first arrived in Italy."

"About me?"

"Yes. You will like it, I think."

"I am so glad Angelo is here. I'm tired of being with adults all the time. Babbo says I am smarter and more mature than children my age because I've grown up surrounded by old people. That's good, I suppose. But I'm tired of old people. I want to play hide-and-seek and tag. I want to have someone to tell my secrets to. I want to slide down the bannister, jump on my bed, and climb out my bedroom window and sit on the roof with a friend, and not just the ones in my imagination.

Angelo is only eleven, two years older than I am, and I'm already as tall as he is. He's kind of small. Nonna says that is normal. Girls mature more quickly. She says he will catch up. But he is very handsome, and he has very beautiful eyes. They are far too beautiful for a boy, though. Of course, that is not his fault. His hair is curly like a girl's as well. He'll have to keep it short and never wear a dress. Otherwise he will be prettier than I, and I don't think I like that idea."

Angelo scowled at Eva, and she snickered at his displeasure.

"You *are* very handsome, you know," she teased. "Even if your nose is too big for your face."

"I don't think you have to worry that I will be prettier than you," he huffed. "You're the prettiest girl I've ever seen." When he realized what he'd said, his face flushed all over again.

"I didn't like that one," he said quickly. "Read me another."

And so she did. She read him confession after confession, and he listened as patiently as a priest.

1938

17 November, 1938

Confession: Sometimes I'm afraid to sleep.

I dreamed my old dream last night, the dream I've been having since I was nine years old, the one I don't understand but that seems to understand me. As always, it is dark in the dream, but the darkness is crowded. I can't see anything but the flash of moonlight through the small window high up on the wall and the slats that ring the darkness on all sides. I am moving, and I am scared.

I know I must reach the window, and suddenly my fingers are clutching at the ledge beneath the small opening, and the toes of my shoes are shoved into the slats that I've used as a ladder to reach it.

"If you jump they will punish us." Hands grab at my clothes, and I shake them off, kicking desperately.

"They will kill us!" a woman wails below me.

"You must think of the rest of us!"

"You will die if you jump," someone else hisses, and the consensus grows around me. But I can't listen.

My head fits through the opening, and the air against my face is like water. Like life. A waterfall of cold hope. I open my mouth and gulp it in, unable to quench the thirst clawing at my throat, yet I'm fortified by it anyway.

I force my shoulders through the window, clinging to everything and nothing, wiggling to free myself, and I'm suddenly hanging, headfirst, over a world that is racing and clattering, yet I can still hear my heart pounding in my chest.

Then I'm falling.

Eva Rosselli

CHAPTER 2
ITALY

Her father woke her, saying her name and shaking her fiercely, rescuing her from her dream.

"Eva! Eva!" He was afraid. She could hear it. And his fear made her afraid too. She opened her heavy lids and looked at him, and his face melted into relief.

"Eva! You scared me!" His voice broke, and he gathered her up, her tangled covers between them, his arms circling her back. His neck smelled like sandalwood and tobacco, and the comfort she drew from the scent made her limp and drowsy.

"I'm sorry," she whispered, not sure exactly why she needed to be sorry. She'd been asleep. That was all.

"No, *mia cara*. I should have known. When you were small you would sleep so deeply, Fabia would lay her head against your chest to make sure you were breathing. I suppose I forgot."

After a few moments, he let her go, and she slumped back against her pillows.

"I was dreaming," she said.

"Good dreams?"

"No." It hadn't been a good dream. "The same old dream. The one I've told you about before."

"Ahh. Did you jump this time?"

"Yes. I suppose I did. But not with my legs. With my whole body. I fell. Through the window. I let myself fall. Then I woke up."

"In dreams, we always wake up when we're falling. We always wake up before we land," her father soothed.

"That's good. Because landing will be very painful. Landing might kill me," she whispered.

"Then why are you jumping . . . in the dream? Why do you always want to jump?" her father asked.

"Because if I don't, I will die for sure." It was the truth. And in the dream she knew it. Jump or die.

Her father patted her cheek like she was eight instead of eighteen, almost nineteen, and she grabbed his hand and kissed his palm. He closed his hand over the kiss, the way he used to do when she was little.

He was almost to the door when she asked him, "Did I scream? Did I scream and wake you?"

"You screamed, but you didn't wake me. I was already awake." It was three in the morning, and she noticed suddenly how old her father looked. It scared her, worse even than the dream.

"Are you okay, Babbo?" she asked fearfully.

"*Sono felice se tu sei felice.*" I'm happy if you're happy. It was what he always said.

"I'm happy." She smiled at him affectionately.

"Then all is well in my world." Again, what he always said. He switched off her lamp, and her room was bathed in darkness. But he hovered at the door.

"I love you, Eva." His voice sounded strange, like he was crying, but she could no longer see his face.

"I love you too, Babbo."

Eva's father, Camillo Rosselli, knew what was coming. He thought he had sheltered his daughter from it, or maybe she was just Italian enough, young enough, naïve enough, that she completely missed the gathering storm and thought only of dancing in the rain. Most of her friends had no idea she was Jewish. Eva didn't remember she was Jewish most of the time. She had no sense of being different. She'd noticed the cartoons mocking the Jews, the occasional derogatory sign, and the articles in Santino's papers. Those things always infuriated her father. But it just seemed like politics to Eva, and politics in Italy was for the politicians, not the people—the people mostly shrugged and went about their lives.

Sure, she'd heard Camillo arguing with his brother, Augusto. But they argued constantly. They had argued at least once a week for Eva's entire life.

"Jews are the pure blood of Italy. The synagogue preceded the church," Augusto would say.

"This is true," Camillo would answer heatedly and pour more wine.

"We lost friends and family in the Great War. All in the defense of our country, Camillo. Surely that counts for something."

Camillo would nod and sip, sip and nod.

"I trust the Fascists more than the Communists," Augusto would add.

"I see no reason to trust either," Camillo would retort.

And that is where Augusto and Camillo would not see eye to eye, and they would spend the evening smoking, sipping, and arguing about Il Duce and the Blackshirts versus the Bolsheviks.

"No freedom-loving Jew can support an ideology that uses force and intimidation to gain followers." Camillo would point a long finger at his younger brother.

"But, Camillo, at least they don't seek to take our religion from us. The Fascists are as disdainful of Catholic conservatism as we are. It's about nationalism. Revolution, even."

"Revolution rarely helps the Jew." Augusto would groan loudly and throw up his hands in disgust. "When was the last time you went to temple, eh, Camillo? You are more Italian than you are Jewish. Does Eva even know our prayers? Did you even realize today is Shabbat?"

Camillo would shift guiltily in his seat, but his answer was always the same. "I know it is Shabbat, and of course Eva knows the prayers! I am a Jew. I will always be a Jew. Eva is a Jew. She will always be a Jew. Not because we go to the synagogue. Not because we observe holidays. It is our heritage. It is who we are, who we will always be."

Lately, they had talked more and more about the growing anti-Semitism in the reports on the radio and in the newspapers. Camillo's brother-in-law, Felix Adler, with his clipped German-Austrian accent, so different from the rising and falling, rolling Italian the rest of the family spoke, had even threatened to leave Italy when the *Manifesto della Razza* had been published in the newspapers last July, causing an uproar that ruined August. The family had vacationed on Maremma, just like they did every year, escaping the heat of the city for the seashore. But the Manifesto of Race had come along with them and occupied their thoughts and hijacked their happiness.

"Mussolini is building a case against us. He is saying we Jews haven't served our country well. It is our fault that wages are low and taxes are high. It is our fault that housing is limited, food is scarce, and schools are crowded. It is because of the Jews that there are no jobs and crime rates are soaring, you know," Camillo had said, shaking his head in disgust.

Augusto would scoff. He was always more optimistic than his older brother. "The only newspapers that are printing things like that are those trying to get government money. They spew the nonsense and cozy up to the Fascist powers that be. Nobody believes it. Italians know better."

"But Italians are allowing it. It is being tolerated. Whether our friends like it or not, it is being tolerated. We Jews are tolerating it! We are not so long out of the ghetto that we have grown a sense of righteous indignation. We hope that the worst won't happen, all the while expecting that it will, so when it does, we aren't surprised. You know, Augusto, someone leaned some old rusted gates against the wall across from the café on Via San Giana where I drink my coffee every morning. There was a sign on them. It said, 'Put the Jews Back in the Ghetto.' It's been there for over a week. No one has taken it down. I didn't take it down," he had added in a shamed murmur.

"The king will put a stop to it. Mark my words," Augusto pushed back.

"King Emmanuel will do what Mussolini tells him to do," Camillo had predicted with finality.

Eva had heard it all, but they were all old men to Eva. Camillo, Augusto, Mussolini, and the king. Old men who talked too much. And she was a young woman who was not inclined to listen.

On September 5, 1938, a week after returning from the seashore, a new law, authored by the Fascists and signed by the king, declared that Jews could no longer send their children to public or private Italian schools or be employed in any capacity in any Italian school from kindergarten to university. It was the first of many laws to come.

Eva had finished secondary school the spring before, and instead of applying to university, she decided to explore her options. Camillo had warned her not to wait to apply, but she had dragged her feet. She just wanted to play music for a while. She was a member of the Orchestra della Toscana and had been for two years, and she was the youngest violinist ever to win first chair. Plus, she had three boyfriends who kept her very busy—a Jewish boy who played the cello, a Catholic boy who played hard to get, and a Firenze policeman who looked handsome in his uniform and loved to dance. She was juggling them all with no plans to stop any time soon. She was young, beautiful, and life was good. So she didn't apply. And suddenly that door was closed to her.

The morning after the bad dream, Eva awoke to a different sort of nightmare. When she walked into the kitchen looking for breakfast, Santino was sitting in his regular spot at the scarred table where Fabia served his coffee—she said the dining room was for Camillo and Eva— and he was reading from *La Stampa*, a national newspaper he read every week from cover to cover. Three other papers were stacked beneath it, and every so often he ran his hand down his face, from eyebrows to chin, saying *"mio Dio"* like he couldn't believe what he was reading. Fabia was crying.

"What's wrong, Nonna?" Eva asked, going to her side immediately. Her thoughts rushed to Angelo, the way they always did, worried that something had happened to him.

"There are new laws, Eva," Santino said grimly. He tapped the page of newsprint he was holding. "More laws. Against the *ebrei*. The Jews."

"Where will we go?" Fabia asked Eva. "We don't want to leave you."

Eva could only shake her head in confusion. She took the paper from Santino, knowing he had a spare, and began to read.

Fabia was crying because it had suddenly become illegal for non-Jews to work in Jewish homes. She and Santino were Catholic. According to *La Stampa*, the new Racial Laws prohibited Jews from owning homes, property, or businesses above a certain value. Jewish-owned businesses couldn't employ more than one hundred people, and they had to be managed by non-Jews. Camillo's glass factory, Ostrica, had more than five hundred workers. His father had started the company, and Camillo had gotten a chemical engineering degree so he could be the best glassmaker possible, and he had made it hugely profitable. But none of that mattered now.

Not only could Jewish teachers not teach at the schools and universities, but no textbooks written by Jewish authors were allowed in Italian schools. Jews and non-Jews were no longer permitted to marry. Jews could not be legal guardians of non-Jews.

Camillo's father, Alberto Rosselli, had been born in the ghetto. It had only been sixty-eight years since the Jews in Italy had been freed and given the full rights of Italian citizens. And those rights had been taken away again. Now Jews couldn't hold political office. They couldn't serve in the military. Foreign Jews weren't allowed in Italy at all, which meant Felix Adler, Camillo's brother-in-law, had four months to leave, and going back to Austria was no longer an option.

Eva read the list over and over, examining the language, the details. Then she read it again, not able to fully comprehend what was happening, what had already happened.

Uncle Augusto, Aunt Bianca, Claudia, and Levi came over, and the family all talked in varying tones of incredulity, until they lapsed into nervous silence as the day wore on. Augusto could only scratch his head. "Why does this keep happening? Why the Jews? It is always the Jews!"

Camillo told Santino and Fabia that there were ways around the laws, and he would think of something. He told everyone not to worry, but for the first time in Eva's life, she didn't believe him.

By late afternoon, Eva couldn't stand the black mood in the villa and grabbed her hat and her pocketbook and walked to the seminary. It had been three years since she'd visited Angelo there.

In the beginning, Fabia and Eva would visit Angelo at the seminary almost every day. It made the transition easier for him, and they would walk to the trattoria and have a gelato or play a game of checkers in the piazza in his hour of free time. Padre Sebastiano, the director of the seminary, was indulgent with Angelo, giving him certain allowances due to his circumstances and regular donations from Camillo. Fabia would crochet, Angelo and Eva would talk and laugh, and Angelo would be fortified until they came again.

Slowly but surely, Angelo shed his little-boy-lost persona and became a true Italian seminarian, blending in with all the other boys who attended school with the goal of becoming Catholic priests. But when he turned fifteen, Angelo told Eva to stop waiting outside for him. He said it was frowned upon and the other boys teased him. Eva had laughed and said, "But we are family!"

He had looked at her then, his mouth pursed like he wanted to say something. He had waited until Fabia's attention was elsewhere.

"What, Angelo?" Eva huffed, her hands on her hips.

"You and I are not related, Eva."

"But we are family, Angelo!" She was hurt by his rejection, but he was unyielding, the way only Angelo could be.

"You are too beautiful, and I am too attached to you. And you are *not* my sister or my cousin or anything close," he repeated firmly, almost as if the truth of it made him sad. "The other boys think you are beautiful too. And they like to say things about you. And me. So I need you to stop coming here."

Things had changed between them after that. Eva stopped waiting outside the gate for him, and even though the seminary was only five blocks away from the villa they both called home, she only saw him on school holidays or on the weekends when he missed his grandparents. They still talked and laughed when they were together, and she still played the violin for him, but things had definitely changed.

She needed him now, though. She needed to talk to him, to tell him her world was falling apart. Their world. For their worlds were intertwined by their families, whether Angelo wanted to claim her or not.

She walked down the street, finding herself looking at the familiar buildings and people of her neighborhood through new eyes. No one acted any differently. No one stared at her or pointed a finger at her, yelling, *Ebreia!* Jew!"

Donna Mirabelli was walking toward her on the street, and when she reached Eva, she smiled warmly, greeting her the way she always did. The shops were open; the earth had not opened up and swallowed Italy whole. The laws were silly, Eva told herself. Nothing would change.

This time, Eva didn't wait at the gates for Angelo to appear. She walked across the piazza; past the fountain where John the Baptist stood in the center, his arms outstretched and surrounded by doves; and let herself in through the entrance with the neat little placard announcing to visitors that they had arrived at the Seminario di San Giovanni Battista. John the Baptist was the patron saint of Florence, and everything was named San Giovanni something or other. The door opened into a small foyer where a tired-looking priest with thinning hair was typing away at a little desk. A few students traversed the wide staircase beyond him. They stopped in their tracks when they saw her. Apparently, female visitors were unusual. The typing ceased and the priest looked up at Eva expectantly, removing his glasses.

"I need to see Angelo Bianco. Please. It is a family matter."

"Wait here, Signorina," he said politely, setting his spectacles down and smoothing his cassock as he stood. He walked swiftly to the double doors to his left, and Eva wondered if there was another set of stairs or if Angelo was just beyond the doors.

When Angelo appeared, his forehead creased with concern, his blue eyes wide, his hands outstretched toward her—he already had priestly mannerisms—Eva did her best to smile and put him at ease, though she wanted to throw herself at him. His hair was parted neatly and slicked down, tamed but not smooth. It rippled like the surface of the sea on a breezy night, dark and glossy. She fought the urge to run her fingers through it, freeing the curls. She gripped his hands instead and found herself fighting off tears.

"Can you walk with me?" she asked in a rush.

"Eva? What is it? Tell me what's wrong. What's happened?"

"Everyone is fine. It's not anything like that. I . . . just, please, Angelo. I need to speak with you."

"Give me a moment," Angelo acquiesced, and turned, walking as swiftly as his limp would allow. He was back a few minutes later with the wide-brimmed black hat typical of seminarians, and the cane he had stopped resisting.

"Can you just leave with me?" She felt like she was going to be detained at any moment.

"I am twenty-one years old, Eva. And I am not a prisoner. I've told Padre Sebastiano that I am needed at home and will be back in the morning."

They walked across the piazza and out into the street, but Eva didn't want to go home. Not yet.

"Can we walk for a bit? I've spent all day listening to Fabia's tears, my father's strategizing, and Santino's hammering. Why does he always find something to hammer when he's upset? Uncle Felix has been playing the violin all day—terrible, terrible songs—and when he's not, he's pacing."

"The laws." Angelo didn't ask. He already knew.

"Yes. The laws. I can't go to school now, Angelo. Did you know that? I should have enrolled last summer, like my father told me to do. They are letting Jews already enrolled in the universities continue with their studies. But I wasn't enrolled. Now I can't. No new Jewish entrants allowed."

"Madonna," Angelo breathed, the word sounding like a curse instead of a plea. They walked in silence, both of them lost in helpless fury.

"What will you do instead of school?" he asked finally.

"I wanted to teach music. But there will be many Jewish teachers looking for work now that they can't teach at the regular schools."

"You could teach private lessons."

"Only to Jewish students."

"Well . . . that's something, isn't it?" He tried to smile encouragingly. Eva frowned back at him.

"Maybe I will marry a nice Jewish boy and have fat Jewish babies and live in the ghetto! And maybe we will be run out of our country like the Schreibers were run out of Germany, like my Grandfather Adler is being run out of Austria, like Uncle Felix is being run out of Italy."

"What are you talking about? Who are the Schreibers?" Angelo tipped his head in question.

"The Schreibers! Remember? The German Jews who came to stay with us?" Eva couldn't believe he'd forgotten. When Adolf Hitler became chancellor of Germany in 1933, things started to go very badly for Germany's Jews. Laws had been passed, just like the laws being passed in Italy.

Eva stopped walking, her stomach churning. They had thought it couldn't happen in Italy. But they were just like the Schreibers. They were just like all the refugees that Camillo had opened his home to. For two years, they had had people in the guesthouse. Different families. All Jews. All Germans. And none of them stayed long. The Rosselli villa was a place to regroup before permanent plans could be made. All the refugees were quiet, and they kept to their rooms.

The Schreibers had a daughter who was Eva's age and one a little older—Elsa and Gitte. Eva thought they could all be friends—she spoke German—but the German girls never came out of the guesthouse. Eva complained in the beginning that they might as well not have guests at all. To her, having guests meant entertainment. Fun. Camillo explained that the refugees were tired and afraid, and none of this was fun for them.

"Afraid of what? They are in Italy now." Italy was safe. Italians didn't care if someone was Jewish.

"They have lost their homes, their businesses, their friends. Their whole lives! Mr. Schreiber isn't even Jewish."

"So why did *he* have to leave?"

"Because Mrs. Schreiber is."

"She is Austrian," Eva retorted, so sure of herself.

"She is an Austrian Jew. Just like Mamma was. Just like Uncle Felix is. It is illegal under the new laws in Germany for a German to be married to a Jew. Mr. Schreiber was going to be sent to prison even though he was married to Anika long before the laws were passed. So they had to leave."

The Schreibers were the first. But there had been many more. A steady stream, actually. Some were more open than others, relating horrors that seemed impossible. Uncle Augusto had even scoffed at some of the stories. Privately, of course, and only in conversation with Camillo, who grew increasingly gray during those two years. What couldn't be denied was that most of the refugees they took in, even if for only a short time, seemed to be in varying states of shock, and there was an ever-present nagging tension among them, as if any moment, the local authorities would swoop in and arrest them.

"I don't remember them, Eva," Angelo said softly. "But I do remember there being strangers for a while."

"For two years, Angelo! Then they just stopped coming. Babbo said they couldn't get out of Germany anymore." Eva hadn't really understood what that meant. She had just shrugged and life went on. But there were no more skittish Jews at the villa. Until now. Now their villa was full of skittish Jews.

Eva clenched her fists and stopped walking, needing every ounce of strength to keep her tears behind her lids. But they seeped out the corners and dribbled down the sides of her face. She turned and blindly walked the other direction, looking for someplace to let them fall without an audience. Angelo followed, a silent shadow, his slightly uneven gait oddly soothing. Eva walked without realizing that she'd known her destination all along.

She found herself just outside the San Frediano gate on Viale Ludovico Ariosto, standing at the entrance to the old Jewish cemetery. Her mother wasn't buried there. Her Rosselli grandparents weren't buried there either. The old cemetery had closed in 1880, almost sixty years ago, long before they died.

The tall cypress trees that lined the path leading from the entrance made her feel safe. They always had. Her father had brought her there once, long ago, and showed her where his maternal great-grandparents were buried. They were Nathans, and he was proud of the name. He said Nathan was a Jewish name with an impressive history. Sadly, Eva didn't remember it. But she loved the cemetery and had come back alone many times, setting her smooth stones on those Nathan headstones, vowing each time to ask Camillo more about her ancestors. But she never did. Very few stones decorated these headstones now. Sixty years was a long time to carry memories and leave pebbles in their place.

She had no stones with her today. No pebbles or pretty rocks. No weight in her pockets and far too much heaviness in her heart. The timeworn headstones reminded her of a mismatched chess set—some stones were fat and curved, others tall and ornate, but most were short and tottering, like ancient pawns. Eva liked to imagine the shape of the markers was a caricature of the person buried there, and she took pride in the royal stature of her ancestors' monuments. She wove her way to the far corner, to the little bench that someone had erected long ago to sit with long-dead loved ones. Angelo followed, still silent, but he'd pulled off his hat, as if wearing it among the graves was sacrilegious. It was ironic, she thought. Jewish men covered their heads—signifying themselves beneath God—for prayer and religious rituals, but she didn't tell Angelo.

"What is this place, Eva?" he asked, sitting beside her carefully, his hands in his lap, his hat in his hands, his cane leaning on the bench between them. Eva fought the urge to knock it down. She was tired of things that came between them.

"It's an old Jewish cemetery." She kicked at the blanket of fallen leaves and untended grass at her feet and upended a little rock. Leaning down, she retrieved it, brushed the dirt from its surface, and shined it between her palms. Then she stood and placed it on the base of the oldest Nathan headstone and sat back down next to Angelo. He reached for her hand and turned it over so he could see her palm.

"Why did you do that?" Angelo took out his handkerchief and started gently removing the grime from her hands. His tenderness wiped away her anger too. Eva's lips trembled, and she wanted to lay her head against his shoulder and cry out all her fear and confusion.

"Eva?" he prodded softly, when her answer never came. She swallowed back the feelings in her throat and tried to speak. Her voice was low, barely a whisper, when she finally responded.

"The story Babbo told me is that in ancient times it wasn't common to mark graves with a headstone or any kind of marker. Jews did it, but they did it to avoid inadvertently stepping or bending over a grave and desecrating it or becoming impure from the body beneath the ground. I don't know, exactly. It's a mitzvah." Eva shrugged, a uniquely Italian shrug that said, "I don't know, but knowing isn't very important."

"What's a mitzvah?"

"Something—a holy act or tradition—that elevates the mundane to the divine." Again, the shrug. "So before the days of headstones and markers, every person who walked by the grave added a rock, building it up, so the monument became permanent. I guess eventually someone thought of adding a bigger rock with a name or birth date, so people would know who was buried there. And now? Now we do it as a sign of remembrance."

"Something that elevates the mundane to the divine," Angelo murmured. "That's beautiful." He was done with her hands, and he gently returned them to her lap, ever respectful, ever careful. Eva didn't want her hands back. She needed Angelo to hold them tightly, to grip them in his and tell her everything was going to be all right. The emotion swelled again, and her thoughts were so loud, so insistent, that she pressed a trembling hand to her forehead so they wouldn't escape. But the devastation of the day had peeled back her defenses, and she found herself blurting out all the things she shouldn't say.

"I thought I would marry you someday, Angelo. Do you know that? I wanted to marry you. But that can't happen now, can it?"

He gasped but didn't answer. She finally made herself look at him, and his blue eyes clung to hers. There was awareness there—her words shocked him, but her feelings didn't.

"That was never going to happen, Eva. In one year, I will be able to receive the Holy Orders, and I will become a priest. I am going to be a priest, Eva. My path is set," he said firmly, but there was tension in the set of his lips, and the hand he raised to her cheek shook slightly. She pulled away in disgust, brushing at his hand like he was a persistent fly. Her feelings kept bouncing back and forth between tenderness and outrage.

"No. It can't happen because I'm a Jew. And it's now against the law for Catholics to marry Jews. It's against the law for me to love you, Angelo. It should make it so much easier for you now."

"What are you talking about, Eva?" Angelo kept his voice neutral, soft, like he was trying to calm a fretful child. But she wasn't a child, as Angelo was well aware.

"I've seen the way you look at me, Angelo. You want to be a priest, but you love me."

"Eva!" The word was like a whip, and Eva flinched. "You can't say things like that." He stood abruptly, his cane gripped in his hands. "We have to go. It will be dark soon, and after a day like today, your father will wonder where you've gone."

Eva stood, but she wasn't finished. "Babbo says so many boys become priests because of family pressures. Because they can get an education they may otherwise not get. He worried that you were forced into the seminary because your father and your grandparents wanted you to go and because you never felt like you had a home."

"It wasn't like that for me, Eva. You know that. You know being a priest is what I want."

"But you were a child." Her voice was hesitant. "How could you have known what it would cost?"

"It has cost me very little compared to what it has given me." His eyes were so clear, so guileless, yet so fierce, that it was all she could do to hold his gaze.

"God makes me strong. He gives me courage. He gives me peace. He gives me purpose." His voice was filled with conviction.

"And he can't give you those things unless you're a priest?" Eva asked sadly.

"No. No, Eva. I don't think he can. Not in the same way." He held out his arm—a peace offering—and Eva slipped her hand through it, letting him lead her out of the cemetery. They picked their way among the graves, and Eva was suddenly glad for his arm. Her anger and despair had boiled over and left her cold and weak, tired. She numbly placed one foot in front of the other until Angelo spoke again.

"I would have been a soldier. A pilot. If I'd been born with two good legs, I would have been a pilot. I've dreamed of flying since I could walk. Maybe it's because I couldn't run like the other boys. You don't need to run if you can fly. Now, with war in the air and Mussolini passing these insane laws, I'm grateful for my bad leg. I'm grateful I won't have to drop bombs and fight for things I don't believe in."

"Is the Catholic Church the only thing you believe in?"

Angelo sighed. "Eva, I don't understand what you're asking me."

"Do you believe in people? Do you believe in me?" Her voice was tired; she really wasn't trying to fight. Not anymore. Fighting with Angelo was like kicking a wall—she only ended up hurting herself.

"I put my faith in God. Not people," he said softly, stubbornly, and Eva wanted to slap him.

"But God works through people. Doesn't he?" Eva insisted.

He didn't answer but waited for her to continue, looking between her face and the road they walked along, the lengthening shadows giving them a sense of privacy. He hadn't even pulled his arm away, and Eva let herself cling to it.

"My father used to believe in Italy. Uncle Augusto even believed in Fascism. Fabia believes in the Pope, Santino believes in hard work, and you believe in the church. Do you know what I believe in, Angelo? I believe in my family. I believe in my father. I believe in Santino and Fabia. And I believe in you. The people I love most in the world. Love is the only thing I believe in."

"Don't cry, Eva. Please," Angelo whispered, and his voice broke in distress. Eva hadn't even realized she was. She raised a hand to her face and wiped at the moisture that clung to her cheeks.

"These laws are going to destroy all of us, Angelo. It's only going to get worse. I believe that too."

1939

29 June, 1939

Confession: I've never hated anyone before. Not a single soul.
But I'm learning.

There are more Racial Laws. Angelo raced home when he heard, only to find us completely unaware of what had transpired. He became the bearer of bad news—there is never good news anymore, it seems.

Jews can no longer practice their trade among non-Jews. Doctors, lawyers, journalists—all the trained professions. In one day, they lost their livelihoods. And that isn't all. We are banned from popular resorts and vacation spots. We can't spend our holidays at the beaches, the mountains, and the spas. We can't put advertisements or death notices in the newspapers. We can't publish books or give public lectures. We aren't even allowed to own radios.

I laughed at that one and said to Angelo, "We can't own radios? What about electric razors? Babbo loves his new electric razor—don't get too attached, Babbo! What's next? Washing machines? Telephones?"

Angelo didn't laugh. Instead, he stared down at the decree in his hands.

"You can still own a telephone. But your names will no longer be listed in the telephone directories, and you are barred entrance from certain public buildings." No one had laughed after that. The absurdity of it all was the most insulting part. And the insults never seem to end.

Eva Rosselli

CHAPTER 3
VIENNA

"My father won't leave his apartment. He says the last time he did, a German soldier made him scrub the sidewalk. The bleach burned his hands, and he can't play his violin." Uncle Felix threw himself onto the sofa and buried his face in his hands.

"They stormed his house and took his art, his valuables. He is living in my old bedroom, with nothing but his violin—which he is lucky to have—and he is worried that he can't play because of the sores on his hands. There is a German commandant living in his apartment, sleeping in his bed, eating off his plates, and sitting at his table! But he still thinks he will be able to wait it out. He still thinks it will all blow over. Many of his friends have already been arrested. Musicians, artists, writers, academics, taken to a work camp! How long will they last, Camillo?" Felix wailed the question from behind his hands.

Eva's father just shook his head. Uncle Felix didn't really need him to give any estimation on the life expectancy of the imprisoned Austrian artisans. They both knew.

"Every day they are arresting Jews. I have to go get him. I have to get him out of Austria. I have to bring him here."

"Felix . . . you can't," Camillo reasoned gently. "They are deporting Jews from Austria, not letting more come in! If you are lucky you will be turned away at the checkpoint. If you are not, you will be detained and deported. There is no scenario where you will reach Otto and be able to get him out. I am doing all I can. Otto has to apply for a visa, though. He must wait in line like all the others and show them his passport. He must tell them he has family and a place to stay here in Italy." Camillo had been over this time and again with his aging father-in-law, but Otto Adler was weary and stubborn, and the incredibly long lines outside the emigration office were intimidating. Many waiting in line were often subjected to the kind of indignities that he had suffered recently. Scrubbing paint from a wall or political slogans from a sidewalk, or licking the cobblestones, or picking up horse dung with their bare hands.

"I have told him. But he won't listen," Felix mourned.

On March 12, 1938, Austria had welcomed Hitler with open arms. *Anschluss*, they called it. Union. But Otto Adler said the word was just Nazi propaganda to reframe a forced incorporation of Austria into Nazi Germany.

Otto Adler had watched it all from his apartment high above the street, a street that was thick with thousands of people waving the crooked cross, raising their arms, and calling out to the motorcade that moved slowly down the street. It was a military parade, with Adolf Hitler himself standing in an open command car waving and acknowledging the jubilant crowds that were welcoming him, the Austrian-born conqueror, into their beautiful city. It was like nothing Otto Adler had ever seen before. A parade, but more than that. The cheering crowds treated Hitler like a savior or messiah.

Otto was not impressed, and he refused to be part of the celebration. He turned his back on the parade, resuming his practice. But the onlookers were as thick as flies, and the sound from the street seeped through the windows and the walls, making it impossible for him to drown them out, even with Tchaikovsky's Violin Concerto in D Major singing from his strings.

"*Sieg heil, Sieg heil,*" they intoned, throwing off his rhythm and making him curse. He shrugged and changed his tempo to keep time with the chanting. He was good at adapting.

"That is the problem with so many Jews," he told his son in a letter. "They don't adapt. They haven't assimilated. But I have. I have been welcomed into the arms of the highest society. I have played for royalty and dined with dignitaries. I am not afraid of the little *Führer*. I will adapt, and as long as I have my music, I am happy. I don't need much."

Still, he hated to see Austria bow to the Germans. All of Austria lay prostrate, letting Hitler roll right over them with his tanks and fiery words, and they celebrated the invasion.

Eight months later, and mere days before the Racial Laws were passed in Italy, Nazi Stormtroopers and Hitler Youth implemented and carried out violent pogroms against the Jews. In cities throughout Austria and Germany, rioters looted and vandalized Jewish businesses and homes. They burned nine hundred synagogues and damaged or destroyed seven thousand Jewish businesses. Instigators attacked, spit on, and threw Jewish men and women into the streets, killing ninety-one of them. Police rounded up, arrested, and sent thirty thousand Jewish men to concentration camps. And when it was all over, the Nazis presented the Jewish community with a bill for the damages, claiming they had caused it to happen.

All this terror had a beautiful name. *Kristallnacht*, the Night of Broken Glass. Otto Adler wrote to Camillo and told him he could have made a fortune. Ostrica would have had business for a year just replacing the smashed windows and the shattered glass in the streets. Then he'd confessed and told Felix he was finally afraid. He wasn't adapting anymore.

"How can you compromise with people who don't want you to exist? They want us to disappear. I can't adapt to death!"

1938 had been a very bad year to be Jewish. 1939 was even worse.

Angelo went home from the seminary that day, expecting to accompany Camillo, Felix, and his grandparents to Eva's concert, only to find that she'd been asked to resign her position and leave the orchestra. No explanation. Just dismissal. She hadn't really needed an explanation. The reason was obvious. Another member was dismissed as well, the Jewish cello player she'd dated off and on the year before.

"I don't care. It's their loss," Eva said defiantly. Her chin was high and her eyes were bright. She obviously *did* care. But Felix cared even more. The news was yet another, very personal blow to the teacher who had spent years molding her into a classical violinist.

Felix wasn't adjusting well to any of the laws. He'd been in Italy for thirteen years and had become a citizen after five. But his citizenship was revoked with the new laws. Camillo had managed to get him an exemption. Angelo didn't know how, but he knew it usually had to do with money and bribes, which Camillo had gladly paid. For the time being, Felix was safe, though his father was not. His father's precarious fate in Austria and the continual insult of the Italian Racial Laws had made the handsome forty-five-year-old Austrian look sixty. His blue eyes were heavily shadowed and his light-brown hair had turned almost completely gray. He was gaunt and quiet and spent far too much time in his room.

"I was the best they had, by far," Eva said again, her eyes on her uncle Felix. "I don't need an orchestra to be a violinist."

"You are already a violinist. No one can take that from you," Felix said stiffly. But his posture belied his words.

Eva watched her uncle retreat with helpless anguish written all over her face, and Angelo had to bite his inner cheek to keep himself from cursing out loud, condemning the outrageous laws and the constant strain on the family he loved.

"Let's go, Eva," he said suddenly. "Let's walk. You need air, and I need gelato." He didn't need gelato. He needed to kick someone, to throw rocks through windows, something. He thought about the shop he'd seen along the main piazza the previous week.

It was an apothecary shop, one he'd frequented before. They sold a salve that soothed the ache and protected the stump of his right leg from being over-chafed when he wore his clumsy prosthetic. It was painted a cheery, welcoming yellow. But it didn't welcome everyone. A sign in the window said, "No Jews Allowed." And next door another shop upped the ante. "No Jews and Dogs Allowed." As if the two were synonymous. Angelo had swallowed back the bile rising in his throat and opened the door. A tinkling of bells alerted the shopkeeper of his entrance.

"*Buongiorno*, Signore," a woman had called out from behind a row of shelves.

Angelo hadn't answered, but retrieved the salve he liked from its usual spot and set it on the counter, waiting for the woman to ring him up. She had eyed him warily, his failure to reply to her friendly "good morning" apparently noted.

"How can you tell?" he had asked, unable to help himself.

"*Scusami?*"

"How can you tell whether or not someone is a Jew? Your sign says no Jews allowed."

The shopkeeper blushed and her gaze slid sideways. "I can't. And I don't care. I also don't ask."

"Then why the sign?"

"There is a certain amount of pressure, you know. The Fascisti leave us alone if the sign is on the door. I'm just trying to protect my shop."

"I see. And the shop down the street? Do the Fascisti have something against dogs too?"

She snickered, as if he were making a joke, but her smile faltered as he glowered down at her.

"I have shopped here for years. But I won't be back unless that sign is taken down," he said softly.

"But you are not a Jew, Signore," she protested. His black seminarian robes and broad hat made that clear.

"No. And I am not a dog. Nor am I a fascist pig." He'd left the salve on the counter and turned to leave the shop.

"It is not that simple, Signore," she had called after him, and he'd glanced back at her crimson face. It had embarrassed her. Good.

"It is exactly that simple, Signora," he said. And it was. With all his heart, he believed it was. Black and white. Right and wrong.

"I need to be back before sundown. It is Shabbat," Eva said quietly, pulling Angelo back to the present, but she grabbed her hat and gloves with an eagerness that betrayed her own need to escape for a while.

They meandered purposefully, stopping to purchase their favorite gelato in huge portions, determined to forget the world around them for a moment, needing to laugh, needing to forget, needing to pretend that their lives were sweet and simple, if only for an hour or two.

But they would have had to walk with their eyes closed. The world was not sweet or simple anymore. The proof of it was all around them, and neither of them was blind.

"We don't look like that, do we?" Eva said around a spoonful of ice cream, staring down at the weekly paper someone had left behind near the park bench where they sat to eat their treat. She slid her foot over the pages to keep it from flapping in the breeze. A cartoon labeled "Race Defilers," depicting a Jewish man with exaggerated features carrying an unconscious Aryan female into his private office, was front and center. Eva picked it up and studied the cartoon thoughtfully. Then she looked up at Angelo and squinted her eyes.

"That looks more like your nose than mine!" She was trying to laugh it off, her voice light and purposely unaffected.

"I have a Roman nose." Angelo tried to laugh too, but his stomach churned. He'd seen too much of that kind of mockery and "humor" in the Italian press. It had been an ongoing campaign, worsening with the "scientific" manifestos on race, and the blame for all the country's problems that was constantly focused on the Italian Jews who made up less than 1 percent of the country's population.

Angelo read all the national newspapers, a habit he'd cultivated when he felt homesick for America. If he was to be an Italian, he had to understand Italy. And he'd tried. But even as a twelve-year-old boy, painstakingly reading the politically charged *La Stampa*, he wondered if the papers represented Italy or just the government.

"He looks a little like Mussolini," Angelo said, wishing he could make Eva laugh like she used to.

"Yes. Mussolini . . . and Signore Balbo, who conducts the orchestra," Eva added drily, and Angelo crumpled the piece of newsprint in his hand. He thought about the picture he'd seen in a newspaper of an Austrian woman sitting on a bench that said, *"Nur Für Arier"*—For Aryans Only—and he wondered how long it would be before Eva was not allowed to even sit on a bench in her own country.

"You never used to observe Shabbat," Angelo said, not because he cared, but because he needed to change the subject.

"Yes. I know . . . funny, isn't it? I never really thought about being Jewish until I started to be persecuted for it. Babbo's always celebrated learning above everything else, but we decided that we'd better see what all the fuss is about. We're becoming devout." She winked at Angelo and shrugged.

She had grown up in the last year. She still kept a few men on a string, but the string was getting longer, the dates fewer and further between. When she wasn't teaching violin lessons to Jewish children for little or no money, she was at home, practicing. Her life had narrowed dramatically to her music, her family, and a few Jewish friends who were as watchful and reticent as the Rossellis had become.

"And what have you learned?" he asked, sounding like Father Sebastian. He smirked to soften the effect.

"A great deal. But I haven't learned the most important thing."

"No? And what would that be?" he asked.

"Why do people hate us so much?"

∞

"They've taken my father," Felix cried. "He's been arrested."

"How do you know?" Camillo asked, his face pale, his hands extended toward Felix.

Felix held up the letter. His hand was trembling like he was stricken with a disease, the paper flapping like he was shaking the terrible truth from it.

"The maid. It is illegal for her to work for a Jew, but the German commander living in my father's apartment needed a housekeeper, so he hired her to cook and clean for him. She cared about my father, and I think she's watched out for him as best she could. She said she would have called me, but she was nervous about speaking freely. There are always listening ears on the phone lines. But she thought I should know. When she arrived at the apartment on the fourteenth—two weeks ago!—my father was gone. When she asked the *Kommandant* where he was, he told her 'it was his turn.'"

"Where have they taken him?" Camillo pressed.

"She doesn't know for certain. She writes that the whole building was cleared. There are no Jews left. The officer told her soon there would be no more Jews in Vienna."

"I read that some of them are just being relocated to Jewish ghettos." Camillo started pacing, trying to remain positive, his thoughts scrambling for solutions.

"The maid thinks he will be sent to a work camp. Her brother works at the train station, and he told her that every day the trains leave early, before the sun rises, so the people of Vienna won't see them leave. He says they are loaded with Jews. He says the trains have been going to a place called Mauthausen, near Linz."

"But Linz is not too far from Vienna. This is good!"

"This is not good, Camillo! None of this is good. He will die." The certainty in Felix Adler's voice made Eva wince and Camillo collapse onto a chair. He looked completely defeated.

"They wouldn't let him bring his violin. The German officer was looking at it when the maid arrived for work. He told her he's going to send it to his son in Berlin. He's going to send my father's violin to his son," Felix repeated, suddenly enraged, and he swept his arm across the table, upending the lamp and the radio they weren't supposed to own.

❧

"What are you playing, Eva?" Felix Adler sighed from the window overlooking the garden. "I don't recognize that. It sounds a little like Chopin, but it's not."

"It's Chopin mixed with Rosselli, sprinkled with Adler, and doused with anger," Eva murmured, her eyes closed, her chin gripping her violin.

She expected him to scold her, to tell her to "play what is written!" But he was silent. She continued playing, but she opened her eyes, watching him as she let her bow flit over the strings like a bee flirting with a flower. His hands were clasped behind his back, his feet together. It was the way he stood when he was deep in thought or when he was listening.

She and Uncle Felix had had a love/hate relationship since he'd arrived in Italy in 1926, two years after her mother's death. She had been only six years old and was not prepared for the maestro that was

Felix Adler. He had come to Italy with the express purpose of molding her into an Adler violinist, and he had come to Italy out of love for his sister, which he reminded Eva of frequently. It was her dying wish. He'd acquired other students, and he'd played with the Orchestra della Toscana, but his focus had been Eva.

Eva had challenged him at every turn. She was willful and distracted, easily bored, and known to disappear when it was time for lessons. But she had a gift. She had a remarkable ear, and what she lacked in discipline, she made up for in musicality. She loved the violin, she loved to play, and Felix had eventually learned to forgive her for the rest, though it was forgiveness bestowed grudgingly.

It had taken him a while to realize that she wasn't really reading the music he put in front of her. She was listening and copying. If she didn't understand something, she would ask Felix to show her. After a few demonstrations she could play bar after bar from memory.

Teaching her to read music had been torture for both of them. She'd hated it, he'd hated it, and they'd hated each other half the time. He made her do everything she despised and rarely let her do what she loved. Long notes and scales and sight-reading, day after day.

"I don't want to practice long notes! I want to play Chopin." Eva would stomp her foot.

"You can't play Chopin."

"I can too! Listen." Eva immediately launched into a Chopin nocturne, complete with every variation he'd purposely played, just to test her.

"You can't. You are parroting. You are not reading. You are listening to me and playing without looking at your music and seeing the music as you create it."

"I see the music in my head. And it doesn't look like little black dots and lines! It looks like rainbows and flying and the Alps and the Apennines. Why can't I just listen and play?" she had whined.

"Because I won't always be here to demonstrate! You have to be able to read the notes and turn the notes into music, both in your head and on your instrument. You are composing, but the greatest composers can see the notes when they hear music. They don't see the Apennines! And you will never be able to record your compositions if you don't understand how to read and write music."

She had learned, eventually. But she still relied far too heavily on her ability to mimic, to embellish, to adapt.

The word *adapt* made her think of her grandfather, who hadn't been able to adapt after all.

"Uncle Felix?" Eva lowered her violin and bow, interrupting her reverie and her freestyle composition to stare at her uncle's rigid back.

"Please keep playing, Eva," he said quietly.

"What would you like me to play, Uncle?"

"Play whatever you wish. Something else mixed with Rosselli and sprinkled with Adler," he said, and his shoulders began to shake. She'd never seen her uncle cry, and in the last months, he'd cried twice. She didn't know what to do to comfort him. So she played. She played Chopin's Nocturne in E Flat Major because it was hauntingly beautiful, but she drifted off into her own arrangement and ended up playing something that didn't sound like anything she'd ever played before. When Eva finally lowered her violin, Felix had sunk into a chair and dried his eyes on a handkerchief he still held wadded up in his hand. He met her gaze, and his eyes were so sad her heart ached in her chest. But he smiled at her with tenderness and began to speak.

His voice was tired, his words measured. "In my life I've only been good at one thing. The violin. Not as good as my father. Maybe I could have been. But I drank too much and lost my temper too often. I came to Italy because I failed in Vienna. I came to Italy because I was in love with a woman who wasn't in love with me. And for the last thirteen years, I've taken it out on you. If you hadn't been so strong, I might have broken you. I might have made you hate me. But you fought back. You shrugged me off. And now I listen to you and I am in awe."

"You are?" Eva asked in amazement. These were things she had never heard before.

"When you play, Eva, I feel hopeful. They can take our homes, our possessions. Our families. Our lives. They can drive us out, like they've driven us out before. They can humiliate us and dehumanize us. But they cannot take our thoughts. They cannot take our talents. They cannot take our knowledge, or our memories, or our minds. In music, there is no bondage. Music is a door, and the soul escapes through the melody. Even if it's only for a few minutes. And everyone who listens is freed. Everyone who listens is elevated.

"When you play, I hear my life lifting off your strings. I hear the long notes and the scales, the tears and the hours. I hear you and me, together in this room. I hear my father and the things he taught me that I passed on to you. I hear it all, and my life plays on, his life plays on, over and over, when *you* play."

Eva set her instrument down and, with tears streaming down her face, knelt in front of her uncle and slid her arms around him, pressing her cheek to his thin chest. He embraced her gently, and they stayed in sorrowful silence, listening to the wind as it wailed a mournful strain not so different from the one Eva had composed, wondering if the wind would be the only witness, the only whisper, when the death in Austria came for them too.

10 August, 1939

Confession: I am nineteen years old, and I've been kissed many times. But I've never been kissed like that.

It felt like drowning but not needing to breathe. Like falling but never hitting the ground. Even now, my hands are shaking, and my heart is so swollen and fat it feels like it's going to burst, or I'm going to burst. I want to cry. I want to laugh. I want to bury my head in my pillow and scream until I fall asleep, because maybe when I go to sleep I can relive it.

I can't believe it happened, yet I think I've been waiting for it to happen for the last seven years, ever since I conned Angelo into kissing me the first time. I've been waiting for him for so long, and for a couple of hours tonight, in a little world that was only big enough for the two of us, he was mine.

But I don't know if I will be able to keep him. I'm afraid when tomorrow comes, I'll be waiting for him again.

Eva Rosselli

CHAPTER 4
GROSSETO

Angelo had been surprised when Camillo announced he was still taking the family to the beach house, considering the new set of Racial Laws that had been passed earlier that summer. But Camillo had made the reservation before the law was passed, and he stubbornly maintained that he had been renting that particular lodge from the same family for twenty years, and he would keep on renting it for twenty more. So that August, only months before the war broke out, they all boarded the train for Grosseto, confident in Camillo's ability to make everything all right.

The first few days of Angelo's planned five-day retreat were spent sleeping, eating, playing checkers, and debating everything and nothing, simply because Camillo and Augusto enjoyed discussion, and Angelo enjoyed listening to them argue. In the last few months they argued less, as Fascism had revealed itself and Augusto had been proven wrong. But they still found points of disagreement and seemed relieved that they had.

Eva walked a lot, her feet flirting with the surf, dancing in and out of the waves until she was wet and cold. Then she would lie on her big white towel and fall asleep in the sun until she was almost dry. Then she would repeat the process. Her porcelain skin had grown rosy and brown, making her look decidedly more Italian than Austrian. Her hair and eyes were dark, but her skin was unquestionably less olive than Angelo's was. His skin turned smoky after an hour in the sun, and within a few days, he looked like he'd spent his life casting nets with the fishermen of Grosseto.

Umbrella-shaped maritime pines fringed the beaches, and one afternoon Angelo found himself stomping around in the cork-oak woodlands, where aristocratic families still hunted for wild boar, losing himself in the shade and the scents and the quiet. As the shadows grew longer, and his skin grew sticky with sweat, he tromped out of the woods and headed back toward the beach, eager for a quick swim in the cool, clear waters.

Clouds had rolled in, and the sky was no longer the guileless blue it had been earlier in the day. Still, even with rain threatening, Angelo shrugged out of his shirt, removed his shoe and his prosthetic, and hopped through the waves until he could immerse himself in the Tyrrhenian. Before too long, Eva was treading water beside him, and they kicked and splashed and floated on their backs until distant thunder rumbled and urged them back to the shore.

Rain was coming, but the air was still warm, and they toweled themselves off and let the heat dry their hair as they watched the storm move toward them.

"What's that?" Eva inclined her head toward his pile of abandoned clothing and forest finds. He rarely saved anything, impatient with clutter and generally unsentimental, but he'd thought maybe his *nonno* would like that afternoon's discovery.

"I found a quiver of black-and-white porcupine quills."

"Hmm. Well, I saw some spotted pink flamingos in the lagoon," Eva countered, her eyes on the water. She was smiling slightly, letting him in on the game.

"That's nothing. I woke a barn owl and he dove at my head," he shot back. "And I killed a wild pig with my bare hands. I thought about bringing him back for dinner, but then I remembered pigs aren't kosher."

Eva pursed her lips, clearly trying to come up with a better story.

"Well, I found this." She handed him a shell, still completely intact, still hinged at the back. He took it and peered inside. The interior was smooth and empty, the life inside long gone.

"No pearl?"

"No. Just sand."

"But the sand can become a pearl," he offered, handing the shell back to her.

"The sand doesn't really become a pearl, silly. It doesn't become something else. It's just hidden. The grain of sand is still there beneath the layers of nacre—"

"Nacre?" he interrupted. It wasn't a word he'd heard before.

"The mineral substance that the oyster coats the grain of sand in."

The mention of the oyster had its same old effect, and Eva's eyes touched on his briefly before she glanced away. Another time it probably wouldn't have registered. But here they were, sitting in roughly the same spot where they'd sat seven years before when the skies were clear and no storms threatened.

"You mean mother-of-pearl? How did you know that?"

"Babbo. He is a chemical engineer, Angelo. He knows the actual name of every substance known to man."

"So the little irritant becomes a beautiful pearl." He winked at Eva and tapped her nose.

"Are you calling me a little irritant?"

He laughed, unable to help himself. She had always made him laugh.

"Yes. I am. A beautiful irritant."

"Keep it up, and I will steal your fake leg and you will have to hop back to the house."

"You're so heartless," he said in mock horror.

"A heartless irritant." She swiped at him and he blocked her easily, stealing her shell in the process.

Thunder belched through the sky once more, not nearly as polite and distant as it had been before. Eva and Angelo, still bickering good-naturedly, quickly dressed and gathered their few things. They weren't quick enough, though, and with a solid crack, the swollen skies suddenly split above them. Rain peppered the sand, and Eva squealed. Angelo couldn't run very well, and Eva wasn't inclined to let him get drenched alone, so they looked around for immediate shelter.

Hand in hand they struggled across the sand toward the trees and the little fisherman's shack that sat back from the shore. The lock was broken and the shack abandoned, though an old net and a rusty fishing pole still remained among the dust and the cobwebs.

Clothes clung to limbs, black hair to burnished cheeks, and they tumbled, laughing, into the shack, the damp walls and the earthy darkness making the space feel more like a medieval dungeon used for torture than a respite from the storm.

Eva picked up the pole in one hand and tossed Angelo the net, and within moments they were quarreling once more as they fenced, saying things like "*En garde*," and "Feel my wrath," and "Take that, fool!"

Eva made the mistake of lunging too deep and Angelo easily swiped her "sword" away.

"Surrender, knave!" he said with a sneering twist of his lips. His black curls were clinging to his forehead and his blue eyes danced with Eva as she sashayed around him, pretending she was a skilled swordsman. She was laughing and relaxed, the old Eva, and his heart softened as he looked into her grinning face.

She sensed the shift in his attention and she feinted, as if to kneel, only to step forward and grab at his arm, pivoting as if to throw him over her shoulder in a move that was more ancient wrestling than fencing. He dropped his net and pulled her against him aggressively, her back to his chest, his forearm resting firmly beneath her breasts, one large hand wrapped around her rib cage.

He had meant for it to be part of the game. Clearly, he hadn't thought. His body hugged hers from his chest to his thighs, her hair brushed his face, her female scent tickled his nose, and his mouth was poised at the silky whorl of her ear, ready to demand her surrender.

They stood frozen for several long seconds, locked in the strange embrace, eyes closed, mouths slightly open, trying to breathe without movement, without sound, and growing lightheaded in the attempt. Eva's hands had risen to Angelo's arm when he pulled her to him, and she stood motionless against him, her hands gripping the hard length that held her hostage. She didn't dare say his name, didn't dare utter a sound. Surely, it would break the spell. Then she felt his lips move ever-so-softly against the lobe of her ear, skim the uppermost edge of her jaw, then travel back again. Eva resisted the sweet shudder that slid down her spine, but Angelo felt the tremor and his lips left her skin. But he didn't pull away or loosen his arm.

Eva slowly turned her head, feeling his breath mark a path across her cheek as she raised her face and lifted her chin. Then it was her breath tickling his cheek and warming his lips. Again they paused, muscles tensed, straining to feel everything, to miss nothing, and still not cross any lines. Their eyes stayed closed as they neared that line, stood toe-to-toe, and then stepped over it, into each other.

Mouths touched. Pressed. Retreated. Brushed, retreated. Pressed, sought, then slid away. And still their eyes remained closed. Denying everything.

Amy Harmon

Eva turned as Angelo shifted, and the dance began again, the angle different, more direct, less accidental. *Accidental. Innocent. Sweet.* The words slipped through Angelo's foggy mind, and he nodded slightly. Yes. That was it. Innocent.

With his mouth pressed against Eva's, that slight nod lifted Eva's full top lip, separating it from the lower one, and Angelo explored the space between them with an unintentional touch of his tongue. Unintentional. Innocent. Sweet. So incredibly sweet. Just like that kiss so long ago.

But the sweetness pulled him under like Camillo's wine. Then he was drinking deeply, pulling every last drop from Eva's mouth, unable to stop. It was like nothing he'd ever tasted before, and she cradled his face, letting him sip away, slip away, lost in the flavor, the texture, the heady heat of her mouth on his.

Then they opened their eyes.

Dark and heavy met blue and blazing, and Angelo ached to close his eyes again, even as he lifted his mouth and dropped his hands from her body.

"Eva," he whispered, and his torment made her tremble.

"Again," she pleaded, and her eyes begged. "Again, Angelo."

"Madonna," he breathed. "Madonna," he pleaded. But the lovely Madonna, mother of his precious Jesus, couldn't hold a candle to the madonna before him.

They moved as one, bodies coming back together, the renewed contact so welcome and wondrous that their sighs slid around them like a hushed hallelujah chorus. Then there was only pleasure and pressure, mouths and momentum, as one kiss grew and multiplied and became something new, something neither of them had known before.

Outside the storm abated, welcoming a rainbow of soft pastels reflected in silvery puddles that neither of them saw. Outside, Fabia called for them, telling them to come in for supper. But neither of them heard. Outside, the air chilled with the evening, but neither of them

66

felt the cold. Outside, Camillo Rosselli worried, puffing on his pipe, wondering what the future would hold for the two young people who had always loved the other but didn't belong together. And as their fires were banked, they both smelled the smoke.

They left the fisherman's shack with their virginities intact, but they didn't go inside to safety and sanity. Instead, they drifted up into the fragrant, rain-damp evergreen forest that stood sentry on one side of the vacation home, unwilling to part, unable to stop touching, to stop kissing, to walk away from each other and into the place where separation would surely invite guilt and regret, at least for Angelo.

When they finally parted and Eva tiptoed up to her room, drunk on love and dizzy with desire, smiling against the palm she pressed to her lips to keep from giggling, Angelo sat on the veranda and tried not to think at all. He too kept his hand pressed to his mouth, but it was not to keep from laughing. He could smell Eva on his fingers.

His body tightened all over again and his breaths grew painful. He was in exquisite agony. He had never known such pleasure, and not just in her body and her skin. Not just in her mouth and her sweetness. Not just in the way she touched him and made him tremble. It was more than that. It wasn't just pleasure, it was joy.

He'd been warned about the dangers of the flesh. Seminarians were counseled extensively, cautioned endlessly, and threatened with their very souls when it came to bridling passions and denying every carnal impulse. But no one had told him he would be filled with this immeasurable joy. He felt close to tears, and it wasn't simply because he'd just fallen into the snare every seminarian secretly dreads and simultaneously dreams about. It was love that made each touch feel like redemption and each kiss feel like rebirth. Not lust. Not pleasure. It was *love* that created joy.

He'd known for a long time that he loved Eva, but he had never admitted to himself that he loved her the way a man loves a woman. He had never allowed himself to ruminate on the idea. He'd locked it away the moment he'd decided to marry the church and forsake all others.

"Angelo?"

Angelo dropped his fingers from his mouth as if he'd been caught with his hand in a cash register. Camillo stepped out onto the veranda and looked around, obviously expecting Eva to be out there too. When he saw that she wasn't, he eased himself into a chair to the right of Angelo and filled his pipe as if he had all the time in the world. It wasn't late, though Angelo and Eva had missed dinner. Everyone else was still awake inside the house, and low murmurs and tinkling laughter filtered out into the loamy air. Angelo hoped no one had noticed the length of time he and Eva had spent alone.

Camillo puffed and purred, smoke billowing from his mouth in fragrant clouds. Angelo had always loved the smell of his pipe, and he closed his eyes briefly, letting the scent mingle with the salt and the sea, the evergreens and the rain, before he exhaled and then breathed in deeply once more, savoring the aroma.

"You might be our only hope, Angelo," Camillo said after a time. Angelo had grown drowsy in the comfortable darkness, the inevitable adrenaline crash leaving him weak and loose-limbed.

"What do you mean, Camillo?" Camillo had never allowed Angelo to call him anything else.

"You know, you could marry Eva and take her to America. You are an American citizen. And if she were your wife, you could get her out of Italy. Out of Europe. You could make sure she is safe from what is coming."

Angelo was so stunned he could only sit, staring off into the darkness like it held a forest full of jesters, waiting to laugh at Camillo's incredible suggestion. He sat still for so long, with his face so blank, that Camillo leaned forward and peered into his eyes.

"She would never leave you," Angelo said finally, offering the only response that came to his mind.

"Ha!" Camillo barked softly, and puffed again, slumping back in his chair. "I knew it."

"You knew what, Babbo?" Angelo said, slipping and calling him by Eva's pet name.

"I knew you wouldn't pretend with me," he said. "You love Eva. And she loves you. You are a priest and she is a Jew."

"And you are a poet," Angelo said mildly, though his heart was galloping.

Camillo laughed softly. "That I am. A great poet and philosopher. That is why I smoke this pipe. It gives me the look I desire."

"I am not a priest yet," Angelo murmured. It was a silly thing to say. He had spent nine years in the seminary. Nine years. And now, he was in the final months of his training. His ordination had been scheduled.

"That's like a man who is betrothed saying he is not yet married."

It was exactly like that, and Angelo had no response. He was too honest and too shell-shocked by the whole evening to play games. Camillo was right. He couldn't pretend. And reality was starting to penetrate the fog he'd been in.

Angelo wasn't a stupid man. He wasn't blind. He wasn't deaf. He wasn't dumb. But he'd been a fool. He'd thought he could love Eva and not be in love with her. He'd thought he could be close to her and not be too close. He'd thought he could have Eva and have God too.

And he couldn't.

He was not the exception. He was the rule. He was not Saint George, slaying dragons for his God. He was simply Angelo Bianco, being slain by the wiliest serpent of all—Satan, flaming red, with seven heads and ten horns—which John spoke of in his Book of Revelation.

"I still want to be a priest, Camillo," he whispered, and his chest ached at the admission, as if he were betraying Eva. He *was* betraying Eva. Just like he'd betrayed the church and betrayed himself. The last few hours had been the sweetest of his life, but they had not been his finest.

"I know," Camillo said. "I know you do. That is why you are sitting out here alone instead of somewhere with Eva. That is why you've spent all these years treating her like a sister and letting me treat you like a son."

"You are my family," Angelo said, emotion rising in his chest.

"Yes. But you can still save her." Camillo met his gaze with a frank expectation that confused Angelo all the more.

"But . . . I thought you meant . . ."

"Marriage? No. It's illegal, first of all. Catholics can't marry Jews, even though we've been marrying each other for decades in Italy. Even though Santino's Catholic uncle married my Jewish aunt thirty years ago," he scoffed, disgusted. But he waved his hand in the air, dismissing his derision as well as the mention of the convoluted family connection that had brought Santino and Camillo together in the first place. He continued. "And second, you're right. Eva wouldn't leave. It is a distinctly Jewish trait. We would rather die together than be separated from our loved ones." He puffed his pipe, letting the silence cleanse his mental palate. "Ah, who knows? Maybe that isn't a Jewish trait. Maybe that is a human trait." He waved his hand again. "Regardless, I know she will not leave me to save herself."

"I don't understand, Camillo. What do you want me to do?" Angelo hoped Camillo could tell him exactly, give him instructions, make the path ahead straight and narrow.

"You are our only hope because you will be in a position to help many people, Angelo. The church is already helping refugees. Did you know that?"

Angelo shook his head. The question was, how did Camillo know?

"I have been looking for ways to help my father-in-law. I have been working with DELASEM—"

"What?" Angelo had no idea what DELASEM was.

"The Delegation for the Assistance of Jewish Emigrants," Camillo supplied. "There are growing networks, Angelo. And the Catholic Church is quietly assisting where they can. The Catholics may save our souls after all," Camillo said, smiling around his pipe. "Or maybe just our lives. But I will settle for that much."

"What can I do?" The instructions seemed very vague.

"With the threats of war, Ostrica's contracts have gone up tenfold. The government is our largest contractor. They don't pay well, but they buy huge volume. We are just happy they haven't taken the company in the name of the greater good. We specialize in fine handmade glass, but we invested in the machinery to do heavier, industrial-grade glass when Mussolini started posturing and war looked like it was going to become inevitable. We are richer than we've ever been, and a large percentage is going to DELASEM. I have even donated a large portion to the church with the caveat that you are the trustee of the account and have a right to dictate where, within the organization of the church, that money goes. I would ask that you make sure that it goes to feed and hide refugees and those who are sheltering them. Can you do that? Will you do that for me?"

"How?" Angelo asked again.

"Become a priest. Just like you've always planned. And if worse comes to worst, use your connections to hide us. I need you to save our family, Angelo."

❧

Eva lay awake all night, gloriously giddy, caught in the haze of remembered kisses, only to fall into a fierce depression when she contemplated the future. The last year had convinced her there were no happy endings, only happy interludes, and somehow the interludes made the endings even worse.

She ended up falling asleep near dawn and slept until noon. She took a leisurely bath, dried and curled her hair, painted her toenails red, and finally slunk down the stairs at about three o'clock, certain that everyone would take one look at her and see her feelings stamped all over her face. She was terrified of that first glance with Angelo, because then she would know if he felt the same. Maybe she just wouldn't look at him at all.

Fabia was in the kitchen breading and frying sardines. Santino was fashioning some kind of hat decoration from the porcupine quills Angelo had found, and the rest of the family was gathered on the veranda, sipping lemonade laced with something stronger, enjoying the slightly cooler temperatures, courtesy of the previous night's storm.

They all greeted Eva warmly with no mention of her late morning or her absence at dinner the night before. Angelo wasn't on the veranda. She breathed a little easier as she wiggled beneath her father's arm on the porch swing, leaning against him and closing her eyes so she could avoid seeing Angelo if he eventually joined them. But it wasn't Angelo who made his way up the walk in late afternoon.

It was not uncommon for the manager and his wife—an older couple who had always been unfailingly polite and welcoming—to stop in every now and then and check on their guests. They managed the whole row of beach houses for one of Italy's wealthiest families, though Eva could never remember which one. The couple was greeted warmly all around by the group gathered on the veranda. But the warm reception changed almost immediately into something cold and damp.

The elderly man and his wife stood side by side in front of Camillo, as if they needed moral support to do the immoral deed.

"I'm sorry, Signore," the old man said. "I know you have come here for many years. And we don't mind. We are happy to have you join us. But people are complaining. They recognize you from past years, and they know you are Jews. The new laws . . . you understand."

Camillo stared at the couple for a moment, disbelieving. Eva straightened, pulling away from him as he rose, clearly needing to face this unexpected assault on his feet.

"We will refund your money, of course," the woman added hastily. She extended an envelope to Camillo. He took it, opened it slowly, and looked at the lire inside. Eva could see his humiliation, and her own face grew hot with outrage. She reached out and took her father's hand. He stiffened briefly, then squeezed her fingers.

"I see," Camillo said slowly, calmly. "When exactly would you like us to go?"

"As soon as possible. You understand. We don't want to lose more business or get in trouble with the *carabinieri*." The man shrugged like it couldn't be helped. "Eh, what else can we do?"

"We will leave in the morning, then," Camillo said stiffly.

The old woman looked at her husband and her husband looked back at Camillo. "It would be better if you left tonight, Signore."

The silence on the veranda felt like standing in front of a blazing furnace.

"It is a full day's trip back to Florence, and we have people in our party who are getting on in years," Camillo said softly but firmly. "We were just about to sit down to a late lunch and we will need to gather our things. We will leave in the morning."

The woman reached out and yanked the envelope from his hands.

"Then we will need this to cover our losses," she snapped. "And don't blame us if the *carabinieri* show up and throw you out. They won't be as nice as we have been."

The old man looked at his wife, his face reflecting the shock that Eva felt. The woman had grown hostile with very little provocation.

"I'm sure tomorrow will be fine," the old man said, backing off the veranda, his hat in his hands. "Come now, Guida," he commanded his wife. His wife turned away, but she didn't return the envelope.

When Angelo finally showed up and heard the news from his sobbing grandmother, he left the house again, slamming the front door with wall-trembling force. He'd stormed off to the manager's cottage only to come back a half hour later looking shaken and sick. No one asked him how the conversation had gone.

He was as silent as the rest of them as they dined on Fabia's fried sardines, green salad, and tomatoes. From the frozen expressions and weary eyes all around the table, one would think the crucifixion was at hand and not simply the last supper. Eva didn't think anyone would appreciate her attempt at levity, and kept her Catholic wordplay to herself.

They packed their things in an embarrassed stupor and retired early, none of them wanting to talk about the aborted holiday. The next morning, they left the house as clean and tidy as they'd found it, and climbed into the hired cars that would take them and their luggage to the train station in Grosseto.

Eva didn't want to look back, but as they pulled away, she found herself turning in her seat to see the house disappear around the bend. They wouldn't be coming back to Maremma Beach. There would be no more white-sand vacations and fresh fish from the market in Grosseto. There would be no more stolen kisses. Of that she was almost as certain. Those things were only memories now, and the memories had been tainted.

15 August, 1939

Confession: I am afraid of rejection.

A rejected infant will often die, even if its basic needs are met. A rejected child will spend his whole life trying to please everyone else, and never please himself. A rejected woman will often cheat, just to feel desirable. A rejected man will rarely try again, no matter how lonely he is. A rejected people will convince themselves they deserve it, if only to make sense of a senseless world.

I'm convinced there is nothing worse for the human heart than rejection, but over the past year, I have grown accustomed to it. I expect it. Accept it. Roll with it, instead of against it. I hate this about myself, and sometimes I wonder where the old Eva has gone, the girl who had fire, the girl who secretly believed she could do anything, be anything, and love anyone. Then I remember. She was rejected.

Eva Rosselli

CHAPTER 5

ROME

Angelo wasn't expected back at the seminary for three more days, and he used the first two to visit with Monsignor Luciano in Rome. He confessed his feelings for Eva, told him of the intimacy they'd shared, and he asked him for counsel and absolution. The monsignor gave both, but he didn't hide his dismay very well.

"There is no future in this, my son."

Angelo thought about Eva, her bright smile and laughing eyes, the way her mouth had felt beneath his. She loved him. He loved her. Surely, there was a future in that. But Monsignor Luciano continued, as if he heard the doubt in Angelo's silence.

"Even if you didn't become a priest . . . she is a Jew, Angelo."

"Yes, she is."

"You can't marry a Jew."

"Because of the laws?"

"Yes. But that isn't what I'm referring to. You are Catholic. You can't marry her because she isn't a believer."

"She believes in God." Angelo felt the sting of affront, a desire to defend, even as he recognized what his mentor was saying to him.

"Which God?" Monsignor Luciano pressed. "Certainly not Jesus."

"Do you really think God is a God of conditions, Monsignor?" Angelo found himself arguing. "Maybe the only condition is love. Love for him, for each other. She doesn't reject Jesus. She just doesn't know him," Angelo tried to explain.

"And are you confident that you could help her come to know him?" Monsignor Luciano probed.

Angelo thought about that for a moment before coming to a conclusion. "I don't know, Father. But even if she accepted Jesus as her savior, I don't think she would be baptized."

"Why?"

"Because she is . . . Jewish." Angelo threw up his hands, frustrated by his inability to find a better explanation. "It is her heritage. It is her history. It is more than religion. It is who she is. Who her father is. Who her ancestors were."

"But it is not who *you* are," Monsignor Luciano said quietly, folding his hands and looking at Angelo.

Angelo reared back, almost as if he'd been slapped. He turned away from the monsignor, not wanting him to see the reaction his words caused.

It was not who *he* was.

That was the crux of the matter. He was not Jewish. He'd been raised and loved by Jewish people, but he was not one of them. The hurt and rejection he had felt when his mother died and his father left him in Italy reared its scaly head and burned him all over again.

The church is the best place for you, Angelo. You won't be a burden. His father's final words to his son. He was older and wiser now, and he could rationalize his father's decision and his grandparents' desires for him, but the feelings, the insecurity, had never gone away.

"You know what is best, Angelo. You know what is right. Now you must go forward and not look back," the monsignor said, and Angelo could only nod. The church *was* the best place for him. Deep down, he believed it. Angelo didn't belong with Eva. It was not who he was.

Angelo spent his final day of vacation back in Florence with Eva, trying to find a way to tell her nothing had changed and nothing could change. He took her to all his favorite places, trying to share his feelings, to explain what drove him. Instead, he ended up sounding like a tour guide in a city she already knew and loved.

She was quiet, and he could feel her depression. The art and the architecture didn't feed her spirit the way it fed his. He tried harder, pointing out a fresco there, a statue here, telling her what he loved and what he appreciated, so she could appreciate it too, and little by little her face relaxed and her smile came back as the art came to life.

The only thing he wanted to show her inside the Palazzo del Bargello, amid the sprawling expanse of some of the world's greatest art, was Donatello's statue of young Saint George, shield in hand, eyes facing a threat no one else could see.

"Padre Sebastiano brought a group of us here about two years after I came to Italy. This one statue changed everything for me. I couldn't look at anything else. The rest of the group moved on, but I couldn't move. Another priest saw me staring at the statue, and he told me the story of *San Giorgio* and the dragon."

He relayed the tale that had moved him, altered his thinking, and redirected his life. As he talked, Eva's eyes were fixed on the sculpture, like she could almost imagine how he had looked, standing there all those years ago, a boy who wanted to be a saint.

"He risked everything," Angelo said as he finished the story, "and even though he died for his beliefs, he lives on because of them too."

He met Eva's gaze then, and her eyes were sad. Maybe she saw the truth, and it hurt her.

"After that, Don Luciano, the priest I met that day, kept tabs on me and even sent a letter to the seminary, asking for periodic updates on my schooling and progress. Don Luciano is now in Rome. He's a monsignor. I'm hoping I will be able to learn alongside him at some point." It was his fondest wish.

In the Piazza del Duomo, they stood in front of the bronze baptistery doors, and he pointed out the life of Christ, so painstakingly illustrated, engraving after engraving, panel after panel.

"The first time I saw these I could only stare. It was like being in love, when your eyes can't look away without instantly wanting to go back," he breathed, his voice an awed whisper, but Eva just nodded, her eyes on his face instead of the baptistery doors.

Angelo turned away from the baptistery. "Now to Santa Croce."

"Santa Croce too?" Eva asked, groaning as if she were five. She was teasing, but beneath her banter was a growing despondence. The more they saw, the wider the gulf between them grew. They walked the short distance, a few city blocks, between the Duomo and the basilica, their conversation mild in the August heat. The forecast had threatened rain, but the sky was cloudless, the breeze nonexistent.

"Have you been inside?" he asked as they began to cross the Franciscan basilica's lengthy piazza.

"Yes. On school outings, and once with Uncle Felix. He made me play my violin outside, remember? I drew a crowd. He was quite pleased with me that day."

"I do remember! You told me all about it. You were quite pleased with yourself too, if I remember right." Eva always came alive in front of a crowd, and when she'd told Angelo about the numbers she'd drawn, he had wished more than anything he could have heard her play.

"Playing for an audience is a million times better than playing alone," she said, confirming his thoughts.

"Well, I love Santa Croce. It's charming, less intimidating." Angelo winked at Eva and she just shook her head and sighed.

He studied the towering white edifice ahead of them, the arched doorways, the intricate carvings, the height crowned with several crosses and a blue six-sided star that made him think of the ugly yellow stars some of Camillo's refugees had worn on their clothing. The reminder depressed him. Thank God Italy had not resorted to pinning labels on her Jews.

"Less intimidating?" Eva countered doubtfully. She rubbed her head, and he could have sworn he heard her whimper. He was invigorated by the art, but Eva seemed overwhelmed by it all. Or maybe it was him. Maybe he depressed her.

"Catholicism is so . . . ornate," she said, trying to take it all in.

"That is one of the things I love about it. It's complicated and beautiful and there's nothing easy about it. Everything is symbolic, ritualistic. Like a beautiful woman, it makes you work."

Eva harrumphed. "What do you know about beautiful women?"

"I grew up with one. I think I know plenty."

"Ha!" she laughed. He was trying to be sweet, though he was also being truthful. "I'm not complicated, Angelo."

"You are to me." He eyed her briefly, then looked away.

"No. You make me that way. You are far more complicated than I'll ever be. I'm not sure what drives you. I have never been able to understand your passion for . . ."

"God?" He finished her sentence.

"No. I don't think your passion is for God, exactly. I think your passion is for ascension."

Angelo could only stare at her in stupefaction.

"Ascension?" he asked, incredulous.

"You aren't hungry for power. You aren't hungry for riches. You aren't hungry for women or fun or music . . . or pleasure."

"Am I really so bland?" He laughed at himself, and Eva laughed too, but she pressed her point.

"You are hungry for purpose, for meaning, for . . . martyrdom . . . or maybe just sainthood."

"I think you just described the ambitions of every good priest," he said, strangely relieved.

"Yes. I did, didn't I?" Eva looked a little stunned.

"Why are the synagogues so plain, do you think? Is it because Judaism is much more . . . bare? Simplistic?" It was Angelo's turn to search for the right word.

Eva thought for a moment. "They aren't all plain. But unlike Catholicism—a religion that has had unfettered centuries to decorate"— she shot him a wry look—"you only need the Torah and ten Jewish males to have a synagogue. The rest can be cobbled together. My father says it's because Jews, as a people, have had little chance to settle. We are always on the move. The exodus never ends. We have been unable to make roots. So our roots are in our traditions, our families. Our children."

Angelo could see Eva suddenly struggling with her emotions, and he reached for her hand. Her tears made him want to tear at his clothes and pull at his hair. He hated to see her pain. He hated the terrible injustice of it all, and he could only watch helplessly as she fought for her composure.

"It's happening again, Angelo. All over again. The exodus."

He could only nod. Agreeing. But then she looked up at him, and her eyes were fierce, glittering with anger and unshed tears.

"Our rituals are all about our children. So different from Catholicism where they take a man and ask him to make vows that deprive him of his roots, of children, of family. There will be no descendants of Angelo Bianco. Your tree ends with you."

Angelo shook his head, but he didn't bother to defend the church or himself. Eva was angry, and she had a right to be. The anger and the hurt and the longing for things to be different, both in the world and with them, was like a tangled ball of string, interwoven and indistinguishable. He understood that. And in a way, he felt it too. Angelo didn't think Eva blamed him for the way things were. But she did blame him for the way things could never be.

"I didn't come here to see Santa Croce. It is wonderful, but some other time. Come on." Angelo released Eva's hand and gripped her elbow, tugging her toward the picturesque cloisters to the right of the massive church.

They worked their way around until they stood at the columned entrance of the renowned Pazzi Chapel.

"Filippo Brunelleschi's Pazzi Chapel, famed for its Renaissance architecture," Eva parroted. She was Florentine, after all, and Camillo Rosselli was her father, a man who valued learning above all else. But Angelo was pretty sure she'd never seen beyond the exterior.

"Very good. Now come inside and sit with me," he demanded.

She followed obediently, stepping into the quiet chapel. She was clearly expecting more extravagance, more opulence. Instead, Angelo watched as her face softened and her chest rose and fell, deeply at first, as if she couldn't find her breath. Then her hand rose to her chest and she left it resting there, as if her heart had attempted to break out and fly up into the soaring, simplistic beauty of the domed interior.

"You like it," he said, more than a little pleased. He led her to the stone bench that lined the walls beneath the long windows and the arched pilasters that made up the rectangular perimeter of the room. Angelo sat down with a sigh, stretching his legs out before him, his hand rubbing absently at his knee. There was always a little pain when he wore the prosthetic, like a shoe that rubs in all the wrong places. He didn't mind the pain for the most part. It reminded him of his weaknesses and made him thankful for his strengths.

"This is where the monks of Santa Croce would have sat, once upon a time. This was a meeting room, a chapter house," he softly explained to Eva. They were alone in the chapel, but the space demanded reverence.

"I wonder how the violin would sound in here," Eva mused, her eyes on the light that poured through the oculus at the top of the dome overhead.

"Wonderful. This space, with you on the violin. Paradise," Angelo said, wishing he could hear it. The strain he'd felt between them all day had dissipated at the chapel doors, and they sat in companionable silence.

"The plan of Brunelleschi's chapel is the circle and the square—a rectangular base with a conical central dome. Every space is divided geometrically. The dimensions are mathematical, every proportion is perfect. Everything is in harmony; nothing is superfluous. The white plaster of the walls, the gray stone pilasters, even the glazed terra-cotta circular paintings, are mellow, serene, and balanced," he explained in hushed tones.

"I can feel that," Eva said, nodding. "I like it here." She paused and then added with incredulity, "I've lived my whole life in this city. How have I not been inside this chapel before?"

"You were born in Florence. You take it for granted. But I was born in New Jersey. It is not exactly known for its art. Even as a boy, and a pretty sad, homesick boy at that, I recognized that this city was special. If you look down on Florence from the hills surrounding her, you see the domes, the bell towers, the medieval castle ramparts, and it's almost as if no time has passed at all—like the Renaissance is still in full swing. There's a sense of timelessness, of being transported back five hundred years when chapels like this were being built."

"You've climbed the hills? I haven't even climbed any hills," Eva teased.

"You doubt me?" Angelo smiled and tapped his prosthetic leg with his cane.

"No." She smiled too. "I think you were born with half a leg so the rest of us could keep up."

"Ah, Eva. Spoken like a true sister."

"I'm not your sister, Angelo," she said softly, and he didn't argue. Funny how they both employed or rejected the familial relationship when it suited their own purposes. But he needed to confess something, and he couldn't wait any longer.

"Eva?"

"Yes?" There was fear in her voice.

"Do you remember a year ago, in the Jewish cemetery, when you told me that Camillo worried that I had been pushed into the seminary, coerced a little?"

Eva nodded.

"I didn't want to admit it then. I was afraid if I admitted it, you wouldn't let it go. But your father was right."

Eva's eyebrows shot up at the admission, but he continued lightly, determined to get it all out.

"Before he left me here, my father told me what was expected of me. He told me my uncle had made inquiries and recommendations, and that I would be entering the seminary. He reassured me I would be cared for and taught. He told me that because of my leg, physical work, the kind he did, wouldn't be an option for me, and the church was the best place for me. 'It will be hard for you to provide for a family, Angelo. Your duty is to be able to provide for yourself and not be a burden to others,'" Angelo quoted softly.

"He said that?" Eva's cheeks pinked, and her hands clenched in outrage.

"He did," he said, nodding. "Forgive him, Eva. I have."

"You could have been anything you wanted to be, Angelo. You still can."

"Ah, there she is again. The girl who thinks I can walk on water."

"I'm Jewish, Angelo. I don't think anyone can walk on water."

He shook his head at her irreverent humor and smiled in spite of himself.

"When I'm here, I feel like I can simply immerse myself in space. All my life I have been physically imbalanced because of my leg, but in here, everything makes sense. Everything is simple. My mind and body are in harmony. There is balance."

"But you can't live here," she said. Angelo thought her intention was probably to tease, but her voice sounded plaintive.

"No. I can't. But I can do my best to carry that peace inside of me, that sense of purpose. I didn't want to be a priest in the beginning, Eva. But I have come to believe it is what God wants for me. I started to believe it the day I saw Saint George. I don't know how, and I don't know why, but I have to defeat my own dragons. We all do. This is the way I will defeat mine."

Eva's face was pale, and Angelo could see her pulse hammering at her throat. His own pulse pounded in his head, and he felt a bead of sweat trickle down his spine under the shirt he wore beneath his seminarian's robes.

"The art I've shown you today is old, ancient. But the art centers on one thing. It is the story of Christianity. And that gospel is a living, breathing thing, still inspiring and moving men and women today. It is the thing that separates us from chaos, from selfishness, from being lost. It is the breather of hope and the light in the dark. It has always been enough for me, more than enough. I fell in love with the Catholic Church through the art, then I was asked to give my life to her. It was easy for me, don't you see? When you love someone that completely, you will do anything for them. I feel that way about the church and about God." He hesitated briefly and then, with a deep breath, said, "And I feel that way about you."

Eva's eyes snapped to Angelo's, and he saw a flash of joy in their deep brown depths before it flickered out with the realization that there was more. He wasn't finished.

"I would do anything for you, Eva. Anything." He thought of what Camillo had said about not only blessing lives, but saving Jewish lives, and it gave him the strength to continue. "But I can't have you *and* the church. I need the church, Eva. I need the church, and I believe the church needs me."

She didn't respond. Not at all. Not a glance or a sigh. Not a word.

"Eva?" The question was soft. But he knew. He could feel it between them, dark, thick, slippery. Dangerous.

She turned and raised her eyes to his.

His breath caught in his throat as he rose stiffly from the stone bench and stepped away. He had to step away from her.

Dear God. What had he done?

She didn't just love him. She was *in love* with him. And he was unable to give himself to her. The truth he'd been skirting rose in his chest like spilled oil—dark, thick, slippery. Dangerous.

He took several steps away, turned, and walked back. She rose to meet him. Her eyes shone and her lips trembled.

Kyrie, eléison. Lord have mercy. *Christe, eléison.* Christ have mercy.

"I can't," he whispered.

"You can," she whispered back, almost pleading, abandoning all pretense. For a minute he let the possibility pull at him again. Could he? He shut his eyes and tried to imagine walking away from the church. His father's words echoed in his head. *You belong in the church. It is the best place for you. Your job is to not be a burden.* He pushed the words away, but Camillo's voice rose up as well, and the chorus was deafening. *You will be in a position to do so much good. Save my family!* And finally, Monsignor Luciano's parting salvo. *It is not who you are, Angelo.*

"I can't, Eva," he said more firmly. "I won't," he added, his voice harsh. He would be strong. He would not lose the battle in this moment. Not even for Eva.

"You already have." Her voice was mild, but the pain was sharp, making her mouth twist wryly. She mocked herself, and the agony in her face echoed in his chest. She was reflected in him, and he in her. It had always been that way. When she was in front of him, she was the only thing he could see. She filled his vision. But his eyes were single to a different glory.

He closed them briefly and took a deep breath. When he opened them again, only steel remained.

"It was wrong, Eva. On so many levels. You know it. I know it. Neither of us can afford to let it happen again. It won't happen again." He kept his hands clenched at his sides, holding himself firm.

"I love you, Angelo." The last truth, and maybe the only truth that really mattered.

"And I love you!" he shot back. The truth was terrifying to him, but not as terrifying as turning from the only course he truly believed in.

"But not enough?"

"More than anyone I've ever loved before."

"But not enough," she repeated.

"We are only as good as the promises we keep, Eva. And I've made a promise. You don't want a man who can't keep his promises, do you?"

Their eyes caught and held. And he saw the moment she believed him. He recognized her defeat, saw her acceptance. He saw Eva, the little girl who had always given in to his whims and followed his lead. She knew he wouldn't yield. Unyielding Angelo, she'd called him. She'd told him once that his virtue was as disheartening as it was admirable. He didn't feel virtuous at the moment.

She nodded then. An acknowledgment, an acquiescence. A muscle in his jaw jumped and his lips firmed. Without a word he held out his arm. But she wouldn't take it.

"Please just go, Angelo. Just go," she whispered.

"I want to walk you home. I need to see that you are safe."

"I need you to leave me now." Her voice grew stronger.

"I won't do that," he insisted, willing her to yield once more.

"You already have," she said again. And when her eyes rose to his, the little girl was gone. "Go, Angelo."

It was his turn to yield.

With a heavy heart, he turned and left the quiet chapel, knowing this time, and forever more, Eva wouldn't be following.

1940

10 June, 1940

Confession: I still love my country, even after what she has done.

Italy has not been loyal to her Jews, but in my heart, bruised and betrayed as it is, I am still Italian, and my soul quakes at the thought of what is to come for my country, even if she has rejected me.

We are officially at war. Italy invaded France and simultaneously declared war on Great Britain. No more rumors or threats, no more posturing and pounding of chests. Italy is at war, allied with Germany. We are allied with a country led by a man who hates Jews.

I wonder how many men, how many Jews, will have to die for Hitler to declare himself the winner. Germany already invaded Denmark and Norway, rolling over them without mercy. Belgium surrendered in only eighteen days. Next is France. When England falls there will be no one left to stop them.

America wants no part in the war. I want no part in it either. Jews are not allowed to fight anyway. Non-Italian Jews resent us for it. Impromptu work orders are popping up all over the city, run by the Fascist police. Jewish men and boys, and sometimes women too, can be randomly pulled from their homes or off the street to shovel gravel or dig ditches or *move bricks from one place to another. It is our patriotic duty, the Fascists say. They say it is the least we can do, as if we made the laws that banned us from military service. Better banned than forced to fight with Hitler, I suppose. But it feels wrong to sit by while others fight, even if they die for terrible things.*

Angelo has banned me too. Banned me and abandoned me. Just like Italy. Last November he was ordained to the priesthood, and I haven't seen him since.

Eva Rosselli

CHAPTER 6
SHIVAH

Two days after Italy entered the war, Camillo interrupted Eva and Felix in the music room, and the desperate look in her father's eyes had Eva's palms sweating and her heart racing.

"There are immigration officials here, Felix," Camillo said grimly. "Police. *Carabinieri.*"

Felix froze, his bow in midair, his violin positioned for the swelling high point that would never come. Resignation shrouded Felix's features, and his hands fell to his sides even as his shoulders slumped. He set his violin carefully on the settee and placed the bow beside it.

They all descended the stairs slowly, as if pulling against an invisible band that sought to draw them back to the security of the music room, to the safety of Paganini and Bach, to the comforting routine of long notes and scales.

Three Italian policemen stood in the entry. Fabia had ushered them in and offered them refreshment. She never could get used to the fact that she wasn't supposed to open the door like hired help. She was no longer a domestic. She was the lady of the house, but no one could convince her of that. In her mind, nothing had changed. Camillo's maneuverings were just that, maneuverings. It was his home, and she was his housekeeper. Beloved. But still the housekeeper.

"Felix Adler?" one policeman asked briskly.

"Yes. I am Felix Adler," Uncle Felix replied wearily. He looked almost relieved, as if he had been anticipating the visit and was grateful not to wait any longer.

"We have an order for your arrest."

"I see." Felix nodded slowly and clasped his hands behind his back, strangely docile. He was neither the fiery maestro nor the melancholy philosopher anymore.

"But he is an Italian citizen!" Camillo was not resigned. He looked stricken, as if he had somehow failed again. Otto and now Felix.

"He is a foreign Jew. His citizenship was revoked with the 1938 laws." The policeman showed Camillo his orders. It had all kinds of official-looking stamps on it. Italians loved their stamps.

"But he received an exemption," Camillo insisted.

"It has been revoked as well." The officer folded the paper and tucked it beneath his arm.

Camillo reared back in shock, and angry color bloomed high on his cheeks. "When? Why?"

The policemen ignored Camillo and addressed Felix once more. "You will come with us, please."

"Where will you take him?" Camillo said, his voice shaking with outrage.

"He will be detained for a time. Eventually, he will be sent to Ferramonti, or maybe Campagna in Salerno. Somewhere in the south."

"But he will stay in Italy?" Camillo asked helplessly. He looked at his brother-in-law, but Felix didn't comment. Felix's quiet acceptance was almost as unsettling as the arrest order.

"Most likely. Don't worry. We are not like the Nazis. He will not be mistreated. We are at war, and this is for the security of Italy. That is all. It is simply internment. Nothing to be afraid of," the Italian officer reassured them. He'd noticed Eva and had puffed out his chest and smiled at her as if she would possibly welcome the attention at such a time.

"May I pack a small bag?" Felix asked politely. Eva could only stare at her uncle's blank face as he waited for an answer.

"Yes. But quickly. There is not room or time to gather all your belongings. Your basic needs will be provided for."

Felix nodded agreeably and walked from the room. The officer trailed him, as if those being arrested had been known to make a run for it, but he stayed at the top of the staircase, dividing his attention between Eva and Felix's room. Felix had left his door ajar and they could hear him moving about, opening and closing drawers, letting everyone know he was doing as he was told.

When the gunshot came it was oddly muffled, yet it reverberated through the house like a slammed door. For several stunned seconds, no one moved. The officer at the top of the stairs was the first to react, walking briskly to the room where his detainee had disappeared.

They all stood, frozen, eyes lifted to the balcony overlooking the parlor, waiting for an explanation. Then they heard a shout and a string of Italian curses mixed with pleas to the Madonna.

Camillo began to run, taking the stairs two at a time, a sight Eva had never seen before. Camillo Rosselli didn't run. His response had Eva racing up the circular steps behind him, but before she could enter Uncle Felix's room, her father turned and, with shaking hands, bade her to remain outside.

"Wait, Eva!" he commanded. "Let me go first."

The *carabiniere* was suddenly back, his face pale, his upper lip shining with perspiration. He shut Felix's bedroom door behind him, as if the matter were closed.

"He is dead," he said. "He has shot himself in the head." His voice was matter-of-fact, but his throat worked like he was trying not to be sick. He shoved his black cap back on his head, avoiding Eva's gaze for the first time since he'd arrived at the villa. She immediately shoved past him and reached for the door, bursting through into the masculine space that smelled like shoe polish, coffee, and the soap Felix used when he shaved. But there was another smell. Blood. It smelled like blood and an acrid scent Eva would later come to recognize as gunpowder.

"Eva!" Her father grabbed at her arm and pulled her back. But not before she saw the crimson pool that crawled like a living thing beneath the closet door and across the terrazzo floor.

Felix Adler had stepped into his closet, closed the door, and calmly killed himself.

∞

As far as families were concerned, they definitely weren't typical— Angelo was sure most Jewish families didn't include a Catholic priest and his Catholic grandparents, but they were the only family Felix Adler had. Felix didn't have any parents left—he only had Santino and Fabia. He had no siblings, just Camillo, a brother-in-law. He wasn't married and he didn't have children, though he'd treated Eva and Angelo as though they were his own. Thus, Camillo, Eva, Santino, Fabia, and Angelo gathered at the synagogue before the service, the five of them charged with the duty of *avelim*, official mourners.

Angelo had come from his little parish as soon as he received word, and Eva had fallen into his arms, the strain between them temporarily forgotten for a more immediate concern. They'd had no contact since his ordination. No letters, no telegrams, no friendly visits. It had been seven months since he'd received his Holy Orders, seven months since he'd been home.

Now they stood side by side, Eva's arm wrapped around his as Rabbi Cassuto offered what little explanation he could for something inexplicable. Eva herself had had little to say. She had not been far from Angelo's side since the moment he'd arrived, and though she'd clung to him, letting him know she needed him, she'd been silent—she even wept quietly—as if Felix had taken sound with him. The maestro was gone, and the music was too.

Camillo wanted her to play at the service, but she just shook her head, and he'd seemed to understand. He found another student of Felix's to play something by Mendelssohn, something Felix would have appreciated, and the matter was dropped.

Before the service began, they ripped Felix's shirt, a ritual called *keriah*, or tearing, symbolizing their separation and the loss in the fabric of their family. He had been torn from them, and as each of them rent a piece of the garment, they recited the passage from the Book of Job. God has given, God has taken away, blessed be the name of God. They would wear the strip of cloth attached to their clothing and would keep it there for the seven days of shivah.

God had not taken Felix away. Felix had chosen to go. And though suicide was treated as seriously in Judaism as it was in Catholicism, there was no judgment, and Rabbi Cassuto was the first to add, "*Baruch atah Adonai, Dayan Ha-Emet*"—Blessed are you, Adonai, truthful judge. Felix was a casualty of war, Rabbi Cassuto said, and that was the end of it.

Angelo had conducted his first funeral a month before. A beloved mother and wife in his impoverished parish who'd died unexpectedly. He'd been terrified of failing the family in their time of need but found that as long as he kept his focus on the deceased and on her loved ones, and stopped worrying about himself, he was fine. He'd conducted the funeral service in Latin and Rabbi Cassuto spoke in Hebrew—Eva had to translate what she knew—but the sentiments were mostly the same. We are made in his image, and to him we return.

After the service, they'd joined the long procession to the grave site, stopping seven times as if to show the difficulty of the task, the pain of the ordeal. And when Felix's casket was eventually lowered into the ground, they shoveled dirt over his final resting place, committing him back to the earth. It was beautiful and painful. Just like life. Just like coming home. Just like seeing Eva again.

They went back to the villa and spent the rest of the day welcoming a steady stream of friends and neighbors, until eventually, just like the other rituals of the day, that too had come to an end. Now he sat next to Eva on a stool so low that his prosthetic stuck out in front of him, his eyes on the candle that had been lit the moment they returned and had been burning ever since.

"What does *shivah* mean?" he asked, wanting to pull her from the solitude of her silence. She was so withdrawn he was worried about her.

"It means 'seven,'" she answered immediately.

"Ah, I see. We stopped seven times today. And you will sit shivah for a week. Seven days." Strange. It had been seven months since he'd been home.

"Yes."

"Why is seven significant?"

"It's from Job. When he lost everything, his friends sat with him for seven days and seven nights, grieving with him and for him."

They fell into silence once more, and Angelo was at a loss, sick at heart, helpless to the point of tears, frustrated that he couldn't hold her and make her laugh, that things between them couldn't be easy and comfortable, the way they once were. He fisted his hands in his hair and found himself confessing.

"I can't stay, Eva. I would like to. But I have responsibilities that can't wait."

"I know," she said softly. "Thank you for coming."

"I would take it away from you if I could. I would take it with me. I would take your pain and bear it for you." He would happily endure her sorrow if it meant she wouldn't have to.

"I know," she said again, as if she truly believed him. "I know you would. But sadly, that is not how pain works, is it? We can cause pain, but we can so seldom cure it."

"Talk to me. Maybe that will ease it. Tell me what all of this means." He swept his hand around the room, including the candle and the covered mirrors, the low stools and the meal of condolence that the family had eaten. It had been a strange mix of eggs and bread and lentils—not the kind of comfort food he would have chosen. "Tell me about the candle," he suggested, giving her a starting point.

"A member of the family lights the candle immediately upon entering the home. It's called the shivah candle, and it burns for the entire seven days."

Angelo nodded, encouraging her.

"The candle reminds us of the soul of the one who has gone, and also of God's light. After all, he created our souls with his light. It's from a psalm, I think."

"The light of God is the soul of man," Angelo quoted.

"Yes." Eva nodded. "That's the one." She stopped talking, a contemplative expression on her face, and Angelo pressed her, not wanting her to slip away again.

"And these stools?"

Eva looked startled, as if she'd forgotten he was there for a moment. "Oh. Well, we are closer to the ground. Closer to the loved one who is now in the ground."

Symbolism. He was a Catholic priest. If he understood anything, he understood symbolism.

"And the mirrors?" he prodded. The mirrors were all shrouded in dark cloth.

"Grieving is not a time to worry about appearances. There should be no judgment in grief. People should be allowed to grieve in any way they need. It is a kindness to the mourners. Shivah is about those left behind."

He reached over and took her hand in his, needing to give comfort, and they sat, staring at the flickering candle, holding hands across the space between their odd little stools.

"I sat shivah after you were ordained," Eva blurted out suddenly. "I didn't realize that was what I was doing. But for a week I didn't leave the house. I couldn't. I covered the mirror in my room so I wouldn't have to look at myself. And I slept on the floor. You left me behind, and I was grieving." She laughed hollowly and let go of his hand. Angelo didn't know what to say, but somehow she'd given him some of her pain to bear, because all at once his heart was heavy with shared sorrow.

She had come to his ordination. She, Camillo, Felix, Santino, and Fabia. His family. He had wondered often about her impressions of that day. What had she thought as he lay, prostrate on the floor, his arms folded beneath him, his forehead pressed to the ground, his eyes closed, letting the litany of the saints roll over him, through him?

Kyrie, eléison. Lord have mercy. *Christe, eléison.* Christ have mercy. *O God, make me worthy. Make me better. Help me to be a valiant servant. Help me to be more than I am,* he had silently prayed, wanting only to be better, to be worthy.

Donatello's Saint George had risen in his mind and moisture had fallen from his eyes. "Help me slay my dragons," he had whispered. "Help me resist the serpent. Help me resist. Help me. Help me."

"O God the Father of Heaven, have mercy upon us. O God the Son, Redeemer of the World, have mercy upon us. O God the Holy Ghost, have mercy upon us," the voices around him had intoned.

His hands were anointed and bound, consecrating them, sanctifying them, that whatsoever they blessed would in turn be blessed by God. The bishop had placed his hands upon his head, asking him if he could swear obedience. He had said yes. Yes to obedience. The bishop asked him if he could give his life to God and forsake personal wealth. He had said yes. Yes to poverty. And finally, he had said yes to celibacy. Forsaking the pleasure of the flesh for the joys of the kingdom of God. He had said yes. He had promised his life and his heart and his loyalty.

Yet still, he had wondered. He had wondered if, as Eva watched, she felt the same stirrings that moved him whenever the Eucharist was raised and voices were lifted in worship. He wondered if she saw the beauty and understood. He had wanted so badly for her to understand. And he desperately needed to stop caring.

She leaned toward him suddenly, and Angelo thought for a moment that she was reaching for his hand once more. Instead, she tugged on a loose thread hanging from the sleeve of his cassock and tore it free. She held the little string between her fingers, smoothing it over and over.

When he left for Rome the next morning, the string from his cassock was tied around the piece of fabric from Felix's shirt and pinned to her blouse.

In August, two months after Felix's death, Eva's father took her to the beach—a day trip, he called it. That's all they were allowed anymore. Day trips. They couldn't stay at the resorts or rent a cottage. So they took the train from Florence to Viareggio, walked the ten minutes from the train station, and kicked off their shoes and walked in the sand, pretending it was all the vacation they really needed.

Camillo's ankles were skinny knobs sticking out below his rolled slacks. He took off his hat and let the breeze sift through his salt-and-pepper hair as the sun glinted off his spectacles. Eva shouldered their lunch and tucked her shoes inside the hamper so she wouldn't have to carry them. The beach was crowded, a forest of umbrellas and laughing children, and Eva longed for the beaches of Maremma with stretches so isolated you could walk and never see another soul.

Eventually, they found a place to sit and spread their lunch on a blanket, watching everything and nothing, trying to enjoy the change of scenery, if only for each other. The wind kicked up once, spraying them with sand and surf, and their lunch became decidedly crunchier.

"It's funny, isn't it?" Camillo said vaguely, his eyes on his feet.

"What's funny, Babbo?"

"There is sand in my sandwich and sand between my toes." He shook one foot and then the other, as if verifying that there was, indeed, sand between his toes.

"That isn't terribly funny," Eva teased.

"It is irritating me. Sand everywhere, in my food, in my clothes, rubbing against soft skin, every crack and crevice. I don't think I like eating on the beach. No matter what I do, I can't seem to avoid it." His voice was thoughtful, like he was puzzling something out, solving a riddle. Eva just waited, accustomed to her father's roundabout way of expressing himself.

"But sand is my business. Sand, soda ash, and lime. Without sand, there wouldn't be glass. My father named the company Ostrica—oyster—because the oyster takes the sand and makes it into something beautiful. Like we do. We take the sand and make it into glass."

"I didn't know that! Grandfather Rosselli was a romantic."

"We want to make the mundane beautiful. Isn't that right?" he asked. Eva remembered the conversation she'd had with Angelo in the cemetery, when she'd explained what a mitzvah was.

"Everything is a mitzvah to you," she said softly, and wrapped her arm through Camillo's, her eyes on the horizon, her thoughts on Angelo and oysters. No matter how hard she tried, everything reminded her of Angelo.

"Not so. I am just an oyster, hiding in my shell, turning sand into glass." His voice was so melancholy, the ache beneath it so audible, that she pulled her eyes and thoughts back to his face.

"What are you talking about?"

"I'm really no different from so many others, I suppose. I have been hoping it would all right itself."

"What?"

"The world, Eva. The terrible state of the world. I thought I could just juggle, strategize, bend myself and my circumstances around the laws. And I have. I've managed to keep the business afloat, keep our home, provide for you and Santino and Fabia. But the world isn't going to right itself, Italy isn't going to right herself. Not without help. I can't continue hoping and doing nothing. I can't continue hiding in my shell and making glass. I have to do more. We all have to do more. Or we will all die."

"Babbo?" She heard the alarm in her voice, and her father turned to her with sorrow-filled eyes.

"I have to go get your grandfather, Eva. I owe it to Felix."

"In Austria? But . . . isn't he in a . . . camp?"

"The Germans can't possibly want one old man. He won't be a good worker. I will buy his way out. Trade something of value. It is what I'm good at. I'm a natural-born salesman. You know that. I will get him and I will bring him here with us. Then Angelo will help us hide him until the war is over."

"How will you get him out?"

"Eva, Ostrica provides bottles to many wineries in Austria. I have been to Austria dozens of times, and I have every reason in the world to travel there for business. I am an Italian citizen, and my documents clearly show that. No one will question me. I have identity papers for Otto claiming that he is also an Italian citizen."

"How did you get false papers?" she cried.

"I have a very good printer at Ostrica. You remember Aldo Finzi? He makes labels for bottles—beautiful labels—and we have been making passes, Eva. We are making false papers for refugees. It is some of the best work Aldo has ever done. I didn't want to tell you. What you don't know can't hurt you."

"Oh, Babbo," she moaned. "If you get caught with Grandfather, they might arrest you both. They could take the factory if they discover you are forging documents there."

"I do not own the factory," Camillo said lightly. "How can they take it away?"

"Does Signore Sotelo know?" Gino Sotelo was her father's best friend and non-Jewish business partner.

"Yes. Gino knows. And if something happens to me, I hope he will let Aldo continue his work. It is work that will save lives."

Her stomach rolled and her heart plummeted. She was worried about her father's life most of all, and what he was planning to do would put it in terrible danger. Eva didn't really believe her grandfather was still alive in Austria. He'd been arrested, taken away, and Uncle Felix had lost hope. Then they'd lost Felix too. But they'd lost him incrementally, inch by inch, indignity by indignity, until there was nothing left when he finally pulled the trigger.

"Don't worry, Eva. I will be fine, and I will bring Otto back. I can't leave him there. He cannot save himself. No Austrians are being allowed to leave anymore, especially Austrian Jews."

"You can't go! Please don't go."

"I have everything in order. I won't draw attention. I will be courteous and quiet, just like I always am. Invisible. And everything will go smoothly, you'll see."

"If something happens to you I will have no one left. No one," Eva cried, abandoning her courage for honesty. She couldn't let him go.

"I will be fine. But no matter what happens to me, you will always have Angelo. He promised me. You will always have Angelo." Her father's voice was fierce, as if he could make it so by sheer will.

"Oh, Babbo, you don't understand! I will never have Angelo." She looked out at the horizon, squinting into the sun, letting her eyes burn as she cried. "I don't have Angelo, I don't have Uncle Felix, and soon I won't have you."

1943

16 September, 1943

Confession: I never feel safe

*Just last Wednesday, people were dancing in the streets saying the war is over
for Italy. Italy surrendered to America and an armistice had been granted.
Everyone said the Americans would be arriving soon and our soldiers would
be coming home. Some even said the Racial Laws would be revoked. But on
Saturday, the Germans moved in and occupied Florence. They have taken
control of everything north of Naples. The celebration is over but the war is
definitely not. The sides have just changed.*

*We've had no word from Babbo. I try not to think about him at all
because it hurts too much. Maybe I'm weak, but I've heard rumors about
the labor camps. Some say they are death camps, and I'm afraid I'll never
see Babbo again. So I put him out of my head completely and I put one foot
in front of the other. Forgive me, Babbo.*

*Angelo is here. He's back. He says everything is going to get worse, not
better. He thinks I need to go back with him to Rome. I don't know why
he thinks Rome will be safer for me. The Americans bombed Rome in July,
and so far, no bombs have fallen in Florence. But he says he can hide me.
He's been helping Jewish refugees since the war began. Santino and Fabia
will be alone, but Angelo says I only endanger them. Santino and Fabia*

are afraid for me, and they begged me to go. They think Angelo can keep me safe. They don't know that Angelo makes me feel things that aren't safe. He makes me reckless and angry. He makes me sad. And I know he doesn't feel safe with me.

     Eva Rosselli

CHAPTER 7
THE VILLA

Angelo had made the trip from Rome to Florence twelve times in the last eighteen months, and none of the visits were of a personal nature. He had a reason to visit his hometown, knew the city and its residents well, particularly those within church circles, and he spoke English, enough French to get by, passable German, and of course, flawless Italian. He was young and handsome, drawing some attention wherever he went, but his black priest's robes, stiff white Roman collar, and his missing limb gave him an alibi that many Italian men did not enjoy.

There were Jews hiding across Italy, but there were twice as many soldiers running for cover, trying to avoid being shot on sight or rounded up and sent to Germany to labor in work camps. Italy's surrender to the Americans on September 8 had put her citizens and her soldiers in an impossible situation. They were now Germany's enemies instead of her allies, and the Germans considered the soldiers, when they found them, prisoners of war. More than one young priest had been hassled by the Gestapo, and a few had found themselves in jail until someone could come and vouch for them. Angelo didn't have that trouble. He was exactly who he said he was, which made his movements a great deal easier.

That morning he had escorted a group of foreign refugees from Rome just as he'd been instructed. He'd separated the eight refugees on the train so that if one was caught the others might still have a chance. He'd told them all to pretend to sleep so when they were asked for their documents they could sleepily hand them over without speaking and giving themselves away.

The trip took six hours, but the refugees had played their parts. It had all gone as smoothly as he had hoped. He'd escorted them from the Stazione di Santa Maria Novella and from there to the nearby basilica with the same name. At the basilica they were met by another priest who would take them on to Genoa. From Genoa, someone else would take them on, hopefully, to safety.

There were other refugees who were escorted into the Abruzzi, where smugglers and a local priest would bring them into Allied territory. Angelo didn't know who. None of them knew who was involved beyond their initial contact. It was safer that way. If one person was caught they couldn't betray what they didn't know. It was a network of volunteers who were blind to all but their part. No real mastermind, no official organization. Just desperate measures by willing people. And it worked only through the grace of God and the goodness and courage of each individual.

But Angelo hadn't come to Florence just for the foreign refugees. Not this time. This time, Angelo was going home, and the visit was very personal. He'd known the trip was inevitable, that the day would come. He'd been watching and waiting. When Benito Mussolini was overthrown in July and General Badoglio took his place, Angelo had waited, holding his breath. Many thought the old laws would be repealed and all would be made right. That hadn't happened. When the Americans started dropping bombs on Rome and the San Lorenzo district was destroyed, he reconsidered, wondering if Florence wasn't the safer place to be. But when the armistice was announced, and the German tanks rolled in and occupied Rome, he knew he couldn't wait any longer.

The war had hurt Florence—aged the ageless city—and her head was bowed with long-suffering, like a widowed bride. Like in Rome, there were Germans everywhere, long lines for rations, and the people didn't amble. They darted to and fro, as if rushing made them harder to hit. Harder to see. Harder to oppress. As a people, Italians were exuberant and effusive, and they didn't hurry. Italians meandered.

Not anymore. Now they scurried.

Angelo let himself in through the big gate. It wasn't locked. He would have to scold his grandfather. The days for open gates were long past. He walked across the silent courtyard of the place he had once called home, a place where he and Eva had played in the fountain and broken a few windows when he'd tried to teach her American baseball. He was pleased to see the villa looked the same. His grandparents had taken care of it. The flowers still bloomed in riotous color, and the walks were neatly swept with no debris or sign of the calamity that had gripped Italy in its fist. The heat had eased, and the September air was balmy and the skies a brilliant blue. The beauty made him uneasy, as if the mild weather and the soft breeze conspired with the Nazis to lure them into complacency.

Angelo wondered if his grandparents' tender care of the palatial home would simply make it a bigger target. A property in the heart of the city, easily accessible. It rose up behind a high wall on a main thoroughfare. Beautiful. Well maintained. Irresistible. Just like Eva and the wall she'd built around herself. But walls wouldn't be enough. It was time for her to hide. He had to convince her to leave Florence. Eva and maybe his grandparents too. They would be better off out of the city, away from the property that could only bring them unwanted attention.

Camillo had been gone for almost three years. Three years and no word whether he lived or died. The only word they'd learned was Auschwitz. It sounded like a sneeze. Harmless. But when it was whispered among the fearful it became something else, the Grim Reaper come to call, the Black Plague. There were only rumors, but the rumors were enough to make some Jews flee with nothing but the clothes on their backs, looking for a hiding place. It made others cower in their homes, hoping that the plague would somehow miss them, spare them, and pass over, as it had once, anciently. But so often it didn't.

The wisest ones hid. Camillo Rosselli had not hidden. He'd been so confident his Italian citizenship would protect him. Camillo had been sent to Auschwitz. And that was all they knew.

Angelo raised the knocker and let it clatter against the burnished red door. His eyes fell to the right, to the place where the mezuzah had once hung. He remembered the day Camillo took it down. It was 1938, and his shoulders had been set, but tears streaked his face. He'd transferred the home from his name and given it to Santino and Fabia to protect it from the Racial Laws. When Angelo had asked him why he cried, he told him he was ashamed.

"I remove it because of fear. A better man would fight for his God. But I am not that man. It shames me to say, I am not that man."

The door opened slowly, and Fabia peered out into the afternoon sun, shading her eyes and squinting up at him.

"Angelo!" she gasped, dropping the hand that shaded her eyes so she could clap her own cheeks and then his. She pulled him forward by the face, her arms stretched to reach him. She was even smaller than he remembered. Or maybe he had grown.

"Angelo, my beautiful boy! Santino, look who's here!" Fabia called over her shoulder into the dim foyer, its cool expanse drawing Angelo's eyes. But it wasn't rest and refreshment or even his grandfather Angelo sought, but Eva.

"You are so big," his *nonna* exclaimed, drawing his eyes back to her wrinkled face. "So handsome. *Mamma mia!* You look like your father." Fabia promptly burst into tears, which hadn't changed. She couldn't talk about "her Angelino," his father, without crying. It had been so long since she'd seen him. Angelo suspected they would never see him again. The thought bothered him more for his grandparents than for himself.

His grandfather tottered from the back of the house on bowed legs, clapping and calling Angelo's name. His white hair was unchanged, thick and waving back from his sun-browned skin. His blue eyes, the eyes Angelo saw staring back at him from the mirror each day, were bright and relieved.

"You came home! You came home, Angelo. Tell us you can stay a while. We have missed you."

Angelo kissed Santino's cheeks and bent to hold him close. Unlike his eyes, Angelo's height was not something he'd inherited from his *nonno*. When he straightened and stepped back, his gaze moved to the figure descending the wide marble staircase that rose grandly from the formal entry.

Eva wore a dress of deep blue that made her skin look like cream, pale and smooth against the sapphire hue. She was thinner and her dark hair was shorter, brushing her shoulders in smooth curls as was the fashion. She used to wear it longer. Maybe age had made her more aware and careful, more mindful of the opinions and attention of others. He hoped so. It would make her safer. Eva greeted him with a soft hello, her lack of enthusiasm contrasting noticeably with Fabia's tears and Santino's clapping.

He greeted her just as soberly, wishing he could embrace her like a sister, wishing he could convince himself that was all she was, all she would ever be. His eyes clung to hers briefly, looking for forgiveness and finding none. Eva's eyes were guarded. She was young, only twenty-three years old, but she wore the same vibrating tension he had observed on so many others he had helped and sheltered throughout the last few years, and it made her seem much older than she was.

But she was still the most beautiful girl he'd ever seen.

She reached the last stair and approached him, holding out her hands. He clasped one of hers in both of his.

"Is that how it's done?" she asked softly. "Is that a priestly greeting?"

He felt a flash of anger at her mocking tone and immediately rose to the bait, pulling her into his arms and embracing her tightly, albeit briefly.

He felt her jerk, as if she hadn't expected the contact, and her gasp tickled his neck before he stepped back from her. She still smelled like the jasmine that Fabia grew in pots beneath the windows. It mingled with a subtle hint of something new, as if the sadness she wore gave off a scent of its own. Her grief had grown stronger since he'd seen her last, but then, life had delivered some heavy blows, and Eva had absorbed them all. Her jasmine-scented sadness was justified.

It had been too long. He should have come back sooner. But he'd been trying to move on, he'd been trying to let *her* move on. He wondered if they would have to start over from the very beginning, and if they did, would they manage to find common ground, a place where a Catholic boy and a Jewish girl could be friends, even family, once again? There'd been a time when she would have followed him anywhere. He wasn't sure she would follow him across the street anymore, but he was going to do his best to convince her.

The evening meal was meager—nothing was plentiful in wartime— but Eva brought out a bottle of her father's Austrian wine and there was laughter and reminiscence, even if it was flavored with forced levity. Eva participated, but her quick smile had slowed considerably, weighted down by strain. In fact, it wasn't present at all. The sparkle in her lustrous eyes was more nervous than mischievous, and there was a wary tilt to her head, as if she were listening for calamity to strike. Eva had always been grace in motion, as if the music she created on her violin was just beneath her skin. Now there was a stillness in her posture as if she were poised to bolt. He hated it, and his own tension increased considerably.

There was talk of what came next. Fabia was sure the old Racial Laws, the laws inspired by Mussolini's desire to placate Hitler, would be revoked now that Mussolini had been toppled and Germany was no longer Italy's partner in the war.

"It's going to get worse for a while, Nonna," Angelo said softly.

"Worse?" Fabia cried, likely thinking of the losses Eva had suffered, the food shortages, the deaths of thousands of Italian young men on the Russian front and in North Africa, all for a war and an ideology most of the country didn't support.

"You have to come back with me, Eva. To Rome. That's why I've come." Angelo turned to Eva, ignoring the stunned faces of his grandparents.

"Rome will be no safer than Florence," Eva protested immediately.

"It's farther south, closer to the Allied line. And no one knows you in Rome. You have false papers, yes?"

She didn't answer. She just stared, probably wondering what he knew and how he knew it.

"A false identity card won't do you any good here, Eva." He continued as if she'd given him an answer. "Too many people know you. Too many people know you are Jewish. Your papers will actually get you in more trouble. That's what got your father in trouble. He was recognized using false papers. You use them, and they will torture you until you tell them where you got them, until you give up Aldo Finzi and Gino Sotelo and Nonno and Nonna too."

Three pairs of eyes widened and Eva's chair shot back from the table. "How did you know about Aldo Finzi and Signore Sotelo?"

"I know all about them. They've been helping us for years. And I know all about what you've been doing too. "

"Us?" Eva asked sharply.

"The church," Angelo answered, unwilling to mention names, partly because he knew so few of them, partly because by not naming them, they were safer. To give the whole church credit—or blame—was disingenuous. He'd seen many pastors and parishioners who'd needed their arms twisted and their salvations threatened. But there were many who helped, in whatever way they could, opening their doors, their cellars, and their hearts to one refugee after another. He'd witnessed nuns opening cloisters that hadn't been breached by a man, any man, ever. Jewish children were hidden in Catholic schools, Jewish mothers were wearing Catholic veils, and Jewish men were becoming monks—albeit temporarily—and learning Catholic prayers in order to stay alive, and no one was trying to convert them.

"Do you really think my friends and my neighbors will run to the Fascisti and give me up? I know many of the local police. Some of them are even friendly. They are Italians first, Fascists second. And most of them hate the Germans."

"But the Germans are in charge now. Not the local *carabinieri*. And what about when they offer lire for the betrayal? When they start offering three thousand lire for every Jew? How desperate are your friends? How desperate are your neighbors? Someone will turn you in, Eva. I've seen it happen. Some Italians even think that the sooner all the Jews are found, the sooner this all will end. Give the Germans what they want so they will leave. That's what some believe."

Santino and Fabia jumped in then, trying to soothe Eva, trying to placate Angelo, trying to talk their way out of the threat they didn't want to face. It was so much easier to hope it was all going to get better. Angelo knew it wouldn't.

The subject was dropped for the sake of peace, and they all eventually retired to their separate quarters, Angelo back in his old room at the rear of the house—the servants' quarters, though he'd never been a servant. There were times he had wished his presence in that house were that clearly defined, that simple to explain or justify.

He paced in his room and finally forced himself to kneel before the old cross Nonno had hung on his wall to say his prayers. It was the Hour of Compline, an hour that should be spent filled with praise and gratitude, but Angelo found himself veering away from praise and reciting psalms of entreaty. "Make me know your ways, O Lord. Teach me your paths. Lead me in your truth and teach me, for you are the God of my salvation. For you, I wait all the day."

Since becoming the pastor of a tiny parish at twenty-two years old, he had been begging God for direction on an hourly basis. It was a never-ending chant in his head. He didn't see that changing any time soon. When he was finished, he stood and scrubbed at his face, feeling renewed. He washed his hands and calmed his breathing, and then left his room, slipping through the halls and mounting the stairs, determined to resume his campaign. He was not leaving Florence without Eva.

She answered his knock as if she'd been expecting him, and Angelo breathed a silent prayer of relief that she hadn't changed for bed. He didn't need to see Eva in a flowing dressing gown, regardless of how much it covered. She immediately retreated to the window overlooking the gardens Santino tended so carefully, the tennis court where she'd regularly trounced Angelo, and the moonlit darkness that was, to Angelo, menacing in its tranquility. It made his stomach feel hollow and his palms itch, as if the Gestapo stood in the shadowed corners of the yard and aimed their guns at the beautiful girl limned in gold and framed perfectly in the window. He walked to her and pulled her back, drawing the heavy drapes. She looked at him with eyebrows raised and didn't protest. But she immediately left his side, retreating to the opposite side of her room.

"You told me once that you believed in me. Please, believe me now. The things I've been told, Eva. The brutality I've witnessed. The soldiers who have made it back to Italy have seen the camps. They've seen the trains overflowing with Jews. Train after train. And the refugees have stories. None of it is propaganda. People don't want to believe, Eva, but I need you to listen. I need you to believe me again."

"When did I say that? 1938? Five years ago I believed in you. Now, I believe in nothing. I will stay in Florence with Fabia and Santino, and I will do my best not to die or be arrested and sent off to a camp. Okay? You can go back to Rome and your church and continue being Padre Bianco with a clear conscience. You tried. I refused. End of story."

"Madre di Dio!" Angelo cursed beneath his breath and then immediately berated himself, turning the curse into a silent prayer. *Madonna, please. Mother of Jesus, help me control my temper and save this girl.* He added a plea to his own mother and to Eva's mother, Adele, on the off chance that Jews and Catholics all went to the same heaven.

The longer he remained on this earth, the more sure he was that mankind had no clue about God or heaven. Not when they used him as an excuse to kill, to punish, to discriminate. He loved God. He felt God's love in return, but he felt no special claim to that love simply because he'd been raised a Catholic, simply because he was a priest.

"I have work to do here, Angelo. If you know what I've been doing, as you claim, then you know I can't leave."

"What does your rabbi say?" He had her there. He knew exactly what her rabbi said. Rabbi Cassuto had already hidden his wife and children in a convent. Angelo had helped arrange it. Soon, the rabbi would go into hiding too. The DELASEM offices the rabbi helped run were closed. All the Jewish aid from the organization would go completely underground from this point on.

Eva just looked at him, her throat working.

"I can't just hide, Angelo," she whispered.

"I will help you. I will hide you."

"That's not what I mean. If I go to Rome, you have to let me do what I can. I want to help . . . I want to do what you're doing," she insisted, but he could hear her weakening. He didn't let the relief he felt show in his face. He really hadn't thought he would be able to convince her.

"You're not in a position to do what I'm doing," he confessed. "But if there is a way for you to help, I promise, I will tell you."

"Why do you care, Angelo? Really?" she asked quietly.

Angelo blanched and stepped back, as if Eva had walked across her bedroom and slapped his face. His cheeks stung like she had.

Eva's expression was stony, her eyes black, as she stared him down, her arms folded across her chest.

"That's a stupid thing to say, Eva." He sounded like the boy he'd been, and hated that he was Angelo in this house and not Padre Bianco, ever patient and unflappable.

"Is it! You've gone out of your way to make me feel invisible. I don't exist to you, Angelo. I'm a Jew. Hitler doesn't want me to exist at all. Remember?"

For a moment they both remembered. Too well. But it had absolutely nothing to do with her being Jewish. And she knew it. Angelo's breath grew labored as the vise that was Eva became impossibly tight around his heart. Eva was the vise . . . and the vice. That's what she'd become for him, and he couldn't deny it.

17 September, 1943

Confession: I'm going to Rome with Angelo.

I don't know what else to do. It's too quiet and everyone is nervous, waiting. Rabbi Cassuto is urging everyone to leave their homes and hide. He says there are reports of Fascist fanatics—militarized squads—rounding up Jews and antifascists, and no one is stopping them. The Germans have deported thousands of Jews from Nice in France, Jews who had been protected by the Italian army, an army that is now disbanded. Rabbi Cassuto says the Germans won't leave Italy, and now that we are not on the same side, they won't respect our laws or citizenship. The Italian government can't protect us anymore, even if they wanted to. No one can. Uncle Augusto, Aunt Bianca, Claudia, and Levi are in Rome already. Levi is studying law at the Pontificium Institutum Utriusque Iuris—the only university that will allow Jewish students. Uncle Augusto seems to think the Vatican will be able to protect the Jews in Rome. But Uncle Augusto hasn't been right yet.

Eva Rosselli

CHAPTER 8

ROME

Eva and Angelo boarded the train early, and Santino and Fabia saw them off, their lined faces wreathed in encouraging smiles even as their eyes worried. The platform was crowded with the normal bustle and cluster of people preparing for a journey, people disembarking while others jostled to get aboard. All around them, passengers were hurrying, Germans were watching, and whistles kept blowing, making them rush through their good-byes and raise their voices to be heard over the din. The four of them pressed together, arms linked, heads bent to hear last words and expressions of love.

"Take care of her, Angelo," Eva heard Nonno say as he patted Angelo's lean cheeks.

Angelo kissed Santino's forehead and embraced him tightly. "Remember what I told you, Nonno. No resistance. If the Germans show up at your door, give them what they want. You need only worry about yourselves. Camillo wouldn't want you and Nonna to be harmed protecting his possessions. The only thing he would care about is Eva, and I will keep her safe. I promise."

Strangely enough, Fabia didn't cry. She looked too frightened to cry, and her little hands shook and her smile wobbled, and Eva resisted the urge to tell Angelo she had changed her mind, gripped by a sudden, terrible premonition that this was the last time she would see Santino and Fabia, that they would be whisked into the ether the way her father and Uncle Felix had, never to be seen or heard from again. Her panic must have shown, because Fabia grabbed her hands and the fear in her face was replaced with stern affection.

"We love you, Eva," she said firmly. "We have lived good lives. We have been happy. Don't worry about us. We have each other, and we will be fine. Someday the war will be over and we will be together again. And you will play for me, yes?"

"Yes," Eva whispered, unable to hold back her tears. Fabia hugged her close and spoke into her ear. "God sees you, Eva. He sees Angelo too. And he is a loving God."

Eva embraced Fabia tightly, but her mind resisted the sentiments. Either God saw everyone or he saw no one. Too many were crying out for him to see them with no response.

Angelo touched her arm and picked up her heavy suitcase, setting his own small bag atop it, gripping it beneath his arm as he leaned into his cane and allowed his tiny *nonna* one more embrace. Eva clutched her little valise and her violin, and together they boarded the train, promising to send word as soon as they arrived in Rome.

"They will be all right. They have nothing to worry about," Angelo said softly. He didn't say, "now that you're gone," but Eva heard the words anyway. Those who sheltered Jews would not be safe now that the Germans were in charge.

"This is your pass." He handed her a document and she took it, confused.

"I have a pass, Angelo."

"A priest would not be traveling alone with a young woman he is not related to. You are my sister now. See?" He tapped the document she was holding, and she looked down at it. It looked completely authentic—from the different stamps, to the emblem on the front, to the type inside. And Eva would know. She'd been helping Aldo make false papers since her father had gone to Austria and never come home again. But her name was now Eva Bianco, and she was not a Jew.

"How?"

"Aldo," he said briefly. "I asked him to make it a while back. Just in case."

"I'm from Naples?" she asked, her voice pitched for his ears only.

"No one will give the Germans any information they seek south of the Allied line. They have no way to verify you aren't who you say you are."

"Except I don't speak with a Neapolitan dialect."

"A German won't be able to tell. You speak Italian. They don't. And if they do, you can fake it. You've always had a great ear, and a German won't be nearly discerning enough to distinguish dialects."

Their hushed conversation ended abruptly when a couple with a child entered the compartment and sat across from them. A heavy-set man followed a few minutes later and sat on Angelo's right. Unless they wanted to discuss inanities, which was far too much work, they wouldn't be talking much on the trip. It was better that way. Eva didn't need to talk to Angelo. She didn't need Angelo at all. She was going to go see her uncle Augusto as soon as they arrived, and she had every intention of moving in with him, Aunt Bianca, Claudia, and Levi. She would stay with them until the Germans left Italy. She would assist Angelo in refugee work where she could—she had grown adept as a printer's apprentice if he could find her a press—but she wasn't going to hide in a convent, as Angelo had suggested the night before.

The first hours of their journey passed without incident, but at the station in Chiusi, several German officers boarded the train with a civilian translator wearing a black armband, signifying his Fascist affiliations.

"Documenti!" the civilian shouted, and people started to scramble for their papers. Eva's palms grew damp and her breaths short. There was always a first time for a false pass, and this was hers. Aldo had always told her his documents were without equal. She would know soon enough.

Angelo seemed completely at ease, and when the German approached and demanded their passes, Angelo bowed his head in a priestly fashion and placed his in the officer's hand.

The German looked at Angelo's pass for what seemed an eternity. He talked quietly to the Italian interpreter, and though Eva spoke fluent German, she couldn't hear what he said. Finally, he leveled pale, suspicious eyes on Angelo, who did not seem at all alarmed by the scrutiny.

He then looked at Eva sitting next to Angelo, and his eyes narrowed further. He stuck his palm in front of her face. "Papers?"

She placed her identity card in his hand, the one Angelo had given her only hours before.

The German eyed the document with the same suspicion.

"Bianco, eh? Interesting. Her name is the same as yours?" He looked at Angelo. His companion rushed to translate.

"She is my sister," Angelo lied calmly. He was a very good liar, Eva thought.

"Sie ist meine Schwester," the translator repeated.

"I do not think this is your sister. I think this is your wife," the German said.

The translator rushed to spit out the words they already understood.

"For all I know you are a deserter," he continued. "An Italian coward, a soldier running from your responsibilities. I do not think you are a priest."

"She is my sister, and I am a priest. Not a soldier. Not a deserter." Angelo pulled up his cassock and tapped his prosthetic, drawing the attention of the German inspector. "I was never a soldier. Men with one leg do better as priests."

Convinced, but not happy about it, the soldier handed back their papers with a huff and moved on to his next victims. He'd been so intent on Angelo, he'd hardly looked twice at Eva's pass, other than to pounce on her name. Eva slid her pass back into her bag and allowed herself to breathe, just for a moment. Her eyes slid to Angelo's and he met her gaze, smiling slightly. There was no privacy, no chance to celebrate the tiny victory, but when he tapped his nose, she tugged her ear, an old baseball signal he'd taught her once, and turned her eyes out the window so she wouldn't smile back at him.

Eva marveled at the ease with which Angelo bared his prosthetic. It hadn't always been that way. He had made her wait six months before he'd shown her his leg. She'd been dying to know, and he'd been reticent to share. In exchange for the privilege of seeing the leg that "wasn't there," she had read him confession after confession, journal entry after journal entry, and he had listened like she was the most fascinating person in the world.

He hadn't looked at her that way in a very long time.

In fact, Angelo tried very hard not to look at her at all. Even now, his eyes were trained out the window, watching the countryside streak by, a blur of colors and shapes, the speed erasing the details and the definition, until it looked more like a smeared painting than real life. The way Angelo was now, she could almost believe that the boy he'd been had not been real either.

Eva pulled her journal and a pen from her valise and opened it to a blank page, needing to do something to take her eyes from him, to forget him, but instead she remembered the first time she heard his name.

Angelo. Angelo Bianco. White Angel.

She had loved him instantly. They had both known loss. That much was true. But Angelo had felt his loss early, and he'd felt it keenly. Eva had hardly felt it at all. Maybe that was part of the problem. At an early age, Angelo had learned to let go. Eva's experience came later, and when it did, it came all at once.

She hadn't felt her mother's loss when it happened. She felt it more now, now that she was the only Adler left. Sadly, her mother would always be dying in her memories, and her father would never be dead. That's what happened when you said good-bye to someone, watched them board a train, and they never came home. Somewhere, inside, you always believed they would come back.

Going to Austria had been a fool's errand. She'd known it when she heard her father's plan. He'd reassured her by telling her she would always have Angelo.

You will always have Angelo. He promised me. You will always have Angelo.

He'd been wrong about that too. Angelo had never been hers, and he never would be. Except for once, for a few hours, in Maremma. The memory brought the same ache it always did.

"You still write in that old thing?" There was a smile in Angelo's voice, and Eva looked up from her fat leather-bound journal. It wasn't the same old book Angelo remembered. She'd filled up four of them, but she'd always picked the same style, as if the style itself gave her life constancy.

"Yes. Not very often, obviously," she answered, closing the book and wrapping the elastic band around it, keeping the pages tight and the book closed. She slid it back into her valise and folded her hands.

"Do you still write confessions?" he asked gently.

"No," she lied. "I've decided confessions are only for priests." She realized how confrontational she sounded, and she shrugged, shaking off her words. "I just write to record events. That's all."

"What were you writing about . . . just now?" he pressed, and she found herself glowering at him. He reached up and smoothed the crease between her brows.

"I'm just making conversation, Eva. I'm not interrogating you. Stop glaring at me."

She turned her face away, and his hand fell back to his lap. They sat in silence for several moments until she relented with a sigh.

"I was thinking about Maremma. The train ride. It was awful." She didn't specify which trip.

"But we still went. Every year," he said, smiling. She didn't want him to smile. The flash of white teeth beneath his well-shaped lips made her flinch and look away. It actually hurt when he smiled at her.

"I'll never go back," she said tightly. She closed her eyes so she could pretend to sleep, but instead she thought about the last time she'd seen the red shingled house with the big veranda, surrounded by forest and sea, the best of both worlds.

Camillo's determination to get around the Racial Laws had been very impressive to Angelo. At the time, it had given him a great deal of hope. After the first round of laws were passed in 1938, Camillo had deeded his home to Santino and Fabia, with promises to continue on exactly as they had all done before. He and Eva would pay "rent" for the two rooms they occupied. That rent was equivalent to what he'd been paying Santino and Fabia as a monthly salary, so nothing changed. Camillo continued to pay all the bills from a household account, and things had all moved forward quite seamlessly.

Gino Sotelo became sole owner of Ostrica Glass Factory on paper, but the two had written up a contract where nothing changed at all, and they filed the contract with a lawyer in the United States and put a large amount of money in a trust with Angelo's name on it. Angelo was still an American citizen, so it worked. Camillo went to work, but he didn't get paid. If anyone asked he was just consulting.

It required trust. What had Eva said so long ago? Sometimes God works through people. It was true. People were all Camillo Rosselli had to work with, and he'd managed to get around the laws, just like he said he would, trusting the people closest to him. He'd made all the right moves, until he'd made the wrong one.

Angelo knew Eva wasn't sleeping, though the rhythm and vibration of the Rome-bound train was making him a little drowsy. Eva was trying to keep him at a distance. She'd mentioned Maremma and retreated into herself. He could hardly blame her. It had the same effect on him, and his memories of Maremma weren't nearly as long and complicated. He was surprised Eva had mentioned it at all. It had been devastating, the way it all ended.

When he was younger, he would stay for the full month of August, just like the rest of the family, but as he grew older and his studies intensified, an entire month just wasn't feasible. Plus, as much as he loved his family and the seashore, three weeks of sun, sand, and Eva's beauty weren't healthy for a young seminarian, regardless of whether or not they called themselves cousins. But his *nonna* would beg and plead and cajole, and he would inevitably show up, if only for a few days.

Angelo loved the beaches of Maremma. It was a place filled with memories bathed in warmth and washed in white—white sand, white shells, white towels, and the white sundress Eva had worn that long-ago summer when he'd received his first kiss.

It was Eva's first kiss too, though he was pretty sure she'd received plenty since then. Eva had convinced him that they needed to see what all the fuss was about. She was twelve that summer and he was fourteen—still too young and far away from the priesthood to worry about his immortal soul if he kissed a *signorina*. Eva's suggestion had seemed logical. Enticing even, and he had shrugged and let her pull his face to hers.

Her lips were soft, but his were sandy, and she had wrinkled her nose and laughed when their mouths touched.

"That tickles!" She brushed at his lips and they tried again, but neither of them closed their eyes. They stared at each other, even when they were too close to see anything but eyelashes and freckles.

They stayed frozen, lips touching, until Eva started to laugh again. Angelo pulled away and scrubbed at his mouth, embarrassed.

"I think we're doing it wrong," he muttered.

"Really?" Eva frowned, her laughter fading. "What else should we be doing?"

"Well, for one, you could close your eyes."

"But you didn't close yours!" she argued.

"I'll close mine too."

"Okay. What else?"

He had a pretty good idea that kisses involved tongues. He wasn't sure how, as that seemed extremely wet and a little disgusting. But he thought he would try just a tentative stroke. He wouldn't tell Eva it was coming, then if it didn't work he could claim the attempt was inadvertent.

"Tip your head so we don't bonk noses," he instructed.

"Okay. And come closer so we aren't stretching," she suggested.

They tried again, and he made sure there was no sand on his lips. They leaned in and simultaneously closed their eyes, tilting their heads instinctively. It was much better, especially because Eva wasn't laughing. Angelo's tongue tiptoed out and touched her top lip. She tasted like sunshine and grapes. She stiffened in surprise but didn't pull away, and his hands fisted handfuls of sand as her tongue hesitantly returned the caress. Then his tongue was touching hers and her grape-and-sunshine flavor was in his mouth and tickling his nose, and his eyes were rolling back in his head, completely drunk on sensation.

That was when his *nonna* discovered them. She shrieked their names and swatted them both on the heads, crossing herself and praying between the slaps. They were grounded from each other for two days, and Camillo sat them both down for a serious talk.

When he was finished with his strange, rambling lecture about men and women and babies and kissing, Eva just laughed and bounced up from her seat. She placed herself in her father's lap and looked him in the eye, her face deadly serious.

"Babbo! It was disgusting. It was like kissing an oyster! I never want to kiss another boy for as long as I live."

"It was?" Angelo interjected, stunned that the experience had been so very different for him.

"You don't?" Camillo looked as shocked as Angelo felt.

"No! It was a silly dare. Angelo is like my brother. I am his sister. It will never happen again, Babbo. Don't worry. Now please, I need my friend back. I don't want to spend my holiday all by myself."

"Angelo?" Camillo was looking at him, his eyebrows raised.

"Huh?" He was completely lost, and his feelings were more than a little bruised.

"Was kissing Eva like kissing an oyster?" Camillo pressed.

Angelo's eyes darted between Eva's face and Camillo's spectacled gaze, then back again. He always tried to tell the truth. Especially to Camillo. Should he tell him it was nothing like kissing an oyster? Should he tell him it was the most amazing fifteen seconds of his life? Eva had widened her eyes comically and tilted her head, giving Angelo a look that said, "Play along, you idiot!"

Oh.

Oh!

"Um, yeah. Maybe not like an oyster . . . but it was slimy and a little disgusting. Like kissing Nonna, maybe," Angelo lied.

Eva laughed, not offended in the slightest.

Camillo narrowed his eyes at his daughter, and she grabbed his face and kissed his cheeks.

"Don't worry, Babbo. Angelo is my brother. Now may we please go to the beach?"

The memory made Angelo smile. Eva had been devious and oh-so-convincing. Camillo had sighed and off they had gone. But they weren't left alone again, even once, for the rest of the summer. And there was no more kissing. It was as if a decision had been made. The response of their elders had made the pathway clear: if they wanted to remain in each other's lives, kissing was not an option.

They had never talked about it. Never admitted to each other that it was a beautiful first, a precious memory. But for years afterward they couldn't mention oysters without grinning at each other, and when they did, Eva would get a look in her eyes. She got a look in her eyes, and Angelo got a pain in his chest.

He rubbed his hand over his heart, absentmindedly casing the old ache. His hand found his cross and he traced it, closing his eyes and trying to say his midday prayers, but the sway of the train and the shape of the girl beside him made his mind flit away, back to white beaches and forbidden kisses.

CHAPTER 9
THE CHURCH OF SANTA CECILIA

A gong sounded and a whistle blew, and Angelo awoke with a start. They were in Rome. He'd fallen asleep after all. Eva had too, and her head was tucked against his shoulder, as if she'd tried to prop it up against her seat, only to lose the battle to gravity. A surge of tenderness for her had him closing his eyes and asking for strength for the umpteenth time since he'd first seen her yesterday.

She stirred against his shoulder and pulled away with a jerk. He finished his prayer and stretched his arms, giving her time to compose herself. He straightened his collar and ran his hands over his closely cropped curls—as long as he kept them short, the waves conformed to the shape of his head, keeping the curl relatively tame—before placing his wide-brimmed black hat on his head.

"We're here," he said gently, finally turning toward her.

She nodded, a quick dip of her head, as she re-pinned her little white hat. She slicked a fresh coat of red across her lips and snapped her handbag closed, tucking it back down inside her small valise.

They stood and made their way off the train, the exhaust and bedlam of the station invigorating, even if the September day was still too warm.

"I have a place for you to stay. It's not far from where I live," he said, tossing the words over his shoulder as he wove in and out of the crowd, using his cane to clear a path.

"I'm going to stay with my uncle. I sent a telegram. They're expecting me," she called out behind him.

He stopped abruptly, and Eva cursed under her breath as she collided with his rigid back. He resumed walking almost immediately, but when they reached the street and set down their luggage, waiting for a bus that could take them across town, he murmured his displeasure into her ear.

"They live in a predominantly Jewish neighborhood."

Eva raised one delicate eyebrow and pursed her lips, waiting for him to continue.

"Living with a Jewish family is the most foolish thing you can do. You might as well wear a star on your chest."

"Are you saying they're in danger?" she murmured, keeping her voice as low as his.

"Yes! Eva, that's exactly what I'm saying." He shook his head, incredulous. "Staying with your uncle will completely undermine the whole reason I wanted you to come to Rome, a place where you aren't known, a place where your name, your address, and your religion isn't on some Fascist list, easily accessed by the SS. A place where no one can point you out."

"I want to see them, Angelo. I haven't seen them in two years."

The bus pulled up and Angelo moved toward it, still lugging her suitcase and his much smaller bag.

"This is our bus," he said, though she had no idea what that meant or where it went.

They boarded, sliding into a seat near the front, stowing their bags on a rack above their heads. When the bus lurched and groaned and eventually resumed its route, Eva tried to find out.

"Where do *you* live?"

"I'm not far from your uncle. I live on the west side of the Tiber near the Basilica di Santa Maria."

Eva had no idea where that was. His landmarks were meaningless to her.

"Do you live with other priests?"

"I live in an apartment with Monsignor Luciano and his older sister, a lovely old woman who spends her days making lace when she's not playing housekeeper. She likes to pretend I'm her son. She takes very good care of both of us."

"I thought you lived in a . . . a rectory. Isn't that what a priest's home is called?"

"I used to. After I was ordained, I served in a village just south of Rome for about six months before I was assigned as a curate at the Church of the Sacred Heart east of Trastevere, not far from the Colosseum."

"A curate?"

"An assistant to the parish priest. I served there for two years. In that time, I got to know the area very well."

"And now?"

"Now my duties have changed."

"You don't conduct Mass every day?" She had always imagined him feeding wafers to open-mouthed parishioners and giving long sermons. She realized suddenly how little she really knew about Angelo's daily life.

"I attend Mass every day. Several times if my duties allow it. But no. I am an assistant to Monsignor Luciano, who is a senior official with the Roman Curia."

"What is the Roman Curia?'

"It is the administrative arm of the Catholic Church."

"You work in an office?" She was stunned.

"Yes. I do. When I'm not running all over the city, I work in an office in the Vatican. It is a busy time for my department. It will only get busier."

"What is your department?"

"Migrant assistance."

She stared at him, bemused. "There is such a department?"

"In a manner of speaking, yes. The official description is to promote pastoral assistance to migrants, nomads, tourists, and travelers. The congregation is overseen by a cardinal. Monsignor Luciano serves Cardinal Dubois. I assist Monsignor Luciano. My job is to attend the monsignor in whatever duties he assigns, but I rarely sit at a desk and type, if that's what you're thinking. There are lay secretaries and assistants to do that. I tend to be the physical liaison, and I mostly do legwork."

"How interesting. The one-legged priest doing legwork."

"Yes. Ironic." He smirked, and his blue eyes glinted. She didn't smile even though she wanted to. It was too easy to fall back into their old ways, poking at each other and teasing one another. It wouldn't be good for her. It would make her miss him too much when she returned to Florence. She resolved to guard herself against him even as he spoke again, the humor absent from his voice.

"I want you to stay at the Santa Cecilia. It's a cloistered convent, but there are rooms available for boarders along the entrance block. It's in Trastevere, and you won't be too far from your family." He sounded as if he were giving an order, dictating what she would do, and she opened her mouth to refuse.

"Please, Eva," he implored so softly that she could almost pretend it didn't happen.

"I don't want to be alone," she murmured, hating herself for her vulnerability.

"Better alone than arrested," he said, but his eyes were compassionate.

"I'm not sure that's true, Angelo," she answered. "I'm not sure of that at all."

"Eva." He sighed. "You don't mean that."

"How do you know, Angelo?" she asked sharply. "How can you possibly claim to know how I feel?"

He shot her a look that said he knew exactly how she felt, and she turned away with a shake of her head, dismissing him. He knew nothing.

"I told my family I was coming," she reiterated. "They are expecting me. I'm sure they would like to see you too." Angelo started to shake his head, anger tightening his mouth and causing the groove between his eyes to deepen into a canyon.

"I will see them, we will have dinner with them, and then you can lock me in the convent if you must," she added before he could resume his campaign. Angelo exhaled with relief, and the rest of the ride was spent in stony contemplation.

∞

They had to change buses and catch another before taking a streetcar that let them off two blocks from 325 Viale Domina. It was two in the afternoon, and they'd been traveling since six o'clock that morning. Angelo looked remarkably un-wilted, his black cassock and wide-brimmed hat traveling much better than Eva's slim red skirt and white blouse. She felt filthy and wrinkled, and she removed her hat so she could smooth her hair as they waited for someone to answer the door. The building was neat and clean, the corridors wide and airy, but the residence was a decided step down from Uncle Augusto's Florence home, which was now being rented to non-Jews for a ridiculously small amount of money. The door opened an inch, and a brown eye appeared in the gap.

"Eva! Angelo!" The door was flung open, and Eva's cousin Claudia, decidedly less plump than she'd once been—war rations were only good for one thing—pulled Eva into the small parlor, reaching out a hand for Angelo as well. Eva took quick note of the polished floors, the pictures on the walls, and the pieces of furniture from their home in Florence. The homey atmosphere and the effort to make the apartment comfortable eased the knot in Eva's stomach. She had worried about her uncle and aunt, about her cousins and their life in Rome. From the looks of it, all was well.

"We've been waiting to eat. Levi got fruit. He's a black-market guru, you know. He manages to get things no one else can." She prattled easily as she led them into a sitting area teeming with people.

"Eva, you remember Giulia, don't you? Mamma's sister?" Giulia Sonnino was much younger than her older sister, barely thirty years old if that, and Claudia and Eva had always looked up to her, more like a sophisticated older cousin than an aunt. Giulia was still lovely, but she was hugely pregnant, and she smiled wearily at Eva and Angelo and tried to stand to greet them. Her husband, Mario, pressed her right back down into the sofa and stood in her stead.

Mario Sonnino was a physician, a tall, slender man with kind eyes—a Jewish trait, according to her father. "We Jews have kind eyes and quick minds," he would say. Eva didn't know if it was true. Camillo had claimed so many things as Jewish traits, but Mario reminded Eva a little of her *babbo*, so maybe he was right.

Eva had attended Mario and Giulia's wedding when she was twelve or thirteen, and she and Claudia had thought Mario very good looking. Plus, he played the violin, which made him a kindred spirit from the start. He wasn't especially handsome—Eva could see that now—but he wore his goodness all over his face, and he was clearly devoted to his wife. Eva smiled at him warmly and shook hands with the little girl who hung on to his leg and dimpled winsomely when she was introduced.

"This is Emilia," Mario said. "And the boy who is determined to beat Levi at chess is our oldest, Lorenzo." Lorenzo, a little boy of about eight or nine and missing his two front teeth, heard his name and grinned, lifting his head from the chessboard in front of him. Levi stood from the game and approached Eva and Angelo in three long strides, swooping Eva up in a huge hug that had her laughing and little Emilia squealing and begging for a turn.

"Me, me! Swing me, Cousin Levi!"

"Yes! Swing Emilia!" Eva laughed as he set her down. Levi shook hands with Angelo, then Aunt Bianca started ushering them to the dinner table where the simple meal was quickly consumed. The conversation volleyed from one topic to the next, the time apart requiring a great deal of catch-up. When Angelo stepped in to field some questions, Eva turned to Giulia to inquire about her pregnancy.

"When is the baby due?"

"We have a month," Giulia sighed, as if a month was an eternity. "I'm very ready now, though our circumstances aren't the best."

"Do you live here in the building?"

"No. We are in the old ghetto," she answered quietly. "Mario's a doctor, but he lost his practice. We had a home in Perugia . . ." Her voice faded off and Eva didn't pursue the subject.

"Will you be staying here with Augusto and Bianca?" Giulia asked politely, shifting the focus to Eva.

"I'm not sure," Eva hedged, not wanting to start a possibly uncomfortable conversation. Of course, her answer didn't go unchallenged.

"What do you mean?" Claudia chirped up from across the table. "Of course you are. You will stay in my room."

"I've made arrangements for Eva," Angelo interjected, and Claudia immediately frowned.

"But . . . why?"

"Eva will stay here," Uncle Augusto said, as if his was the final word on the subject.

"It's not safe," Angelo said quietly. "It's not safe for any of you, honestly. You need to change apartments, Augusto. Or leave Rome."

"But Rome is the safest place for Jews! The Germans have been on their best behavior. We'll be fine here. Your Pope is our best defense. The Germans don't want an international public relations problem with the Vatican. One in three Germans is Catholic. Did you know that, Angelo? That's why I brought my family here. "

"The Pope is in an impossible position. He holds no power over Hitler. He couldn't save the Jews in Germany; he couldn't save the Jews in Poland. He couldn't save the Jews in Austria. He won't be able to save the Jews in Rome."

The table went silent and Eva winced. Angelo put down his fork and stared at Augusto soberly.

"If you won't hide, that is your choice. But Eva won't be staying here." He lowered his voice, as if the walls had ears. "At the very least, let me get you false documents that you can use if the Germans do come knocking."

"Like the documents Camillo used? Documents like that?" Augusto retorted, pushing his chair back from the table in disgust. He didn't rise, but he leveled a finger at Angelo.

"My brother pretended to be someone he was not. They caught him. And now my brother is gone."

A week after Camillo Rosselli went to Austria to find Otto Adler, the Italian police had shown up at the Ostrica Glass Factory in Florence, asking questions. The Gestapo had contacted them. Camillo had been recognized in Vienna by someone who knew he was Jewish and knew he was not the person he was claiming to be. He was claiming to be Gino Sotelo, his non-Jewish partner at the glass factory. Camillo would have been far better off with his own papers—an Italian Jew was safer than a man with false papers.

Gino Sotelo had pled ignorance and innocence, and they'd believed him, only because Camillo Rosselli had claimed he'd stolen the pass, unbeknownst to his old partner. It was a lie—Gino had known everything—but it saved Gino from charges, and it saved Camillo from having to tell authorities it was a fake pass, protecting the forging operation that was ongoing at Ostrica.

It didn't save Gino from having to tell Eva that her father had been arrested. He had arrived at the villa, his hat in his hands, his face gray, and told Eva that her father was not going to be coming home any time soon. The only information police could give Gino Sotelo was that Camillo Rosselli had been sent, along with other Jewish detainees, to a labor camp called Auschwitz.

"Three years." Augusto held up three fingers, underlining his words. "And we've had no word. I won't do it. I won't do anything to endanger my family. No fake papers." He slapped the dinner table, and little Emilia stuck out her lip at the sound, as if she'd been slapped too.

"That's your choice," Angelo repeated. "But Eva isn't staying here."

Eva bit back her irritation. She didn't like being discussed as if she weren't there to speak for herself. But she remained silent. Uncle Augusto had always been too quick to choose optimism. Optimism could get you killed.

They remained an hour longer, but the days were growing shorter and a new curfew had been announced with the arrival of the Germans. Mario Sonnino followed Angelo and Eva to the door and walked with them to the street, chatting amiably, but when they moved to leave he touched Angelo's arm, halting him.

"I want documents," he whispered. "For my family. As soon as the baby is born we are leaving Rome. Can you help me?"

Eva and Angelo both nodded, and Eva gripped his hand. "It may take a few weeks. And if Angelo can't help you, I will."

Angelo shot Eva a cautionary glare, but he didn't argue with her. Not there.

Mario nodded gratefully. "Thank you. Thank you both." He scribbled his number and his address on a scrap of paper and handed it to Angelo.

"Eva?" Mario stopped her as she turned away.

"Yes?"

"Don't come back here," he murmured. "The *padre* is right."

∾

The distance to the Church of Santa Cecilia was relatively short, and within fifteen minutes, Angelo was leading Eva toward a stately, gated edifice tucked at the far end of a cobbled piazza. There were hundreds of churches in Rome, big and small, ornate and old, famous and obscure, but the arched entrance of the Santa Cecilia was quietly welcoming as Angelo led Eva beyond the tall gate into a courtyard lined with roses and benches.

A rectangular pool with a large vase at the center encouraged quiet conversation and meditation, though the space was completely empty. Rows of windows overlooked the courtyard on each side, several stories that made up the convent on one side and an ancient bathhouse on the other. Angelo said the church was named for Cecilia, a noblewoman who was locked in her bathhouse for three days—a murder attempt—only to come out unscathed and singing. The bathhouse had been turned into a chapel, and Cecilia had since become a patron saint of music. Eva tried to imagine what a bathhouse chapel looked like, and determined that she would sneak inside at some point if the nuns refused to show her.

They walked into the nave, looking for the abbess, and found it as empty and silent as the courtyard. The nave was rather gray and depressing, the arch of the ceiling too low for transcendence, but the statue of a woman beneath the altar made up for it. The sculpture was unlike any Eva had ever seen before. It was lifelike and lovely, yet so forlorn. The woman appeared as if she were sleeping, but her face was turned into the ground, strands of hair obscuring her profile, and the gash on her neck told a different story.

"Is this Saint Cecilia? What happened to her?" Eva asked, her eyes clinging to the slim white column of the woman's throat.

"After failing to kill her in the bathhouse, they attempted again. They tried to behead her."

"Tried?"

"The legend is that three blows with an ax did not accomplish the task. She died slowly, converting many in the process," Angelo answered.

"What was her crime?" Eva asked, unable to look away from the statue.

"It was politics. She was an outspoken woman," Angelo said wryly, as if he thought Eva could relate. There was a smile in his voice, but Eva couldn't smile. She could only stare at the martyred saint.

"Oh, Father Bianco! We expected you much sooner," a woman called out in surprise, distracting Angelo from his response. Eva turned toward the voice and watched as a diminutive woman with sagging jowls and sharp eyes approached them at a speed that belied her age. She'd entered the nave through a door to the left of the apse.

"Mother Francesca, this is Eva," Angelo said simply, as if he'd already told the ancient nun all about her.

"You'd best be off, Father," the abbess directed. "There is trouble with the Holy Sisters of Adoration. A pilgrim has died, and there is some disagreement about what should be done."

"I will check on you tomorrow, Eva," Angelo said, and with a quick bow toward the abbess, he was striding back toward the entrance, cane tapping, his small suitcase swinging. Eva could only stare after him, wondering again why she'd agreed to come to Rome.

"Come," Mother Francesca commanded, and without waiting to see if Eva was coming, followed Angelo out of the nave and through the courtyard. Eva grabbed the large suitcase Angelo had carried all day, and juggling her valise and violin in her other hand, struggled to catch up. The nun led her through a small door to the left of the entrance wall. As they ascended a narrow staircase, the nun offered some information.

"The convent is shared between the Benedictine nuns and the Franciscan Missionary Sisters of the Immaculate Heart of Mary. But we are smaller in numbers than we once were, and the convent is past its prime."

Eva wondered how long it had been past its prime. Two hundred years? Three?

"These rooms were used for lay staff, but we have no use for a large staff anymore. We have both a cloistered community as well as nuns who serve in an active apostolate beyond these walls. We use these rooms for boarders. The little bit of income is much needed. Especially now."

Eva nodded, wondering how long the stack of banknotes she'd brought with her would last. The value kept falling. Before long, they would be more useful as toilet paper. The jewelry she brought would get her a little further.

The abbess opened a door and stepped aside. The room contained a narrow mattress on a metal frame, a wooden cross nailed to the wall above it. A simple chair, a chest of drawers, and a small closet lined the opposite wall. Mother Francesca flipped on the desk lamp, indicating this was home.

"This is your room. Washroom at the end of the hall. It is for shared use, but you are the only boarder here at the moment. A luxury. Vespers at six. You are expected to attend."

"But . . . I am not Catholic," Eva protested.

"You are now."

18 September, 1943

Confession: I don't like nuns.

I am tired, but sleep is as elusive as Angelo has always been. The convent is too quiet and it smells old. Why is it that all of Rome smells so old? Or maybe it is just me, and I can't get the scent of loss from my skin. I feel as ancient and crumbling as the walls of the old temple the bus trundled past today. But at least the temple doesn't have to hide. I've been here less than twelve hours, and I miss Florence so desperately I want to start walking. Florence smells like flowers. It smells like jasmine and Fabia and my father's pipe. After all these years, I can still smell him in the rooms of the villa, and I am both comforted and tortured by the scent.

I'm lying in a little bed in a strange room, listening to the walls say nothing. I tried to play my violin, but the echo in the room made my skin crawl, like I was the Pied Piper of dead nuns. I didn't want to summon ghosts or rats, so I put my violin away.

I went to Vespers as instructed and watched the nuns sing and an old priest conduct the service. There were more nuns behind a little opening on the other side of the apse. They never come out, apparently. I wonder if that's what Angelo wants for me. Maybe he thinks I can just hide in this little convent until the war is over, and then he'll pat himself on the back because he saved me.

What am I being saved for? I look ahead at my life, even a life where there is no fear or worry that the Gestapo will swoop me up and send me away, and I can't find the will to be hopeful.

Eva Rosselli

CHAPTER 10
THE JEWISH GHETTO

The "pilgrim" who had passed was an old Jewish woman who had been left behind when her son and his family fled to Genoa. The nuns of the Holy Sisters of Adoration had taken her in, and she'd passed peacefully in her sleep, sitting in front of a window in a white wimple and a borrowed black veil looking like one of the nuns who hid her.

Angelo promised the abbess to pay a visit to the rabbi at the main synagogue first thing in the morning to see if clandestine funeral arrangements could be made. Otherwise, they would be burying her among nuns with a cross on her grave. It was all they could do. She'd died among them; she would be buried among them too. Maybe when the war was over they could remove the cross and put a Star of David in its place. And maybe they could restore her name. Maybe someday her family would return and lay stones on her grave, the way Eva used to do for ancestors she never even knew. But the odds were that Regina Ravenna would be hidden in the ground under a false name and a meaningless cross, and no one but the Holy Sisters of Adoration and Angelo would ever be the wiser.

The knowledge and responsibility weighed on Angelo. He wanted to keep records but didn't dare. He wanted to keep ledgers and lists of names and family members so that he could account for every person he felt responsible for. But records and lists were incriminating. So he'd devised a method to keep it as straight as he could, kept any necessary papers in the Vatican, and prayed that God would preserve his memory so no one would be lost to forgetfulness.

He made his way home long after the curfew, but was not stopped, fortunately. He had a pass that allowed him to be out when his duties demanded it, but if he were challenged, he would have to lie about the old woman he'd attended to. And the old woman was a paperless Jew.

The last year or two had been one lie after another. Sometimes he missed the simple little village where he'd spent the first six months of his life as a priest. Eat, pray, sleep, serve. That was all he did. Plus, the streets were so narrow and the road to the village so winding and steep, it was unlikely the Germans could send in their tanks without getting them lodged between buildings. Then he was called to Rome, and he'd gotten a crash course in service and survival on the streets of the Eternal City.

Then Monsignor Luciano, his sponsor of sorts, the man who had kept an eye on him for so many years, brought him in to assist him at the Curia. A totally different kind of experience. At the Curia he'd met Monsignor O'Flaherty, an Irish priest at the Vatican who was deeply involved in refugee work. And Angelo's double life had begun. He'd begun traveling from one end of the city to the next, every church, every monastery, every convent, and every college. And he'd made note of numbers, rooms, availability, and access.

And the people had started to come. A Jewish mother needed to hide her sons. A rabbi, fearing he was a target but unwilling to leave his congregation, still wanted to protect his family. The word had spread, and people came. The church was now in the business of hide-and-seek, and Angelo was the eyes and ears, a young priest with a limp and an affinity for languages, with a special understanding of the Jewish people. He understood their dietary needs and their worship practices, and he was just another cog in the wheel of clergy who had begun the enormous task of trying to hide the hunted.

They'd started with foreign Jews who had been ordered to leave Italy in 1940 but had nowhere to go, just like Felix. But since July, the tide had turned, and with the fall of bombs and dictators, the church was hiding Italians.

The monsignor instructed him to find alternative methods of hiding refugees, and Angelo remembered Aldo Finzi. He made a trip to Florence and asked the little man to help him. Together they'd distributed over two hundred passes to Jews who could hide in plain sight if they had the right paperwork. This made room for the Jews who couldn't blend in due to language or physical appearance. It was harder to hide the Jewish men. They couldn't just pretend to be non-Jewish Italians and be absorbed into the populace. Young Italian men of a fighting age were expected to be doing just that . . . fighting. Soldiers had to hide from the Germans too. And there were so many children. They had three convents throughout the city that were full of Jewish orphans. Some of them could be placed with families, but children presented a specific danger. All it would take was one wrong word, a forgetful comment, and the child, along with the family that sheltered him, would be exposed. They'd branched out into the countryside, but transporting them was difficult too. The whole operation was difficult and made more challenging every day.

Angelo wasn't working alone—there were hundreds of fathers and sisters, monks and nuns—opening their doors and closing their eyes to the danger all around them. But sometimes Angelo *felt* incredibly alone. It was safer not to share, safer not to confide, safer to handle as much as he could without involving anyone else. And he was tired.

That night, he fell into bed after hasty prayers, his leg aching, feeling wearier than he'd ever felt, but his mind kept returning to Eva. She'd watched him leave the chapel without protest, her face blank, gripping her violin like it was all she cared about in the world, and he'd walked away without looking back. He'd had to. She was safe and he was needed elsewhere. But it reminded him too much of August of 1939 when he'd walked away and left her in the Pazzi Chapel.

They'd come back from Maremma, back to reality, with a new knowledge of each other and of the world they found themselves in. Angelo had known what he had to do, and he'd done it. But the memory haunted him still.

On September 26, less than ten days after Eva moved in with the sisters at Santa Cecilia, Lieutenant Colonel Kappler, the head of the German SS in Rome, demanded fifty kilograms of gold be delivered to German headquarters on Via Tasso. If the Jewish community failed to do so within thirty-six hours, two hundred of Rome's Jews would be rounded up and deported.

Lines of Jews formed outside the main synagogue on Lungotevere de' Cenci, desperate people donating all they had to keep the dragon at bay. Angelo forbade Eva from going anywhere near the synagogue, but she ignored him, taking every piece of gold jewelry she'd brought to Rome and waiting in line to add her offering to the pile. Uncle Augusto was among the elders assisting with the weighing and the counting, and when he saw Eva, he reassured her once more that the extortion was a "good sign."

"The Germans are logical men. Taking our gold makes much more sense than taking our people," he said. Eva could only shake her head. Nothing about the Jewish persecution was logical or rational.

But she gave her gold with a glimmer of hope that it was exactly as her uncle said.

Eva was leaving the synagogue when she saw Mario and Giulia Sonnino standing in line with their two children. Giulia was so hugely pregnant that Eva convinced those waiting in front of her in the line to let her move ahead, so she wouldn't have to stand for hours. The Sonninos donated their wedding rings and a Swiss pocket watch that had been in Mario's family for three generations. Giulia joked that the thin white line on her finger was proof enough that she wasn't a loose woman, but there were tears in her eyes when she left her thick gold band on the pile. Eva waited with their children until they were finished and walked with them back to their ghetto apartment, merely a block from the huge synagogue.

"We need pictures, and they need to be official quality," Eva murmured. Mario nodded once, understanding immediately what she was referring to.

"We will get them to the printer. He will add them to the passes so he can stamp the picture when he stamps the pass. It makes it more complicated. But it is the only way to keep them authentic. We can add your fingerprints and signatures when we have the passes, but we need the pictures as soon as possible."

Angelo was being impossibly close-lipped about his maneuverings, refusing Eva's help at every turn. He was determined to keep her tucked in the convent and out of harm's way, but she was slowly going crazy. She knew the Sonninos were on the bottom of a very long list of those in need of false identity cards, so she decided to make them her responsibility.

"I have them," Mario said softly. "And I have pictures for ten other people in the community who will need passes as well." He looked at her apologetically. "I don't mean to take advantage. But these people have nowhere else to turn."

Eva left Mario and Giulia's apartment with the twelve pictures tucked into her brassiere and a promise to be back with the passes as soon as she could arrange for their completion. She simply had to get past Angelo and get back to Florence to see Aldo. She would buy a round-trip ticket, work all night, and return to Rome the next day. If Angelo would let her, she would deliver pictures and obtain more passes for his refugees as well.

She found him at the synagogue, standing in line with several other priests from parishes across the city. Angelo had managed to gather a significant amount of gold from non-Jewish Romans who wanted to contribute but thought they might be turned away by the "rich Jews." Old stereotypes persisted, apparently.

No one was turned away. The average contribution was an eighth of an ounce, and the fear of failure was palpable. The lieutenant major of the SS "graciously" extended the deadline by four hours and then four hours more. Then rumors started to circulate that the Pope would step in and donate Catholic gold if the Jews failed to gather the required amount. Uncle Augusto relayed the rumor to Angelo, grinning like a Cheshire cat. "What did I tell you, Padre? We have nothing to worry about in the shadow of the Vatican."

Miraculously, the number was reached without a donation from the Vatican, and more than one hundred and ten pounds—fifty kilograms—of gold, consisting of every last precious thing sacrificed by an already impoverished people, was delivered to German headquarters before the deadline on September 28. The Jews of Rome congratulated themselves, Augusto opened a bottle of wine, and a collective sigh of relief echoed down the cobblestone streets.

But the very next day, trucks pulled up in front of the synagogue and emptied out the rabbinical library—every book, every sacred scroll, and every precious document. Then they cleared out all the offices, carrying out filing cabinets full of records, contributor lists, and community members. Jewish leaders watched helplessly as every last piece of paper was confiscated by the very Germans who had promised to leave them alone only the day before.

The city held its breath once more, but the week passed uneventfully. Then another. Eva bought a ticket for Florence and informed Angelo she was going. Regardless of the lull, time was running out for the Sonninos. He argued heatedly, but when she wouldn't relent, he arranged to go with her, and they set out for Florence again, less than a month after Eva had arrived.

The trip went without incident. No one stopped them. No one questioned them. No one looked twice at the two of them. They saw no one they knew and no one they knew saw them, except Aldo, who welcomed them to his little workshop at dusk. He reported the same thing. All was peaceful in the City of Flowers—but his expression echoed the nagging feeling none of them could shake.

They spent all night setting type, tightening the string and screwing down the plates, adjusting the ink, refilling the feedboard, and churning out card after precious card. Then they attached pictures and stamped the seals, printed emblems, and assigned names of southern places that the Germans would have no way to verify. They dried, cut, trimmed, stacked, and started all over again with different samples from different places guiding their efforts. Eva and Angelo took quick turns napping on a corner cot, and they finished the long night with a stack of hope and blackened fingers. Aldo's fingers were perpetually stained, but Angelo and Eva spent twenty minutes scrubbing their hands raw to remove the evidence of the night's activities.

They boarded the six a.m. Rapido for Rome with fresh clothes and red hands without ever seeing Fabia and Santino. It couldn't be helped, but Eva realized Angelo had probably been in Florence dozens of times over the last two years without ever seeing her.

"I forgive you," Eva murmured, closing her eyes as the gong sounded and the train pulled away from the station, right on time.

"You do?" he answered just as softly. He sounded as tired as she felt.

"Yes. I do. But maybe I shouldn't. How many times have you come to Florence since the war broke out?"

"Many times," he confessed.

"And I never saw you. Not once."

"No."

"Why?"

He opened one of his eyes and looked at her. She'd already opened hers.

"You know why, Eva."

Something hot and needy sliced in her belly, and she closed her eyes once more, unable to continue the conversation without revealing her longing for the forbidden. Her lips tingled and her palms grew damp and she had a hard time drawing breath. It took her a long time to drift off and nothing more was said on the subject of knowledge and forgiveness.

Isaaco Sonnino, a healthy seven-pound baby boy, was born on October 15, 1943. He was delivered by his father but was passed quickly to Eva, who washed him, diapered him, and bundled him in the thin white blanket Giulia had set out in preparation. Eva had never held a baby before, never diapered one either, but she managed with the help of Isabella Donati, an old woman from across the hall who had been a business owner before her shop was closed by the Racial Laws. Her husband was gone, her two sons lost in the Great War, and she claimed there was nothing left for her to do and little left to fear. She was as calm and comforting as a breeze in summertime, and Eva liked her immensely. She made a note to herself to convince the woman to come to the convent at Santa Cecilia. There was room, though Angelo had placed two families there in the last week. Eva would like her company, the nuns would like her soup, and Signora Donati would be safe.

Eva had come to the apartment late that afternoon with the precious passes in hand. All that needed to be added were the fake names, the signatures, and the fingerprints. But Giulia was already well into her labor, and Eva tucked the passes away and stayed, making herself as useful as possible, playing with the children, timing contractions, and eventually, in the early hours of the morning, watching a baby come into the world.

Signora Donati went home at midnight, but the curfew made it too dangerous for Eva to walk home, and so she stayed, putting the other children, who had slept in fits and spurts throughout the long night, back to bed. As the hour approached morning, Mario made his way out the front door, bleary-eyed but smiling, claiming he needed to be the first in line for rations with another mouth to feed. Lorenzo and Emilia, bedded down in the living room, were awakened once more, and they were irritable and hungry.

Eva warmed what was left of the soup and let them fill their bellies in hopes they would sleep again. When they finished, she brought out Mario's violin and tuned the strings by ear, plucking and tightening until Emilia grew impatient and begged for a song.

"Can you play the bird song?" Little Emilia started to sing in lisping Yiddish, a song about being a free bird and a loyal little friend, something Eva herself had been taught as a child, and Eva felt her own fear abate.

"I don't know that one very well. Sing it a few more times so I can learn it."

The little girl kept singing, and before long Eva was moving the bow across the strings, matching Emilia's sweet voice with the wail of the violin.

"Something else," Emilia said suddenly, with the limited attention of the very young.

"Something happy," Lorenzo grumbled, unable to resist the lure of distraction.

"But you need to sleep! We've been awake all night! And your mother is sleeping now. I will play something from America. How about that? But you must lie down and close your eyes," Eva insisted.

The children climbed under their blankets on the makeshift bed and closed their eyes obediently.

Eva left the smallest lamp on and curled up on the sofa, determined to get the children to sleep before their father came home. He would need sleep too. It had been the longest night of her life, and Eva longed to close her own eyes and grab a few minutes of rest.

She notched her violin between her shoulder and her chin and channeled a little Duke Ellington, smiling as she thought of Angelo shaking his hips and his head, the first time he'd introduced her to jazz music. It had been during the week at the beach house, the time he'd kissed her for real. The one time he'd loved her. Then he'd donned a cassock and rejected her once and for all.

"It don't mean a thing if it ain't got that swing." Those were the only words she could sing, and only because Angelo had told her what they meant. He'd laughed when she'd tried to say them, her mouth tripping over the blunt words. But she wasn't a singer, and the words weren't important. The song was fun and fast, but she didn't want fun and fast, and she changed the tempo, the melody curling from the strings, making the song unrecognizable, haunting even. Angelo said jazz was all about lament. She could hear it now. The dissonance of the song, stripped down and robbed of its tempo, made it sound like a song for Shabbat.

"That's not happy." Lorenzo yawned, but his eyes were closed. Emilia was asleep already.

"But it's beautiful. And beauty is always joyful."

"It doesn't sound like American music," he mumbled. Then he was quiet.

Eva played for a few more minutes, her eyes heavy, her limbs loose, and her head drooped as she slid the violin to her lap. Dawn would come soon, and when Mario returned, she would stumble home. But she would sleep until then.

She came awake and to her feet when screams pierced the night. Pounding feet and a series of gunshots rang out from somewhere outside. Eva scrambled for the window, pushing the curtain aside so she could squint down at the still-darkened streets to make out what was happening below. It was raining, and the darkness was inky and slick. Then she saw them. Germans. SS officers in their gunmetal-gray raincoats and bulbous black helmets, almost blending into the night. They lined the alley, and as she watched, one lifted his weapon and shot at the sky, sending the message that no one should try to get past them. Answering shots came from farther off.

The building came awake with a start, and as Eva watched, one family, then another, staggered into the dark streets, still in their bedclothes, holding children and clutching each other. They were herded immediately into the back of a waiting truck. The Sonninos' apartment was four floors up, and it was only a matter of time before the Germans were pounding at the door.

Giulia called out from the bedroom beyond, and Eva raced from the window, stepping over the children who had miraculously remained asleep.

"It's the SS, Giulia. It looks like they have surrounded the building, maybe the whole ghetto. I can't be sure. But they're loading people in the back of trucks."

Giulia rose gingerly, tucking her newborn between two pillows and pulling a robe over her nightgown. She staggered and Eva reached for her, sliding her arm around her narrow back. She was too thin. And now she had a baby to nurse. But at the moment, that was the least of their worries.

"Mario. He isn't back yet?" she whispered, looking past Eva toward the small sitting room.

"No. But that is good. If he isn't here, they can't arrest him."

Giulia started to shake, and Eva knew with a sick surety that if the Gestapo arrested Giulia, she wouldn't last a week. Nor would her children.

"We have to hide, Giulia," she said firmly. "We have to hide somewhere. Think. Where can we hide?"

Giulia shook her head numbly, her eyes wide and unblinking. "There is no place. There is nowhere, Eva."

Eva left Giulia and ran back to the window. People were filling the streets, soldiers were shouting instructions, and every so often another shot rang out. Eva hoped it was simply a shot into the sky like the first shot had been, warning shots, shots designed to incite fear, and not shots aimed at anyone in particular. If the shooting was to instill fear it was working. Yet Giulia's children slept on.

"We will hide here," Eva said briskly. It wouldn't work. It couldn't. But it was something.

"Here?" Giulia squeaked.

"Help me!" Eva started shoving the rectangular table with the thick marble top, the table that had been too heavy for the previous tenants to attempt to take with them. If she could get it in front of the door and turn it on its side it would reinforce the door if the Germans tried to break it down. It was the only thing she could think of.

Giulia was suddenly next to her, pushing with all her meager strength, and they scratched and scraped their way across the wood floor, inching the table toward the door.

When they were two feet away, they tried to ease it over, but the weight was too great and it crashed to its side, as high as the knob and extending several feet on either side of the doorframe.

Eva gave it a final shove, snugging it up under the doorknob. She wondered suddenly if it had been used this way before.

"Is the door locked?" Giulia said feebly, her breath harsh from the exertion. There was blood on her nightgown and drops of it trailing across the bare floor. Eva didn't know how much bleeding was customary after so recently giving birth, but she pretended she didn't see it. There was no time for compassion.

"It's locked. But I want you and the children to go into the bedroom and get in the closet. You have to keep the children quiet. No matter what. I will keep the table pressed against the door. Maybe they will think there is no one here, and they will leave. But we have to be absolutely quiet. If they come in, I will tell them I am the only one here."

Eva didn't wait for Giulia to respond but ran to the sleeping children, scooped up little Emilia, and raced to the narrow closet, tucking her into the corner, her small body propped against the back wall. She curled into it like it was her mother's breast, and didn't even let out a whimper. Giulia was rousing Lorenzo, helping him stagger into the bedroom, his eyes still closed. Eva trusted that Giulia could handle her children from there and shut the bedroom door behind them.

She could hear the clatter of boots on the stairs.

She ran to the front door and threw herself down, her back against the table, her legs extended to the opposite wall that made up the narrow entryway serving as a divider between the kitchen and the sitting room. She braced her feet and closed her eyes. She found herself reciting some of the words from the Amidah. "Oh, King, you are a helper, a savior, and a shield. You are mighty forever, you are powerful to save." She couldn't stand and take three steps back, as was customary, and she left words out, but if God cared about such things at a time like this, he wasn't a god who would bother to save them. Her lips moved over the words, adding, "Deliver us!" as she repeated them.

The apartment door shook beneath the pounding of an upraised fist.

"*Öffne die Tür!*" a voice demanded in German, and Eva slapped a hand over her mouth to muffle the shriek that tried to break loose. There was no sound from the bedroom beyond.

"*Öffne die Tür!*"

"Oh, King, you are a helper, a savior, and a shield. You are mighty forever, you are powerful to save," she mouthed against trembling fingers.

"Open the door!" Another voice shouted in badly accented Italian. Fists beat against the door once more. The doorknob rattled and there was an emphatic shove from the other side, but the lock held with the heavy table as reinforcement. Again, a powerful shove. Eva's legs started to tremble with exertion.

Two shots rang out above her head, stunning her, and her legs buckled momentarily. German cursing could be heard from the other side of the door. Apparently, the shooter hadn't warned his comrades to cover their ears. There were two holes in the wall about a foot above Eva's braced legs. The bullets had easily penetrated the door and buried themselves in the old plaster wall. A cloud of dust lazily floated down around her. Terrified tears ran down Eva's cheeks, and the prayer died in her throat, but she didn't move and she didn't scream.

"No one lives there!" a voice rang out in the hallway. "It was damaged during the air raids in July. It's been condemned."

"Something is pushed against the door," the German argued.

"Debris. The ceiling collapsed in several places. People died." Eva realized suddenly that the voice belonged to Isabella Donati. The woman's calm demeanor made her a convincing liar. Her claim that the residents had died should comfort the SS—they wouldn't need to locate dead Jews. Another shot rang out, right above Eva's head. Then another, and the table bucked at her back.

One German barked at the other, and then, miraculously, Eva heard them moving away, retreating down the hall to the next apartment. She waited, breath held, listening for their return. She waited for what felt like hours, until there were no more boots, no more cries, and no more confusion in the hall. The silence felt false, like the silence in a room where death waits behind the door, knife raised, waiting for the unsuspecting victim to turn her back.

Eva's legs gave out when she tried to stand. Her muscles ached, and delayed shock stole her equilibrium. She moaned and steadied herself on the wall, looking down at the table that now had a web of cracks extending in every direction. Either the last bullet, the bullet she'd felt at her back, hadn't penetrated the marble, or it had miraculously missed her.

She stumbled across the parlor and into the bedroom, crossing the tiny space and flinging the closet door wide, anxious to share the news of their deliverance. Giulia shrieked, one arm extended, clutching her baby, who was latched onto her breast, as if to ward off any would-be attackers. She blinked rapidly at the light, her eyes trying to adjust after an hour spent hiding in the darkness. Apparently, Lorenzo was also temporarily blinded. He barreled out of the closet like a demon freed, and crashed into Eva, fists thrashing, fighting as if his life depended on it.

"You can't take us! Leave us alone!" he shouted.

"Lorenzo! It's me! It's Eva. Shhh! They are gone! They are gone!"

She wrapped her arms around the flailing child as the fight left him, and her eyes found his mother once more. Giulia staggered to the bed and sat weakly upon it, one hand buttoning her gown, the other wrapped tightly around her now squalling infant.

"They're gone," Eva reassured. "But they've cleared the building. They've taken everyone else." How many? There were hundreds of Jews living in the ghetto neighborhood. Hundreds.

"Oh, God. Oh, dear God," Giulia moaned in horror. "Mario. What if they arrested Mario?"

Eva could only shake her head helplessly. "Where's Emilia?" Eva asked suddenly, realizing the little girl was absent.

"She's in the closet." Giulia laughed hollowly. "She slept through it all."

The sudden pounding at the front door had Lorenzo crying out and Giulia staggering to her feet, babe in arms.

"Quiet!" Eva hissed, urging them back toward the closet as she raced for the door, determined to hold it closed once more.

"Giulia! Giulia!" A desperate voice, barely muffled by the door. A key scraped in the lock and Mario Sonnino pressed his face to the small crack in the now opened door.

"Giulia!" he cried.

"It's Mario!" Eva called, her voice cracking with relief. "Giulia, it's Mario!"

"Papà!" Lorenzo shouted, racing from the room, ahead of his mother.

"Help me move the table!" Eva instructed, shoving at the heavy furniture, and the little boy was at her side, pushing it out of the way.

Mario fell through the opening, grabbing at his son with one arm, embracing his wife with the other. Eva took the baby from Giulia and held the tiny body against her chest, kissing his downy head and patting his little back. The baby quieted instantly, but Eva's heart was slower to calm. The stress of the last hour was slowly unraveling her control.

"They are rounding up all the Jews. Going from house to house. I ran all the way here. I was in the queue when the news hit, and everyone left the line, running in different directions, afraid for their lives. I didn't get our rations, Giulia," Mario said sadly, as an afterthought. "I thought I was too late. I thought they'd taken you and the children and left me behind."

"You were lucky!" Eva spoke up. "If you'd arrived when they were still here, you would have been taken. And you might have given us away."

"How did you manage? How?" Mario was weeping now, relief and joy seeping from his eyes, unchecked. "Is everyone all right? The baby? Emilia?"

"We hid in the *ripostiglio*." Lorenzo puffed out his small chest and placed his hands on his hips. "And we were so quiet they thought no one was home!"

"You hid in the closet? All of you?" Mario whispered. His gaze lingered on his wife's face, noting her pallor and the strain that tightened her mouth and lined her eyes.

"Not Eva! Eva held the door closed," Lorenzo offered up.

All eyes were suddenly on Eva, Mario's wide with awe.

"Your neighbor told them no one lived here. I don't know if they would have moved on if not for her." Eva's mouth trembled.

"Signora Donati is gone," Mario whispered. "Her door was wide open. All the doors are open. All down the hall. All, except ours. The SS police must have entered each one, making sure no one was left behind. It looks like the phone lines have been cut too."

"They didn't find us!" Lorenzo crowed.

"Where will they take them, all those people?" Giulia asked quietly.

"I don't know." Mario shook his head in disbelief. "But it won't stop with the ghetto. I heard someone say they have addresses. Names. Rome is no longer safe for Jews."

"My sister and her family!" Giulia cried, suddenly realizing, now that Mario was safe, that she had others to be worried about. The same thing had just occurred to Eva. Uncle Augusto and his family needed to be warned.

"I have to go." Eva thrust the baby into Giulia's arms and turned toward the door, halting as she realized she was shoeless.

She ran to the lumpy sofa, shoving her feet into her shoes and her arms into the long red coat she had always loved. Now she wished for a coat in the drabbest brown, something that wouldn't draw attention or admiration. She needed to be invisible. Hadn't Babbo always said, "Keep your head down and your manners in place"? The thought of him made her stomach clench painfully. She missed him! Oh, God, she missed him so much. Had the SS dragged him away like Isabella Donati? Loaded him up in the back of a truck, never to be seen or heard from again?

"Oh, Eva. Be careful!" Giulia warned.

Eva kissed her cheek and embraced Lorenzo before looking up at Mario.

"Will you be okay without me?" she asked softly. "I will come back when I can, and we will finish your new documents. Giulia needs to be in bed, resting. But you know you can't stay here. If you have nowhere else, come to the Convent of Santa Cecilia. We will figure something out."

"I will take care of my family," Mario said firmly, but his eyes found hers and held. "Thank you, Eva. Don't worry about us. We are the lucky ones today. Do you have your pass?" She nodded, knowing that he wasn't referring to the papers that labeled her a Jew. He was referring to the fake ones, the ones that claimed she was Eva Bianco from Naples.

"Mamma?" a sleepy voice said from the bedroom doorway. "Are we playing hide-and-go-seek? I want to count." Little Emilia was rubbing at her eyes and yawning widely, completely oblivious to the terror of the morning. Her parents laughed quietly, and the laughter broke into grateful tears as they clung to each other and to their small children.

Eva slipped out then, letting the young family have a moment together, her mind on what remained of her own family, and the danger they all faced.

CHAPTER 11
TRASTEVERE

The alley leading out onto the Via del Portico d'Ottavia was eerily quiet, the four cramped blocks wedged between the Tiber and the Teatro di Marcello gutted of their inhabitants. The dome of the church in the nearby piazza peered down at Eva, making her feel exposed and small. She wanted to run from doorway to doorway, from tree to bush, hiding herself in spurts, but she made herself walk at a leisurely pace.

It was early, but not terribly so, and the streets were filling with Romans going about their day. It was as if the terror of the predawn was just a strange mirage, shimmering in and out of focus. She saw a single German truck, thick flaps obscuring its cargo. She didn't duck her head or slink. She walked, telling herself that running would only draw attention, even as her stomach twisted more tightly with each step. She walked across the Garibaldi Bridge and down the wide Viale di Trastevere, too unfamiliar with her surroundings to duck onto side streets. It took too long, and when she finally turned onto the narrow street lined with palms and little stores, she was numb with fear. The street was too quiet, just like Via d'Ottavia, and she finally started to run.

She was almost to their building when strong arms wrapped around her from behind and dragged her back. When she cried out, a hand clamped around her mouth as she was pinned between a man's chest and an alcove wall.

"Eva, shhh! Be still." It was Angelo. The relief was almost as great as the despair as she turned and wilted against him.

"*Grazie a Dio!*" he cried, and pressed his sandpaper cheek against hers before pulling away so he could cradle her face in his hands. Angelo had failed to shave, a testament to the kind of morning it had been, and his blue eyes were wild beneath the unruly black curls drooping dejectedly over his brow. Their eyes clung, gratitude and relief giving way to a baser need, a need for affirmation, even celebration, and suddenly his mouth was on hers, kissing her fiercely, desperately verifying that she was indeed safe, present, and accounted for.

Eva froze beneath the onslaught, but only for a heartbeat. Her hands rose to his face, her mouth opened beneath his, and in those few stolen moments, there was euphoric frenzy. Lips, teeth, and tongues that tasted truth and reaffirmed life. The dam broke, and there was only unbridled feeling, stripped of duty and civility, of pretense and propriety. There were no lies between them, no space.

But the suspension of time could only last so long. Eva pulled back, gasping for breath, and with oxygen came remembrance.

"Angelo, the SS are coming," Eva cried, hands gripping, lips pleading. "I have to warn my uncle."

Angelo still held her face in his hands, his relief and lust slower to dissipate, and he forced his gaze from Eva's lush mouth to meet her pleading eyes. She immediately began to shake her head, refusing the dreadful compassion she saw in his face.

"I know. I know, Eva. The SS are everywhere. All over the city, they are rounding up Jews."

"Oh, no. No, Angelo. Oh, please, no."

"I went to the apartment, Eva. I went there first. When the nuns said you never came home last night, I thought you must have been caught. I thought I was too late. I thought they'd taken you too." His breath caught and he swallowed back the black nausea, the horror of that moment so fresh he could still taste it.

Eva closed her eyes, as if closing her eyes would protect her from what he knew.

"Maybe they were warned. Maybe they left before the SS arrived," Eva said hopefully, her lips trembling around the words.

"They're gone, *cara*," he said gently, unable to keep the truth from her. "I saw the truck. I saw the truck drive away, Eva. I saw your uncle climb in. I think he must have been the last. And he saw me."

Eva's legs wobbled, and Angelo was there, wrapping his arms around her, bracing her as her tears began to flow and her strength left her.

"Where did they take them?" she cried, the wail only a whisper against the wall of his chest.

"I don't know. But we will find out. We will find out, Eva."

He smoothed her hair with a trembling hand and kept her locked in his embrace. It was several long moments before either of them had the ability to say more, stricken into silence, as if a meteor were jetting toward them, promising certain annihilation, and no matter where they turned, where they hid, the results would be the same. So they stood, waiting for the world to end, wrapped in each other's arms, breathing, unable to process thoughts into words. But after a time, brain function returned, and with it, a terrible realization.

"The gold. All that gold that was gathered . . . the gold they insisted upon. It was a lie, wasn't it? They wanted to make us think we were safe," Eva said.

Angelo stepped back so he could meet her gaze. Then he cursed angrily, one of the American words he'd taught her to say more than a decade ago. He dropped his arms from around her and gripped his hair, repeating the ugly word over and over. His eyes were bright with outrage. "Yes. It was all a lie. They are pulling our strings, watching us dance."

∞

The Jews apprehended in the daylong Roman roundup were transported to the Italian Military College and held there, under armed guard. People had gathered outside, a substantial crowd—curious bystanders and horrified neighbors who had witnessed the arrests, gawking and gossiping as people are inclined to do. They watched as truck after truck unloaded terrified prisoners into the college courtyard. SS guards pushing and shoving them with shouts and directions that almost no one understood. Twelve hundred Jews, more than half of them women and children, many of them in their pajamas without food or blankets, were told they were being sent to labor camps in the east. Eva's uncle, aunt, and cousins were among them.

The Pope could have looked out of his window and seen the crowds, the military college a mere six hundred feet from Vatican City. Angelo even hoped that the Pope might intercede. After all, he'd known about the gold, even offering to make up the difference if the fifty kilograms wasn't raised. And these were mostly Roman Jews, protected by Italian law. But there was no Italian law anymore. There was only the *Führer's* law. And the *Führer* wanted all Jews deported. The *Führer* wanted *Judenrein*—a world clean of Jews.

Angelo and Eva had wound their way back to the Church of the Sacred Heart, gathering information on their way. Angelo knew everyone, and everyone knew the young father. He gave comfort and instructions as they went, sending people scrambling for this or that, listening patiently, acting quickly. He was a natural leader and a good priest. It suited him. Eva stayed with him, and no one seemed to think it odd or unseemly that they were together. War made a mockery of convention.

When they arrived at the church, Angelo had deposited her firmly in a basement room recently vacated by a janitor killed during the air raids that had left portions of the city in rubble. He'd been running through the streets, terrified. They'd found him shoeless and minus an arm, sitting against the church doors, seeking sanctuary he wouldn't find. The entrance was still lightly stained with his blood, and his rooms weren't much more hospitable. A mattress on an old spring frame, an oddly ornate yet faded Victorian-era chair, and behind a small partition, a little sink, a cracked oval mirror mounted on a bare joist, and a toilet.

"You will be safe here, for now. The bedding is clean. The bathroom too. We knew we would need the space before long. I will tell Suora Elena you are here. She, or one of the other sisters, will bring you something to eat. I don't want to bring you back to the convent until I know for sure they weren't visited during the roundup."

"Almost no one knows who I am. No one, Angelo. I don't need to hide here. I could come with you to where they are holding my family. I speak German! Maybe I can help in some way."

"No. You have to stay far away from all of that. All it would take is someone pointing you out, recognizing you, and you would be inside the college with the others. All it takes is one, Eva. One person telling the wrong person. And I may not be able to save you."

She started to follow him out of the basement room. "Maybe we can find a back entrance, an unlocked door. Maybe we can get my family out. There has—"

"No!" Angelo's roar was so enraged, so full of fury, that Eva stopped midsentence and stared at his livid face. Her eyes immediately filled with frustrated tears, but Angelo pushed her back, as deep into the minuscule space as he could get her, pressing her against the back wall, his arms braced on either side of her head.

"No, Eva. You avoided arrest twice today. Twice. God smiles on you, Eva, in so many ways, but I won't let you do this. I will go. I will do everything I can to save as many as I can. But if you insist on coming,

I will tie you to that bed. I will tie you up, and neither of us will leave this room."

"You act as if you aren't in any danger!" Eva put her hands on his chest and pushed him back, angry because he was angry. "But I know better. Priests have been tortured, shot, hung from bridges, shipped off in trains loaded with the Jews they've tried to help. In fact, non-Jewish Italians caught helping Jews are sometimes worse off than the Jews themselves."

"The only thing that matters to me, the only thing in this whole world that truly scares me, is something happening to you. Do you know that? I think I could face anything, endure anything, if I knew for sure you were safe and well. I cannot serve the way I need to serve. I can't be the kind of priest I need to be, and be full of fear. My faith is being drowned by my fear for you. You aren't the only one who has lost their family. Your family is my family, Eva. I've lost them too! And I can't lose you. Please. Please, Eva. If you have any feelings for me at all, you will stay here until I come back for you. You will let me do what I need to do, knowing you are out of harm's way. Please."

Eva could only nod, shocked at his vehemence, touched by his sentiments. She sat down on the thin mattress and nodded once more.

"I will wait. But you have to come back here. No matter what happens, no matter how late it is. You have to come back, Angelo."

Eva lost her battle with sleep, making the hours of waiting easier to endure. She wrapped the thin blanket around her shoulders and pulled her knees into her chest, pretending that she was an oyster in a shell, a maker of glass, and nothing more. She fell asleep to the drip and creak of the basement walls, a prayer on her lips and the echo of cries and gunshots from the morning still haunting her thoughts.

When she awoke she was afraid, caught in her old dream, the one with the crowded darkness and the need to escape, to jump, though jumping was almost as terrifying as staying put. She opened her eyes, trying to convince herself that the darkness was empty and she was stationary. No one grabbed at her clothes and pulled at her legs. The light that flickered was not from moonlight penetrating the cracks in her consciousness. It was an oil lamp, turned down so low it glimmered without lighting the space around it.

"Angelo?"

The wick was lengthened, the flame danced, and the light grew, casting a glow over Angelo in the odd Victorian chair, sitting in the dark like he didn't want to wake her.

She sat up and reached for the water Suora Elena had brought her. There was bread too, and she split it in half and brought it to Angelo, insisting that he eat. He relented and they ate in silence, the bread doing little to fill the empty dread in both their bellies. When they finished, Eva made him drink. Then she crouched in front of him and peered up into his face.

"Tell me."

Angelo was silent. Eva took his hands in hers, giving him something to hold on to.

"Tell me, Angelo."

He answered with a deep breath, as if it required courage to speak.

"I walked around the perimeter of the college. I even found an unlocked door, just like you said. Being a priest, with Vatican City so close by, I was sure I could simply keep walking or come up with a plausible excuse if I was caught." He paused, then added quietly, "I saw Levi."

Eva's heart leaped in her chest, hope giving her a fleeting smile. But Angelo's grave face in the lamplight stole it from her lips, and her heart resumed beating with a despondent thud.

"He and several other boys had already discovered the unlocked door. They were standing near it, arguing among themselves. I beckoned to them, whispering that there was nothing to stop them. The back was completely unguarded. They would have been able to slip away, Eva."

"But they wouldn't leave," she whispered knowingly, seeing her cousin in her mind's eye, insisting that he couldn't leave his family.

"They wouldn't leave," he confirmed. "One boy argued that if they left, others might be punished."

"So they stood by an unlocked door, and refused to use it," Eva moaned.

"Can you blame them? What would you have done, Eva?" he said softly. "I know I would not have been able to save myself if I couldn't save you with me. They wanted to stay with their families."

"They are all going to die," Eva whispered.

"Maybe not," Angelo protested, his voice just as soft.

"They will be sent to camps. You've heard the reports. You've heard, Angelo. You know. They are death camps."

"Some still say those are rumors, British propaganda." He didn't want to take her hope from her.

"Angelo, you know!" Eva's face crumpled and she covered her tears with shaking hands. "You heard what the soldiers said. They've seen the crematoriums. They've seen the mass graves."

"We got some out, Eva," he offered, needing to give her something, anything, to hold on to, needing to rid his mind of the images her words evoked.

"Some of the Jews had Italian names. Non-Jewish Italian names. We convinced them to line up with the non-Jews who were arrested by mistake. One of the prisoners spoke German, and he was keeping everyone calm, translating for the Germans, telling people what to do so there would be no reprisals.

"The Germans said if anyone lied they would be killed on the spot. But bravado won the day. The officers let all those insisting they were non-Jews go. I vouched for several of them, swore they were my parishioners." Angelo stopped talking and Eva wrapped her arms around his neck, pulling him to her, horrified by the risks he'd taken and moved by his courage.

"It was awful. They confiscated their belongings. The guards told them it was to provide for those who couldn't work when they arrived at the labor camps. Those who were too sick, too old, or too young. But I saw the most valuable items being pocketed by the officers. And there was a woman giving birth, Eva. Right there on the concrete floor. They wouldn't take her to a hospital! She gave birth to a healthy baby girl." Angelo's voice broke, and for a moment he couldn't speak. He had wanted to give Eva hope, and he'd lost all of his. His arms moved around her, embracing her as she was already embracing him, and he buried his face in her hair.

"The more I see, the harder it is to believe in God. What kind of priest can I be if I don't believe in God anymore?" he confessed, his voice thick. "Some days it hurts too much to believe."

"It hurts more not to believe," Eva whispered back, stroking his hair. "I'm starting to think God is the only reason *any* of us are still alive."

His arms tightened desperately, and his voice was a harsh whisper against her neck.

"I have to get you out, Eva. I have to get you out of Rome. But I don't know where to send you, all alone as you are. I don't know where you'll be safe, and I'm afraid if I can't see for myself, every day, that you are alive and well, I will lose my mind."

"There is nowhere that is safe, Angelo. I am as safe here as I am anywhere else. I left Florence but I won't leave Rome, and I won't leave you," she added gently. Seeing his devastation made her want to be strong, if only for him. It made her long to be honest. When loss was a constant threat and a terrible likelihood, there was no time for pretense. She held him as he held her, neither of them speaking, finding a temporary peace and comfort in each other, if nothing else. She fell asleep with her head on his shoulder.

❧

In the inky dark, always blackest before dawn, Angelo walked to his apartment, only a few blocks from his old parish and the Church of the Sacred Heart where he'd left Eva for the second time in twenty-four hours. When daylight came, she would be safe enough, with her false papers, to walk back to Santa Cecilia on her own. The nuns had not been visited in the daylong raid, making Angelo breathe a little easier. None of the convents, churches, or monasteries where he had refugees hidden had been included in the *razzia* by the SS. His people, Jews and Catholics alike, were safe for the time being. And after today, there would be so many more that needed to hide.

Angelo needed to sleep for a few hours, and then he would return to the Italian Military College and see what more could be done for the Jews being held there.

He let himself into the modest flat, leaving his cane and his hat by the door and unbuttoning his cassock, eager to be free of it, to wash himself and fall face-first into his bed.

He jerked in surprise when he heard his name being called from the sitting room. Monsignor Luciano was sitting in pajamas and a dressing gown next to an unnecessary fire, a closed Bible in his hands as if he were comforted by its heft but too tired to open the cover.

"Monsignor! Are you just waking up or have you been awake all night?"

"A little of both," Monsignor Luciano said with a smile in his voice. "It was a terrible day. My sleep was troubled."

Angelo didn't want to sit, he needed to sleep, but he sensed his mentor had waited there for him, and he fell heavily into a chair opposite the monsignor and closed his eyes.

"Where have you been, Angelo?" The tone was kind, not accusatory, but still Angelo weighed his words.

"Eva's uncle, aunt, and cousins were arrested today in the roundup. After I spent all day trying, I had to tell her I could not obtain their release," he said. It was the truth, but the simplicity of the truth was in itself a lie. Words did not exist that could fully express the horror of the day, the desperation, and the gut-sickening realization that he was almost powerless to save anyone.

"I am worried for you, my young friend," Monsignor Luciano admitted quietly.

"Why?" Angelo was worried too, but he doubted his concerns were the same as the monsignor's.

"This is the girl who made you question your decision to become a priest. This is Eva." Monsignor Luciano clearly hadn't forgotten Angelo's agonized confession or his counsel to Angelo after that terrible, wonderful trip in August of 1939.

"Yes, it is." Angelo nodded, his eyes on his mentor.

"You love her."

"Yes. I do. But love in itself isn't sinful," Angelo said simply, another truth that skirted a lie.

"True. But it is distracting. And you've promised your heart to another."

"God's heart is big enough for all of mankind, yet mine can't be big enough for two?"

"Not when you're a priest. You know this, Angelo." The monsignor sighed. "You know the dangers."

"I have loved her since I was a child. It isn't something new, something I haven't grown accustomed to. My heart is God's." Truth. Truth. Truth. And still, a lie.

"We are at war. War has a way of stripping us of perspective. War is about life and death, and it paints everything in shades of now or never. We do things we otherwise wouldn't because *never* is so frightening and *now*, so comforting. 'Let us eat and drink, for tomorrow we may die.'"

"You are quoting Isaiah. You must be worried."

Luciano laughed ruefully. "Do not change the subject."

"You may think I'm rationalizing. And I probably am. But I know one thing. She makes me serve him better. In fact, she is the very reason I serve."

Monsignor Luciano raised his eyebrows and folded his hands, ever the patient father, listening as his child tried to talk his way out of hell.

"In every Jewish face, I see her. I think it would be easier to ignore their plight and say, as some have done, it was foretold. They crucified our Lord. Some say that, Monsignor. You know they do."

Monsignor Luciano nodded his head once, slowly, and Angelo knew with a flash of intuition that the monsignor had said the very same thing himself at one time or another.

"But Eva didn't crucify our Lord. Her father didn't either. Not a single Jew living on this earth crucified our Lord." Angelo felt his neck getting hot and his temper building in his chest. He paused and took a deep breath, reminding himself that the monsignor was not the one persecuting the Jews.

"They are just people. And many of them, most of them, are good people. Camillo and Eva loved me and gave me a home; they are my home. Signore Rosselli would never admit it, but I know that he gave a great deal of money to the church so that I would be allowed to attend seminary. I believe he donated again so that I would have a position waiting for me when I became a priest. I never waited in line, Monsignor. Unlike so many others, after ordination I was immediately assigned a parish. It was that money and your influence, not anything I did.

"Camillo gave my grandparents a home, and when the laws were passed—those ridiculous laws—Camillo Rosselli signed his possessions and all his property over to them. He asked that they would return a portion if the laws were ever revoked. And if they weren't, he asked that they look after Eva and give her a home when he was gone, should she need it.

"When I see a family running for their lives, no home, no country, no one to protect them—hunted—I see Eva, and it makes me try harder. It makes me pray harder. It gives me purpose, Monsignor. I see Eva."

"Try instead to picture our Lord. Instead of seeing Eva, you should see our Lord. Our Lord was a Jew too, Angelo." The monsignor's voice was pleading, trying to redirect his focus to a safer place.

"Yes. He was. And if he were on earth today, the Germans would arrest him too. They would arrest his mother. They would arrest the apostles. They would load them all aboard a northbound train, traveling for days without a place to sit. They would make them stand in their waste, no water, no food. And when they finally arrived at their destination, they would work them to death or gas them immediately."

"Angelo!" The monsignor was aghast at Angelo's crass response. Angelo almost laughed out loud at his horrified expression. But he didn't laugh. He didn't cover his head and cry either, which was what he wanted to do. It was crass. But it was true. Funny how that worked.

"Here is the difference, Monsignor. Jesus gave himself willingly. He could have saved himself. But he was God. And he chose. Eva is just a girl. She wasn't given a choice. The Jewish people have been stripped of choice. They have been stripped of liberty. They have been stripped of dignity. And they cannot save themselves."

Throughout the next day, Angelo watched the military college where the Jews gathered in the roundup were being held. It was close enough to the Vatican that he could see portions of the courtyard from the window in Monsignor Luciano's office. He arranged for food to be delivered to the prisoners, as much as he could gather and cobble together with permission from his higher-ups. The soldiers made them leave it in the courtyard. He wasn't certain anyone inside received any of it.

There was little movement. German soldiers with submachine guns guarded the facility, and no one left. But in the early-morning hours of October 18, forty-eight hours after the raid began in the old ghetto, army trucks started leaving the Italian Military College. When Angelo arrived at dawn he managed to arrange for a Vatican car to follow the row of trucks at a distance. The trucks didn't go through the regular terminal, nor were the prisoners put aboard passenger trains. He and Monsignor O'Flaherty, the Irish senior official who had cleared the food delivery, watched as the trucks filed into the loading platform at Tiburtina Station. Men, women, and children, many still in their pajamas, the clothes they were arrested in, were loaded into freight cars, packed in at full capacity with barely room to stand and no room to sit. The doors were shut and locked. The empty trucks left and returned again, several times.

All day they watched. Truck after truck arrived at the loading dock, and the process was repeated. The day was warm, but the cars were never reopened. The people inside never received water, and the cattle cars had no bathrooms. Angelo and Monsignor O'Flaherty could only watch from afar—a pair of cassocked spies sharing a set of binoculars. They couldn't hear the crying children or the questions that must have been raised among the crowded occupants of the trains. But they voiced some of their own.

Why would the Germans want to transport all those people hundreds of miles just to kill them? And what reason would they have to kill them in the first place? It would be completely irrational. Surely, they would be put to work. It was the only logical conclusion.

But Angelo knew. He'd had a group of refugees from Czechoslovakia that had told him about the trains. And the evidence was in front of his eyes. The words he'd said to Monsignor Luciano in the early-morning hours of the previous day were riveted in his head: *They would load them all aboard a northbound train, traveling for days without a place to sit. They would make them stand in their waste, no water, no food. And when they finally arrived at their destination, they would work them to death or gas them immediately.*

"Why won't the Pope do something?" Angelo cried, watching yet another transport arrive. "Can't he intercede? These are Rome's Jews! They were guaranteed this wouldn't happen. And it's happening! We are standing here doing nothing to save them."

Monsignor O'Flaherty put down the binoculars and rubbed at his tired face, crossing himself and muttering a quiet prayer before he turned to Angelo with wounded eyes.

"I can't answer that, Angelo. All I know is that sometimes we only see our corner of hell. The Pope has to consider what intercession in one place will mean in every corner, to all people. If he starts making demands for these Jews, what will Hitler do? The line is so tenuous, Angelo. Lives hang in the balance of every decision. Many lives. More lives than these. The church is hiding thousands of Jews and caring for people in every community throughout the world. We can't continue doing what we're doing if we draw a target on the Vatican walls, now can we?"

Angelo had no answer, and he could do little but watch as his corner of hell continued to widen. Finally, at two p.m., eight hours after the first trucks arrived at the loading dock, the cargo train—pulling twenty freight cars filled with more than twelve hundred of Rome's Jews—left Tiburtina Station.

20 October, 1943

Confession: Uncle Felix was right about long notes.

Uncle Felix used to torture me with long notes, the most tedious, painful, boring exercise known to violinists all over the world. One note, sustained endlessly. No volume change, no variance, no vibrato. Babbo hated long notes almost as much as I did. The music room was on the other side of his library at the villa. One day I heard him heave a book at the wall after I'd been playing long notes for more than an hour. It ruined my concentration, and I stopped, falling just short of my record.

Uncle Felix shouted, "You will never master this instrument if you do not master the long note, Batsheva!" I was so frustrated I yelled back, "And you will never master Italian if you only speak in German!" Babbo heard that too. And I was grounded for a week for my impertinence.

I play my long notes when I'm alone in my room at the convent, and for the first time in my life, I'm comforted by them. I'm comforted by my ability to master that one continuous sound, though my arm aches and my spirit longs for music.

Life is like a long note; it persists without variance, without wavering. There is no cessation in sound or pause in tempo. It continues on, and we must master it or it will master us. It mastered Uncle Felix, though one could argue that he simply laid down his bow.

I wonder what the nuns think of this exercise, the long note that wails from my room, night after night. I would think if anyone understood the power of constancy, it would be the nuns of Santa Cecilia.

Eva Rosselli

CHAPTER 12
VIA TASSO

Two days after the raid, looters, realizing the city's Jews had been forced to leave their belongings behind when they were arrested, had moved into the ghetto and started taking anything and everything of value. In the darkness before dawn of the third day, Mario Sonnino and his little family walked the dark streets to the Church of Santa Cecilia and rang the bell on the gate.

"Father Angelo told us to come here," Mario said when Mother Francesca peered at him through the iron bars.

"And Eva," the little girl chirped up. "Is Eva here?"

Mother Francesca took one look at the tired mother, an infant in her arms, and the two children holding their father's hands and ushered them through the gates and up the stairs to the room next to Eva's.

Eva came awake to the sounds of a baby crying and the padding of nuns' feet scurrying down the corridor, trying to make accommodations for the new arrivals. She jumped out of bed and dressed in the dark.

Another bed was brought into the little room, and a crib was fashioned out of a large crate. Mario and Lorenzo would stay on the lower floor where two other Jewish males were boarding. The nuns had rules about these things, but Mario could only nod gratefully. He'd had a plan in place, but it was too late to implement it.

"The escape routes have closed. The Germans have shut down the port of Genoa, and the Swiss border is too dangerous. Giulia and the children would not be able to make it, even if it weren't. It's too grueling a trip. I don't know where to go, Eva. We have the false passes but nowhere to live. And my pass won't be sufficient to hide me."

"I was worried about you. I should have come to check on you myself! Angelo wouldn't hear of it. He said the ghetto was too dangerous," Eva said as she helped Giulia unpack their small suitcases.

"It was. But don't worry. Father Angelo came himself. And he told us to come here before the sun rose. It is the safest time to be on the streets. There was a family who offered to hide us, another doctor and former colleague of mine. But it is getting too dangerous. It's not just the Germans we have to look out for."

Eva knew what he meant. The Blackshirt Brigades, OVRA—the Organization for Vigilance and Repression of Anti-Fascism—and the Fascist House, all Italians—were reporting to the Gestapo. They were actively hunting Jews and spying on other Italians.

"I didn't want to endanger his family." Mario stopped suddenly and looked at the ground as if he were ashamed. "Yet we are here, endangering these women," he whispered brokenly.

"You will be safe here. And so will the nuns," Eva replied firmly. "It was the right choice."

In the days that followed, Angelo brought two young sisters, one fifteen and one sixteen, who had escaped the *razzia* when their older brother had forced them out an upstairs window and told them to flee across the rooftops, promising them that he wouldn't be far behind. He'd been shot instead. An older couple and another young family with two little boys, not much older than Lorenzo, followed shortly thereafter. A pair of brothers in their early twenties and a man and his young daughter rounded out their numbers. The small convent was starting to burst at the seams with new "boarders."

It was illegal to take in boarders without legal documents, and only Eva and the Sonninos had papers that wouldn't get them immediately arrested. It was also illegal not to list all boarders on an official register. But then again, at this point it was illegal to be a Jew in Rome. Mother Francesca had fretted about their growing numbers and the official register that she had to produce if the police asked. Angelo had pulled her aside and reminded her how the mother Mary herself had been turned away time and time again and ended up giving birth to the Savior of the World in a stable.

"We can't turn them away, Mother. They have nowhere else to go."

Angelo also had letters from cardinals asking all religious institutions to open their doors to refugees and do what they could to shelter them, and he used the letters without remorse or restraint. He'd told Eva that the pastors throughout the countryside around Rome had reminded their parishioners that Jesus was a Jew in order to coax them into opening their doors. Catholic guilt was a powerful tool, and Angelo and his brothers showed no qualms at wielding it.

In the days that followed, Angelo and the abbess gave instruction in catechism and liturgy and taught lessons in paters and aves to the refugees, a crash course in Catholicism on which they were continually grilled. The refugees who had false papers and whose accents or appearance would not give them away went with Eva to the *municipio* to obtain food coupons and proper residence permits. Aldo was able to get forged documents to Mario Sonnino consisting of release papers from the Italian army and a doctor's labor permit. He shouldn't flaunt it, but it would give him a measure of cover if he were discovered or detained.

Even with some of the boarders able to register for ration cards, the numbers at the convent—the numbers at every convent and monastery throughout Rome—were far greater than the rations allotted. Mario knew where Levi had gone to buy items on the black market, and he and Angelo braved a few clandestine meetings to secure butter and milk, two things Giulia Sonnino desperately needed. She wasn't well, and she wasn't producing enough milk for her new baby.

But Angelo was resourceful. Two weeks after the raid on Rome's Jews, a woman in his old parish lost her baby in a house fire. Somehow Angelo got wind of it and brought the poor mother to the nuns of Santa Cecilia, giving the woman a roof over her head and providing little Isaaco Sonnino with a wet nurse. If there was a need, he found a way, his abilities as a goalie translating beautifully to his abilities as a wartime priest. Scramble, protect, defend.

Angelo inspired the same ingenuity and respect among everyone he served, and he never stopped moving. He'd drawn some attention from the local Italian police, who had questioned him on more than one occasion, but he'd just blessed and genuflected his way out of trouble every time, doing as much business as he could from inside Vatican City, where the law of Rome could not touch him. But he was adamant where Eva was concerned. She would not risk herself. It was his one stipulation, until it was taken completely out of his hands.

❦

He sat on the long bench, slumped, his cap in his hands, a German officer alone, and people scurried past him. He seemed unaware of the discomfort he was causing, the fear and derision in the looks tossed his way.

Eva had spent the morning in long ration lines, the one thing Angelo would allow her to do, and she had very little to show for it. She had brought Mario's violin with her that morning, instructed to barter with it if there was anything worth bartering for. There had been nothing. Now, several hours later, she was waiting for a streetcar to take her back across town.

She still had fifteen minutes to wait. At least. And she was tired, her feet hurt, and watching the big German occupy the whole bench suddenly filled her with a rage and an insolence her father would have trembled to see. She could almost hear his voice in her head.

Invisibility is our best weapon, Batsheva!

Invisibility may have worked for Camillo Rosselli, a thin, slightly stooped man of indeterminate years. But it didn't work especially well for a beautiful woman. Eva had learned that long ago. Her best weapon was to make others stare. Stare, and assume she had every right to be exactly where she was. She sat down next to the man, her back stiff, her violin case in her lap. She perched with her nose in the air, reminding herself that he was the interloper, an unwelcome visitor to her country. He could move if she made him uncomfortable.

He looked up in surprise—she felt him jerk—and she turned her head and eyed him in haughty rebellion before looking away. He continued to stare, his gaze heavy on her face.

"Can you play?" he asked in German. Eva pretended not to understand. He sighed. He leaned over and tapped the violin case.

"Can you play?" he said again. He mimed the action, and Eva noticed how tired he looked, how dark the hollows were beneath his eyes.

She nodded once. A sharp inclination of her chin, and looked away again.

"Play," he said simply, tapping at her case insistently.

She shook her head. No. She would not play for him. He fell back dejectedly, and she thought that would be the end of it.

"My father could play. He loved music. Beethoven and Mozart. Bach . . . he loved Bach." He was speaking so softly Eva could have shut him out. But his voice broke on the last word, and his sorrow was palpable. Eva almost felt sorry for him.

"Play," he demanded again, his voice rising. He leaned toward her aggressively and jerked the case from her hands. Eva instantly stood and stepped back. It was not her prized Stradivarius, but she wasn't foolish enough to grab it back, even if it had been.

He set her case on the ground and opened it. He pulled the violin and bow free and stood, shoving them at her. She bobbled and almost dropped them, but he didn't care.

"Play!" he yelled, his pale face suddenly ruddy with anger. A child started to cry, and Eva realized they were drawing attention. But no one stepped forward. No one intervened. *Invisibility* was the word of the day. She was too shocked to respond, and stood staring at him, her bow extended like a sword.

"Are you an idiot? Play!" he roared. Then he drew his pistol from the holster at his side and pointed it at her face.

With a quick tightening of her bow and a hasty tuning of the strings, she lifted the violin to her shoulder, and turning her face from the unwavering pistol, notched it beneath her jaw.

His father loved Bach. That is what he had said. Without looking at the German officer, Eva began to play "Ave Maria," the version by Bach and Gounod, the one that had made her weep for her own mother and vow to master the violin if only to feel closer to her, to understand her.

From the corner of her eye she saw the gun lower slightly, but only a bit, and Eva squeezed her eyes shut and concentrated on keeping the tone clear, the tremolo controlled, and the shaking in her legs, where it wouldn't affect her performance. She had shunned invisibility. Look where that had gotten her. Now her only weapon was to play, and play well.

The first sustained note was shy, hesitant. But Eva bore down, gripping the instrument fiercely, her chin pressed against the faded varnish like she was embracing a lover. The melody shimmered and strengthened, and before long she was coaxing a soaring aria from the singing strings that not even a trained soprano could match. Still, Eva heard it all as though she listened through a waterfall, her heart drowning out the sweet, silvery slides and the quivering crescendos, and she wondered in the part of her brain that knew only thought—the part that watched as if from a safe distance—if this would be her final performance. She wondered if it was worthy of her uncle's sacrifice, her uncle's time, of all the hours she had spent practicing, hearing Babbo grumbling and Angelo begging for more.

Then it was over. Complete. Eva lowered her bow from the strings and raised her eyes to her oppressor. He had dropped the gun to his side and his face was streaked with tears. He carefully re-holstered his pistol and turned away. He hesitated, his back to her, and Eva wondered if she would be asked for an encore. Her chest burned and she realized she needed to breathe. Without turning around he said softly but distinctly, *"Vergib mir."* Forgive me.

He walked several steps, his spine stiff, his arms clasped behind his back. Then he resumed walking with a brisk determination, like he knew exactly where he was going. The streetcar was coming, the screech of the wheels on the track music to Eva's ears. The German officer headed toward it, as if he thought he could brandish his gun and make it stop, the way he'd pointed his gun and made her play. As it neared, he quickened his step, and with a composure that struck Eva as instantly familiar and terrifyingly predictable, he threw himself in front of the streetcar. The sound was hell unleashed, a shrieking, tearing, grinding groan, and the car bucked on the track, attempting to swallow the man whole and spewing him out again.

People were screaming and pointing, and within seconds— minutes?—a siren blared, then another, a cacophony of banshees in the bright-blue day.

Eva walked on wooden legs to the case that lay thrown open on the ground. She carefully placed her violin inside, closed it, and sat heavily on the bench. She resumed waiting for a streetcar that was already there, a streetcar that wouldn't be taking her anywhere. Her hands shook and her stomach revolted, and every horrified breath felt like fire in her throat. Yet still she sat, composed, her terror held inside the bony cage that sheltered her war-torn heart and her shrapnel-riddled lungs.

Then there were Germans with whistles and clubs, pushing onlookers into a cluster, yelling in a language no one seemed to understand. But Eva understood.

"Someone pushed him!" an officer shouted. "Who pushed him?"

The terrified crowd looked around, as if to find the culprit, and one woman pointed toward Eva, as if to say, "Her!"

"She was with him," the woman said in Italian. "That woman with the violin. She was with him."

Several of the officers and a handful of horrified onlookers followed the woman's pointing finger to the bench where Eva sat. The Germans may not have understood what the woman said, but they understood her gesture.

Eva rose from the bench, shaking her head.

"Nein," she said. "No! He was not pushed. He walked right in front of the streetcar. I watched him." Her voice rang out in German, and two of the officers broke away and came toward her.

"What is your name?" one barked, his hand on his gun.

"Eva," she answered numbly. She couldn't remember her last name for a moment. Then she remembered she wasn't supposed to say it and was grateful for the shock that had stalled her tongue.

"Documents?" He waited with an outstretched hand.

She fumbled in her pocketbook and rushed to set her fake pass in his hand. He looked at it for several seconds and handed it back.

"You will come with me."

"Wh-what? Why?" She realized she asked in Italian and repeated the question in German.

"Ten civilians for every German. That is the *Führer*'s rule. You saw what happened. Who should we take instead?"

"But he killed himself," Eva shot back.

"So you say. Come with me."

"He walked in front of the streetcar!" Eva cried out, this time in Italian, her eyes on the onlookers, knowing someone had to have witnessed the suicide. The people stood huddled, frozen, eyes wide, mouths closed, and no one said a word.

"No one was even close to him!" Eva pressed. "He just stepped in front of it. Someone had to have seen the same thing I did!"

Then one woman nodded. Then another took courage, and before long, several people were agreeing, adding their voices to Eva's claims. The German officer either didn't understand or he didn't care to, but he took Eva's arm and marched her toward a jeep parked haphazardly in the middle of the street. He snapped at two of the officers and shouted orders at several more, and Eva was shoved into the back of the army vehicle and taken away. Whisked off the street, easy as you please, and there was nothing she or anyone else could do about it.

The German police had converted a row of buildings on Via Tasso into their headquarters. It was an odd choice, just a modest thoroughfare of apartments and schools that was bracketed on one end by a crumbling arch and the Sanctuary of the Scala on the other. Red banners with large swastikas hung down the front of the largest structure, looking official and garish against the dull yellow exterior.

Inside, it was a construction zone guarded by soldiers with machine guns. The Germans had been in Rome for less than six weeks, and by the looks of it, they were anticipating a long occupation. Walls had been torn down and reconfigured, offices sectioned off, and a long row of dark cells, rooms without toilets or beds, stretched down one corridor, and many of the cells were filled. Eva was deposited in a room that looked more like a closet and locked in. It was so dark it took her eyes several minutes to adjust. She could hear an occasional cry or barked command, and she put her hands over her ears to block it all out. Then she focused on what she would say if given the opportunity. Her mind kept tripping back to the melancholy German in his last moments.

She had hated him on sight. She'd hated him even more when he'd held his gun to her head. But then she'd seen his tears and felt his despair. She didn't hate him now. She couldn't. She understood him too well.

"Forgive me," he'd said.

She did forgive him. Wholeheartedly. And she forgave her uncle Felix as well. For three long years she'd pushed all thoughts of him away. But there, in the dark, she could feel him with her.

They left her in the closet-like room for hours. Eva had no way of tracking the time, but she desperately needed to go to the bathroom, and her throat was so dry it was sharp when she tried to swallow.

When a soldier finally arrived and ushered her out, she was given a drink and allowed to use the bathroom—another dark closet with a bucket on the bare cement, overflowing with waste—before being led up a flight of stairs into an office that made the lower floors look like a different planet.

A uniformed German of medium height and compact build waited for her inside a large office beside a large mahogany desk, as if sitting were beneath him. His uniform was crisp, his manner brisk. His pale eyes were sharp, and his tone was sharper.

"I am Captain von Essen. What is your name, Fräulein?"

"Eva Bianco." She'd been rehearsing her lines for hours.

"Why are you in Rome, Miss Bianco?"

"My brother is a priest at the Vatican. I came here to be closer to him and to find a job."

"What is your brother's name?"

"Angelo Bianco. He works for the Roman Curia."

"No job in Naples?"

She shook her head. "No."

"You speak German very well. But you sound Austrian."

She nodded.

"Surely, you didn't learn to speak German so well in school."

"I learned in school, but I had a music teacher who was Austrian."

"Is that so?"

"Yes."

"What kind of music?"

"He taught me to play the violin. I spent a great deal of time with him."

"And where is your teacher now?"

"He is dead." She thought he would ask for details, and he seemed to consider doing so, but changed tacks.

"A German soldier is dead too. He was a very dedicated officer. I am having trouble believing he would just walk in front of a streetcar."

"But he did," Eva said quietly. Firmly. He met her gaze and then lowered himself into his chair and steepled his fingers in contemplation.

"You did not push him?"

"No!"

"And you didn't see anyone else push him."

"No. No one pushed him. He seemed very . . . upset."

"And how would you know this?"

"He held his gun to my head and demanded I play my violin for him," Eva said simply.

Captain von Essen raised his furry blond eyebrows and leaned forward.

"And did you?" he asked.

"Yes."

"Show me." He pointed toward the door. Her violin case had been set against the wall, just to the left of the entrance. It had been taken from her, along with her documents, when she'd arrived. She wondered why he was asking her questions he obviously already knew the answers to.

She stood and retrieved the case, willing strength to her limbs. For the second time in one day, Eva was being ordered to perform, wound up tight like a jack-in-the-box and told to play for her release.

"Do you know any Wagner?" the German asked curiously.

Eva stiffened, hearing Felix's voice in her head. *No Wagner. He doesn't care much for Jews. So I don't care much for his compositions.*

"Not well enough to play."

"Hmm. What a shame. But there are so many wonderful German composers. Mozart, Chopin . . ."

"Mozart is Austrian. Chopin is Polish," Eva corrected him. She knew she sounded belligerent and was pleased at her tone. She wasn't sure at what point she'd stopped being terrified. Maybe sitting in the dark with thoughts about suicide had tipped the balance.

"But Austria no longer exists. You must know. Austria and Germany are one in the same," he reasoned.

Eva just nodded, not trusting herself to speak.

"Play Chopin," he demanded.

Eva lifted the violin obediently. Shutting the captain out, she found the thread of music in her memory, the variation she'd played for Uncle Felix. Chopin mixed with Rosselli, sprinkled with Adler, and doused with anger.

"Genug," the captain said briskly. That's enough. The music didn't seem to impress him. Eva stopped immediately.

"Others have verified your claim. It appears you have done nothing wrong. You are free to go." He stood once more, as if it had all been a formality to begin with, as if the hours she'd spent locked in a four-by-eight room were just an oversight. She stared at him stupidly, wondering if he was toying with her.

"Can you type?" he asked abruptly.

Eva stared at him blankly, trying to switch from Chopin, to freedom, to this new line of questioning.

"Yes." Her answer sounded more like a question, lifted on the end, confused.

"I need a secretary who speaks German."

Eva could only sit in frozen horror.

"You want me to work here?"

"Yes. Here. We will compensate you well. You will run errands. You will file. You will type. You will get coffee. Nothing too difficult. No one will hold a gun to your head and demand for you to play your violin." He didn't smile, though Eva was sure he was attempting to be humorous. "You said you needed a job," he prodded.

"Yes. Yes, I do." Her mind reeled with the horror and the possibilities.

"Then it is settled. Six days a week. You will have Sundays off. Be here Monday morning at eight. You will leave at five. Your brother—the priest—is here. He's been waiting for you. You must tell him you were treated fairly." It was not a suggestion.

Eva could only stare in amazement once more. Angelo was there?

"It is after curfew. We will have a car take you both home. You will report back on Monday." He waited for her to stow her violin and then handed her her fake identity card. It had held up twice now. She would have to tell Aldo.

He had a soldier escort her to the reception area where two Germans with submachine guns were parked on both sides of the entrance and two more behind a large desk. Angelo sat on a metal chair with his head bowed. His hat had been removed and he held a cross in his hands. When she approached the bottom of the staircase, he raised his head halfheartedly, like he'd been lifting his head all day to disappointment.

He shot to his feet, his eyes on her face, scouring her expression for duress. She tried to smile to put him at ease, but the twist of her lips felt strange, and the effort made her feel like weeping, so she gritted her teeth and let the soldier lead the way.

"There is a car out front," the young German said to Angelo. "You will both be taken home. Please follow me." He strode briskly for the door, expecting them to do as he said. Angelo took Eva's arm, clutching her so tightly she would have bruises. She welcomed his grip, though the irony that she would leave German headquarters bruised only by Angelo was not lost on her.

Their armed escort held open the door of a shiny Volkswagen for them, waiting as they slid into the backseat. He leaned down, his gray turtle-shell helmet pointing toward them.

"Address?"

Angelo answered for both of them, supplying the address that Eva assumed was the apartment he shared with Monsignor Luciano and his sister. The German snapped his heels together and shut the door firmly. He relayed the directions to the driver, and seconds later the car pulled away from the curb.

The streets were quiet, Romans hiding obediently in their homes waiting for sunrise when they could start the process all over again. She and Angelo didn't converse. The German at the wheel shot them a curious look in the rearview mirror, his eyes lingering on Eva and then flitting to Angelo before looking away. Angelo had released her arm when she'd climbed into the vehicle, and he didn't take it up again.

"There was a woman hung from a streetlight today. A partisan," the driver said conversationally, in German. Neither Angelo nor Eva responded. "She asked for last rites. Were you aware, Father?" he pressed.

Angelo nodded once, but his hands balled into fists.

"When you said your sister had been brought in, Father, there was talk going around that the partisan was your sister. We don't have many women at headquarters. Not yet. Fortunately, I was wrong." He commenced whistling like it was truly a happy occurrence.

With the streets bare, the ride took a quarter of the time, and before long, Eva and Angelo were stepping out onto the dark sidewalk in front of a building Eva didn't recognize and watching the black Volkswagen pull away.

10 November, 1943

Confession: I never used to pray.

Prayer wasn't something I ever thought about when I was younger. It wasn't something that mattered to my father, and so it didn't matter to me. Then one day it did matter. So I started to listen. And I started to pray.

The prayers of the Jewish people have been passed down, generation after generation, and when I say the prayers, they are like lullabies. In the prayers I feel my parents, and their parents, and their parents before them. I feel them all, singing to me, and they are not gone, but just away. We are apart, but not forever. So I will keep saying the prayers. I will never stop, and because of this, I will always be a Jew.

Angelo does not pray the way I do. He calls his God a different name. But I'm convinced God is not just my God or Angelo's God. He is God. He wouldn't be God if he was only God to some of his children . . . would he? Whether or not his children call him by the same name. I call my father "Babbo." Angelo refers to his father as "Papà." Does it matter what we call him? Does it matter how we pray, if our devotion is pure, if our love for him leads us to love and serve and forgive and be better?

I guess it does. Sadly, it does. Because my prayers could get me killed.

Eva Rosselli

CHAPTER 13
THE CHURCH OF THE
SACRED HEART

"Come with me," Angelo said softly. He turned, not taking her hand, not holding her arm. He acted as if the buildings had eyes. He walked swiftly, his cane clicking on the cobblestones, and turned up a narrow alley. He walked in the shadows along the back of the building until he reached the rear entrance of a large church surrounded by a high wall. Eva realized belatedly that it was the Church of the Sacred Heart. They'd just approached it from another direction.

Angelo groped beneath his stiff white collar and pulled up a chain that was hanging around his neck. Several keys hung from the links, and he selected one and unlocked a gate. It opened soundlessly, as if the hinges were kept well oiled. He closed it behind them, a careful clang, and led Eva up a little path that ended at the back door of the church. With another key he unlocked the rear entrance, and they slipped inside.

The scent of incense and candle wax assailed her, and beneath that heavy fragrance, the smell of old stone and damp corners. Vespers was over, and the minimal lighting from the wall sconces was mellow and muted. Angelo genuflected before the cross and slid into a pew, indicating that Eva should sit as well.

"Why are we here?" She had known Angelo wasn't taking her to the convent when he gave the German soldier a strange address. But she'd thought he was taking her to his home.

"I didn't know where else to take you. There is nowhere else where I can speak freely."

"You don't trust Monsignor Luciano and his sister?"

"I trust them. I just don't want to endanger them. And every time I turn around, there is a new threat." He clasped his hands and rested them on the back of the pew in front of them. "What happened today, Eva?"

"I saw a man die. A German soldier. He killed himself. Just like Uncle Felix. I was waiting for the streetcar. He held a gun to my head—"

"*Mio Dio!*" he moaned, and he dropped his head to his forearms.

"He held a gun to my head, Angelo," she repeated. "And he told me to play my violin. So I did." The whole bizarre incident felt like a Greek tragedy, acted out by unfamiliar actors on a makeshift stage.

"When I was done, he asked me to forgive him. Then he walked away."

"How did he die?" Angelo asked.

"He threw himself in front of the streetcar. He knew exactly what he was doing." Eva pressed her hands into her eyes, wondering how she would ever forget what she'd seen, forget what it had sounded like. "Then there were people screaming, and I just sat there. Before I knew it, I was being taken away. I told the soldiers what happened, but they didn't believe me."

"They believed you. You wouldn't be alive if they hadn't. You would be swinging from the streetlamp with that poor girl they hung today." Angelo stared at her gravely, his blue eyes gray in the flickering shadows.

"Who was she?"

"Part of the resistance. A partisan. She was even younger than you, and she was murdered in the street." He looked away and scrubbed at his face with open palms, and Eva knew she wasn't the only one scarred by the day.

"How did you know I was there, Angelo?" she asked, her eyes on the blue-robed virgin who looked at them from her corner perch with patient acceptance.

"One of the nuns from Santa Cecilia was in the ration line, and she saw them take you away. She came to the Vatican and found me." He rubbed his hands over his head once more, and his throat moved convulsively. "I have never been so scared in my life, Eva," he whispered.

"I have," she replied softly. "Several times." He looked up at her, and he didn't look away for several seconds. He just looked at her, drank her in, and she held his gaze.

"I was offered a job, Angelo."

"What?" he gasped, the spell between them broken.

"The captain who questioned me. Captain von Essen. He needs a secretary who speaks German." Eva pointed at herself. "I do."

"Eva, *mio Dio.*" Angelo was shaking his head again. "No. You can't do it."

"I have to. What possible reason would I have to refuse? The convent needs the money."

"No! You will hide. When you don't show up, he will find someone else. He doesn't know where you live. He won't be able to find you."

"But he can find you, Angelo. He knows where *you* work. He knows who *you* are."

"I will be fine," he snapped.

"No. You won't. And I am going to take the job. Maybe I can help in some way. I will be in a position to hear if there is going to be a raid—"

"Eva!" Angelo grabbed her shoulders and shook her so hard her teeth rattled. "This is madness!"

"No. It isn't! It's war. And I will do my part. I will not sit by while others die. If I can help, I will."

"Your job is to stay alive," he cried, still gripping her by the shoulders, his face inches from hers. He was furious, but under the fury was a desperation she recognized. It was the desperation she felt when her father told her he was going to Austria to find her grandfather. But she understood her father now like she never had before. He had been compelled to act. Action was life, even if it ended in death.

"No, Angelo. My job is not to simply stay alive. My job is to live. Not hide. Not wait. Not hope that it will all end. You can't tell me not to fight, Angelo. I don't tell you what to do! You can't tell me not to try to help in some way."

"Eva—"

"If I can't fight, then I might as well swallow a bullet like Uncle Felix or throw myself in front of a streetcar like that German soldier. I'm this close to hopeless, Angelo." She held her fingers an inch apart. "Resistance is all I have left. Don't you understand?"

He looked down into her face, wanting to comfort her, wanting to comfort himself, needing to save her, needing to save himself.

"Resistance." He repeated the word like it was his own and dropped his forehead to hers, closing his eyes and willing himself to move away. "Resistance," he said again. "I do understand," he said softly. "I understand completely."

His own resistance was shot, and he released Eva's shoulders and pushed himself up from the pew.

"I don't want you to walk in the dark. It's after curfew, and it's too far. Can you stay here tonight?" he asked Eva tiredly. He looked at her long enough to see her nod, then he walked away, but he didn't leave the church. He approached the altar, lit a candle, and used his cane to sink down to his knees in front of the cross. He buried his face in his hands and for several long minutes he prayed. He didn't know if Eva watched or if she'd retreated to the little basement room that she'd used once before, leaving him alone. All he knew was that his resistance was failing him, and he had no armor against her any longer.

He started with his face in his hands. It was the way he always prayed, the way he'd been taught to pray. It kept him from sight and distraction, cradling his face that way, as if he covered himself from everything but the words he spoke. But before long, he was overcome, and he found himself prostrate, the way he'd lain during his ordination, his arms extended in front of him toward the wooden cross that hung above the altar.

He was just a man. Young, crippled, scared. But he would give his life for Eva. And he would give his life for the people he was trying to save. That had to count for something, it had to. He'd broken a promise. He'd held Eva in his arms, and he'd knowingly, willingly broken his vow. He'd kissed her. Yes, he'd been vulnerable. Yes, he'd been scared. Yes, it was forgivable, even understandable. But there is a consequence for every broken promise, and he feared the consequence would be an innocent life. Not his life, but someone depending on him.

"Please don't let my weakness be reason to withdraw from me. Please don't let my love for Eva endanger her or remove her from thy grace," he said without sound, his lips moving around the silent words.

That was what he feared most, that his own sin would cause a cessation of blessings, of divine intervention. And he could not risk it. There were too many people counting on him.

When he'd gone to see Monsignor Luciano before he was ordained, the monsignor had read him the account of David and Bathsheba in the Bible, and the name Bathsheba had not escaped him, essentially the same name as Eva's. At the time, it had struck him how King David hadn't averted his eyes as Bathsheba bathed. He hadn't looked away from her beauty, shielded her from his gaze. He hadn't stayed away, not after he'd discovered she was married. Not after he'd realized who she was married to—loyal Uriah, who had faithfully fought for his king and country. Not after he'd gotten her pregnant and created a mess. Not after he'd had Uriah put in death's path. He'd persisted in his sins, making them worse every step of the way.

Was Angelo doing the same thing, persisting in his sins by being near Eva? Was he willfully looking at her beauty and not averting his eyes when he should? The problem was, he didn't know how to stay away from Eva. He didn't feel like it was a choice. She was not another man's wife, another man's responsibility. She was his responsibility. He'd made a vow to God, but he'd made a promise to Camillo. And Eva was his. She had been his from the moment they met.

"Create in me a pure heart, O God,
and renew a steadfast spirit within me.
Do not cast me from your presence
or take your Holy Spirit from me.
Restore to me the joy of your salvation
and grant me a willing spirit, to sustain me.
Then I will teach transgressors your ways,
so that sinners will turn back to you."

He recited David's prayer like it was his own, and when he finally finished and rose to his knees, he raised his head, his eyes seeking the candle he'd lit and the cross above it. A candle and a cross, the only thing that separated him from being hopelessly lost.

But there were several candles now, and Eva sat nearby, her head bowed in her own prayer. He didn't disturb her but watched as she prayed, her hands outstretched toward the candles she'd lit. When she raised her head and saw him watching her, she curled her fingers and stared down at her palms.

"What are you doing?" he asked softly.

"It's Shabbat."

He nodded. She was saying her prayers beneath a cross. If it didn't bother her, it certainly didn't bother him. She continued speaking, her eyes on her bent fingers.

"With our hands, we reach for things we shouldn't have and we grasp what isn't ours. The way I have always reached for you." She raised her eyes then and looked at him steadily. *The way I have always reached for you.* Angelo's pulse quickened immediately, but he didn't look away. *We reach for things we shouldn't have and we grasp what isn't ours.*

Her eyes returned to her hands, and she traced one finger over the opposite palm as she spoke, as if she were anointing it the way the bishop had anointed Angelo's hands at his ordination.

"With our fingers we touch the filth that is all around us. Our fingernails collect dirt, the lines in our palms become stained and soiled, yet when we raise our hands in prayer or supplication, we demonstrate that even that which is sullied by the world can commune with the spirit. That is why during Shabbat, when we hold our hands toward the candle, we curl our fingers away from the flame, allowing the light to be reflected in our fingernails. Even our fingernails, the part of us that is most unclean, can still reflect God's light. At least, that's how I understand it." She smiled ruefully and let her hands drop to her lap, but her eyes stayed fixed on the candlelight.

Angelo raised his hands the way she had done, palms up, curling his fingers toward his chest, so he could see the light reflecting in his nails. He would never have the hands of a scholar, though he supposed he qualified as one. They were large and rough. They looked as if they belonged to a peasant, not a priest. They were his father's hands, he realized suddenly, the memory rising from somewhere in his past. His *papà* was wrong. He could have been a blacksmith instead of a priest. He had the hands to prove it.

"Fire purifies," he said softly, looking at the dirt on his palms. The floor in front of the cross obviously needed a good scrubbing.

Eva nodded. "When we wash our hands and say a blessing in the morning, we pour the water with our right hand over our left, which signifies kindness before might. When we wash we are also remembering the close of Shabbat and the flame or power that purifies."

He shifted his raised palms so they were no longer tipped toward the candle but tipped toward her.

"I keep reaching for you too, Eva," he confessed. "I keep trying to grasp what isn't mine." He dropped his hands and tried to rise, his bad leg making him awkward and clumsy and his exhaustion making it worse.

Eva rose with him.

"I have always been yours, Angelo," she said, echoing the very words he'd thought while he prayed. She *was* his. "But you have never been mine."

It was true. She had always come second. But now? Now, instead of coming second, he was simply being torn in two. The priest and the man warring with each other. The scripture about serving two masters flitted through his head.

"Angelo?"

"Yes?"

"Life is hard," Eva whispered, so softly he strained to hear. Then she laughed without mirth, just a quiet huff of disbelief. "Life is hard. What an understatement! *Hard* is too mild a word for the trouble we've seen. Life is hell shot with just enough heaven to make the pains of hope all the sharper. Life is impossible. Ugly. Agonizing. Inexplicable. Torture." She stopped and he waited, and when she spoke again, her voice was no longer a whisper. She still spoke softly, but there was steel in her words, and he heard her conviction.

"But there are some things that don't have to be hard, Angelo. Loving me doesn't have to be hard. Being with me doesn't have to be hard. You don't have to long for me and fight thoughts of me. You don't have to beg God for forgiveness day after day and pray a dozen rosaries because you're in love with me. It doesn't have to be hard, Angelo. It can be the easiest thing in the world. It can be the only thing in our lives that *isn't* difficult. If you stop being a priest, no one will die. No one will lose his soul. In fact, there is not a single person on this planet who will suffer at all. You can be mine. I can be yours. And it can be easy."

Her words clanged through his head and his heart like the old parish priest of the Church of the Sacred Heart was ringing in Lauds, seven hours early. He shook his head in disbelief. No. It couldn't possibly be easy.

"What about God?" he asked.

"God forgives."

"What about my vows?"

"God forgives."

"You are so sure about the nature of God?" Angelo's voice was mild, even mocking, but his eyes were troubled, his brow furrowed.

"Angelo, there are only two things I know for sure. The first? I love you. I've always loved you. I love you now. I will love you in fifty years. I love you. Second: No one knows the nature of God. Not you, not me, not Monsignor Luciano, not my father, not Rabbi Cassuto. Not even Pope Pius XII. No one."

Angelo's lips twitched, and he began to laugh. He laughed soundlessly for several minutes, the pressures and the pain of the day giving the laughter a manic flavor. But still he laughed, and Eva, smiling slightly, waited for him to get control of himself. He did, eventually, sighing and wiping at his eyes.

"And what about the people who are depending on me right now, my beautiful prophetess? The Curia, the parishioners, the Jews I am hiding, the network we've created? Do I just take off my robes and run away with you?"

"You continue on. I continue on. Until it's done. Until the war is over."

"So you will pretend to be a Catholic, and I will pretend I am still a priest?"

"No. I will pretend I am not Jewish, and you will continue to pretend, at least in public, that you aren't in love with me. Just as you've always done." Eva smirked at him impishly.

"Ah, Batsheva," he said tenderly, and leaned toward her and kissed her forehead, hardly trusting himself to do even that. "I don't know whether you are wise or just devious."

She stared up at him for a long time as if she were thinking it over. Angelo was too tired to put up any walls. Too raw. Too afraid of losing her to forces that were beyond his control. The world was raging all around them. And he couldn't stop spinning.

"I am neither wise nor devious. I just don't have the time or luxury for a moral dilemma. There is truth, and there is self-deception. I suppose we all have need of both. Good night, Angelo." She turned and walked toward the little door to the left of the apse that led to the basement room.

He could only watch her go.

25 November, 1943

Confession: I am a spy.

Not all grape growers want to make their own wine. Many sell their grapes to wineries, and the wineries then produce the wine under their own label. My father made a fortune providing bottles to wineries—bottles they got to hand select. He had molds for bottles of all shapes and sizes, so the bottle was as unique as the wine. It was a great selling point, and Babbo always insisted that wine tasted better in Ostrica bottles. "The shape is important," he would say. "Many do not know this. But trust me. Shape is everything."

Each day that I go to work, I am reminded of my father's glass molds at Ostrica. It's been two weeks since I started working at Via Tasso, and I have been careful to mold myself into the perfect secretary, to do all that is required of me quietly and efficiently, so I don't bring attention to myself. Angelo worried that like Ostrica's bottles, I was hand selected for my shape and my beauty, but so far, it seems as if my German language skills are all Captain von Essen truly wanted. Angelo stops by the convent almost every night before going home to make sure I've survived the day.

The Romans won't even refer to Via Tasso as German headquarters. It is regarded with such loathing and fear that it is simply called laggiù—*down there. They whisper, "So and so was taken down there."*

Amy Harmon

I rarely venture beyond my little desk outside the captain's office and the small kitchen and lavatory down the hall. I run errands, relay messages, type endless reports, make coffee, and do whatever the captain asks. But I hear things, and I feel them. It is a grim place to be, though the offices are separated from the prison that haunts my dreams. I've seen the cells of the prison, I've been inside one, and though I was never tortured, I am sure many are. So I listen and I watch and I pay attention, hoping something I learn will be of use.

      Eva Rosselli

210

CHAPTER 14

FLORENCE

Angelo stepped off the train in Florence and was met by a frantic Aldo Finzi wearing the robes of a priest, robes that Angelo had made sure he had, just in case. It was November 27, 1943, and the time had come for disguises in Florence.

Ostrica had been raided, Aldo's home had been ransacked, his printing press destroyed. They were looking for him, but not just him. The SS, Italian and German, were looking for all of Florence's Jews, and they weren't doing it quietly. "Rabbi Cassuto has been arrested," Aldo cried, his eyes wild as they walked from the train station, unsure of where to go now that hell had descended on the city. "He was arrested with a priest and several other members of the underground. I was afraid it was you, Angelo. That's why I'm here. I thought it was you."

Angelo had come to Florence for that very purpose—to meet with Rabbi Cassuto and deliver the last of Camillo's money. He had been delayed at a checkpoint and missed his train that morning, and that delay may have saved his life. Angelo put his arm around Aldo's shoulders, reassuring him, but he was leveled by the news. He had come to know Nathan Cassuto through DELASEM. Camillo Rosselli had introduced them after Felix's death and made sure that the young rabbi knew how to contact Angelo when he needed funds.

The rabbi was a tall, handsome man with kind eyes and a gentle demeanor. He'd been a doctor before the Racial Laws had made it impossible for him to practice. Fate, opportunity, and a rare, second rabbinical degree made him a candidate for a different vocation, and what a terrible, tragic time to be a rabbi. Yet he hadn't wilted under the pressure or succumbed to the temptation of the "wait and see" attitude that so many Jewish leaders and their congregations couldn't resist. He'd warned his people tirelessly, telling them to hide, to get out, and he'd stayed behind with those who couldn't. Now he'd been taken.

The streets were absolute chaos. Germans with bullhorns rode up and down the neighborhoods demanding that residents—all residents—come out of their homes. They were to bring no possessions, no weapons—guns were illegal to all but the police—and they had three minutes to be outside. If the Germans found them hiding in their homes, they were shot.

It was the Roman *razzia* all over again, but there was nothing stealthy about this raid. It took place on the streets in broad daylight, in full, garish colors and surreal pageantry.

Three blocks from the train station a family was being lined up against the wall, their hands in the air. The father was trying to reason with the soldiers, talking wildly with his hands, pointing and gesturing. A soldier knocked him in the side of the head with the butt of his rifle and the man dropped, his animated hands coming to final rest at his sides. His hysterical family was executed against the wall, and the man was left in the street, lying in a growing pool of blood. A soldier put a bullet in his head to make sure the family wouldn't be separated in death.

Angelo and Aldo saw Jewish children being torn from their mother's arms and loaded into trucks while their sobbing parents were loaded into another. On the corner, mere feet from the seminary where Angelo had obtained his degree, a teenaged boy was shot in the back as he tried to flee from a member of the Italian SS. Angelo had to walk around his body to escort Aldo inside the gates. Father Sebastiano and several other monks had gathered the seminarians together, and their heads were bowed in prayer. The Germans had been and gone, and no one had been harmed or discovered, though Angelo knew for certain there were a few Jewish boys hidden among the seminarians.

"Wait for me here," Angelo instructed Aldo. "You will come back with me to Rome. But I have to make sure my grandparents are safe, and I need you off the streets."

"I have the type for the documents. I break it up after every session, but I was able to grab it, all my samples, and my province stamps. I also have a stack of finished documents and a hundred more that need pictures and names. Everything is in a suitcase in a locker at the train station. If you can find me a printing press in Rome, I can continue with my work."

Angelo didn't know how he would manage it, but they would find a press, even if they had to put one in a cloister. He kissed the little man's cheeks and promised not to be long, striding down the street, his heart galloping sickly, his sights set on the villa.

The SS beat him there.

When he arrived, several soldiers were overturning beds, opening closets, tapping walls, and peering into dark corners. A captain stood in the courtyard with Santino and Fabia, a clipboard in his hands. A member of OVRA, recognizable by his black uniform, had taken the lead in the questioning, though his translation skills left a great deal to be desired. Angelo's grandparents had obviously been ordered from the house and were now being questioned about the whereabouts of

Camillo and Eva Rosselli. As he approached, a weapon was leveled at him, but he was greeted civilly.

"You are Angelo Bianco?" the SS officer asked. Angelo's blood ran cold. He hadn't lived in Florence for four years. But they knew who he was. They knew his connection to the residence.

"Yes," he answered in German. He wouldn't mind leaving the Italian Blackshirt guessing about the conversation. He looked familiar to Angelo, and familiarity with your enemy is often portentous of bad things.

"Can you tell me where Batsheva Rosselli is?" The Italian jumped in immediately.

"No." Santino was shaking his head. "We haven't seen her in months."

"I find that hard to believe. You are her family. Surely, she would tell you where she was going." The OVRA official said this with such certainty that Angelo was sure the man must know Eva personally.

Angelo realized suddenly who the man was. He'd courted Eva, years before. Eva had said she liked him because he looked good in a uniform and he was a great dancer. It had made Angelo jealous, though he'd never admitted it, even to himself. His robes were hardly masculine, and his inability to dance was well established. It had rubbed at him, Eva's enthusiasm for things he couldn't do with her.

The policeman had even dated her a few times after the Racial Laws were passed. And now he was here, looking for her, asking after her whereabouts, so he could assist the German occupiers in arresting and deporting her. The name came to his mind instantly. Georgio. His name was Georgio De Luca.

"Georgio! It is you! I didn't recognize you at first." Angelo greeted him with forced levity and clasped his hand, patting it affectionately as if he and the Italian thug were dear old friends. Then he turned to the SS man and, in German, clued him in on the Blackshirt's romantic interest in the woman they now searched for.

"I thought maybe Georgio and little Eva would marry. They were quite taken with each other!" he lied effusively. The German's eyebrows rose dramatically.

"So you don't know where Eva is?" the Italian shot back instantly, his eyes hardening. He didn't like Angelo undermining his credibility with the Germans.

"We have it on good authority that she is engaged to be married and living in Naples," Angelo lied. "But with the difficulties in communication between the north and the south, you understand, we have not heard from her in months."

The German didn't like being left out of the loop, and he cleared his throat expectantly. Angelo instantly translated.

"Interesting. I could have sworn I saw her with you in September, Padre. You were at the station boarding a train to Rome."

Angelo did not translate this. He just shook his head and shrugged, adopting the old Italian response to anything sticky or uncomfortable. Shrug and shrug some more. I don't know. Don't ask me.

The German SS officer seemed a little unsure of himself. His men had returned to the courtyard. He waved them back to the truck and turned to Angelo.

"It is against the law to hide or harbor Jews, Father. I hope you aren't hiding Miss Rosselli. It would not go well for you or your grandparents. Think of them."

Angelo nodded immediately. "Of course. You can rest assured, sir. I want only to do the right thing." He bowed subserviently and turned to Georgio De Luca. "And Georgio. So nice to see you again. If we do hear from Eva at some point, I will tell her you came by."

Georgio flushed angrily and stomped to the jeep. The German officer clicked his boots and followed him, a deep groove between his brows. They rolled out of the courtyard, through the gate, and Angelo, Santino, and Fabia stood in silence and watched them go, badly shaken.

The house had been searched from top to bottom, various valuables removed for the "support of the Reich," but his grandparents were unharmed, and the house had not been commandeered. But had Eva stayed in Florence, she would have been arrested. They had known exactly where to find her.

"It's time for you to leave Florence, Nonno," Angelo told his grandfather. "Go stay with your brother." He had a feeling the Gestapo would be back.

"Where do you live, Fräulein Bianco?" Captain von Essen asked Eva out of the blue one morning. She had delivered his coffee and the stack of reports that he'd had her type.

The question surprised her. She'd had to list her address for her employment file when she'd begun work at Via Tasso. He could look in her file for the information. She was guessing he already had.

"I board in the guest quarters at the convent of the Church of Santa Cecilia." There was no reason to lie. It was easy enough to verify, and boarding at a convent made sense, especially if it had been arranged by her brother, the priest. Still, she didn't like shining any attention on the convent. She wasn't the only one boarding there, or hiding there.

Something flickered across the captain's face, as if he was a little surprised she'd answered truthfully.

"I thought you would live with your brother."

"No. He is the assistant to Monsignor Luciano of the Curia. Monsignor Luciano and his sister are natives of the city, and they still own the family apartment they were raised in. Angelo would have lived in a religious college with other assistants and priests who work at the Vatican, but he wanted to be more accessible to Monsignor Luciano. Monsignor has had some health issues in recent years." Her answer was very logical. Very smooth. Very reasonable. But her stomach twisted anxiously.

"I see." The captain smiled and nodded amiably. "Where is that church, exactly? I am not terribly familiar with the city."

"Just west of the Tiber, in Trastevere. Are you familiar at all with Trastevere?" So forthcoming. So conversational. No secrets from the boss.

"Ah, yes. Trastevere," he said as if it were all making sense. "Isn't that a Jewish neighborhood?"

Eva stared at him blankly, having anticipated his question. "I don't think I've ever met a Jew. How would I know if I had? Everyone at the convent is Catholic." She sounded simple. Stupid, even, and the captain laughed and patted her hand.

"That is a long way to work each day. Now that it is growing dark so early, I must remember and let you leave earlier so that you will arrive home before curfew."

Angelo had said the very same thing the day before, worrying that she was not getting home before dark.

"That would be very generous of you. I have worried about getting detained."

"Then that is what we will do. You may leave at four thirty today. That will be all." She turned to leave, and he called out after her.

"Oh, Eva?" It was the first time he'd called her Eva and not Fräulein Bianco, and she stiffened at his familiarity but turned with a smile.

"If you are to see a Jew or hear of Jews in your neighborhood . . . you will tell me." It wasn't a request. "We will reward you, of course."

Eva nodded, feeling bile rising in her throat. She left his office quickly. Just the day before she'd overheard soldiers talking about a Jewish girl in Rome who had reported dozens of her fellow Jews. Her favorite thing to do was walk through the marketplace at the busiest times of day or walk by ration lines and wave and call out to friends and community members, revealing their identities, only to have the SS men who followed her around swoop in and arrest the unfortunate people who'd been outed by one of their own. She was of great help to the SS, and they rewarded her with lire and freedom.

Eva wondered if the girl ever considered what would happen when she was the last Jew left, when she was of no more use to the Gestapo. Eva promised herself that if she ever discovered the girl's identity, she would find a way to kill her. She'd told Angelo what she'd heard, and he could only shake his head in disgust, but he'd cautioned her to forgive, just like a good priest should.

"Your hate will only harm you," he said.

"Just as long as I can harm her too. I would very much like to harm her."

Angelo laughed at her fire and tweaked a lock of her hair, like they were children again.

"What if someone pointed me out on the street, and just that quickly I was gone? What then, Angelo? Would it be so easy for you to forgive?" she wondered aloud.

He had looked at her soberly, his smile fading.

"Remember when I told you not to come to the seminary anymore to visit me with Nonna?"

"Yes. You said I was not your sister or your cousin and you were too attached to me. You were very rude about it." She was teasing him, but he *had* hurt her feelings.

"I was trying to protect you, Eva."

"What does this have to do with forgiveness?"

"I told you not to come anymore because some of the boys had taken notice of you. They had started asking questions. They wanted to meet you. I refused. They thought you were my cousin and couldn't understand why I was so protective."

Eva laughed a little, but Angelo didn't.

"I hit one of them. One of the boys. I split his lip and gave him a black eye because he said if he had a cousin like you, he would make sure he was alone with you as much as possible."

Eva's eyebrows rose faintly.

"Father Sebastiano thought they were taunting me about my leg. I let him believe it, but I recognized then that my feelings for you weren't very brotherly. And that's when I knew I would have to protect you . . . from me. My instincts, where you're concerned, are to go to war. I don't know that I could forgive someone who hurt you. But most of all, I would never forgive myself for not protecting you."

Angelo *was* protective. There was no doubt about that, and Eva spent the rest of the day worrying over how she would tell him that the captain had been curious about her address and whether or not she had seen or heard of any Jews in the area. Angelo was already worried about her association with him. As a priest, Angelo was immediately suspect, and by association, so was she.

Lieutenant Colonel Kappler, the head of the German SS in Rome, had become fixated on Monsignor O'Flaherty, convinced that he was the director of the underground in Rome. He was right, unfortunately. Lieutenant Colonel Kappler had established checkpoints on every street, and Vatican passports were receiving more and more scrutiny. One of Monsignor O'Flaherty's helpers—an Italian priest—had recently been arrested under allegations of resistance work. He'd been tortured and executed.

As a result, O'Flaherty had limited his meetings with any of the helpers in his organization to within the Vatican walls so that he wouldn't, by association, make them targets of the colonel as well. Since then, code names had been given, and O'Flaherty's foot soldiers were on high alert. O'Flaherty said Angelo was his "foot soldier with one foot," and as a result, his code name was O'Malley, after a famous Irish pirate.

Eva had met both Monsignor Luciano and Monsignor O'Flaherty when she'd first arrived in Rome and efforts were being made to collect the gold the Germans had squeezed out of the Jews. Monsignor O'Flaherty was rumored to be a bit of a ladies' man because he attended every party and swanky soiree, but he joked that there was safety in numbers and that if he wanted to know what was going on in the city, he had to rub shoulders with the people who knew. He'd smiled widely and talked with her at length, and she'd liked him immediately, though she struggled a little with his Irish-flavored Italian. Monsignor Luciano had been decidedly less friendly. She had the feeling he didn't approve of her. When he'd been introduced to Eva, he extended his arms, the way so many priests did, but he never touched her.

It was something Eva had noticed early on in many of the Catholic clergy, this embrace that was never consummated. It left her feeling bereft. Maybe Jews were more demonstrative, more physically affectionate. Or maybe that was just Camillo, just her family. Her father had kissed her cheeks whenever he greeted her, as if he didn't see her every single day. Every single day until, one day, he was gone. Until he'd boarded the train, waving reassuringly, and he'd never come back.

Deep down, in that part of her soul where Eva kept painful truths tucked away, like grains of sand that chafed and bothered, she knew Camillo wasn't coming home. And she prayed every day that he wasn't suffering. That was another grain of sand, rubbing her raw when she allowed herself to think about him at all. If he were gone, she would learn to endure. She *had* learned to endure. But if he were suffering, that she couldn't abide. Her loved ones were her Achilles' heel. She supposed it was good that she had so few loved ones left. If she was going to be a spy, it made her less vulnerable.

In mid-December, charged with the task of emptying garbage cans and finding a crate of office supplies that had been delivered but that no one could account for, Eva stumbled across an out-of-the-way janitorial closet that wasn't being used for cleaning supplies or paper, envelopes, or typewriter ribbon.

It wasn't even locked.

Shoved in the corner, behind a small row of empty shelves, was a barrel overflowing with gold. Gold that had once belonged to Rome's Jewish population, still in the very same container it had been collected in. Eva touched it in horrified disbelief, running her hands over it, sifting through the bracelets and the pins and ropes and chains. There were gold teeth and rare coins and wedding bands. She picked up a dainty ring and realized it was Giulia's. Giulia had given her ring to keep Rome's Jews from being slaughtered. But they'd been taken anyway, some of them reduced to ash, and Giulia's ring sat in a closet at Via Tasso collecting dust—ignored, forgotten, and completely insignificant to the men who had extorted it.

Suddenly, Eva was crying, the tears sliding down her cheeks and falling into the barrel filled with the only remains of so many who were taken. It had all been a charade—a tactic—and the sheer, malevolent gall of the shakedown was almost more than she could bear. They hadn't even needed the gold. They hadn't even sent it back to Germany. It was inconsequential, as inconsequential as the Jews themselves.

Filled with fury, Eva shoved Giulia's ring on her finger, determined to return it. Then she stuck her hands deep into the barrel, and sifted the pieces through her fingers, looking for something, anything, that might have belonged to her family. Augusto had given a gold watch chain, several tie pins, and a gold ring. Bianca had given much more than that. She opened her hands and looked at the treasure, her angry tears making it all run together in a shiny tangle, one piece indistinguishable from the next.

She released the treasure and stepped back, sickened by the sight but unsure of what to do. It might take all day to find Bianca's jewelry, and Bianca was gone. But the gold didn't belong here. It didn't belong to the Germans. Without a plan or a purpose, other than to balance the scales of justice, to take back what was stolen, Eva started filling the pockets in her slim skirt.

Two handfuls in she realized that wouldn't work. She emptied her pockets and took the little garbage can she'd intended to empty and dumped out its contents. Then she put four handfuls of gold in the bottom and covered it back up with the trash. She paused over a thin, gold-plated nail file and impulsively slid it into her shoe, where it rested between her foot and the left side. It was a pathetic weapon against the danger all around her, but she felt better immediately. She wiped her eyes, straightened her blouse, and smoothed her hair. Then she opened the door and flipped off the light, and with her back straight and her head high, she walked up the stairs and back toward the offices on the third floor, swinging the can from one hand, easy as you please.

The money her father had set aside to aid the refugees was gone, used up by the unending, overwhelming need of so many. It had been gone for a while, and the money in an account in the United States was difficult for Angelo to access. She would return to the closet every time Angelo and Monsignor O'Flaherty needed money for their refugees. The gold would go a long way. Merry Christmas and Happy Hanukkah.

15 December, 1943

Confession: I am an unrepentant thief.

I found gold at the Via Tasso, gold that had been extorted from Rome's Jews, and I took some of it. I put it in my hat and pinned my hat to my head to hide it on the bus ride home. It worked quite well, though a chain was tangled in my hair when I removed my hat. When I showed it to Angelo, he didn't cry the way I did when I found it. He yelled instead. He yelled at me and told me I was the most foolish woman he'd ever met. When I yelled back and told him I would be taking more, and I would keep taking it because it didn't belong to the German thieves, he cursed, kicked the wall as hard as he could with his prosthetic leg, then hugged me so tightly I could hardly breathe. I could feel his heart pounding against my cheek, and though I don't want him to be afraid for me, I can't find it in myself to regret taking the gold. I will take more, and more, and more. I will take every last piece. They won't miss it, they stole it, and we need it. They've forgotten it's even there.

Giulia wept when I returned her wedding band. When I told her and Mario where I'd found the gold, they were as sickened and angry as me. But they didn't yell at me for taking it. Instead, they started devising ways to get the entire barrel out of German Headquarters. Mario insisted it could be traded on the black market for everything from milk to shoes and safe *passage to Switzerland, and he pressed Angelo to take the gold and use it. Angelo has so many to look after, so many people to be afraid for, but I think the main reason he took it was so I wouldn't try to barter with it myself.*

Mario must have sensed his hesitation, because he told him that that much gold could save hundreds of lives. Angelo nodded and agreed but said he was more worried about my life and the danger I put myself in by taking it.

I reminded him that I am not the priority. He didn't argue, but I could see his response all over his face when he looked at me. I am his priority. I'm not sure when it happened, but I am his priority.

The gold file I took from the barrel and slid in the side of my shoe is still there. It isn't much of a weapon, though it is quite sharp. Still, it reminds me of what has been done to us, and it gives me courage.

Eva Rosselli

CHAPTER 15

CHRISTMAS

The day before Christmas Eve, first thing in the morning, Angelo cornered Monsignor O'Flaherty in his office and bade him to follow him to the loading dock at the rear of the Vatican where the kitchen and the service entrances were located.

"I have a surprise for you, Monsignor. An answer to our prayers."

"Which prayer, Angelo? I've put up quite a few different ones as of late."

"Food, clothing, supplies. Presents."

"Presents?"

"Didn't you say some of our smallest pilgrims are in need of Christmas cheer?"

"What magic have you done, Angelo?" O'Flaherty's eyes lightened with hope.

"I haven't done anything, really. One of my refugees found a pot of gold," Angelo said with a bad Irish brogue.

"Whatever do you mean?" O'Flaherty gasped.

"You've met Eva. She is the one who works at Gestapo Headquarters."

"Ah, yes. Eva." O'Flaherty narrowed his gaze on Angelo's face. "Monsignor Luciano has mentioned her as well."

Angelo didn't want to know what Monsignor Luciano had said.

"She found the gold that Kappler demanded from the Jews. The fifty kilograms. It was in a storage closet at Via Tasso, pushed back in the corner like no one knew what to do with it."

The monsignor crossed himself and released his breath. "Dear Lord. What a travesty."

"She found a ring that belonged to her aunt's sister. A woman we're hiding. She took some of the gold. Handfuls of it. And the next day she went back for seconds."

The monsignor looked at him with wide eyes and a gaping mouth. Angelo wondered if he had looked the same when Eva had told him what she'd done. She was too fearless for her own good.

"Well, it certainly doesn't belong to the Germans," O'Flaherty said, shaking his head like he still couldn't believe it.

"No. It doesn't. But she didn't take it for herself. She gave it to me, and I used it to buy all of this." He lifted the flaps of the truck and O'Flaherty whistled, low and slow, when he saw the interior, filled to overflowing with food and toys and miscellaneous supplies.

"It's Christmas, Monsignor. We have presents to deliver."

The monsignor began to laugh and spin, and before Angelo knew it, he was being pulled into an Irish jig.

"Father, I can't dance!" he yelped, trying not to fall flat on his backside.

"Sure ya can!" The monsignor laughed, but he released Angelo to finish the steps alone, laughing and kicking up his heels.

"Eva wrapped all of them and labeled them so we can gift them appropriately. The Jews celebrate Hanukkah, not Christmas, but she says it doesn't matter. She says we can all celebrate Christ this year, as it is his church protecting her people."

"I like this girl." O'Flaherty laughed, and he danced a few more steps.

Angelo liked her too, but he didn't offer commentary.

"Well. I guess we should be about the Lord's business, then." Monsignor O'Flaherty clapped him on the back. "Let's go!"

They set out across the city, delivering goods and blessings to the children hidden in monasteries and convents where there was never enough to eat, a great deal of need, and very little cheer. It was a bit of a risk for O'Flaherty to leave the Vatican at all, but one he frequently took, and as members of the Curia, it was not suspicious whatsoever for the monsignor and Angelo to be together delivering Christmas cheer to convents and monasteries throughout the city.

"Your Eva. Tell me about her," the monsignor insisted from the passenger seat. Angelo was driving and enjoying himself thoroughly. He didn't get the opportunity very often, and he never let his prosthetic stop him.

He looked over at the monsignor, wondering at his use of the word *your*, but he didn't protest or disagree.

"Growing up, we were as close as two people can be," he said. "My grandparents worked for her father, in his home. I came to Italy when I was eleven, and I lived with her family when I wasn't at the seminary. I love her more than my own life." It was the truth without all the complicated subtexts and side stories.

"Yet you became a priest," O'Flaherty said thoughtfully.

"Yes."

Monsignor O'Flaherty looked out the window and said nothing for a while, as if his thoughts were tangled up in Angelo's twisted choices.

"She is a beautiful girl," he said quietly.

"Yes." Angelo braced himself.

"I hear she plays the violin."

"She does. She's been classically trained. She's very accomplished."

"I wonder if she can play any Celtic music," O'Flaherty mused, and Angelo relaxed. "I miss it."

"She can play almost anything by ear. I will ask her if she can oblige you."

"She doesn't work on Christmas, does she?"

"No."

"Then she should come with us tomorrow. We won't be able to make all our deliveries in one day. We will go to the schools on Christmas Day. She should see the fruits of her labor."

"The fruits of her thievery," Angelo said with a small grin.

"That too!"

Eva borrowed a wimple and a veil for the deliveries. If they were stopped, which they probably would be, considering the checkpoints all over the city, she would need to look as if she belonged in a Vatican delivery vehicle with two Catholic priests, and it would mean fewer questions and explanations at the seminaries and schools as well.

They introduced her to the monks and the nuns as Sister Eva, and left it at that. Monsignor O'Flaherty had a personality that outshone everyone in the room, and Eva and Angelo hung back and let him hug and laugh and generally draw the attention to himself. But Eva was lovely and oddly alluring with her covered hair and veiled figure, and she was impossible to ignore completely.

The final stop was the Seminario di San Vittorio, where the oldest boys stared with wistful smiles and the little boys surrounded her with wide eyes and careful hands, touching her borrowed robes like she was the Virgin herself, come to visit on Christmas Day.

They were all receiving haircuts, lined up in a long row. The older ones were being taught to shave, and Eva had the grand idea of soaping up the dirty little faces of the youngest boys and giving them "shaves" as well, making them sit very still, scraping off the suds with the dull edge of a butter knife, and patting their small faces dry with a clean towel. She got smiles and clean, shiny cheeks in the process, and she kissed each one and gave him a piece of hard candy when she finished.

After Mass, they roasted the chestnuts the monks had been hoarding for months in an attempt to provide a Christmas treat. The smell was deep and rich, but the flavor was even better. The chestnuts were continually moistened with a brush as they cooked, then piled into a basket and tossed into the air repeatedly until the burned outer shell flaked off and revealed the white delicacy beneath. Eva proclaimed it the best thing she had ever eaten, and Angelo had to agree. As privileged as Eva's upbringing had been—and by association, his own upbringing—there were some things that privilege could not buy. The scent of chestnuts roasted on a fire the sound of childish voices laughing and the sense of oneness and purpose shared among the impoverished group gave the evening a burnished glow that Angelo knew he would never forget. A child of maybe three or four, a little boy so small Angelo was afraid to hold him too tightly, found his way to Angelo's lap, his newly shorn curls resting against Angelo's chest. His parents had been killed in the San Lorenzo air raid in July. The seminaries and schools run by monks and nuns were becoming orphanages for the lost and hiding.

Eva had brought her violin and played "Adeste Fidelis" and "Tu scendi dalle stelle" at every stop, and she did so again before they left the humble school, making the monsignor weep, the monks bow their heads in worship, and the children sing softly. Even the Jewish children sang, feeling a oneness with the holy child born to poverty. For a few hours they had been released from fear and deprivation, caught up in the festivity and the spirit of the occasion.

> *"You come down from the stars*
> *Oh, King of Heavens,*
> *And you come in a cave*

In the cold, in the frost,
And you come in a cave
In the cold, in the frost.

Oh, my divine baby
I see you trembling here,
Oh, blessed God
Ah, how much it costs you,
Your loving me.
Ah, how much it costs you,
Your loving me."

"How do you know those songs?" the monsignor asked Eva once they were headed back to the Vatican, bouncing down unpaved roads, huddled together in the cab of the delivery truck. He hummed a couple bars and was immediately wiping his eyes once again with the memory of the sweet Christmas melodies. "You are Jewish."

"But I am also Italian," Eva answered easily. "You aren't Italian if you don't know 'Tu scendi dalle stelle.'"

"Ah, forgive me my Irish blunder," he said in English with a purposeful brogue. "Sing it for me, then, lassie."

She sang softly, in a voice as clear and lovely as her violin. She knew every verse, but it was one line that made Angelo's throat close and his eyes smart. *Ah, how much it costs you, your loving me. Ah, how much it costs you, your loving me.*

Angelo could only cling to the wheel, his eyes on the road and his heart on fire, looking out into the starry darkness and feeling the monsignor's gaze on his face.

January of 1944 was as gray and wet as December of 1943 had been. Like everyone else in the occupied city, the convents and the clergy listened on pilfered radios as the Americans seemed to make one misstep after another as they climbed Italy's boot toward Rome. The opening notes of Beethoven's Fifth signaled the nightly reports of the Allied movements from the BBC, and it rarely brought good news. The Germans celebrated and dug in their heels, claiming success at every turn.

But there were small victories. Monsignor O'Flaherty had the inspired idea to let the Jewish population gather for worship services in the excavated church that sat beneath the existing Basilica di San Clemente al Laterano. The basilica was not far from the Colosseum and was under Irish diplomatic protection, providing a measure of safety for the refugees to assemble. The basilica had three tiers, the lowest tier a first century home that had later grown into the fourth-century church above it, built to provide persecuted Christians with a place to worship. The significance of that history was not lost on the Jews and those who sheltered them. It was dank and the walls continually wept with moisture and echoed with the sound of rushing water from the subterranean river that ran beneath the church, but there was peace and a sense of sanctuary within the space.

Despite the danger, Eva and the Sonnino family, along with other members of their underground community, would meet for worship when circumstances allowed. They assembled on the right-hand aisle of the ancient basilica under a faded fresco of Tobias, an Old Testament figure with whom they could identify, clinging to each other and the very traditions that had exiled them and at the same time made them one.

Eva would sit with Giulia and little Emilia, Lorenzo would sit with his father and the men, and they would sing the songs and recite the prayers of those who had come before, doing the best to keep the roots alive, to remember what it meant to be *ebrei*—the beauty, the symbolism, the sense of community and family.

Emilia's sweet voice would rise above the rest, childish and clear, and in that sound was the future and the past. Eva would hold the little girl's hand, singing with her, and as she sang she thought of her father and Felix, of her mother and her grandparents. She thought of freedom and sunshine, of love and hope, and she longed for the days of sand and sea, when Babbo had made glass and life had been simple.

Sand and ash. The ingredients of glass. Such beauty created from nothing. It had been something Babbo had marveled about and something she'd never understood. From sand and ash, rebirth. From sand and ash, new life. With every song and with every prayer, with every small rebellion, Eva felt reborn, renewed, and she vowed to press on. She vowed to push back, to make glass from the ashes, and that courage was a victory in itself.

Eva kept pilfering gold from Via Tasso, and Angelo—priest turned smuggler—managed to convert it into sustenance. But the biggest triumph by far, achieved through a strange series of events and the curiosity of Greta von Essen, was the new printing press for Aldo Finzi to continue his work.

Greta von Essen, Captain von Essen's very bored and very lovely wife, had taken a liking to Eva, probably because Eva, with her German language skills, was one of the few people she could talk to. Greta was a striking woman in her late thirties with no children to occupy her time, so she filled her days with hobbies and housekeeping. She also regularly wheedled Eva away from Via Tasso for lunch and shared intimate details of her life with "Wilhelm" that Eva would really rather not hear.

She broke down and cried in her wine at lunch one day, telling Eva she was a disappointment to her husband and a failure to the Reich. "It is our duty to have children for the fatherland. And I can't seem to have any. Wilhelm is embarrassed of me. He is certain my infertility is the reason he hasn't risen more quickly up the ranks."

Eva patted her hand and made soothing clucking noises, but she was more than happy to oblige Greta when she suggested they finish their lunch and take a detour past a new row of shops, shifting her attention and the topic of conversation from Wilhelm and infertility. They found themselves in a fashionable district a few streets over, lined with dress shops, haberdasheries, perfumeries, and a small but distinguished bookstore with ornate gold lettering in the windows. There was a padlock on the door and a stack of newspapers piled in front of the door.

Greta, an avid collector of everything old or valuable, peeked brazenly through the windows, trying to see what remained inside. It was obvious that none of the inventory had been removed, yet the shop was not open for business.

"What does that say?" Greta asked, pointing at the words on the window.

"*Libri nuovi e rari*—New and rare books," Eva translated quietly. It said, *"Luzzatto e Luzzatto"* in bigger letters just above it. Eva felt the same old nausea rise in her throat. She was certain the Luzzattos were never coming back. Luzzatto was a Jewish-Italian name, and the bookstore had probably been sitting empty since the October roundup. The Germans had put the padlock on the door as if they now owned the place, but Greta was certain she could coax a key and a chance to explore out of her husband.

"There might be books worth thousands of dollars on those shelves. You know how Hitler loves his art and his precious things. Think of what I might find! Wilhelm could present the *Führer* with a one-of-a-kind gift!"

Eva would rather rot than watch Greta find a stolen treasure for Captain Wilhelm von Essen to present to the *Führer*, but she held her tongue, and her self-control was rewarded.

Three days later, Eva accompanied Greta and a German soldier—who seemed relieved to be out of Via Tasso for a while—back to the bookstore. Mrs. von Essen was decked out in a fur coat and a flirty little netted hat shading her big blue eyes, but when they walked inside the dusty establishment, she shed both and dug into her treasure hunt with a gusto that had Eva eager to stay out of her way. The German soldier must have had a similar response. He stepped out on the sidewalk and pulled a lighter from his pocket, more interested in a cigarette break than rows of old books.

She was browsing the titles when she discovered a little door tucked behind a tall row of the dustiest shelves. The door led down a flight of stairs that resembled the excavated sacristy at the Santa Cecilia, but she descended them carefully and found her own treasure at the bottom. Luzzatto hadn't just been a bookseller. He'd been a publisher, and there, in a basement that looked more like a grotto, was a printing press with all the bells and whistles, cranks and trays, to make Aldo Finzi a very happy and productive man.

Best of all, there was a separate entrance leading up to the alley behind the shop and a set of keys hanging from a nail by the door. She tested the keys on the outside entrance, verifying they worked. Then she silently thanked Signore Luzzatto and dropped the keys into the pocket of her coat before climbing the old stairs and locking the little door securely behind her. They were back in business.

CHAPTER 16
FEBRUARY

"Aldo has another batch of documents ready to go," Angelo said. "After you finish work today, he will meet you at the trattoria near the streetcar stop. Order a pastry. He will stand behind you in line. Drop your pocketbook, and he will hand it to you with the pouch of documents. Take your pastry. Leave. Don't talk to him; don't interact with him at all. He is a stranger."

Eva nodded. Angelo hated giving her assignments like this, but he couldn't be everywhere at once, and the bookstore was closer to her than it was to him.

"Trattoria, drop my pocketbook. Leave. I can do that," she assured him.

"Don't go to Santa Cecilia. Meet me at the Sacred Heart. If you're there first, light a candle and pray."

"It is Shabbat."

"Yes. I know," he said with a small smile. "I will try to be there before dark so you can get home. Otherwise, plan on staying there for the night."

"Why don't you want me to go to Santa Cecilia?"

"The Sacred Heart is closer to Via Tasso for you and easier for me to access."

"And if for some reason I am followed or caught, I won't be endangering anyone else," Eva added.

That too. But Angelo refused to consider the possibility that she would be followed or caught. She must have seen the concern in his face, because she immediately changed the subject, and they parted minutes later, Eva heading across town to Via Tasso, Angelo heading the opposite direction to Vatican City.

Eva was running late. Von Essen had brought her a report to type at four thirty, telling her it was of "the utmost importance" and asking her to leave it on his desk when she was finished. He continually forgot that he had told her she could leave at four thirty. He was on his way out, taking some new arrivals on some sort of patrol. He enjoyed patrols. It was something she'd noticed before. His SS uniform was crisp, his weapon at the ready, his boots gleaming like a mirror. They wouldn't stay that way for long. It had been raining all day, making the dreary afternoon seem never-ending, making the hour seem later than it actually was.

She left the headquarters on Via Tasso at five thirty, a half hour later than the prearranged meeting time. She pulled a scarf over her hair to protect it from the rain and ran, hoping it would only appear she was trying to catch a bus or streetcar, rushing to the trattoria, praying Aldo had waited. She slowed to a walk and stood in line for her pastry as instructed, but Aldo didn't fall in behind her. She bought a sweet roll and stood under the dripping striped canopy, eyes scanning, nibbling at the cinnamon-and-sugar-encrusted luxury that should have been savored. She was too uptight to savor it and ended up eating the whole thing without even tasting it. It was six o'clock—curfew—and she needed to get off the street.

And then she saw him, walking briskly toward her, a folded newspaper clutched in his hands. She dusted the sugar from her hands and threw her napkin away, trying to appear casual. She stuffed her icy fingers in her coat pockets and started moving down Via Regala, away from the trattoria and toward Aldo, when a whistle blew and a shout rang out behind her. It was just barely curfew and she didn't think the shout was directed at her, so she kept walking, not even turning her head. But Aldo's eyes jerked toward the source of the ruckus, and she saw him shove the newspaper inside his coat. The document pouch must be inside.

"Keep walking!" he hissed, not glancing at her as he passed. A whistle rang out again. Eva kept walking, just as instructed.

"Buonasera, comandante," she heard Aldo say, his voice cheerful and slow and far too loud. He sounded drunk. "Care for a drink? I'm buying!"

He would be fine. Aldo would be fine. He was an older man with good papers, papers he'd painstakingly created himself. He would be fine. The commander said something in German and Aldo laughed uproariously. She recognized the voice. It wasn't a commander. It was Captain von Essen.

Alarm clanged in her skull, and she did as she was told. Her coat was dark and so was the scarf over her hair. She wouldn't be distinguishable from the back. She kept walking. Her heels clicked against the cobblestones, and she kept her pace steady, her eyes forward. She was at least thirty feet away. Forty feet away. Fifty.

Walk, walk, walk, walk, she commanded, the rhythm of the words and the tapping of her heels urging her to move faster, faster, faster. As she neared the corner she turned, ducking behind a gnarled olive tree and darting a glance back at Aldo, unable to slip away without first knowing how he fared.

Time doesn't stop or give warning. It simply ticks along, marking time, ignoring humanity. Von Essen stood behind Aldo. He had placed the muzzle of his gun at the base of Aldo's neck, almost like he was using the weapon to lift the collar of his raincoat.

Then he pulled the trigger.

Aldo Finzi crumpled to the ground like his legs had suddenly ceased to function. There was no protest—not from Aldo, not from the handful of uniformed men who now surrounded him. Not from Eva. No screams, no exclamations. Just the sound of a weapon being discharged.

And time kept its schedule without a thought for the man whose time had just run out. Tick. Tock. Tick. Tock. Right. On. Time.

Von Essen put his gun back in the holster and pulled a silver cigarette case from a breast pocket. The click of the case counted off another second. The crisp strike of a match, another. A flame swelled and retreated, almost like it took a single breath and exhaled, and the captain lit his cigarette and snuffed it out. He dropped the match on the inert form at his feet and a thin wisp of smoke rose up from the dead man, as if his spirit rose and dissipated in the soggy dusk.

Eva stood, staring, as cold and as silent as time itself. She was the only other person out. Nothing cleared the area as effectively as a German patrol.

"Er war ein Jude," von Essen said simply, his voice carrying down the street. He didn't even try to moderate his volume. Why would he? Aldo was only a Jew. He'd only killed a Jew.

"How do you know?" One of his companions prodded Aldo with the toe of his boot, as if asking him to verify the captain's claim.

"I told him to drop his pants," von Essen said simply.

The soldier used his foot to turn Aldo to his back.

"Can't hide the circumcised dick." Laughter. Ha ha ha. Tick tick tock.

"Leave him for now. It is good for the Italians to see what happens when you don't heed the law. They were warned. All Jews were to report months ago. He didn't. Now he's dead."

They continued back the way they came, unconcerned, their footfalls fading with their voices.

Eva waited until she couldn't hear them any longer. She was still rooted to the spot where she'd turned for one last look. She walked toward Aldo on legs that shook and wobbled like she was as drunk as Aldo had pretended to be. Forty feet, thirty feet, twenty, then ten. It was almost full dark, and though the rain had stopped, the air was still thick with moisture that threatened to fall. The wet streets shone blackly like Aldo's blood. But she wouldn't look at the blood.

Eva kept her eyes on Aldo's face. His eyes were closed, mercifully so, and his glasses were slightly askew, making him look like a child who had fallen asleep reading. She crouched beside him and felt for the newspaper he'd shoved inside his coat. There. It was fat with documents. And it was still warm.

"Oh, God. Oh, dear God," she moaned, feeling the bile rise. She wouldn't think about it. She wouldn't. Gritting her teeth, she dropped the pouch down the front of her dress, ignoring the sticky heat against her skin. The tight belt at her waist kept it from falling through to her feet. Then, purely by feel, she pulled the flaps of Aldo's coat together, wanting to hide his nakedness, wanting to preserve his dignity in death. She straightened his glasses and rose, pulling her coat over the telltale bulge of the pouch. Then she made herself move, one step in front of the other, the cadence of her feet joining the metronome of time marching on and on and on, without relief.

Angelo was waiting. Pacing down the long aisle between the pews, his hands clasped, his head bent. She'd taken too long, and she realized he must have spent the last hours worrying that something had happened to her.

Something *had* happened to her.

He must have sensed her approach, and his head shot up, his face softening with relief when he saw her standing at the back of the church.

"I'm back, Angelo," she said woodenly. "I have the . . . provisions." That was the word they always used to refer to everything and anything. One never knew who was hiding, listening, watching. Provisions were vague. Documents were not.

She turned and made her way to the little door that led to the basement of the church. She needed to get rid of Aldo's blood. Moments later, she heard Angelo descending the stairs. The pattern of his steps—thud, tap, thud, tap, thud, tap—unmistakable. Her mind drifted back to the retreating footsteps of Aldo's killer, and she began to shake. She couldn't unbutton her coat. Her fingers didn't obey her orders.

"Eva! What happened? What took you so long?" He was growing alarmed. She could hear it in his voice.

He reached out to her, but Eva sidestepped him, unable to meet his gaze. Concentrating, she managed to shove the top button through its hole and then the next. When she reached the fifth button, she reached down the neckline of her dress and pulled the pouch free, tossing it at Angelo. He caught it easily and set it atop the small chest of drawers, his eyes trained on her face. He didn't even look at it. Eva wondered if there was now blood on his hands.

Her brassiere was stuck to her chest and she was panting, pulling in just enough air to keep her standing, but not enough to feel the nausea that threatened to rise every time she breathed too deeply.

"I had to walk." Her answer was so delayed it sounded stilted.

"All the way?"

"Yes. All the way."

"But the curfew! Eva, you could have been arrested."

"I had to walk. I have blood on my hands, on my clothes. I didn't dare take a streetcar."

"Blood? Are you hurt? Eva, dammit! Look at me."

He grabbed at her hands, and turned them over. Eva's eyes followed his, unable to avoid it any longer. The blood was minimal, surprisingly. She'd kept her hands in her pockets as she'd walked. There would be bloodstains in her pockets. She pulled her hands from Angelo's, and shrugged her coat from her shoulders.

"*Madre di Dio!*" Angelo cried. The blood on her yellow dress was not minimal. It had soaked through the thin cotton between her breasts narrowing like a tunnel as it reached her belt.

Angelo grabbed her again, this time more insistently, loosening the belt and tugging at her collar. He ripped the fabric and buttons flew as he tried to get to the source of the blood.

She didn't even try to stop him.

The bra beneath looked worse, and Angelo yanked on the clasp and tossed it aside as his hands ran over her skin, across her chest and stomach, his fingers searching for a wound, his face as white as the panties she now stood in, her dress pooling around her feet, her hands covering her breasts.

"It's not mine."

His eyes rose from her skin to her face and his hands stilled.

"It's not my blood. It's Aldo's. He's dead."

"Oh, no," he groaned. "No."

"Yes. He is," Eva insisted brokenly.

"Tell me everything," Angelo commanded, leading her to the sink.

As she talked, tripping over the terrible words, he washed her quickly, his hands deferential, his movements sure, cleaning the blood from her skin.

"I left him lying in the street," Eva whimpered, the horror starting to break through the shock.

"No. You didn't. *They* did. *They* left him lying in the street."

"I tried not to look at the blood. He was drenched from the neck down. The bullet must have come out the other side." She started to retch and shake and abandoned the sink to run to the toilet.

Angelo held her hair and stood silently beside her until she'd emptied herself out. Then he wrapped her in a blanket and led her to the small bed. Somewhere in a very distant part of Eva's female brain, she registered that Angelo was seeing her without her clothes, that he'd *removed* her clothes and washed her, and she mourned for yet another first that had been ruined by war. Or made possible by war. He brought her water and demanded that she drink, and Eva obeyed gratefully, wincing as the cold liquid hit her empty belly.

"Breathe deeply. You have to breathe, Eva."

"Von Essen didn't even ask for his papers. He didn't even ask! He wanted to humiliate him. And then he killed him." Her teeth chattered as she spoke, and she realized how cold she was. She shivered desperately and the blanket fell back down, baring her shoulders and breasts and an expanse of skin that was covered in gooseflesh.

Angelo pulled the blanket up again and forced her to lie down. He pulled another blanket over her and tucked it around her firmly before he lay down beside her and pulled her against him, holding her tightly until her shivering subsided and her teeth stopped clacking together. All the while he talked and encouraged her to talk, as if he knew she needed to get it all out, every last detail.

"It's not uncommon. It happens all the time. The Jewish men are even more vulnerable than the women in that regard. Their very flesh gives them away."

"So Aldo died to deliver documents that are of no use, documents that couldn't even save him?" Eva's voice rose in disbelief, slightly hysterical once again.

"Shh. Shh, Eva," Angelo soothed, smoothing her hair. "Aldo's documents have saved many people. You have saved many people, Eva. You realize that, don't you?"

Eva just shook her head, not ready for accolades just yet. She had walked away and Aldo had saved her, not the other way around.

"It was random. Just . . . random. I was almost to him, maybe ten feet away, when the voice called out behind me. Aldo told me to keep walking, and I did. I walked on, and Aldo walked to his death."

Angelo was silent then, and she could feel his horror—it echoed her own—but his hand was heavy and comforting, a continual caress, as he smoothed her hair over and over again. They stayed that way for a long time, Eva cocooned in threadbare blankets and Angelo's embrace. She started feeling sleepy, the return of warmth and the loss of adrenaline leaving her loose and drained. But she didn't want to sleep. She was afraid if she slept Angelo would leave, and she would dream about terrible things and have to endure them alone.

The thought made her heart kick up and her breath shorten all over again.

"Eva?" Angelo's voice lifted in concern, feeling the return of her tension.

She rolled into him, pressing her lips against his neck, just above the white collar that gleamed like a halo in the darkness. He didn't react at first, as if she'd taken him by surprise. She opened her lips and tasted the scratchy skin of his throat, and felt him swallow back a curse or a groan. She couldn't be sure.

She lifted her face and found the edge of his jaw, pressing insistent kisses along the squared-off plane, hungry for his mouth and for the mind-numbing pleasure she knew would follow. She needed him to kiss her and make her forget everything but him for just a little while. She found his lips, and he responded instantly, feverishly, only to tear himself away a second later.

"Eva. No," he said softly and sat up, releasing her. She tried to follow him, but she was pinned by the blankets he'd wrapped her in, and she squirmed desperately, suddenly frantic to be free of them. She was panting, panicking, suffocating. She bucked, releasing her arms and loosening the blankets around her body. She pushed them down around her waist, then kicked her legs free so that she was stretched out, uncovered and uncowering.

She lay winded and relieved, her eyes on the low stone ceiling, the cold air welcome on her skin. Then she looked down at herself, staring at her body through new eyes, seeing herself as Angelo would see her. Above the plain white panties, her stomach was flat . . . too flat, the deprivations of war taking the softly rounded curve from her belly and her hips, making her more girlish than womanly. But the shadows were alluring, forgiving even, and her breasts were still full and high, the tips a dusky red against her pale skin.

Eva looked from her body to Angelo's face. He was staring down at her unclothed form, his eyes desperate, his jaw clenched, as if fighting against the very demons that had swarmed the dark street and taken Aldo's life. Then he lifted his gaze, and his eyes locked on hers. The raw devotion in his face sent a surge of something hot and powerful slicing through her chest. She had been powerless for so long.

She reached for Angelo's hand and pulled it to her mouth, kissing his palm before dragging his fingers over her lips, her chin, down the length of her neck, and across her chest. She thought she heard him say her name, but there was a roaring in her ears, and she didn't respond. She couldn't. She pressed his hand against her left breast, the base of his palm resting against her thundering heart, his fingers brushing sensitive flesh. She shuddered and closed her eyes. It felt so safe and warm. So heavy and delicious. He didn't pull away, but he didn't curve his hand against her or make the caress his own.

She didn't care.

She was filled with reckless desire, and she slid his flattened palm sideways to include her other breast, the peaks pebbling in response. His hand trembled against her skin, and her belly vibrated like a violin string as the bow was slowly pulled across it. Her body hummed with a building crescendo, and Eva dragged Angelo's hand down over her ribs, across her abdomen, past the hollow between her hip bones. Then she pushed his palm lower, gasping at the contact.

She could feel her pulse there—an aching, insistent thrumming— as if her heart had followed Angelo's hand. Maybe it was her brush with death, watching a life end so violently right before her eyes. Maybe it was just the incessant threat that lurked at the edge of every single moment. But her body burned with desperate life, with frantic need, and the simple weight of Angelo's hand pressed at her center was enough to have her clinging to his wrist, tears leaking from the corners of her eyes as her body tightened and then teetered, tumbling over and over, quaking and pulsing against his warm palm.

And still Angelo was silent and unmoving, an unwilling participant, and as Eva's head cleared and her body cooled, she became instantly hyperaware, her sense and inhibitions returning with her release.

Bliss became intense mortification.

She let go of Angelo's wrist at once and curled away from him, his fingers trailing heavily across her hip as she rolled and withdrew. She pressed her hand to her mouth to muffle the sobs, but now she cried from shame, humiliated by what she'd done, by what he'd seen, by what she'd made him do. And still her body sang softly, betraying her.

She felt him shift and her blankets were drawn up loosely around her shoulders, covering her nakedness and her shame. His hand rose to her face, and he wiped her tears away, brushing them back into her hair.

"Don't cry, Eva. Please don't cry," he whispered. "I understand."

She only cried harder, not able to believe him.

Then he was holding her again, turning her so her face was pressed into his neck, her arms folded between them. His breathing was harsh, and his entire body was rigid, like he wanted to bolt.

"I'm sorry, Angelo," she moaned softly.

"You have nothing to be sorry for."

He pressed his lips to her temple and continued to smooth her hair, reassuring her, shushing her like her father used to.

"Shh, Eva. Shh. I understand."

But her tears continued to fall.

Eva drifted off that way, her face in the crook of his neck, his hand in her hair, tears on her cheeks. When Angelo was certain she was deeply sleeping, he moved away from her, his body aching with need and denial. His left arm was numb and his back stiff from holding such an unyielding position. He hadn't wanted her to feel what she did to him. He didn't want her to know that his will was crumbling.

He said he understood, and he did. She'd been desperate for the affirmation that only the most intense experiences—sex, danger, pain—can provide. He'd heard enough confessions of battle-weary soldiers who had succumbed to self-pleasure or sex or worse in the oddest of circumstances. It was a very natural reaction. He understood. But it had required every ounce of his faith and his self-control not to partake or participate, not to take advantage of her vulnerable moment. But he hadn't stopped her or averted his eyes, and just like King David watching Bathsheba bathe, he suspected that it would cost him.

But first, it had cost her. She had apologized, and he had wanted to thank her. The thought shamed him, but it was the truth. It was one of the most beautiful things he had ever seen—*she* was the most beautiful thing he'd ever seen—and he'd been captured by a sense of surreal wonder, until he'd seen her despair, her embarrassment, and then he'd wanted to cry too.

He'd failed her over and over, and he didn't know what to do. He didn't know how to heal her or hold her or save her. He didn't know how to be what she needed. All he knew was that he loved her desperately.

Desperately.

He wearily climbed the stairs and slipped into the silent church. Lighting a candle, he dropped his tired face into hands that smelled like Eva's hair and groaned out his fears and his failings, asking God not to withdraw because of his weakness, and thanking Aldo Finzi, wherever his spirit had flown, for saving Eva's life at the expense of his own.

8 March, 1944

Confession: I like Greta von Essen.

I can't help but like her. She is kind, and she is sad—a very sympathetic combination. We are all products of the places we are raised, the people who love us or have power over us, and the things we hear, over and over again, as we grow.

Our beliefs don't have to be based on personal experience, but when they are, they can rarely be altered. Greta has been told over and over that she is a beautiful disaster who has failed at the only thing she was created for. Her experiences have not disproved that.

Greta is shallow, but I have a feeling it is only because depth would drown her. So she floats on the surface and does her best to smile vapidly at her life and the man she is tied to. I have let her mother me, not because I want a new mother, but because she needs a child, and if I'm being honest, she provides me a small measure of safety, a buffer against the captain.

I like Greta von Essen, but I hate her husband. When I close my eyes I see his face, calm and cold, the way it looked before he pulled the trigger and killed Aldo.

Eva Rosselli

CHAPTER 17
MARCH

Lieutenant Colonel Kappler sent for Captain von Essen first thing
Friday morning, and the angry shouting that reverberated through the
surrounding offices was the talk of the staff at Gestapo Headquarters by
lunchtime. Eva rarely saw the lieutenant colonel, and she was happy to
keep it that way, but Captain von Essen worshipped him and did everything in his power to please him. Apparently, Himmler himself was
in Rome bearing word of the *Führer's* disappointment with Kappler's
inability to rein in the Italian resistance in and outside of Rome, as well
as to uncover and smash the underground that provided safe haven for
soldiers, partisans, and Jews.

Kappler and von Essen had been drawing up plans all week that
included maps and consults with a thin, patrician Italian man with a
German name, a man named Peter Koch who had established his own
militarized band of Italian Fascists. The maps made Eva nervous, and
the Fascist leader made her skin crawl. Thankfully, there was no sign of
Koch that morning, but when Captain von Essen returned to his own

office an hour later, his face was flushed and his eyes were bright, as if the confrontation with the Gestapo chief had brought on a raging fever.

"Follow me," he commanded as he passed Eva's desk. She grabbed her dictation notebook and a pencil and trotted after him, hoping whatever had possessed him wasn't contagious. He didn't wait to tell her what was on his mind.

"Herr Himmler is in town, and the lieutenant colonel wants to impress him. There will be a dinner tomorrow evening with the most important people in Italy. Rich men, beautiful women, wine, the finest food, the best entertainment."

Apparently, the responsibility for the gala had been delegated to the captain. If the captain was a smart man, he would call his wife.

"What is the nicest hotel in Rome?" he asked Eva.

"The Villa Medici, Captain. It overlooks the Spanish Steps, and it's reasonably close to the Trevi Fountain and all the finest shopping. It's a beautiful hotel."

It was the first thing that came to Eva's mind. She'd overheard two women talking about the hotel, newly restored and renovated with an acclaimed chef, on the streetcar that morning. She parroted what she'd heard, hoping the women knew what they were talking about.

The captain was on his phone immediately, demanding to be put through to the Villa Medici. Eva made a hasty retreat but could hear him snapping out orders and demands.

"Fräulein Bianco!" he called, causing her to jump from her desk and quickly return to his office. "Where can I find entertainment at this short notice? The hotel has a small dinner band, but I need something more. Something special."

Eva was at a loss. She didn't think the captain would be interested in Catholic children's choirs or chanting monks, which were about the only thing she had access to at the moment.

"You." He stood from his chair abruptly and rounded his desk, pointing at her accusingly. "You!" he repeated, practically shouting.

"What?"

"Himmler loves classical music. You are a violinist. A very good violinist, if I recall. Bach, Beethoven, Mozart. You will play. A beautiful Italian woman playing the violin. Perfect." He slapped his gloves against his desk victoriously and reached for his phone once more, as if it were decided.

Eva could only stutter and stare.

"But I would have to practice! I haven't performed in ages. And I have absolutely nothing appropriate to wear to such an affair," she protested.

"I've heard you play. You will be wonderful. You have until eight o'clock tomorrow evening to practice. And Greta will help you with a dress. I will send for her immediately." He waved his hand toward the door, signaling that he was done with her.

"I can't do it! Please, Captain."

"You will do it. I'm leaving you no choice in the matter. Must I hold a gun to your head and demand that you play?" He raised his blond eyebrows and cocked his head, waiting for a response.

Eva stared at him in horror. Did he think this was funny?

"I have all the confidence in the world that you will be able to pull this off, lovely Eva," he said softly. "I know you will not let me down. Now be a very good girl and leave my office."

Greta was ecstatic, rushing Eva from one shop to the next, insisting on dressing her from top to bottom—lacy lingerie and silky hose that were as rare as a cup of espresso made with real coffee beans instead of the chicory most Italians were drinking.

She had the dressmaker squeeze Eva into a red dress so low and tight that Eva broke out in nervous hives and refused to come out of the dressing room.

"Something elegant that I can actually play in, Greta, please! I don't think you are understanding the gravity of the situation. I can't breathe. If I can't breathe, I can't think, and if I can't think, I can't play. If I don't play, your husband and I will face the firing squad."

Greta tittered as if such a thing were preposterous, but she found a sleeveless, glimmering black sheath with a low, square neck that skimmed Eva's body without being tight.

"We will paint your nails, and you will wear red on your lips. Wear your hair down. We want to play up your Italian beauty."

No, Greta, Eva thought. Drawing attention to herself was the most dangerous thing she could do.

As if she could hear Eva's thoughts, Greta added slyly, "When Herr Himmler sees you, he will want to make you his mistress." Greta laughed again, but there was a concerned crease between her brows, as if it had just occurred to her that Eva worked for her husband. Eva's stomach knotted all over again.

"Are you trying to terrify me, Greta?" Eva asked softly. "I cannot think of anything worse than catching Herr Himmler's eye."

"He is a very powerful man." Greta shrugged, her eyes a guileless blue.

"I have no desire to be with a powerful man."

"What kind of man do you want?" Greta asked, removing the pins from Eva's hair so she could see the effect. She ran her fingers through the curls and pulled all the hair to one side, her eyes narrowed thoughtfully.

"A good man. A kind man. A man who loves me." Angelo's face rose up in her mind, but she pushed his image away. She had humiliated herself in front of him, and every time she thought about him, her temperature rose, her skin flushed, and her body felt like a wanton stranger's. They hadn't talked about what had occurred between them after Aldo's death. She couldn't, Angelo wouldn't, so they'd simply gone on, pretending it hadn't happened.

"You are in love with someone!" Greta interrupted her reverie. She was staring at Eva with wide eyes. "I can see it in your face. You are all pink and rosy! Tell me."

"What? No. I'm not," Eva stammered.

"Yes. You are. There is someone. I'm going to be relentless until I find out who he is."

"He is just a boy from home. It is nothing. I don't want to talk about him," Eva said.

"When was the last time you saw him?" Greta wheedled.

"Greta! Please. I don't want to talk about him." She didn't want to talk about him. It was enough that she thought about him constantly, about the hopelessness of loving a man who would not yield, the hopelessness of a life spent hiding and pretending. When the war ended and she went home to Florence, what then? The thought of returning to the time when she'd spent years on end without seeing him was worse than her fear of death. It was worse than Via Tasso. Worse than the convent with the quiet walls and the quieter nuns. It was unimaginable.

Greta pouted, an adorable, practiced expression that Eva was sure she used on her husband. "But what else is there? Love is the only excitement we women have."

"Maybe when the war is over I will think about love. Right now, I'm too afraid to think of anything else. I just want to survive tomorrow night." Eva changed the subject.

"There are worse things than being afraid," Greta said gravely, her sudden sadness catching Eva off guard.

"What?" Eva asked softly.

"Being resigned is far worse. Being afraid lets you know you still want to live."

"Then I must want to live very badly," Eva whispered. "Because I am very afraid."

Greta squeezed her arm, their eyes meeting in the mirror. They were a striking contrast—Greta blond and statuesque, Eva dark and slim beside her.

"I envy you," Greta said wistfully. "You have your whole life before you."

"But none of us knows how long that life will be. My life could end tomorrow."

"All the more reason to wear beautiful clothes and play beautiful music." Greta winked, shaking off the seriousness that had them both frowning. "Now you must be sure and invite your brother. He will be so proud of his little sister. Plus, it will be wise to let others see you have a protector."

The certainty that the night would end in disaster had Eva rushing home after Greta's shopping spree and practicing her violin deep into the night, apologizing to the other refugees, who endured hour after hour of frenzied music. When it grew late, she banished herself to the church to allow the convent to rest, and continued playing and praying, plotting her performance as if her life depended on it, for, deep down, she believed it did.

The dress was simple, but the black silk gleamed and fell around her slim form, giving her an understated elegance. Her hair was carefully curled and deeply parted, tucked behind her ear on one side where a dangling diamond played hide-and-seek every time she turned her head. Her lips were red and her dark eyes softly lined. She was pale, but her skin was pearly and it looked dramatic against the ebony dress.

She stood on a small stage, all alone in the very center, and she raised the roof and the hair on his neck, piece after glorious piece. The audience clapped and there was no conversation, even hushed and polite, when she played.

She'd been waiting in front of his building that morning, her eyes tired and her nerves raw, and when she'd told him about the gala and he'd seen her fear, he had swallowed his own and bit back his insistence that she go into hiding. It had been a constant refrain in his head. *Hide her. Hide her. Hide her.* She'd refused every time. Insisting now would be no different, so he would be strong for her instead.

"Why are you afraid, Eva? You have been doing this all your life. You are a magnificent violinist. You have played for thousands. Surely, you can play for a mere handful."

She had dropped her face into her hands, and he had shoved his fists into the pockets of his cassock to hide his tremors. She was afraid because she would be a Jewish girl in a room full of German police, the same reason he wanted to whisk her away and lock her in the cloister.

"I don't want to share this with them," she had whispered. "My talent is mine. My skill is mine. Mine and Felix's. And I don't want to entertain them. I don't want to give them pleasure or enjoyment. I want to spit in their soup. I want to break dishes and poison their wine. I do not want to play for them."

He had laughed so he wouldn't weep. "You will play. And you will be magnificent. You will be the victor, knowing that you are Eva Rosselli, and they are applauding for a Jew."

Her mouth had trembled, then the trembling became a broad smile. She had curtsied deeply, right there on the street, and when she stood, she had smirked at him. "I think you have a little devil in you, my white angel. I must be rubbing off on you."

She was definitely rubbing off on him. Rubbing him raw and wearing him thin. In the last hour he had aged ten years. He stood at the back of the room, unable to dine while she played, even though his stomach growled at the scents in the room. He'd politely refused the place that had been set for him and kept his cross in his hand and his eyes glued to her face. He was terrified for her and proud of her all at once. He wanted to swoop her up and carry her to safety, and at the same time he wanted the world to listen to her play. He wanted to witness her triumph over the people who would, at the very least, turn their backs to her plight, and at the worst, kill her if they knew who she was. Still, she played, exultant and brilliant, powerful in her vulnerability, a conquering army of one. And the audience had no idea they were bested.

When she finally lowered her instrument and bowed, signaling the end of her performance, she tucked her violin and her bow against her side, and her eyes found his. He could see her terror even as she smiled graciously and inclined her head, acknowledging her audience. Her posture regal, she glided from the small dais, pausing as Captain von Essen stepped forward to assist her down the few steps. He escorted her to the side and seemed to be congratulating her effusively. He should congratulate her. Eva had made him look very good. He murmured something in her ear, his mouth hovering too close, and Angelo saw her stiffen even as she shook her head—smiling but refusing him. He leaned into her once more, obviously insisting on something, and he placed an envelope in her hand.

Angelo felt rage shoot through his belly and his temperature climb beneath his stiff collar. He held himself back, knowing his part, knowing the genteel subservience people expected from him. But he exhaled in relief as Captain von Essen stepped back and Eva moved away from him. She walked toward the exit, nodding and smiling as she made her way through the glittering people and the tables laden with rich foods and the best Italian wine in a city of starving people. She kept walking as she neared him, and he followed her out of the large dining hall to the cloakroom where she'd stored her violin case.

"What did he say?" Angelo asked, his voice pitched just above a whisper. Eva checked behind every coat, behind every wrap, and every corner before she answered him.

"Greta is insisting that I take a room here at the hotel. The arrangements have already been made. Captain von Essen says I have earned it." She showed him the key and the envelope filled with banknotes.

The rage in his stomach turned into an inferno.

"Does he think he will join you there?"

Eva's eyes shot to his face, and she shook her head instantly. "No. I really don't think that's what he's implying. Greta is here with him, Angelo. You saw her. I am well aware of what he is capable of, but he has never been inappropriate with me."

"You can't stay here, Eva. I don't trust him."

"I don't either. But I don't think his intentions are lecherous. I'm worried about something else."

Angelo raised his eyebrows in question.

"I think they are going to raid Santa Cecilia tonight. He knows I board there. He doesn't want me there when it goes down."

"How do you know this?" he asked, the ramifications sending his thoughts in a million different directions.

"He said something in the office today, something about the evening's activities. He was on the phone with Lieutenant Colonel Kappler. I thought he was talking about this." She tossed her hand in the direction of the ballroom and swept a hand down her dress. "But there was another man, by the last name of Koch, who came to the office three times last week. He is some kind of *squadristi* leader."

When Angelo heard the name he swore and crossed himself simultaneously, and then crossed himself again to cancel out his dual reaction. He wondered some days if he was cut out to be a priest. He had a foul mouth. He blamed it on the American in him.

"Koch is a notorious Jew hunter," he said. "He's been on Monsignor O'Flaherty's tail the last few months. Lieutenant Colonel Kappler too. But why Santa Cecilia?"

"I don't think it's just Santa Cecilia. I think it may be every church, convent, and monastery in Trastevere."

"And what makes you think tonight?"

"Captain von Essen told me I should stay here at the hotel to avoid 'trouble.' I asked him if he could just provide me with a car. But he said Trastevere wouldn't be safe tonight."

"We have to get word to the sisters," Angelo said. The Villa Medici was a good distance from Trastevere and even farther from the Vatican.

"There are telephones in every suite. I heard the women talking in the powder room. They were all highly impressed. I'm sure they are all looking forward to eavesdropping on each other's conversations." She held out the key, enthusiastically. He took it, his unease growing as he stared down at it.

"We'll ask for another room. We'll switch," he said abruptly. "Come with me."

They approached the registration desk, but Eva held back when Angelo put a warning hand on her arm.

"Let me," he whispered. "Stand here and look frightened."

"That won't be hard to do," she murmured. Angelo understood completely. His own heart was pounding heavily beneath his cassock. But he smiled easily and nodded at the man behind the glossy mahogany registration desk, who took his hand and kissed it, as if he wasn't sure if Angelo were someone important or not.

"Signore, I need your help," Angelo said, sotto voce. "My sister is staying here at the hotel. She is a renowned violinist and she played for the dignitaries who are in attendance at the gala this evening. She is very beautiful, you understand." He paused so the concierge could verify this truth for himself.

The little man with the slick black hair and the neat little mustache peered around Angelo's shoulder and eyed Eva. His eyes widened slightly. "Yes. Yes. I see," he said awkwardly, as if he wasn't sure whether to agree that she was beautiful or refrain from commenting on a priest's sister.

"She is receiving some unwanted attention from one of the guests. No one especially important. But I would like her to be moved, if possible. Unfortunately, he saw her coming out of her room, and my sister is now a little frightened."

"Oh, yes, Padre. Of course. I understand." The concierge took the key from Angelo's hand and consulted his ledger.

"Will you be staying with your sister?" he asked judiciously. Angelo tried not to react or to think about what those words could entail.

"For a while. I would like to make sure she is all right."

"Yes, Padre." The man bobbed and whisked out two keys with a tidy little nod. Then he crossed himself as if it had been a while since his last confession. Angelo didn't know whether to smile or sigh. He had a tendency to make people chatty or nervous. It didn't hurt that this man was nervous. He'd been easy to persuade.

"Do we need to move the lady's things to her new room?"

"No. That won't be necessary. She was so upset she was ready to leave the hotel altogether. I put her things in the cloakroom while she played. It will be easy enough to retrieve them."

"Very good, Signore. I mean, Padre. Very good." The man bobbed his head and crossed himself again.

The suite was lavish and large behind double doors with a small foyer that opened up into an elegant sitting room and well-appointed bathroom beyond that. The sitting room was built around the large windows that overlooked the Spanish Steps. But Angelo didn't waste time staring out at the backdrop.

There were ten monasteries, convents, and churches sheltering Jews in Trastevere, with more Jews sprinkled among another twenty families in the area. If the whole west side was to be raided, the whole west side would need to be warned. He was put through to the Vatican and reached an assistant of Monsignor O'Flaherty. Angelo asked that he be told that O'Malley had called with news of the Midnight Mass being conducted that evening in Trastevere. Midnight Mass was code for a night raid.

There was a one-word warning that he had put in place with a few trusted runners who had access to telephones, people who could get a warning to a nearby convent, monastery, or religious institution sheltering refugees. Most convents and monasteries were not equipped with phones—few places were—and getting someone to answer, hear the warning, understand what it meant, and then pass it on would be almost miraculous. Angelo began the laborious task of waiting to be put through, via operator, over party lines that were far from private, sharing a message anyone could listen in on. But eventually, one by one, he was able to convey the warning to every runner except for the one for Santa Cecilia. He would have to warn them in person.

"You can't go. What if there is a raid and you are there and Captain von Essen sees you?"

"I have to go," he said simply. "I have to. Stay here. I promise I will come back for you."

She nodded, just once, her face tight and her eyes huge and frightened in her beautiful face. He could see from her expression that she thought it was too dangerous, that to her it felt like her father heading to Austria all over again, destined for disaster. But she didn't try to stop him, and he was struck by her courage. She rose and followed him to the door, a slim silhouette in a long black dress, a candle in the darkness.

"I was so proud of you tonight. Felix would have been proud too. You are a remarkable woman, Eva Bianco. A remarkable woman," he said sincerely.

She looked as if she were holding back tears, and he turned away before he weakened and took her in his arms, pulling the door shut behind him instead. He was halfway down the stairs before he realized he had called her Eva Bianco—not Rosselli—like it was her actual name. Like she was truly his.

CHAPTER 18
THE CRYPT

Angelo was only a block from the Villa Medici, moving as quickly as his leg and cane would allow, when a long black car slid up alongside him and the window was lowered, revealing the top portion of Captain von Essen's face. He was alone in the backseat.

"I'm sure you are aware it is after curfew, and even a man in your position can get in some trouble, Father Bianco," he said silkily.

"I have a permit, and I don't live far. A priest's work is never done." Angelo smiled and sighed, but his heart was pounding. The captain had murdered Aldo Finzi, and there was something very off about him. Maybe it was his tidy ways and his soft-spoken delivery that didn't quite mask his glee at being a proud, card-carrying member of the Reich. He was the kind that inflicted torture while mournfully telling his victims it was all their fault.

"I will give you a ride, Father. Climb in."

Angelo did not want a ride. He hesitated, unsure of how to refuse.

"I insist," the captain said quietly. "You must let me do this as a courtesy to your sister, at the very least. You were there tonight to support her, I'm sure. Now you find yourself in a predicament, walking home after curfew."

Angelo walked around the car, but the driver was quick to hop out and open the door. The courtesy made him breathe a little easier.

"I thought I saw your wife with you this evening, Captain," Angelo mentioned as the door was closed behind him. She was not with him anymore, and Angelo's anxiety rose once more.

"Yes. She was. She had some friends she wanted to visit with. I had business to attend to. A military man's work is never done either, I fear. We have that in common."

"I'm sure that is true," Angelo said politely, folding his hands in his lap.

"Eva was wonderful tonight," the captain murmured. "Magical. It was such a treat to hear her play. Herr Himmler was most impressed. Lieutenant Colonel Kappler as well."

"Yes. She *was* wonderful." Angelo wouldn't let himself think of Himmler or Kappler or the attention they had given Eva. If he dwelled on it, he would do something dangerous, something stupid, and he couldn't afford to do either.

"You two are close, yes? She told me she came to Rome to be near you. I was always close with my older sister. She was like a second mother to me. Of course, that's not how it is with you and Eva, is it? You are the father." He laughed at his play on words.

Angelo bristled but shook his head and shrugged easily. "No, it is not like that. We are only two years apart."

"It is a good thing you are a priest. Otherwise, people might get the wrong idea," the captain said softly. He was quiet then, staring out the window, and Angelo watched as the driver missed one turn and then another. He didn't know where they were going, but they weren't taking him home. The car rolled up in front of the Church of Santa Cecilia, treating the big piazza like a parking lot. The captain reached for the door. Angelo's stomach sank.

"I have some business here. Maybe you can help me with it, Father. You speak German so well, and my Italian is limited. I may need a translator." A truck pulled up behind the Mercedes, and a handful of SS men jumped out, rifles in hand.

"What are you doing?" Angelo gasped, climbing out of the car and rushing to get in front of the men with guns. He stretched out his hands, slowing them, bidding them to stop, praying that the people inside would have time to hide or prepare.

"It is a raid, Father," von Essen said simply. "The Catholic Church is disdainful of our laws. We have reason to believe there are Jews being hidden all over Rome in convents just like this one."

"There is no one here! I know this convent. I know the sisters here."

"But, of course you do. Your own sister rents a room here. But you understand, we must check for ourselves."

"No! I do not understand. Places of worship are sanctuaries. There is a cloister inside these walls. No one violates the cloister. Not a priest, or a German, or a Jew!"

"The Catholic Church—the Pope himself—cannot control a single SS officer. You do realize that, don't you, Father?" The captain smiled at Angelo, but his eyes were cold and flat. He inclined his head to his men, and they immediately ran to the gate and started striking it with their rifle butts, the insistent clanging filling the cold air with dissonance and distress. Through the bars Angelo could see into the serene court-yard, the glass-like surface of the pool around the large urn reflecting moonlight and dark sky. It was late enough that the occupants could be in bed. Angelo prayed they weren't. Sleepy and disoriented would not work in their favor.

He did a mental count of the refugees inside. The Sonninos had documents. But Mario's flesh would give him away if the captain saw fit to go that route again. The two sisters who had escaped the October roundup did not have papers, but the nuns had been coaching them. They had habits, and if they had time to don them, they might be safe. The two brothers had papers and military releases, but their accents were problematic, and they faced the same threat Mario did. Their best chance of survival was to hide. The family with the two small boys did not have passes, and the father and his young daughter did not have false documents either. Their passes labeled them Jews. That made eight people inside who would be immediately arrested and taken if they were discovered, and several more who were extremely vulnerable to detection.

"I want you to call out to them, Father. Tell them to open the gate. Reassure them," von Essen instructed. "Otherwise, we will have to damage their property to gain entrance. We don't want to do that. We are reasonable men."

The clanging ceased as Angelo raised his voice and called out to Mother Francesca, his mind separating from his mouth to pray to Saint Cecilia herself that she might protect the innocents within her walls.

"Mother Francesca, it is Father Bianco. I am here with Captain von Essen of the German Police. He is insisting on checking the premises for Jews." He was almost grateful that he could call out the danger in no uncertain terms but didn't know how that would help beyond scaring them to death. There wasn't time to do much of anything.

Mother Francesca approached the gate with measured steps. Normally, Mother Francesca bustled, too busy about God's work to move slowly. Now she practically dragged her feet, her hands folded piously, her face grim.

"Father Angelo," she greeted, inclining her head slightly. She then looked at the captain.

"Open the gate," von Essen commanded, his eyes holding hers.

She tipped her head as if she didn't understand German. Angelo was quite certain she didn't, but it was clear what the captain wanted.

"Tell her to open the gate!" von Essen snapped. Angelo did so, and Mother Francesca, with great deliberation, slowly opened the gate. The soldiers pushed past her, almost knocking her to the ground, but she clung to the gate and managed not to fall.

Captain von Essen produced a bullhorn through which he demanded everyone immediately come out into the courtyard or be shot.

Angelo took Mother Francesca by the arm, steadying her. He didn't dare ask any questions or draw attention by a hushed conversation, but he translated the captain's command.

"No! We have cloistered nuns here. They cannot come down to the courtyard! They can't come out of the cloister!" she cried, rushing toward the captain. Angelo relayed her concerns.

"Well, then. By all means. We must go to them." He spread his hands, bullhorn in one, as if he were being infinitely reasonable.

"No!" The abbess stamped her foot. "Kill me if you must! You will not go into the cloister."

"You might not be the only one who dies, Mother," Angelo said softly. "They will kill you, and they will still go into the cloister. Live to fight another day."

"Listen to the good father. He is wise," the captain said, smiling. Angelo wanted to spit in his face.

"Go with the sister to the cloister, Schroeder, and take three men with you," von Essen commanded. "You go too, Father. Offizier Schroeder may need some help getting his instructions across."

Mother Francesca led the way, her head bowed as if she carried the weight of the world beneath her veil. She prayed vocally to Saint Cecilia for her forgiveness as she inserted the key into the grille that separated the cloister from the rest of the world.

"Can I at least explain to them what is happening?" she pleaded.

"*Nein,*" the officer said when Angelo translated. "It will only give them time to hide."

But the nuns were ready, standing in a long line with their hands folded in prayer. They didn't need any explanations. Angelo's eyes shot to the middle of the row of bowed heads, black veils, and stiff white wimples. The two sisters were flanked on each side by nuns. Their youth and prettiness drew the eyes, and Angelo could only pray as Officer Schroeder paced in front of the nuns, eyeing each one with equal parts disdain and suspicion. He stopped in front of the youngest sister. She kept her head bowed.

He reached out suddenly and yanked at her wimple, as if to pull it from her head, but the wimple stayed put. The other men snickered, and the officer grew angry.

"Take it off," he snapped. The officer must know that nuns shaved their heads upon taking their vows and kept it short. A woman with long, flowing hair would be instantly suspect.

The youngest sister glanced at Father Angelo in alarm but immediately turned away, as if she knew looking to him wouldn't help her cause. She closed her eyes and took a deep breath, and Angelo did the same. Suddenly, the words that had been so hard for the girl to memorize, the words she'd learned for self-preservation, started to fall from her lips.

"Our Father who art in heaven, hallowed be thy name. Thy kingdom come, thy will be done on earth as it is in heaven." The SS men shifted uncomfortably. She spoke Italian, but it wasn't hard to understand the Lord's Prayer in any language. They were in the cloister, a place completely off limits to the outside world. No man, no woman, no soldier, no priest. These were cloistered nuns, and some of the men obviously knew what that meant.

"Take it off," the officer roared, his face inches from hers, and his spittle flecked her cheeks. She raised her hands and removed her black veil. But she kept praying aloud, and she didn't remove the wimple.

"Give us this day our daily bread, and forgive us our debts"—she looked directly in the face of the blue-eyed German—"as we forgive our debtors."

"All of you. Take them off," he commanded, waving his gun at all the nuns, then yanking at the girl's wimple to indicate what he wanted. When they hesitated, he raised the gun to the youngest girl's head.

"Take them off! Now!"

Angelo tried to control his rage. He was tired of weapons being pulled and aimed at women's heads. Eva had endured the same treatment and had been brought to Via Tasso for nothing more than being in the wrong place at the wrong time. They raised their guns with such impunity, with such insolence. And he could only pray that God saw and would mete out justice in his time and in his way.

The other officers moved nervously, realizing something had shifted in their leader. With shaking hands, the other nuns began to unfasten their wimples too, joining the girl in the recitation of the prayer. "And lead us not into temptation, but deliver us from evil."

"For thine is the kingdom and the power and the glory, forever. Amen," the nuns finished, pulling their wimples free and averting their eyes from the men who stood staring at their shorn heads. Angelo swallowed his gasp. The two young sisters had cut their hair close to their scalps, their tufty hair making them indistinguishable from the other women who stood cowering and vulnerable beneath the scrutiny of the German men. In cutting their hair, they had saved their own lives.

The officer's finger slid down around the trigger. His eyes were a storm and his lips a flat, hard line—a horizon of indecision beneath the tumultuous gaze. He dropped his weapon to his side. He looked like a fool, and he knew it. He holstered his weapon with flaming cheeks and began walking toward the iron grille that had warned him to stay away in the first place. "Let's go."

Amy Harmon

"All is in order," the German officer reported to von Essen when they reached the courtyard. His face was still ruddy with embarrassment, but the darkness gave him a little cover.

Everyone else from inside the convent was assembled in a long line, von Essen standing before them with his hands clasped behind his back like a strutting professor. One of his men held the official register Mother Francesca had been so concerned about. Angelo's eyes went directly to the Sonninos—Giulia holding the baby, little Emilia in her father's arms, and Lorenzo clinging to Mario's hand. Poor Lorenzo. He was old enough to know the danger and too young to understand why any of it was happening. It was the second raid his family would have to survive, the second night they would be forced to beat incredible odds. The woman Angelo had found to nurse baby Isaaco was standing with them, strangely blank-faced, like she didn't care enough about herself to be afraid. None of the paperless Jews were in the courtyard.

The boarders' rooms and the surrounding buildings had been searched while Angelo and the abbess accompanied the raid in the cloister. So far, no cries had gone up and no shots had rung out. Their papers must have passed inspection, and the rooms must not have yielded any clues. At that moment, three soldiers came jogging out of the church toward the captain, and Angelo could hear them discussing the locked door off the sacristy that led to the excavation below.

In ancient times, when a church or structure fell into disrepair, the Romans simply built over it, using the existing structure or what was left of it. As a result, Rome was a city of layered ruins, one era stacked on top of the other. Roughly fifty years ago, beneath the church of Santa Cecilia, the ruins of two ancient Roman houses—one of them believed to be the young noblewoman Cecilia's—had been discovered, and excavations had been conducted. A crypt was built in 1899 at the west end of the excavation, but behind the new crypt, directly beneath the choir, was the original crypt. Angelo wondered suddenly if the refugees were hiding among the dead. It was the best place he could think of.

Von Essen must have thought the same thing. "Father Bianco, Mother, come with me," he demanded, striding after the soldiers who had turned and were loping back toward the church. Sure enough, when they entered the church, the soldiers veered down the left aisle and stopped before the large locked door.

"What is behind the door?"

"It leads to an excavated area below the church. Ruins," Angelo said. "A part of an old tannery, a small household shrine, or what remains of it. Some mosaics. A crypt."

"After you," Captain von Essen said to the abbess. She unlocked the door, and the group proceeded down the stairs that were little more than steps cut into rock. It was dank and smelled of age and earth. It smelled like Rome. Upon reaching the bottom, the soldiers immediately split off and headed in different directions down the crumbling tunnels, unearthed forty years before. With their flashlights out, they searched corners and poked their guns into dark places. There were lights, which Mother Francesca turned on, but they flickered testily, like the disturbance in the primordial space was unwelcome.

"What is back there?" Von Essen pointed with his pistol to a large iron grille that barred the way forward.

"That is the crypt. The tombs of the martyrs Cecilia, Valerian, Tibertius, and Maximus, and Popes Urban I and Lucius." Mother Francesca answered this time, clearly not needing to understand the captain's language to interpret what he was asking. Angelo repeated what she said in German.

The captain's face twisted with distaste but he wasn't to be deterred. "Open it."

"I will not have your men desecrating the tombs." Mother Francesca shook her head and crossed herself. The captain understood she was refusing, and he lost his temper. Clearly, the raid had not produced the desired results.

"Open it!" he roared and pointed his pistol at the defiant abbess. She dug the old key from the sleeve of her robe, and her voice rose in warning.

Von Essen looked at Angelo for translation.

"He who desecrates the tombs of the saints dies the death of the saints," Angelo repeated, straight-faced. "Saint Cecilia died of ax wounds."

The old nun was like a witch straight out of *Macbeth*, casting her spells and portending ominous events. The SS men shifted uncomfortably, but von Essen shook his head and commanded his men to search the space. Mother Francesca hissed and spat like an angry cat circling the tombs and keeping the soldiers on edge. Von Essen's men were clearly ready to abandon their search, and it wasn't long before they were all climbing the stone stairs back to the church above. Neither Angelo nor Mother Francesca mentioned that they had only searched the new crypt. Beyond it, accessible only through a hole tunneled in the wall behind Cecilia's tomb, was the original crypt. It wasn't large, but it was big enough to hide five adults and three children.

"Now, that wasn't so hard, was it, Mother?" the captain asked, as if the whole thing had simply been an agreeable tour of the grounds. He walked to the line of terrified boarders and clapped his hands at their armed guard. "We've wasted enough time here. Let's go." His men immediately obeyed him and marched toward the entrance.

"Father? After you." Von Essen opened his hand in front of him, indicating that Angelo should go first.

"I will walk home, thank you," Angelo said without inflection. He was not going to get in the car with von Essen unless commanded to do so at gunpoint, and maybe not even then. But the captain had resumed his feigned benevolence, and he inclined his head agreeably, snapping his fingers and shooting instructions. The men ran to the truck, hopping up and disappearing behind the black flaps with their intimidation and their guns.

Von Essen followed them, but just before he reached his waiting car, he turned his head to the side and halted, throwing the words over his shoulder, and Angelo knew they were meant for him as much as for the abbess.

"If we discover there are Jews being hidden here, sheltered here, we will be back. We will be back, Mother." Von Essen climbed into the back of his Mercedes, and the vehicles rumbled across the cobblestone piazza and disappeared around the corner as if they'd never been there at all.

The night wasn't over, but Santa Cecilia had survived, and so had her hidden Jews. Now he could only warn others.

"Ring the bells, Mother Francesca," he demanded. "Five times. Let the neighborhood know that the Germans are out."

Before long, the bells of Santa Cecilia rang through the night, loud and insistent, a warning to all within earshot. Those who didn't know about the coded message would simply shrug and hardly notice. Bells in Rome were a daily occurrence. Bells at midnight, not as likely, but not cause for alarm. An answering clanging—five chimes—came a minute later. Then more bells were ringing from farther away, and then more, all in sets of five, coming from different directions. The message was being heard and spread.

18 March, 1944

> *Confession: Tonight, I faced my dragons. Now I'm sitting all
> alone in a beautiful hotel room in Rome, filling pages of sta-
> tionery with my confessions, wondering if those same dragons
> will, in the end, slay me, or worse, slay Angelo.*

*Thinking about dragons has reminded me of my fourteenth birthday. Babbo
hired a family of circus performers who brought in ponies and clowns and
gypsies who performed tricks and read fortunes. It was all very exciting and
authentic, especially the fortune-teller. She was young—maybe eighteen or
nineteen—and quite beautiful, with big round breasts, a tiny waist, and
huge gold loops at her ears. I couldn't take my eyes off her. I think my father
was a little alarmed by the lusty gypsy, but it was the best birthday party
ever, and my classmates talked about it for months afterward.*

*The gypsy had tarot cards and a big round ball that she pretended to
look into as she foretold the future. I wanted her to tell me my fortune, but
got nervous at the last moment and ran and grabbed Angelo by the hand
and pulled him into her little striped tent so he could hold my hand while
she told me my fate. Angelo was sixteen at that time, and he seemed so much
older than the other boys. I had to beg him to come home for the party, and
even then, he hung back and watched, eating cake and listening to Uncle*

Augusto and Babbo argue politics. He wasn't a child anymore, and I was losing him a little at a time.

The gypsy laughed at me when I told her to proceed. I must have seemed very young and foolish. Her eyes were dark and her lips red, and I could tell she thought Angelo was very handsome. She turned over some cards—I don't remember which ones—but her eyes kept going back to Angelo. I don't remember what my fortune was, only that I was disappointed and unimpressed by her predictions. But then she offered to read Angelo's cards. He started to drag me away, clearly not interested, but she stood and pushed him firmly down into the chair I had just vacated. I clutched his hand, indicating that he belonged to me, and she quirked her eyebrows disdainfully.

She told him he would have the love of a beautiful woman who would bear him many sons. I informed her he was going to be a priest. She predicted he would be a hero to many. I told her he was already a hero to me. "You will slay dragons," she predicted grandly, ignoring me. But Angelo grew very still, and his hand tightened around mine.

"You will slay dragons, but not before they slay you," she hissed. And Angelo bolted from his chair, dragging me from the tent.

Eva Rosselli

CHAPTER 19
THE VILLA MEDICI

It took Angelo forty minutes to walk back to the Villa Medici, and every step was rife with dread. He was afraid he would arrive and find Eva gone, that he would walk into the room and see overturned furniture and empty space. He kept imagining her door being knocked down, a *squadristi* of Jew hunters pulling her out into the night and whisking her away.

He didn't trust von Essen, and his insistence that she take a room at the hotel rang hollow. By the time Angelo turned the key and let himself into her room, he was beside himself with worry.

But all was well.

Eva was asleep on the large bed, hugging the edge like she'd fallen asleep while waiting for him and simply tipped over. Her legs still hung off the side. He watched her for a moment, lightheaded with relief, before stumbling to the bathroom and gulping down mouthfuls of water to ease the ache in his chest. It was a grateful ache. A humble ache. An ache that felt like love and longing and loss, though he hadn't lost her at all. But the ache said he could. The ache said he still might. The ache said he'd been a fool.

Eva had made use of the tub. The bathroom still smelled of steam and soap and jasmine, though he didn't know how she managed to still carry that scent with her. The bathtub had an irresistible lure, he had to admit. He pulled off his cassock and dropped it to the floor, and immediately shed the rest of his clothes. The stench of sweat and fear was heavy on his skin, and he was desperate to remove it.

He climbed into the tub, hoping he wouldn't wake Eva, and made the water as hot as he could, which wasn't nearly hot enough. He scrubbed at his skin and washed his hair with the little perfumed bar of soap Eva had used and set to the side. There was a tiny tin of tooth powder and a toothbrush on the vanity, along with a shower cap and a comb, the amenities of a luxury hotel. Angelo rinsed his mouth and scrubbed at his teeth with the brush Eva must have already used, and tried not to dwell on the intimacy of the act or think about her mouth for too long. He pulled his prosthetic and his trousers back on but couldn't stand to don his shirt or the cassock. He shook them briskly and hung them over the door instead, hoping to air them out a bit. Then he went back to watch Eva sleep.

Her position made her look like she'd collapsed, her legs hanging off the bed the way they were. She lay on her side, facing him, the white sheet draped loosely around her, but her face was turned down, baring her slim throat and shadowing her face, so still and so lovely. It made him think of the sculpture of Cecilia, the martyred saint, and he crossed the distance to the bed and knelt beside it, suddenly lightheaded with an irrational dread. He lifted her legs onto the bed, making her roll to her back. She was so limp and lifeless. Before he could stop himself, he was pressing his face to her chest, listening for her heart and running his fingertips over her mouth, feeling for her breath. For several torturous seconds he couldn't find any signs of life. Nothing.

Terror roared and his own heart galloped so loudly that he realized it was no wonder he couldn't hear hers. He was overreacting. He knew he was. He took several deep breaths and exhaled, calming himself. As he did, air whispered past her parted lips and over his fingers, and her heartbeat quickened against his cheek, as if she knew he was there.

Relief washed through him, and he swung her up against his chest, the sheet trailing behind her. He sank into the high wingback chair that sat near the bed, his arms wrapped around her slim frame, and he waited for her to wake up. He didn't let himself stroke the dark chocolate hair that fell down her back and across her shoulders. He didn't let himself gaze into her upturned face only inches from his own. Instead, he stared out the bedroom window into the night and waited, pushing down the tumult and the noise, the clamoring in his chest and the clanging in his temples, internal voices that warned him to release her and run from the temptation that kept him rooted to that chair.

He would just hold her, he told himself. But he couldn't let her go. He couldn't do it.

"Angelo?" The word was a breath, and he shut his eyes, warring with relief and despair. He was embarrassed. He was desperate. He didn't know what he was going to say to her, and he was afraid he'd say too much. So he kept his eyes closed and his lips silent.

"Angelo?" Her voice was stronger and the question more pronounced. He tried to pray but found he didn't want God to help him. He didn't want divine intervention. With that thought he gave in, opened his eyes, and looked down into her face. Her eyes were so dark that he could see himself reflected in them, twin points, his face pale, swimming in the inky depths.

"You were sleeping so deeply it scared me. You must have been dreaming. Where did you go?" he whispered.

"To find you," she whispered back.

"And here I am."

She lifted a hand and laid it against the side of his face, as if testing the veracity of his claim. Her touch—so reverent, so tender—broke him. How could something so gentle cause him to crumble? But shatter he did, and God knows a broken man is a vulnerable man. She didn't pull him to her with the hand that rested on his cheek, or lift her head from where it lay cradled in the crook of his arm. It was all Angelo. He could not make excuses for the action he was about to take.

He bent his head and found her mouth with his own.

He would have liked to think he didn't consciously choose to cross the distance between their mouths, but that would have been a lie. He chose. It wasn't like the kisses in the fisherman's shack or even the kiss in the alcove on the day of the first raid, the kiss that had been without thought or premeditation, the kiss he could blame on circumstance, on a desperate moment. This was a kiss filled with intention.

They were his lips that parted against hers as they found purchase. It was his breath that hitched as the contact, both purposeful and timid, stunned him and scorched him simultaneously. It was all Angelo. No one made him do it.

But once he arrived, Eva welcomed him there. Her hand slid from his cheek to the back of his head, her fingers molding to the shape of his skull as the other rose to his neck, anchoring him where he hovered over her. She tasted him as he tasted her, each of them pressing into the swell of pillowed lips and seeking beyond them to the hot silk of mating mouths and dancing tongues.

For a man who had so little experience with the art of sensuality, there were no tentative brushstrokes or shy imitations. Neither thought about the craft at all. Neither thought about technique or tempo. If there were thoughts, they were reduced to whirling patterns behind closed lids, to curling colors in the bottom of their bellies, to the wash of sensation that built until Eva was pressed against Angelo's chest, her legs straddling his hips. Her arms circled his neck as his arms braced her back, and their hearts created a drumbeat so intoxicating and so demanding, neither of them could do anything but move to its rhythm. Then Angelo stood, one arm anchoring Eva's hips to keep her against him, one arm bracing their fall as they tumbled across the moonlit bed. Eva moaned against his lips and he stilled, instantly contrite, holding himself above her as if he'd broken her in truth, completely different from the way she'd broken him.

He pulled away slightly and looked down into her face. The room was dark, but streetlight and moonlight filtered through the sheer drapes, casting them both in soft black, pearly white, and varying shades of gray.

For a moment they stared at each other in stunned, ardor-filled hesitation, Angelo waiting for permission to proceed, Eva holding her breath, wondering if he would. She didn't urge him, didn't plead, didn't say, "Again, Angelo," the way she'd done in the fisherman's shack a lifetime ago. She waited for him to decide. She wanted him to choose. He could see it all over her face.

Slowly, his eyes holding hers, he raised a hand and touched her cheek, marveling at the silk of her skin, before he pulled the pad of his thumb across her lips, parting them gently. Then he leaned down, his mouth hovering above hers, and whispered, "Again, Eva. Again."

Then he was kissing her once more, drinking from her mouth like a man dying of thirst. It eased the ache in his chest yet intensified it at the same time. He couldn't tear his lips away, but he needed to touch her, to slide his palms against her skin and memorize the valleys and the swells, to make her a part of him and himself a part of her. Finally.

He was so lost in surrender and so desperate to know every part of her that he was unable to slow down, to breathe, to pace himself. He was like a child in a candy store, rushing from one display to the next. If being with Eva meant his life was measured in minutes and hours instead of months and years, so be it.

"I love you, Eva," he whispered, needing to explain his sudden fervor. "I love you so much. And I've wasted so much time." He suddenly felt close to tears, as if the admission had unlocked something inside of him, letting it free. The ache was suddenly gone, and in its place was a swollen heart.

"And when the war is over, will you still love me?" she whispered in his ear, her voice thick with passion, heavy with need.

He knew what she was asking, and his mind tripped and went down, unable to move beyond the moment, this second, where he had her in his arms, the only thing in the whole world that he really wanted.

He closed his eyes, trying to find an answer, trying to make sense of it all, trying to hear God's voice. Instead, he felt Eva's fingers tracing his lips, his closed lids, the line of his cheekbone, the point of his chin. Instead of God's voice, he heard Eva's.

When the war is over, will you still love me?

In that moment, the realization crystallized, and his focus narrowed to the one truth that had come so plainly to his mind. She was the only thing in the world he really wanted. And not in the way most men want women. He didn't want to assuage a need. He didn't want to lose himself temporarily in her body. He wanted to live for her. Beyond the moment, beyond the war. Always.

He'd entered a place, or maybe he'd been walking toward it, or around it, all his life, but the dragons he'd once sought to slay were not the same. The dragons of lust and vanity and greed. The dragons of selfishness and ambition. The dragons of mortality and the need for power. Those dragons were gone, and in their place was unconditional love and a desire to sacrifice and submit, to lay down every need and ambition, for someone else. For Eva. The gospel of love and peace he'd suffered to impart and the God he'd struggled to serve were still the same. The difference was in Angelo.

He didn't have to be immortal. He didn't need to be a hero. He didn't even want to be a saint. He simply wanted to be a good man worthy of Eva Rosselli. He just wanted Eva. He wanted her kisses and her eyes, her smiles and her laughter. He wanted his children in her womb and his mouth on her breasts. He wanted her legs wrapped around his hips and her arms cradling his head as he made love to her. He wanted her promises, her affection and her trust, her years and her secrets. He wanted her prayers and her pride, her tears and her troubles. He wanted Eva. And that was all.

He opened his eyes, and for a moment he could only breathe, sucking in the certainty that no longer eluded him.

Some things didn't have to be hard.

"When this war is over, I will be yours, first, last, and always. And you will be mine."

"Eva Bianco?" She smiled with trembling lips.

"Eva Bianco. In truth."

∞

"Are you awake?" Eva whispered.

Angelo's eyes were closed, his breathing deep, and he didn't answer. He was lying on his stomach, and Eva traced the line of his back but made herself stop at the dip of his waist. If she kept touching him, he would wake up, and he needed to sleep. The sheet clung to his hips and his arms were folded beneath his head in place of a pillow. His skin was dark against the white sheet, making her think of the pale sand and warm days on Maremma when he used to sleep on the beach in exactly the same way. She kissed his shoulder and laid her head against his back.

She was too happy to sleep. Too full. Too alive. Had she ever felt this alive? It was like a humming beneath her skin. Angelo had made love to her. Angelo *loved* her.

"Angelo loves me," she said softly, wanting to hear the words, to make them known, if only to the silent walls. There were no sweeter words in the whole wide world.

"Yes. He does," a groggy voice answered from above her head.

"Eva loves Angelo too," she added, her lips curving around the words. She pressed another kiss to his skin.

"You should sleep a little. It will be morning soon," he said gently.

The thought was like a pinprick to her balloon of joy. She closed her eyes and tried to push reality away, but it penetrated the cracks between her lids and found its way to her mouth, and before she knew it, she was giving voice to the sad truth.

"It will. And life will go on. We will have to leave this room. And we will be afraid again."

Angelo rolled to his side carefully, and her head slid from his back to the bed. He pulled her up and into him, skin against skin, chest against chest, and Eva's breath hitched in time with his.

"Are you afraid right now? Right this minute?" he asked.

"No."

"Are you hurting?" His eyes clung to hers, light eyes heavy with fatigue.

"No. My body is fine." That wasn't quite what he'd asked, but she knew what he meant. She was not in any physical pain.

"Are you warm?" His voice was soft.

She nodded. She was deliciously warm.

"Are you alone?"

"No. Are you . . . scolding me, Angelo?" she asked faintly.

"No." He shook his head, eyes still searching hers. "No," he repeated softly. "I just want, more than anything, to give you peace. To give you rest. To keep you safe." He hadn't told her if Santa Cecilia was safe or if his refugees had survived the night, but she knew he wouldn't be with her now if they hadn't.

"Will there ever be a time when people aren't afraid? The whole world is groaning in agony, Angelo. Can you hear it? I can hear it. I can't stop hearing it, and I'm so afraid. I don't want to be afraid anymore."

He touched his lips to hers, softly first, the only answer he had. And then he kissed her again, more insistently. He could not stop the world from trembling or people from hating. He couldn't make any of it go away—she knew that—but with his kiss, her happiness returned like a waterfall, rushing from her head to her toes, washing the fear away, and she wrapped herself around him, returning the kiss, and finding safety in his hands.

The day dawned cold and clear, a sliver of pale light that grew and grew above the dark horizon and covered the sky above Rome. The war to the south continued. The death in the north raged on. The sorrow in the east was unrelenting. The struggle in the west never ceased. But in a room in an occupied city, with nothing left but love itself, Angelo and Eva held on to each other, and found peace, rest, happiness, and safety. If only for a while.

Monday morning Eva pulled on the red skirt and white blouse she'd worn on the train to Rome—she'd left Florence with four dresses, two skirts, and three blouses. She knew she had more than most, but they were growing dingy from being washed by hand. She'd brought a change of clothes to wear home from the gala so she wasn't riding a streetcar in an evening gown, but she daydreamed about donning the black dress again, just so Angelo could look at her like he'd looked at her on Saturday night. Just thinking about it made her skin feel hot and her breaths grow shallow.

She and Angelo had spent the last twenty-four hours holed up in the Villa Medici, using her payment from the gala to stay another night. They'd eaten well for the first time in forever—fruit and chicken and pasta in a cream sauce—and they pretended the world was only as big as four walls and the two of them.

"I don't want you going to work," he stewed, biting his lip as he lingered at the door. Angelo had washed his shirt and his cassock in the sink and hung them over the rack to dry. He now wore his trousers and the shirt, but his cassock was folded over his arm. Eva didn't know what that meant, but maybe he didn't want to be seen in a cassock and a cross in the luxury hotel. At least not in the early-morning hours.

"I have to. It will be okay. There were no Jews found at Santa Cecilia. Von Essen has no reason to suspect me."

Angelo bowed his head, his chin resting on his chest, and he exhaled heavily. She could feel the tension coming off him in waves, and she hated to part that way. She pressed her body against his and lifted his face until he returned her gaze, his dark brows furrowed over sky-blue eyes, and she kissed his mouth, keeping her eyes open so he would stay with her in the moment.

He responded immediately, wrapping his arms around her fiercely and pulling her off her feet. He'd taken quite well to kissing. He kissed like he prayed, tender and passionate and completely committed to the task. When they parted they were both breathless, and he said no more about her returning to work at Via Tasso.

Angelo needn't have worried. Captain von Essen was in meetings all day. Other than delivering coffee to a room full of uniformed Germans, Eva had no interaction with him at all and went home almost as giddy as she'd arrived that morning.

Tuesday was no different. Captain von Essen stayed closeted in his office. His mood was dark, but even his sneering and his terse commands couldn't penetrate the bubble she'd been floating in. She'd agreed to meet Angelo at the Church of the Sacred Heart, and she ran most of the way because she was too impatient to wait for a streetcar. She didn't care what people thought as she sprinted through the streets with a smile on her face.

He was waiting by the altar, his eyes on the cross. She drew up short, suddenly nervous that he was suffering pangs of guilt and remorse. When he heard her, his head swung around.

He smiled.

Amy Harmon

It was a blinding, beautiful grin that hit Eva between the eyes. Her relief was so great she felt dizzy and weak, and she sank into a nearby pew. But Angelo had other ideas. He strode toward her, his cane clicking, his smile wide, and he took her by the hand, pulling her down the stairs to the little room where she'd known such sadness and fear. Once there, his arms went around her and his lips found hers. He tasted like apples—which meant he'd been bartering with black marketeers—and she licked into his mouth appreciatively, sharing the sweetness, thankful he was safe. He put himself at huge risk every time he ventured to the banks of the Tiber for things he couldn't otherwise provide to those depending on him.

Eventually, he pulled his mouth away. "I was afraid of this," he groaned into her hair.

"Of what?" she panted, not ready to stop kissing.

"Of not being able to control myself. I knew the moment I gave in I would be useless. I would think of nothing else but you. I thought of you constantly before, I confess. But now I have intimate knowledge. I don't just love you; I want to make love *to you*. Every time I close my eyes to pray I can only see you." He groaned again and squeezed his eyes shut as if in real pain. Eva giggled at his theatrics, and she kissed along the hard line of his clenched jaw.

"If I know you, you have not been useless. I'm guessing you have worked nonstop from the moment your knees hit the floor for your morning prayers. You did pray today, didn't you?"

"Yes. Many times."

"And what did you say?"

"I asked God to provide, to save the innocent, to protect the refugees, to ease suffering, to succor the weak, and to help me control my lustful thoughts."

"Did you have many?" she asked sweetly, her lips lingering at the corner of his mouth.

"Yes," he sighed.

"So he didn't answer that particular prayer."

"I really didn't want him to."

She giggled again, and his mouth returned to hers, insistent, hungry, plying happy sighs and sweet promises. When they finally parted, her lips were swollen and her heart was light, and as she fell asleep that night, there was hope in her heart and a prayer on constant replay in her mind—the same prayer she knew so many others were uttering.

"Save us, Lord. Deliver us," she pleaded. "Please, deliver us."

21 March, 1944

Confession: Sometimes I think the Germans are invincible.

American forces landed on Italy's Anzio Beach at the end of January, secur-
ing the beachhead and taking the Germans completely by surprise, but
instead of pushing immediately toward Rome and forcing the Germans to
retreat and pull off the Gustav Line, they stopped, inexplicably entrench-
ing themselves, and the Germans were given ample time to reinforce their
defenses and launch a counterattack. Two months later, thousands of lives
have been lost and the battle rages on. The Americans, only fifty-eight kilo-
meters from Rome on January 22, remain fifty-eight kilometers from Rome
on March 21. I fear this war will never end, and I will be trapped at Via
Tasso forever, smuggling gold and smuggling kisses from a man who won't
truly be mine until Rome is liberated.
      Eva Rosselli

CHAPTER 20
VIA RASELLA

Captain von Essen was very quiet when he arrived on Wednesday. He shut his office door and stayed locked inside all morning. At lunchtime Eva waited for Greta, who had sent word the day before that she wanted to whisk Eva away to some new shop. But Greta never showed. A little worried about her, Eva knocked tentatively on the captain's door and was told to enter.

"Is Greta well?" she asked as soon as she set foot inside.

"Yes," the captain answered, but something flickered in his eyes.

"We were going to have lunch together."

"I see," he said softly. He sat back in his chair and studied her, his head cocked to the side. It was a strange response, considering his wife was technically unaccounted for.

"Sit down, Eva."

Eva perched at the edge of one of the chairs in front of his desk, the same chair she always chose when he insisted she take dictation or instructions. He leaned forward, across his desk, and clasped his hands in front of him, eyeing her quizzically.

"Did you know that not one of our monastery raids was successful last weekend? Not one. No Jews. No partisans. No antifascists. How can that be? The lieutenant colonel was so sure the answer was with the church. But no." Captain von Essen pushed the tips of his fingers together and rested his chin on them, like he was lost in thought. "I went home to my wife so disturbed that she avoided me for three days. But last night she told me something I could hardly believe."

He continued to study Eva but didn't explain what it was his wife had told him. She waited in silence, her stomach in coils of ever-tightening knots. He breezily changed the subject.

"You were wonderful Saturday night, my dear. Wonderful. Such a lucky coincidence for me that you play so well and you were so willing to perform."

Eva thought it better not to remind him how truly unwilling she'd been.

"Thank you," she said simply. "Can I bring you some coffee, Captain von Essen?"

"That won't be necessary. But I do need you to do something for me. Surely, there is a way for you to reach your brother at the Vatican?"

"No. I have never contacted him there." It was the truth, but von Essen raised his brows as if that were hard to believe.

"Ah, but surely they could get a message to him if you needed him."

Captain von Essen picked up the receiver on his shiny black telephone and turned the rotary, waiting for an operator to connect him.

"The Vatican, please," he said and winked at Eva. "Your brother works with a monsignor. What was his name again?"

"Monsignor Luciano," she answered numbly, wondering if the captain wanted her to say Monsignor O'Flaherty. Did he know that Angelo worked with O'Flaherty? Was that what this was about? Von Essen repeated the name to the operator. He waited for several moments, smiling benignly at Eva as she rose slowly from the chair and stood before him, her unease growing by the second.

"Ah. Very good. My name is Captain von Essen of the German Police. I need to get a message to Father Angelo Bianco, assistant to Monsignor Luciano. It is very important." He paused as if he'd been instructed to hold.

"Please tell Father Bianco that his sister has been detained and is being questioned at Gestapo Headquarters."

Angelo was kept waiting in a small holding room at Via Tasso for over an hour. No explanation was given, no answers were provided. He was told to wait, and he did. When he had received Captain von Essen's message, he'd known the end had come. He only prayed it was his end and not Eva's.

He'd informed Monsignor Luciano what had happened and was forbidden to leave the Vatican. Several priests who had worked in the underground had been detained and tortured, some executed, and some sent to prisoner-of-war camps in Germany.

"You cannot help Eva if they have taken her. You cannot save her, Angelo. But you can save yourself. Think of the people relying on you, my son. You must think of them."

He'd kissed Monsignor Luciano's hand and asked that he tell Monsignor O'Flaherty. O'Flaherty would understand, he was certain. And if he could help, he would. He'd taken more risks than anyone.

"We won't be able to save you! The Pope can't intercede. She isn't worth your life, Angelo!" Monsignor Luciano cried, following him down the hall. But Angelo hadn't looked back. He'd left the protection of the Vatican and taken the two buses across town to Via Tasso, knowing full well he was being lured out. But he'd had no other option. Von Essen had known the key to Angelo was Eva. And he'd used it. Angelo wasn't surprised when it was Captain von Essen himself who finally entered the room.

"Thank you so much for coming here, Father Bianco. I would have come to you, but relations with the Vatican are so political, so dicey. Plus, there is the whole matter of diplomatic immunity. I thought it would be easier to have a discussion here, in case things don't go according to plan." He sat down and crossed his legs. His boots were so shiny Angelo could see the reflection of his cross in them.

"You wanted me to come here because you have no authority beyond the white line that separates the Vatican from the rest of Rome," Angelo said calmly.

"But why would I need to do that? You are merely a humble priest. You wouldn't know anything about Jews hidden all over the city, would you?" von Essen protested silkily.

"Where is my sister? Why has she been detained?"

Von Essen threw up his hands. "Oh, no. You misunderstand. She's simply being questioned. And come now, Father, let's not continue the charade. Eva is not your sister, is she?"

Angelo's blood turned instantly to ice.

"It's sad, really. She was playing so beautifully. Everyone was watching her. Listening, enjoying. The music and the girl, so exquisite. Such a beautiful woman. She didn't want to play, as I'm sure you're aware. I had to beg, cajole. Even threaten. She must have been so terrified." Von Essen sighed theatrically.

"But you wouldn't have guessed it by her skill. Everyone was quite taken with her. Especially the wife of Pietro Caruso, Rome's chief of police. Frau Caruso was sure she'd seen the girl in Florence. She'd heard her play years before and hadn't forgotten her. Eva Rosselli was her name. She went back a year later to hear the same orchestra again, and the girl was gone. She asked about her and was told Eva Rosselli was no longer with the orchestra because she is a Jew."

Angelo held himself perfectly still, not allowing a glimmer of reaction to show on his face, but he doubted it mattered. Von Essen knew. He continued in a singsong fashion, as if telling a very quaint story to a group of women at a tea party.

"Imagine then, how happy Frau Caruso was to see her play Saturday night. And imagine how surprised she was that we would have a Jewess entertaining our dignitaries." There was a tiny break in the façade, a flicker of rage on von Essen's face, before he tamped it down again. "Fortunately, Frau Caruso was really quite discreet. She only told my wife. And my wife deliberated and finally . . . told me."

His wife had deliberated. That explained the uneventful Monday and Tuesday. Von Essen hadn't known right away. Angelo wondered why the woman had waited at all. He wondered if von Essen had punished her for it. He imagined so.

"I did some checking up on you, Father Bianco. You came to Italy when you were young. And when you weren't in school you lived with your grandparents. Your grandparents were live-in employees for a Jewish family. A family by the name of Rosselli. I was convinced you were also a Jew disguising yourself as a priest. But no. You are truly a Roman Catholic priest, ordained to the Roman diocese, a servant of God and Pope Pius XII, and a rising star at the Curia. You are authentic. It is Eva who is not. And she is not your sister, though it seems you were raised together."

When Angelo didn't protest or respond at all, but sat frozen in his seat, the captain laughed. It was an ugly laugh, devoid of humor or joy. It was a taunt, a repudiation.

"I imagine you do love her, though I don't think you love her like a sister. In fact, I think you are sleeping with her. She is too beautiful to resist, isn't she? I have hardly been able to keep my hands off her myself. But still, such unpriestly behavior!" Von Essen shook his head and wagged his finger, as if he could hardly imagine such a thing. "I am sure she has been helping you. Sharing information with you. She must have overheard something about the raids last weekend. Or maybe that is my fault. I wanted her to be out of harm's way. And she betrayed me." The flash of rage again, this time not so well hidden. He leaned over the interview table, his eyes sharp and his voice soft.

"But I will make you a deal, Father. I will let Eva go. I like the girl, and I don't want to see her tortured all because of you. So I will let Eva go, give her a head start, a chance to hide before we come after her, so to speak. But I need to know where you are hiding all your Jews. We will find them, you know. Every monastery, every convent. Every school, every church, every religious college. We will raid them all again, one by one. And we will find them anyway. You telling us where they are won't change their fate, but it might change Eva's."

Angelo's mind raced, pinging from one option to another and dismissing it almost immediately. Had the captain hurt Eva? Was she in a cell at this moment, awaiting deportation? Was she even at Via Tasso? His breaths grew shallow and his hands clenched. He didn't know it was possible to hate the way he did in that moment. The hate was so sharp it hurt, so bitter he could taste it on his tongue, so hot he could feel the flames in his chest.

Angelo didn't close his eyes or bow his head, but he began to pray inwardly, searching for faith and strength. He ignored the captain, the soldiers standing outside the door with guns and helmets, empowered by evil men, and he pleaded for help. Prayer was the only weapon at his disposal. The captain leaned back, but he continued his negotiations.

"Ten. Let's start with ten. Ten Jews for Eva. Ten for one, isn't that the rule? I need ten addresses." He handed Angelo a pencil and a sheet of paper. "Or just the names, Father. Just the names of the establishments, and I will place Eva in your care. You give me the list, and you take your *sister* and walk away. Only you and I will know. Eva might guess, but she will be grateful that you put her first, that you value her life above all others."

"I don't have any information for you, Captain. I'm afraid I cannot help you." Angelo answered firmly and without hesitation, not allowing himself to think at all.

"No? Not even for your sister's life?" Von Essen again put exaggerated emphasis on the word *sister*. "I will be sure and tell her." He stared at Angelo for a moment, as if gauging his next move.

Hail Mary, full of grace, the Lord is with thee. Blessed art thou among women, and blessed is the fruit of thy womb, Jesus. Holy Mary, Mother of God, pray for us sinners, now and at the hour of our death. Oh, my Jesus, forgive us our sins, save us from the fires of hell, and lead all souls to heaven, especially those in most need of your mercy. Amen.

The rosary continued through his head like a desperate drumbeat, and Angelo begged Eva for forgiveness even as he prayed that they—that she—would be saved from the fires of hell. He would happily give his life for hers, but he couldn't betray those in his care, and he knew Eva wouldn't want him to.

Captain von Essen stood and leaned out the door.

"Bring the girl in," he said to the nearest guard.

Angelo stood as well.

"Sit down, Father. I have not had you restrained out of courtesy, but I will if I need to."

Angelo remained standing. The captain moved in closer, his hands clasped behind his back, his favorite pose.

"The men are all talking about her, Father. How beautiful she is. She won't fare well here. You know that, don't you? And she won't fare well in a camp. But no one really fares well in the camps."

"May God have mercy on your soul," Angelo murmured, not trusting himself beyond a whisper. His hands ached with the need to close them around the sneering captain's neck.

"She won't be raped—not here, at least. Do you know it is illegal for a German to lay with a Jew? Don't want to sully the bloodlines. We have higher standards than that."

"Oh, my Jesus, forgive us our sins, save us from the fires of hell, and lead all souls to heaven, especially those in most need of your mercy. Amen." Angelo prayed out loud, his eyes locked with the captain's. He repeated the prayer again, enunciating the plea for those most in need of mercy.

The door opened, and a helmeted German pushed Eva into the room, as if shoving and intimidation were part of the routine. Her eyes were wide and her face pale and frightened, but her hair was neat and her clothes tidy, and she appeared unharmed.

"Sit," the captain commanded, and Eva was pushed into a chair, the German soldier standing guard behind her.

"Sit," he commanded Angelo, and this time, Angelo did as he was told, his eyes clinging to Eva's. Captain von Essen sat on a chair, triangulated between them, as if preparing to pit them against each other.

"I have no desire for unpleasantness. My wife is very fond of you, Eva. And she is quite beside herself over all of this."

Eva pulled her gaze from Angelo and stared at the captain stonily, waiting. The captain glared back, as if she had betrayed him personally. Then he continued.

"I have told Father Bianco that all he needs to do is tell me where the church is hiding the partisans and the Jews. Just ten. Not all. Just ten. But he says he can't help me. What do you think about that?"

Eva continued staring steadily at the captain. He raised a brow, waiting for her to respond. When she didn't, he leaned into her, as if confiding in her, and his voice lowered convincingly.

"You can save each other. I have no wish to harm either of you. I just want to do my job. There is a great deal of pressure from Herr Himmler himself." Captain von Essen took her hand. "So why don't you tell me, Eva. Where is your brother hiding his Jews?"

"I am the only Jew he has helped, and that is only because we were raised together," Eva said steadily.

"You must be so very grateful," von Essen said softly. He pulled his weapon suddenly, and Eva gasped, but instead of firing it, he used it to backhand Angelo across the face.

Angelo's head snapped back, and the left side of his face bloomed in hot pain, but he almost laughed in relief. If this was the captain's approach, he welcomed it. Ask Eva the questions, torture Angelo. He wanted to sink to his knees in grateful prayer.

"You have me. Let him go," Eva cried.

"Tell me what I want to know, and of course he may go."

"I am the only Jew he has helped," she repeated, her eyes closing, as if she couldn't watch what came next. This time it was the right side of Angelo's face that took the brunt of the force.

"I am the only Jew Father Angelo has helped!" Eva cried. "You have me. Let him go!" she repeated, tears beginning to slide down her cheeks. Clearly, Captain von Essen thought she would be easier to break. Angelo knew differently. Eva wouldn't talk. She would suffer with him, but she wouldn't break.

"Where did you get your pass? It is very authentic." Captain von Essen changed his line of questioning.

Eva answered immediately, clearly relieved she could answer without endangering anyone. "A man named Aldo Finzi. He worked for my father's company at one time, as a printer."

"A Jew?"

"Yes."

"And where can I find Mr. Finzi?"

"He is dead." Angelo cut into the conversation, pulling the captain's attention from Eva. The captain raised his brows disdainfully.

"How convenient," von Essen said drily.

"I'm sure Aldo Finzi would disagree," Angelo shot back.

"And how did he die?"

"You shot him in the street a month ago near the rail station. Don't you remember?" Angelo challenged.

He'd caught the captain by surprise, and von Essen tipped his head as if searching his memory.

"You shot him in the back of the head after you told him to drop his pants."

Captain von Essen looked stunned that Angelo knew the details. Had he felt so powerful, so invincible, that he hadn't really thought anyone might have seen?

"You killed a man in cold blood," Angelo said quietly. "But I won't name you if you let Eva go." He willed Eva to stay silent. Captain von Essen did not need to know it was she who had seen him murder Aldo.

"You think anyone cares about the death of one Jew?" Captain von Essen said, incredulous. "This is what you bargain with?"

"The war will end. Germany will lose. And you will answer for your sins," Angelo said, spitting the words through bloody lips. "Let Eva go. I will testify on your behalf. The testimony of a priest will mean something. I will say you were a merciful man. You will be able to go back to Germany with your wife, unlike the others who will be punished for their war crimes."

Von Essen laughed. "I don't know how you know about the Jew in the street. But clearly you were there, which makes me even more certain that Eva is not the only Jew you have assisted."

He leaned out the door once more, and two SS men entered the room seconds later.

"Take her back to her cell," von Essen told the soldier behind Eva. To the two new arrivals he directed, "And take the father away too. Keep working him over until he talks. Make sure the girl can hear his pain."

It had been thirty-six hours since they'd been separated. Thirty-six hours of Angelo being questioned and tortured. Thirty-six hours of hell.

Eva had heard him ask for a drink. He'd been given nothing. Instead, he'd been doused in ice water and deprived of sleep. She'd heard him cry out in pain, though she knew he tried not to, for her sake. They'd hurt him. They'd beat him. They'd threatened him with descriptions of what they'd do to her. But he never talked, beyond prayers and the quiet insistence that he had no information.

On Friday, the guards started pulling men from their cells, clearing them out, Jew and non-Jew alike, leaving only Eva and two other Jewish women—sisters—who had been detained and were awaiting deportation on the next train. Eva heard the guards open Angelo's cell and tell him to get up. She rushed to her door and pressed her face to the glass, aching for a better look as they dragged Angelo past. His swollen and bruised face was hardly recognizable, but they hadn't taken his cassock, and his formerly white collar was splattered in blood. He turned for one last look, struggling to stay on his feet.

"Angelo!" she screamed. "Angelo!"

The two remaining guards elbowed each other and walked over to her cell. She moved away from the glass as they unlocked the door, but as soon as it was opened, she fought to see beyond them, desperate to know where Angelo was being taken.

She was immediately pushed back, shoved hard enough to make her fall back against the adjacent wall.

"Come now, Fräulein. You mustn't carry on this way. What will your Jewish friends think?"

"Yes! They might think there is something going on between you and the priest." One of them mimed prayer while pumping his hips lewdly.

"Go to hell," Eva spit out in German, her tears bottled up behind her shocked eyes, her head pounding with denial. Angelo hadn't just been dragged away. Surely, she would see him again.

"Ahh! The little *Fräulein* speaks German!" The officer sounded surprised.

"You speak German," the other said flatly. "Are you a German Jew?"

"Go to hell," she repeated.

He brought his face an inch from hers, his eyes cold and icy. Blue. The same color as Angelo's. But Angelo's eyes were like the sky. Warm. Clear. Endless. Beloved.

"I'm already there, madam. But unfortunately for you, this hell isn't quite as bad as where you will be going. And you will be going there soon."

"Good news, though," the other guard said with false levity. "Your priest won't have to live without you. You know where they're taking him, don't you?"

She waited, knowing that they were going to enjoy telling her.

"He will be executed with all the others. Thirty-three German police died yesterday from a bomb set by partisans on Via Rasella. Ten Italians will die for every policeman who was killed. Via Tasso isn't the only prison we emptied out. The prison at Regina Coeli was emptied too. Every Jew, every partisan, every antifascist we could find. Now we're pulling civilians off the streets. Three hundred and thirty men. Next time, maybe the partisans will think twice about setting bombs."

"There won't be a next time for some of them," the other guard added. "There won't be a next time for your priest. I hope you gave him something to remember you by."

Eva covered her head with her arms and sank to the floor, too despondent to listen any longer. She wasn't even aware when they left.

24 March, 1944

> *Angelo Bianco, my white angel.*
> *They have taken you*
> *and I am lost.*
> *But we were both here,*
> *once.*
> > *Eva Rosselli*

CHAPTER 21
ARDEATINE CAVES

They were lined up and counted, their hands linked behind their heads, and then they were loaded into trucks—just like the Jews on the morning of the October roundup—and taken south of the city to an old quarry not far from the storied catacombs that tourists came to see and Romans never thought about. There were no tourists in Rome these days. Just Germans, beleaguered Italians, and the Catholic Church. Just war, hunger, hopelessness, and death.

Angelo's ribs had been kicked a time too many, and one eye was swollen shut. He hadn't been able to see where they were taking them, riding in the back of the covered truck, but it hadn't taken overly long for them to arrive. When all 336 men—six more than was required—were herded from the trucks and lined up once more, he'd recognized his surroundings. His spirits had plummeted. It was the perfect setting for a massacre.

The German guard kept them sufficiently contained with bound hands and intimidated with pointed guns. No one tried to escape. Why was that? Was hope so powerful that it would cause a man to cooperate to the very end? He'd seen it over and over again. So few people actually fought, because fighting seemed so futile. Fighting back meant certain death. So they all cooperated and hoped.

The hope ended when the killing began inside the quarry. At that point weeping and praying also commenced, and Angelo began dispensing comfort the only way he knew how. Amazingly enough, the German soldiers allowed him to administer rites, and they ignored his prayers and his movement up the line to reach those who would enter the caves first. With his hands bound behind his back he couldn't properly make the sign of the cross, but he moved his right hand in the proper direction and continued on.

He accompanied the second group of men into the quarry, winding through tunnels until they reached a large cave. He kept his mouth moving, administering last rites and hoping God would understand and forgive his own inadequacies and provide for these three hundred thirty-five souls who were looking to him, a fallen man who no longer wanted to be a priest.

Five would kneel. Five executioners would press the noses of their guns to the backs of the prisoners' necks. Five triggers were pulled. Five men would die. Five more would then kneel behind the pile of the dead only to share their fate. Each time, Angelo expected to be pushed forward and forced to his knees. And each time, he was bypassed and allowed to continue the rites for the men who were dying all around him.

A boy and his father knelt side by side and were murdered side by side, their bodies falling into a sloppy embrace, and Angelo wept as he prayed. But he refused to close his eyes. He needed to see, to bear witness, even in his last moments, to what was occurring. The blood of the innocent demanded it.

It took hours.

When the pile of bodies grew too high, they would create another row until the cave was filled with the dead, and then they would move to another opening. Still Angelo prayed, blessing those waiting to die. When the final man was thrown face-first onto the blood-soaked mountain of death, would there be anyone left to die beside him?

As the Germans neared what had to be the end, there was a brief lull as bodies were moved, and more men were led through the dark passageway. Suddenly, Angelo was being shoved from behind and urged to walk. When he resisted, he was grabbed by his bound arms and yanked forward.

"Come with me, Father," a voice said, but he wasn't sure if the voice was in the caves or in his mind. His ears were ringing, the result of hundreds of gunshots, one after another, with nothing to protect his eardrums from the report. He staggered and fell down, his already poor balance compromised by his hearing loss.

Rough hands jerked him to his feet, and he tottered again.

His hands were suddenly cut free from his bindings, and his arms screamed in pain as the blood rushed through his limbs. He was urged forward again, the hand gripping his arm steadying him through a narrow passage that led to a tapered swath of light. The light grew, and the man leading him urged him on until he found himself crawling through a small opening, coming out of the caves about a hundred and fifty feet east of the craggy main entrance where the prisoners had first formed the long line. He stopped and turned around, still not sure what was expected of him. He was on higher ground now and could look down on a semicircle of helmeted, blood-soaked Germans that stood a ways off. Others—those who had guarded the men awaiting execution—leaned against trucks that were now empty, smoking and drinking bottles of cognac. Cognac for courage. More than one officer had grown sick inside the caves, and others had refused to shoot, only to be dragged off or forced to participate by a commanding officer. The assembly of soldiers wasn't nearly as orderly and contained as it had been at the start, and no one had seen him or his unknown deliverer, who tugged on his arm once more and pointed through the trees.

The German soldier had a blunt nose, a wholesome face, and red-rimmed eyes, and Angelo noticed there were blood spatters—small, red, pin-size dots—all over the soldier's cheeks, making him appear diseased.

The soldier's mouth moved around words and Angelo focused on their shape, trying to understand. He heard the words as if he listened through water, and he wondered if his hearing would return, or if it was simply the first part of him to die.

"Go. None of us wants to kill a priest," the man mouthed.

The soldier shoved Angelo away from the rocky outcropping and motioned with his pistol.

"Go!" he growled, sticking his face in Angelo's, his eyes frantic. Angelo heard enough to realize he was being told to flee.

He turned and began to put one foot in front of the other. His prosthetic straps were loose, and he staggered and almost fell, but he didn't dare stop and make the necessary adjustments, expecting a bullet in his back at any moment.

But none came, and he kept walking, limping through the trees toward a road he knew must be there. The terrain was muddy and wet from recent rains, and the trees were just starting to grow leaves again. Some were still completely bare, as if the winter had been harder on them than on others. Angelo wondered, still reeling from shock and horror, if those trees would ever come back to life, or if they would simply stand, skeletal, among the living and wait to be brought down.

He wondered if he would ever come back to life. Then he stopped thinking at all. He just walked in circles, stumbling and slipping, and after what could have been an hour or merely minutes—he wasn't really certain—he reached the road. A sign next to a fork pointed the way to the old quarries at Fosse Ardeatine. Suddenly, a boom rocked the ground beneath his feet. Angelo fell to the earth once more and lay there, reeling, wondering if bombs were falling. He couldn't hear the whine and shriek or see the stars and stripes above him in the sky. The ground rumbled again, then again, and the trees above him shook in whispery terror, their new leaves dancing in the tepid March sunlight.

Then he realized what was happening. The Germans were using explosives to bring down the rocks inside the caves. They were trying to hide the bodies and seal the openings, attempting to cover their tracks, as if more than three hundred people would not be missed.

He crawled back into the shelter of the foliage that lined the road, weak with pain and horror, sick with despair, and waited until the trucks rumbled down the road an hour later, the deed done. Darkness descended, and his cane was gone. His cross too. And Eva would be gone. The truth assailed him like a relentless whip, and he moaned audibly, his agony escaping through his clenched teeth.

Save my family, Camillo had said. *Become a priest and save my family.* But there was no one left to save. He didn't even know if he had the strength to save himself. Still, he rose on shaking legs and willed himself forward. It was a long way to Rome for a crippled man with a broken heart.

∽◎

"He is dead. Father Bianco is dead. You realize that, don't you? You don't have to die. I will let you walk out of here. I will keep your little secret. But you need to tell me where he was hiding the fugitives," Captain von Essen said reasonably.

Eva didn't even bother to look at him. He was an idiot. He'd left himself no real incentive, no bargaining chip. Didn't he realize that without Angelo, she wanted to die? Didn't he realize she had absolutely nothing left to live for? With the gold file she kept in her shoe, she'd scratched his name into the wall of her cell, along with the date and a testimony that she'd been there. That he'd been there. But it was tedious, scratching the words into the walls. She wanted to write one last confession, even if no one but the captain ever read her words.

"I would like a piece of paper and a pencil," she said quietly.

He jumped to his feet and walked to the door. He snapped his fingers and told someone what was needed. A soldier was back within seconds, and Captain von Essen set the paper and pencil down in front of her. He sat down and smiled, nodding his head like he was proud of her, certain she was finally cooperating.

She put the date at the top—24 March, 1944—and she started to write in German.

> *Confession: My name is Batsheva Rosselli, not Eva Bianco, and I am a Jew. Angelo Bianco is not my brother but a priest who wanted only to protect me from the very place I now find myself.*

She wrote for several minutes, filling the page with her final thoughts. When she was done, she slid her paper toward the captain and stared at him dully. He read with growing anger, not having received the confession he sought.

"You are going to die. Do you understand?" he spat.

"We're all going to die, Captain, eventually. If I were you, I would kill me now. Because if I live, I will tell the world who you are and what you've done," she answered, folding her hands. "I will tell Greta that you are a vicious killer. But then, I think Greta already knows what kind of man you are."

"Take her away! She's useless," Captain von Essen called to the guard. Then he stood and looked down at Eva. "Enjoy your trip, Fräulein Bianco."

Eva flinched at the name. Angelo's name. She would never be Eva Bianco.

She had almost felt relieved when she was arrested. The thing she had dreaded, feared, run from, had happened. When it came, she was strangely liberated from the fear. She couldn't dread what had already come to pass. She didn't have to anticipate the horror when the horror was right there. With her arrest came a certain calm, a quiet comfort. It had come. She had known it would. And she could stop fighting.

But then they arrested Angelo, and they tortured him. When they dragged Angelo away, the comfort left, and the fear came back. Fear is strange. It settles on chests and seeps through skin, through layers of tissue, muscle, and bone, and collects in a soul-size black hole, sucking the joy out of life, the pleasure, the beauty. But not the hope. Somehow, the hope is the only thing resistant to the fear, and it is that hope that makes the next breath possible, the next step, the next tiny act of rebellion, even if that rebellion is simply staying alive.

When they told her Angelo was dead, she lost her hope.

◌◞◟◌

"Help me, Saint George," Angelo prayed, beseeching the statue overlooking the church fountain. It wasn't Saint George, but it could have been. Maybe it was Saint Jude, the patron saint of lost causes, the apostle of the impossible. If so, Angelo had a task for him.

"Help me face what is to come," he murmured through lips that wouldn't cooperate. "Help me get to Rome, and most of all, watch over Eva. Take care of Eva, until I can do it myself."

He'd filled his belly with brackish water from the fountain and washed himself as best he could, trying not to think of the blood and death he carried on his skin and in his clothes. Then he turned and stumbled away from the fountain of the unknown saint and continued his painful slog toward Rome. He needed to reach Santa Cecilia before dawn. He had to find Eva.

Hours later, when he limped the final steps and collapsed against the gates of the convent, the church bells began to ring, but Angelo was too far gone to notice.

⁤⁢⸻⤳

Eva was still wearing the gray dress she'd worn to work on Wednesday, still wearing her low-heeled black shoes and her little black belt. She was stylishly filthy. Her hair was matted. It hadn't been brushed in— she thought back—days? How many days? Wednesday she had been arrested. Friday they had dragged Angelo away, Saturday morning she was loaded on a train. It was still Saturday, and she still sat in the stinking darkness of the cattle car, the press of bodies keeping her warm but making her want to climb up to the little window that sat high on the side, just so she could breathe air that hadn't been breathed a hundred times and see a stretch of sky. There were only women and children in this car. The Jewish men detained in the prisons had been taken to help satisfy the numbers required for the reprisal killing. Just like Angelo.

Four days. It had been four days since she'd brushed her hair. Or her teeth. Or looked in a mirror. She had a strange feeling that if she saw herself, she wouldn't recognize her face. Seven days ago, she'd lain in Angelo's arms, the happiest she'd ever been in her entire life. Now she sat shivah over her old life in a train that would take her to her death.

She managed to find a place against the wall. They'd designated a corner for waste, and though no one wanted to use it, they all eventually had. The humiliation of the older women especially, crouched in that corner, trying to maintain their modesty while not stepping in the waste of others, tears of mortification streaming down their faces, was something she didn't think she could ever forgive. It is one thing to kill someone. It is another to degrade and humiliate, to strip away a person's dignity like stripping away flesh. One made a man a murderer. The other made him a monster. Eva was sure many of the women aboard that train would prefer death, clean and quick, to the slow loss of their humanity.

They were on the train for hours. It stopped once and they could hear dogs and commands, the sounds of more people being loaded into the cattle cars, but the doors were never reopened. Eva thought they were in Florence. It smelled like Florence, like home, and she pressed her palms to her eyes, trying not to weep and call out for Nonna and Nonno like a child. She couldn't afford to cry. She was too thirsty.

It was the end of March, and the temperatures were moderate. It could have been so much worse, but it was hard to tell yourself how much more terrible a situation could be, when you were already on the outskirts of hell. The hungry children suffered the most, or maybe that wasn't true. When children suffer, the ones who love them suffer even more, helpless to alleviate their agony.

When the train started to move for the second time, the occupants almost wept in relief, just to be leaving one torture for another, and Eva sank down, pulling her knees to her chest so she wouldn't take up too much space, and rested her head against the side of the car. She had slept deeply that first night of confinement, waiting for the train that would take her away from her life. From the struggle. From everything that had become so impossibly hard. Now she slept deeply again, an ability she'd always had, and in sleep she escaped for a while.

She recognized the dream immediately. It was the dream she'd had a hundred times before. But confusion welled up inside her chest. Was she dreaming? The press of bodies in the darkness felt real. She remembered being loaded into the car, a German with a submachine gun pushing at her back. This wasn't a dream. But she'd been here before.

They didn't veer northeast toward the Brenner Pass, with Austria lying on the other side, but instead hugged the west coast and approached France. They spent a week at a transit camp called Borgo San Dalmazzo in the Piedmont region of Italy, twenty miles from the French border, where they were fed—thin soup and hard bread—and given enough water to wash and quench their thirst. The knowledge that they'd been heading west instead of east was a great relief, though they would be heading due north from that point on, if the reports were true.

"Bergen-Belsen. We're going to Bergen-Belsen!" a woman cried, a thankful smile on her lips. She even closed her eyes and raised her hands to heaven, offering a prayer of gratitude at the development. They weren't going to Auschwitz, and many of the women felt that was cause for celebration.

It was strange how rumors started, trickling down from one mouth to another, crossing great distances to comfort or console, taunt or terrify. Bergen-Belsen wasn't as bad as Auschwitz. Survival was possible. Families could even live together. Sometimes the prisoners were given a little milk and cheese to eat. That's what the rumors were; those were the tales some of the women had heard. But Bergen-Belsen was in Germany. Northern Germany, someone else said fearfully, as if Poland were preferable to Germany. Germany meant Hitler.

"They sent the Libyan Jews that were hiding in Italy to Bergen-Belsen last fall," someone else offered. "Everyone else in Italy has gone to Auschwitz. We are so lucky."

So lucky. They might die more slowly, suffer longer. She just wanted it to be done. Bergen-Belsen sounded like death by a slow drip, Auschwitz was the six a.m. Rapido to the great beyond. She thought she might prefer that. Eva was distantly alarmed by her readiness to die. But only distantly.

❧

When Angelo woke again, Mario Sonnino sat by his bed reading, the lamp casting odd shadows around the humble space. He'd given Angelo something. Morphine, he guessed. Angelo had been in and out of consciousness, waking only to beg for news of Eva and then falling back into oblivion before he could get any answers. But he knew she was gone. Mario said no one knew for sure, but Monsignor O'Flaherty said a train filled with Jewish women and children had left Tiburtina Station on Saturday.

He wished for oblivion again, but knew those hours were behind him. He was wide awake, and Mario helped him sit up so he could swing his legs—his prosthetic had been removed—over the side and use the chamber pot. Hopping down the hallway was out of the question, and he was too sore for crutches. He finished and managed to eat some cold polenta and brown bread and drink a glass of water before easing himself back down on the pillow. Mario hovered for a moment, clearly wanting to be of assistance.

"I set your finger and bound your ribs. They're cracked but not broken. You're black and blue, but the swelling's gone down. I put your nose back where it belongs. How are your eyes? I worried a little about your sight in the right one."

"I can see," Angelo said. "I'll be fine."

"Yes. You will. The ribs will take the longest. But no long-term damage done. Your fingernails might not grow back."

"I'm not worried about my fingernails," Angelo said, his eyes bleak.

"No," Mario murmured. "I don't suppose you are." He sat down heavily in his chair.

"I have to find her, Mario."

Mario swallowed, his throat working against the heavy emotion in the room. "How?" he whispered.

"I don't know." Angelo's voice broke, and he put his hands over his face the way he did when he prayed, but there was no solace in his hands. No solace in prayer. Not anymore. "The Americans are coming. We just needed to hold on a little longer. I just needed to keep her safe a little longer. I've been such a fool. I should have married her in 1939. I could have taken her away, back to America, like her father suggested."

"We all had opportunities to escape. We all had those inner voices that said, 'Flee. Leave.' Those things have haunted me too, Angelo," Mario said, rubbing hard at the back of his neck, fighting the old regrets, the guilt that had kept him up many nights.

"Eva told me once that the roots of the Jewish people are in their traditions, in their children, and in their families. She asked me why the Catholic Church wants to take a man and deprive him of his posterity. She told me there would be no more Angelo Biancos. My roots would die with me." Angelo was so overcome he could hardly speak, but he was desperate to get the words out.

"I am a man who was so impressed by the thought of immortality, of being a martyr or a saint, that I didn't realize that by becoming a priest I was depriving myself of the very thing I sought. Our immortality comes through our children and their children. Through our roots and our branches. The family is immortality. And Hitler has destroyed not just branches and roots, but entire family trees, forests! All of them, gone. Eva was the only Rosselli left, the only Adler left."

The terrible reality of his words silenced them momentarily, and they bowed their heads, shoulders hunched against the weight of such heavy truth, such staggering loss, and it took a concerted effort for Mario to respond.

"You have saved and preserved so many branches, Angelo," he said in a choked whisper. "You saved my family, Eva saved my family, and we will never forget her. We will never forget you. I will tell my children, and they will tell their children. You might not have children who will carry your names, but you will have branches and roots who will honor your names."

Mario wept, and Angelo reached out a hand, thanking him, even as his heart rejected his sentiments. It wasn't enough. He didn't want honor. He didn't want to be a hero. He just wanted Eva, and she had been taken from him. The thing he had feared most had come to pass.

"She loved you," Mario said. It was not a question, and Angelo wondered if everyone around them could see all along what he'd refused to admit.

"Yes. And I love her." He refused to put it in past tense. He would never stop loving her.

"Did she know, Angelo? Did she know you loved her?" Mario asked gently.

"Yes." Angelo wiped at his face, at the tears that wouldn't stop falling. She'd known. He'd been able to tell her, to show her. It was the one thing he was grateful for, and in his heart he acknowledged the blessing he'd been given.

Mario stood and walked to the small chest of drawers in the corner. There was a pile of books placed neatly on top. Angelo recognized them immediately. Eva's journals.

"These are hers. There are several of them. They all look the same, but you can see that she's dated them over the years. You should have them." He set them on the bed, near Angelo, and quietly left the room.

There were four books, all identical. The only differences were in the slight wear on the covers, the dates at the top of each page, and the handwriting that slowly changed and matured, just like the girl herself. But the last book was only half filled, and Angelo found he couldn't look at the empty pages. The empty pages hurt worse than seeing the crowded lines filled with Eva's thoughts, because in the words, she lived. The emptiness mocked him with what could have been, what should have been. He flipped to the last entry and read it just to escape the unfinished chapters.

22 March, 1944

Confession: Kissing Angelo is a mitzvah.

My Jewish grandmother would roll in her grave if I said it out loud. Uncle Augusto would accuse me of sacrilege. But it's true. In him I have found a slice of the divine, a morsel of peace, and when his lips are on mine, his hands on my skin, there is reason to believe that life is more than pain, more than fear, more than sorrow. I am hopeful for the first time in years. And strangely enough, I find myself convinced that God loves his children—all his children—that he loves me, and that he provides moments of light and transcendence amid the constant trial.

Angelo closed the book and wept.

CHAPTER 22
NOWHERE

When they were loaded aboard the train again, a week after arriving at Borgo San Dalmazzo, the numbers had grown to include men, women, and children from other places, who had all been brought to the transit camp. There were twenty cars, with about one hundred Jews loaded aboard each car. Many of the people were there with members of their families, and they clamored to stay together. Eva was alone, so she just let herself be pushed and pinched, as people far more desperate than she clung to each other and fought for better positions. She found a corner and slid down against the wall like she'd done on the first leg of the trip, letting herself drift up and away to numb blindness. It was too dark to try and see anyway.

She curled into herself, fighting to stay asleep, to stay oblivious, and she caught a whiff of tobacco, a wisp of smoke, and she raised her head, wanting to breathe it in.

He was there next to her, looking exactly as he had the last time she saw him. His pipe glowed in the darkness, and his long legs were stretched out in front of him, like he had all the room in the world. In his hand he had a glass of wine. The wine was dark and it glimmered like an enormous gemstone cradled in the palm of his hand. She was so thirsty.

"Babbo?" Eva asked, her voice high and childlike in her head.

"Batsheva," her father said, smiling and swirling his wine. But the smile faded quickly. "Eva, why are you sleeping?" he chided.

"What else can I do?"

"You can fight. You can live."

"I don't want to fight, Babbo. I want to be with you. I want to be with you and Uncle Felix and Uncle Augusto. I want to be with Claudia and Levi."

"You want to be with Angelo," he finished gently. "Most of all, you want to be with Angelo."

"Yes, I do. Is he there? With you?" She would give anything to see him.

"No." Babbo shook his head. "He is not with me. He is there, with you."

"Where? I am on a train! I am being taken away."

Her father touched her face. She could feel his hand, long-fingered and light against her cheek. "Angelo is inside you. His flesh is now your flesh, his branch is your branch."

"No, they killed him. They have killed everyone. And they will kill me too."

"Eva, listen to me. All your life you have had a dream. A dream of this moment. You know that, don't you? You recognize the dream."

Eva nodded, and the fear returned like a deluge, flooding her veins and turning her fingers to ice.

"You have to jump, Eva."

"I can't."

"You can. What do you have to do first?"

"I have to climb to the window." She didn't think she could fit through that opening. And there were bars, dividing it. She couldn't remove the bars.

"You climb up to the window. And then what? In the dream, what did you do next?"

"I breathed in the cold air."

"Yes. You breathe and gather courage. And then what?"

She shook her head stubbornly, resisting. She remembered that wicked relief. That sweet poison of letting go, of giving up. It had released her, temporarily, and she wasn't ready to care again. "I don't think I can do it. I don't want to. I'm so tired, and I'm so alone."

"But you must do it. You are the last Rosselli. You must jump, Batsheva. Because if you don't, you will surely die, and Angelo will die too."

"Angelo is already dead."

"You must jump, Eva. You must jump. And you must live," he whispered, his breath a kiss on her wet cheek. He was so real. Just like the dream that was no longer a dream.

When Eva woke, her father was gone, and her brief respite from trying was over.

In the morning, sore, but able to get around, Angelo packed the books in the small valise Eva had brought with her to Rome. He folded her clothes and put them in the bigger suitcase, clearing out the room because he couldn't stand for anyone else to touch her things. He made her bed, folding the covers neatly, even though he knew one of the sisters would strip them off when he left and wash them. He wanted to take the case that covered the pillow and ended up folding it and tucking it inside the valise, unable to part with the physical reminder of her scent merged with his. He couldn't manage to summon any guilt for taking something that wasn't his. He'd already taken something that wasn't his, and she'd instantly been taken away from him.

He started to shake, the grief and disbelief making him wonder how he was ever going to go on. Movement hurt, thought hurt, breathing hurt. And none of it was because of his battered body. He welcomed that pain, because it distracted him. He made himself walk down the stairs, juggling Eva's things.

Mother Francesca saw him and rushed to his side, scolding him fiercely and trying to remove the cases from his arms.

"What do you think you are doing? You have to rest. At least for a few more days!" she clucked.

"I've been in bed for three days. That's enough rest," he answered softly. "I will take these things home."

"You can't go home! Monsignor Luciano came here. He delivered some of your things. You're to stay hidden until the Americans arrive. If everyone thinks you're dead, they won't be looking for you. You'll be safe as long as you stay here and stay out of sight. He said Monsignor O'Flaherty has been conducting all of his meetings on the steps of St. Peter's to avoid arrest. When he leaves the Vatican he has to wear a disguise! There have been attempts to grab him right off the street. Someone even tried to pull him across the white line the Germans drew on the ground. If they pull him across, he is no longer under Vatican protection and can be arrested. Someone got wind of the plan and turned the tables. The man hired to kidnap the monsignor got a good pounding!"

Mother Francesca's eyes were bright and her cheeks flushed, and Angelo found himself smiling slightly at her obvious excitement over the "pounding." She'd had more excitement in the last few months than she'd probably ever had in her whole life and would ever have again.

But the news put a wrench in his plans. He couldn't sit in Eva's room and wait for the war to be over. If he didn't keep working, keep moving, he wouldn't survive. He would be the next casualty of war's hopelessness. He would be the one walking in front of the streetcar, or throwing himself from a bridge, or inciting a German to shoot him. He felt it in the black despair that coiled in his stomach, threatening to strike, to sink its venomous teeth into his chest and stop his heart.

There was work to be done, and he was going to do it. He would just take a page from O'Flaherty's playbook.

The best way to hide, Eva had said, was not to hide at all. Angelo pulled on a worn pair of trousers and a work shirt that he still had from his time in the hillside parish. Priests were required to wear a cassock when they left their homes, but there had been plenty of work to do inside the crumbling rectory and the ancient church, and he'd worn out a pair of trousers and several shirts in the process. He removed his prosthetic and pinned up the trouser leg so that it was obvious to anyone looking at him that it was missing. Monsignor Luciano had delivered his crutches with his possessions, and with his sleeves rolled, a cigarette hanging from his lip, three day's growth on his jaw, and a worn-out black cap, he looked like a young soldier, aged by war and injury, who had paid his dues and asked only to be left alone.

He would draw attention, and it would be met with either sympathy or a quick averting of the eyes. The Germans might ask for his papers, and he had some he could use, but more likely, he would be ignored. He put his cassock and his cross and a change of clothes in his satchel and looped it over his back, stuffing his real pass in one pocket and his fake pass in the other. He'd need the real one to get into the Vatican.

⌀

The majority of the Jews in the cattle car spoke French. French had been required in school, but Eva was rusty and she had to listen closely to understand. But she didn't need to speak fluent French to know what the man named Armand was attempting. He'd climbed up the side of the boxcar and was sawing at a bar with Eva's gold file. Through everything, the days at Via Tasso and the week at Borgo San Dalmazzo, Eva's file had never been discovered. When the man had asked if anyone had something that might work to cut through the bars, she'd offered it to him.

Armand had been at it all day, trading off with a boy of twelve or thirteen named Pierre who was with his mother, a woman named Gabriele. Gabriele had soaked her scarf in urine from the bucket in the corner, and when the men weren't sawing, Pierre worked it back and forth over the bar, using the corrosive liquid to weaken the metal where the man had attempted to cut through with the file. Armand braced his feet against the side of the car and pulled, with all his weight and strength, against the bar he'd been laboring to weaken.

"It's going to break! I can feel it!" he yelled, triumphant. With a mighty yank he bore down and the bar came free at the top. He grabbed the severed end and hung from it, bending the bar back, creating an opening about a foot wide and a foot tall. He was a very thin man, but he was going to have a difficult time getting through.

"They shoot at the first jumpers," Eva heard the man telling the boy who'd helped him all day and all night long. "So I will go first."

"You can't do this! I am responsible for everyone in this wagon." The protester was a heavier-set man with a bolero perched on his head. "If you jump, I will be punished. *We* will be punished." The man spread his arm to include everyone else, and a woman spoke up from behind him.

"You will die! Someone jumped when we were being shipped to San Dalmazzo. His clothes caught as he was jumping, and he was pulled under. We saw the blood and the strip of fabric hanging from the window when we got off the train."

"We are going to Bergen-Belsen! There is no need to take this risk," another man argued.

Armand could only shake his head in disgust.

"Bergen-Belsen is a labor camp," Armand argued. "Hard labor! And we have done nothing wrong. You act as if being sent to a work camp is our due."

The voices of protest rose again, urging him to think of others.

"No! I am jumping. I would rather die now than die slowly," he shouted. He scrabbled up the side of the car once more, and Eva watched with all the others as he squirmed and wiggled through the small window, trying to get his shoulders to fit. He had just managed to clear his upper body when the sound of shooting commenced. People screamed, and Armand's legs jerked wildly and then went limp. He hung, still wedged in the hole he'd worked so hard to create.

Another man pulled him down. A portion of Armand's head was missing, and the rest was covered in blood, obscuring his face entirely. He was dead. One woman began to weep, but most of the passengers lapsed into silence, careful not to look at the man who had risked it all and died for his efforts.

"Where are they shooting from?" Eva spoke up quietly. "The Germans. Where are they? We are on a moving train. I don't understand."

As much as they would like their prisoners to believe it, the Germans were not all powerful. They did not look down from on high, from the heavens, plucking lives from the earth like God. Instead of scaring her, the shooting made her angry.

"They have a lookout, a guard, and a roving spotlight on each end of the train, in the engine and in the caboose. Wait until the light passes over and then push yourself out. Feetfirst. Not headfirst." The woman named Gabriele spoke up.

"So if you can wiggle through the opening quickly enough, you have a better chance?" Eva hoped she was asking the question correctly. She garbled some of her words and put a vowel on the end of everything—she was *italiana*, after all, but they seemed to understand.

Gabriele nodded. She was holding her son's hand and they were conferring quietly. The boy didn't want to jump anymore. He was understandably afraid that he or his mother would be picked off by the German watch.

"Climb down the side and make your way to the couplings between cars, where you won't be as easily seen. It will also give you the opportunity to turn around and jump outward. Cover your head and roll when you hit the ground. Then stay down. Stay flat. Don't start running until the train has passed, and then wait a bit so the man on the caboose doesn't see you and shoot," Gabriele told her son.

"How do you know this?" Eva asked.

Gabriele shook her head. "I don't. It is just what makes sense to me. I've thought about it nonstop since the first train."

"Do you know where we are?"

"We're in Switzerland, I think. But we may have already crossed into Germany. We need to jump soon. Otherwise, we will be deep into Germany. The deeper, the worse off we'll be."

"I'm not doing it. I'm not doing it. It is too risky," Pierre cried.

"Where will you go?" Eva interrupted. The woman soothed her son and answered softly.

"We are Belgian. We are going to try to get back home. The Germans are pulling back. We think we will be safe if we can just get home. We fled to France when Hitler invaded."

"What happened?"

"The Italian army left—they were actually the reason we stayed safe so long—and the Germans moved into the sector the Italians had once controlled. People were rounded up. My husband was detained and deported. Pierre and I stayed hidden for five more months. But in February, we were discovered. We were put on a train for the transit camp, and we've been waiting there ever since for a group large enough to transport."

"Please, Maman. We don't have to do this. We are strong. We will be all right in a camp," Pierre pleaded with his mother.

"No, Pierre. It is our only chance to go home," Gabriele said firmly, holding his gaze. "You have to jump, and you *will* jump, just like we planned. And you will get to Belgium. You will live, Pierre."

He nodded, but his eyes filled with tears that spilled down his cheeks. He embraced his mother fiercely, and she kissed his cheeks and held him for a brief moment before pushing him toward the window.

He climbed up obediently. No one protested this time. No one tried to make him feel guilty or responsible. They just watched morosely.

Pierre was much smaller than Armand, but maneuvering to get his legs out the small opening first, balanced on the lip of the window, was a feat in itself. He waited, watching for the light. When it swept past, he slid out the window. He didn't hesitate or look back, and with just a brief snag, his shoulders cleared and his head disappeared over the side. They could see his fingertips clinging, then they were gone too. There were no accompanying shots.

Gabriele prayed and wept vocally. Then she turned to Eva.

"Now it's your turn."

"Gabriele. You have to go. Pierre is waiting for you," Eva urged. "He made it. He must have."

"I can't do it. I'm not strong enough or agile enough to survive it. I know it, and Pierre knows it. It is why he didn't want to jump."

"You have to try! Your son will be frantic."

"You go," Gabriele insisted again. "You jump. And stay with my boy. Help him get home."

Eva could only shake her head. "No! You can't do that to him."

"I had no choice. I want him to live." She pushed Eva toward the window. "We have to hurry. The train is moving quickly! You won't be able to find him! The distance grows every second we delay."

"But . . ." Eva protested, thinking of the boy in the dark, waiting for his mother. Gabriele turned on her with fierce eyes, her fingers cutting into Eva's arm.

"*S'il vous plaît*. Please. I've done what I can to save him. Please help me. Save yourself, and help my son."

"I will help you up," someone offered, tugging on Eva's sleeve. It was a middle-aged man with a small child and a wife heavy with pregnancy. They wouldn't be jumping. Eva hesitated once more.

"Go!" Gabriele said, and Eva could only nod helplessly as the desperate mother imparted instructions in an urgent whisper. "Go to my husband's aunt in Bastogne. She will take you and Pierre. She will keep you safe until the war is over. Tell Pierre I love him, and I am proud of him. I will fight, and I will live. And we will be together again. All of us. Someday."

The man who'd offered to help Eva linked his fingers together and braced his feet, creating a step. Eva put her foot in his hands, and he bent his knees and launched her upward, giving her the lift and momentum needed to grasp the lip of the little window with one hand and the remaining bar with the other. She didn't wait for courage or even to see if she was clear to go. She went out the window headfirst. Just like in her dream. She was still clinging to the bar with her left hand, and the action swung her around, her legs pinwheeling for purchase, a shriek on her lips. She hung from the bar for an eternal second before her toes found the edge of the cattle car.

A shot rang out and then another, whizzing above her head. With all her might, Eva let go and pushed away from the train with the balls of her feet, turning as she flew, weightless for a heartbeat, contorting herself like a circus performer. "Slide into home!" Angelo had said when they played baseball. "Slide, Eva, slide!"

She slid through the air, parallel with the ground, flying toward home base. Then she was tumbling and bending, end over end, head, buttocks, hands, back, side, knees, shoulder, stomach, back. Like a rug being beaten against the cobblestones, flapping and connecting, flapping and connecting. And then she was still, lying on her back, staring up at a sky filled with dazzling stars. There was no air in her lungs, and she fought to inhale, unable to reinflate her diaphragm fast enough.

But she'd done it. She imagined Angelo throwing his arms out to the sides and yelling, "Safe!" the way he used to do when she slid home just like he'd taught her.

She smiled as she gasped and choked, sitting up to reach for a breath, ignoring Gabriele's second set of instructions, along with the first. She'd said, "Stay down until the train is gone." Eva hadn't even checked. But the train was slowly disappearing, just a black rectangle in the distance, growing smaller and smaller, quieter and quieter, as she watched. She wanted to lie back down and enjoy her home run for a minute more. She was starting to feel the raw scrape of her tumble, and she knew she would be bruised and sore, but for the first time since Angelo had been dragged from Via Tasso, she felt a glimmer of life. A spark. She wouldn't think about tomorrow. She wouldn't think about how alone she was. She would just celebrate the victory of escape. Of survival. And that was all.

"Maman! Maman!" She heard Pierre, calling and running toward her. He'd probably been running since he jumped, racing after the train, watching for his mother.

Eva rose gingerly to her feet, swaying as the confused blood in her body reoriented itself. It was dark, and Pierre was still a distance off. He was not yet aware it was she, and not Gabriele, who waited for him. She started to walk back toward him, dreading the moment he realized it was her.

She felt a sick flash of sympathy when he pulled up short.

"Where is my mother?" he gasped, out of breath from sprinting along the tracks, running after a train that had carried his *maman* away.

"She didn't jump, Pierre. I'm so sorry."

"Maman!" he called, panicked, and began running once more, racing across uneven ground, tripping and staggering, calling for his mother.

Eva pressed her hands against her aching heart and followed him. She didn't know what else to do. She didn't want to take away his hope. She didn't want to discourage him. But she knew Gabriele hadn't jumped. She'd loved her son enough to part with him if it could save his life. But Eva understood when Pierre sat down and buried his head in his hands. She understood his desolation. Life was small comfort when you had to live it alone.

"What if she decides to jump, and I've given up?" he mourned.

"We can wait here for a while. If she jumped, she will walk back this way," Eva suggested.

"What if she jumped and she's hurt, lying down there somewhere beside the tracks?" He sounded so young and lost.

"We will listen to see if she calls to you," she soothed softly.

He nodded despondently, and they waited, side by side, for a call that didn't come. Finally, Eva could bear the silence no longer. She was cold and sore, and there were trees in every direction. She had no idea which way to start walking.

"Pierre, do you recognize any of this? Do you have any idea where we might be?" she asked gently.

"It is north to Bergen-Belsen. Maman told me the tracks lead north." He pointed in the direction the train had just gone, then pointed straight in front of him. "We were going to go west. West is Belgium. That was our plan."

"There is nothing for me at home," Eva said. There was nothing for her anywhere, but she pushed the thought out of her mind. She would grieve later. Now she had to survive. "I will go with you to Belgium. Your mother says you have an aunt in Bastogne. She said she would come for you there when the war is over."

The boy nodded and brightened a little, slightly reassured that he wasn't completely alone in the world.

"I hope we're still in Switzerland," he mused. "If we are, we will be fine. We can go anywhere and ask for help and directions. But first we need to figure out where we are. The sun is coming up. I'm going to climb a tree and see what's beyond the forest. We can always walk south along the tracks if I can't see anything. Maman said the tracks will lead to a town."

His mother had prepared him to be alone. It was obvious. Eva nodded and waited for him to scramble up a nearby tree. It wasn't long before he was calling down to her excitedly.

"There is a road. I see a road. We will walk to it and see if there are any signs so we can figure out where we are."

Pierre had to climb another tree before they finally emerged from the forest and came upon the road, but they were in luck. There was a sign, but their luck was short-lived. The sign said, "Frankfurt 10 km."

They were in Germany.

28 March, 1944

Confession: I've broken my vows and I feel no remorse.

Eva told me once there were two things she knew for sure. One was that no one knows the nature of God. No one. And the other thing she knew for sure was that she loved me. I find I am reduced to those same assurances. I love Eva. I will always love Eva. And as for the rest? I only know that I know nothing at all.

Many will seek to tell me what God's will is. But nobody knows. Not really. Because God is quiet. Always. He is quiet, and my anguish is so intense, so incredibly loud, that right now I can only do my will and hope that somehow, it aligns with his.

Angelo Bianco

CHAPTER 23
CROSSROADS

The blank pages in Eva's journal haunted Angelo. She'd been snatched up, whisked away, stolen. She'd been taken from him, and her story wasn't finished—he wouldn't let it be—so he would keep writing until she could pick up where she left off.

He recorded his first entry the day he returned to the Vatican on crutches, dressed as a civilian, looking every bit like a man who had narrowly escaped death—multiple times. He'd been hustled into Monsignor O'Flaherty's office, and Monsignor Luciano was called as well.

"You look like you've been through hell," Monsignor O'Flaherty said, tipping Angelo's chin up so he could stare into his badly bruised face. "More than three hundred men were pulled from the prisons and off the streets. No one knows what happened to them. Then we got word that you were alive. Beaten but alive. What happened to you? Where did they take you? And where are the other men?"

"Everyone is dead," Angelo whispered.

"Dear God!" O'Flaherty gasped.

"Where?" Monsignor Luciano cried.

"They took us to the Fosse Ardeatine. They took the men into the cave, five at a time, and killed them with a shot to the back of the head, one after the other. Toward the end, one of the German soldiers sneaked me out through another tunnel. He saved my life. He took other lives, but he saved mine. He didn't want to kill a priest." Angelo stopped, the weight of the memory suddenly more than he could carry. "The soldiers didn't want to do it. Lieutenant Colonel Kappler sent cases of cognac to the caves to loosen them up so they could perform." His voice was bitter, and the horror continued to rise in him like a tidal wave. He closed his eyes and focused on breathing, focused on the here and now, on Monsignor O'Flaherty's hand on his shoulder.

"It is a miracle that you are alive," Monsignor Luciano whispered. "Praise God."

"I am grateful for my life, Monsignor," Angelo said softly. "But it is very hard for me to praise God in this moment. I lived. But three hundred thirty-five others did not. I feel more guilt than anything. I lived, hundreds died, and Eva is gone."

"I have tried to discover where the train was headed, Angelo. All I know is that Eva was on it," Monsignor O'Flaherty offered after a short silence.

"She is young, and she is strong," Monsignor Luciano said, trying to comfort him. "She will be all right."

Angelo bit back a curse. Monsignor Luciano could be incredibly blind and stupid sometimes.

"You can't come back to the apartment, Angelo. You will stay here at the Vatican until Rome is liberated," Luciano continued as if the matter were resolved.

"I will continue on until Rome is liberated, until the people I am responsible for no longer have to hide," he agreed softly.

"And then?" Monsignor O'Flaherty asked, clearly sensing there was more.

"I no longer want to be a priest. I have broken my vows," he said with finality.

He'd broken them willingly. Intentionally. Angelo had taken a vow of obedience, and he'd been anything but obedient. He'd taken a vow of celibacy, and he'd made love to Eva. The only vow he'd kept was that of poverty. But maybe he'd broken that one too. He'd been greedy for time with Eva. Greedy for her touch, her kisses, her love. She'd offered them time and time again, and he'd resisted her, rejected her. Refused her. Until the day he hadn't, and he'd taken her love and her kisses and her touch, and she'd made him a wealthy man, rich in love and promise and possibility. And he'd only wanted more. More. More.

That was what haunted him. He could have had a lifetime with her, and he'd squandered it. He didn't feel remorse that he'd broken his vows. He was remorseful that he hadn't broken them sooner. He should never have made them in the first place. When he told the monsignors how he felt, Monsignor O'Flaherty quietly listened, but Monsignor Luciano grew angry.

"You have broken your vows, but you have been ordained. Sin can be forgiven. You don't just stop being a priest because you sin. You have been ordained—indelibly changed—and you can't be unordained. You know this. You are God's. You don't belong to yourself anymore, Angelo. You don't belong to Eva! You are God's," Monsignor Luciano repeated emphatically, thumping his chest as if God himself resided beneath the cloth of his robes.

"I am Eva's," Angelo said quietly. "In my heart, I am Eva's."

"But she is gone!" Monsignor Luciano shouted.

"She is not gone. She is still here!" Angelo cried, and it was his turn to thump his chest. "She is still here inside me, and I am still hers. I will always be hers."

"Does loving Eva mean you can't love God?" Monsignor Luciano said after a long silence. His anger was gone, his voice subdued, his face haggard. But Angelo was committed to answering honestly, even if it hurt his old mentor.

"No. But I would ask you the same thing. Can I only serve him if I'm a priest? If I'm Catholic? I don't believe that anymore, Monsignor. I've seen too much. I want to do the right things for the right reasons. Not because someone will judge or someone else will wonder. Not because of tradition or pressure. Not because I'm afraid or embarrassed to do anything else. And not because it's what people expect. I want to do his will. But that is what I struggle with most, knowing what his will really is. Not his will according to the Catholic Church, but *his* will."

"We need you, Angelo. Rome needs you. The refugees need you. This church . . . needs you," Monsignor O'Flaherty said.

Angelo could only shake his head. "I have put Eva last for too long. *She* needs me. She needs me to love her enough not to give up on her."

"Tell me this. Is it that you don't want to be a priest, or is it that you want Eva more?" Monsignor O'Flaherty asked.

"I want Eva more," Angelo said honestly.

"And if Eva . . . doesn't survive. What then?" Monsignor Luciano asked.

"I can't think that way, Monsignor. I won't."

"I'm not asking you to give up. I'm asking you to continue on in your duties. You are a priest. That has not changed. And if Eva survives, if she returns to you, then we can talk about leaving the clerical life, about laicization," Monsignor Luciano coaxed.

"I'm not going to wait for her to come back. I'm going to find her," Angelo said.

"You can't simply shrug off your ordination, Angelo. You know this. It is permanent," Monsignor Luciano declared with finality.

Angelo ran shaking hands through his hair, despair and fatigue bowing his back and fraying his nerves.

"Then I am absolved?" he asked wearily.

"You are not repentant," Monsignor Luciano barked.

Angelo searched his heart. Was he repentant? No. He wasn't. "I seek your forgiveness—both of you—for disappointing you, for not being who you want me to be. But I am not sorry for the way I feel or for my actions."

"Then you are not absolved," Monsignor Luciano shot back.

"You are not absolved," Monsignor O'Flaherty concurred softly. "But you can continue with your duties. I forgive you. Wholeheartedly. And I can attest that if you ask, God will forgive you as well. He understands, Angelo. You know that he does. You feel it. He is giving you his peace."

Monsignor O'Flaherty's loving forgiveness, spoken in the soft burr of his Irish accent, had Angelo fighting back tears of exhausted surrender. His anger and rebellion left him suddenly, and he fought to remain upright. He was so tired. So incredibly tired.

"We have a room prepared for you. It isn't much. But you need to rest. Tomorrow will come soon enough. We need supplies. Without Eva's gold, we are low on resources." O'Flaherty sighed.

Angelo reached for his makeshift knapsack and opened it, upending it on the thick rug, revealing what was inside. It was full of gold—chains, bracelets, trinkets, tiepins, and rings.

"The Saturday Eva played at the gala, she took her empty violin case to work, and she filled it to the brim with gold. When she went home to dress for the event, she emptied her case and gave the gold to Mother Francesca. She was worried something would happen that night, and she wouldn't be able to take any more. She was right. Something did happen."

"She was recognized." It wasn't a question. O'Flaherty had heard this part of the story through his own channels.

"Yes. The wife of Rome's chief of police told Greta von Essen that Eva was an accomplished violinist from Florence. A Jew. The captain's wife then told her husband. She could have stayed quiet. She was Eva's friend, and she betrayed her."

"Yes. She did. But maybe she will be able to redeem herself. She is a Catholic. Quite devout, unlike her husband. She goes to Mass at a church on Via Rasella. She was there when the bomb set by the partisans killed the German police." Monsignor O'Flaherty stopped and rubbed at his jaw, thinking. "Father Bartolo is her pastor. He told me she's been there every day for the last two weeks. Maybe she can help you with the answers you need."

Eva stared at the road sign in horrified silence until Pierre spoke up, falsely cheerful.

"It could be worse. I actually know where we are. Bastogne is directly west of Frankfurt," Pierre offered. "Almost a straight path that way." He pointed at the road that intersected the highway they stood beside. There wasn't a soul in sight, which was both encouraging and frightening. The sky was lightening with the coming dawn, and they had nowhere to hide and no place to go, with only the clothes on their backs and the slim gold file Eva had tucked back in her shoe.

"How far?" Eva was trying to remember her geography and failing miserably. She was comforted that Pierre seemed to know his.

"Not far at all . . . by train. Papà used to go to Frankfurt on business all the time. Germans make the best toys. He would always bring me something back."

"How far, Pierre?" He was clearly stalling.

"About two hundred and fifty kilometers," Pierre said quietly.

Two hundred and fifty kilometers. More than one hundred and fifty miles across German occupied territory.

"And how far is Switzerland? Do you know that?"

He shook his head. "No. Not exactly. But it's just as far, if not farther."

Eva sank down beside the road and laid her head on her knees. Pierre sat down beside her, and neither could find the energy for further conversation. They watched in silent despondence as the sun rose in the east, breaking out in hopeful radiance above the tree line.

"Angelo," Eva whispered, watching the spread of light that defied her heavy heart. The beauty made her long for him. "What should I do? What would you do?"

"Who are you talking to?" Pierre asked softly. She'd spoken in Italian, a language he didn't speak.

"The sky, I guess. That is where all my loved ones are."

He nodded as if he understood.

"What is your name?" he asked suddenly.

Eva laughed, just a brief huff of incredulity. The poor boy didn't even know her name. She was a complete stranger. And she was all he had.

"Eva Rosselli." She stuck out her hand and he clasped it in his, shaking it firmly. His fingers were as cold as hers.

"Pierre LaMont." He added his surname to the name she already knew.

"Pierre LaMont. That's not a very Jewish name."

"No. My father wasn't Jewish. Just my mother. But they took my father anyway."

I see you trembling there. How much it cost you, loving me. How much it cost you, loving me.

"They took my father too," Eva said, ignoring the haunting lyric that played in her head. Love often had a terrible cost.

"Was he the one you were talking to?" Pierre didn't seem to find it strange that she was conversing with the sky.

"No. I was talking to Angelo."

"Who is Angelo?"

"Angelo is . . . was the man I wanted to marry. I loved . . . love him very much."

"And what did Angelo say?" Pierre asked seriously, as if a response were entirely plausible. It made a lump rise in her throat and tears brim in her eyes.

"He didn't answer," she said, her voice choked.

"What do you think he would say, if he could?"

"He would tell me to pray. If Angelo were here, he would pray," she supplied immediately.

"We can do that. And then what?"

"If Angelo were here . . ." Eva thought for a moment, and then the answer came as clearly as if a voice spoke directly in her ear. "If Angelo were here, he would tell me to find a church."

Pierre rose to his feet and held out his hand. She let him pull her up, and she brushed at her backside, as if the little bit of dirt and debris she'd gathered sitting at the side of the road could make her filthy skirt look any worse. Pierre walked ahead to the crossroads and turned west.

"Eva, look!" Pierre stopped walking and pointed. "There. Can you see it?"

She hurried to his side and gazed in amazement. He was pointing at a thin white steeple rising above a small cluster of picturesque houses in the distance.

"*Merci*, Angelo," Pierre said simply.

"*Merci*, Angelo," Eva whispered. "Now let us find a priest just like you."

∽◎∾

She was a pretty woman, tall and voluptuous, easily as tall as her husband. But for all her Amazonian beauty, Greta von Essen was as timid and as frightened as a mouse. Angelo had watched her walk into the church, genuflect before the cross, and light a candle. He'd watched her briefly pray and then walk to the confessional, where she'd stayed for several minutes before walking out again and heading for the large doors at the back of the church. That is where he cut her off, standing directly in her path. He wasn't wearing his cassock—he wore his work clothes and an old cap—and she glanced at him nervously.

She looked away, but her eyes returned almost immediately. She tipped her head to the side, narrowing her eyes and pursing her lips, as if she couldn't place him. He saw the moment she realized who he was.

She turned and started walking swiftly in the other direction, toward an exit just left of the apse. Angelo felt a flash of fury and, without thinking, he was pursuing her, almost running, loping awkwardly to overtake her.

"Stop!" he ordered as she picked up speed. "I only want to talk to you. You owe me that much."

She stopped abruptly, as if following orders was second nature. She turned slowly and eyed him with trepidation.

"My husband said you were dead." Her voice was accusing, as if the fact that he wasn't was somehow dishonest on his part.

"I should be. Did he tell you how I supposedly died?"

She shook her head no.

"He wouldn't. It wouldn't make you love or admire him, I promise you that. Did he tell you what happened to Eva?"

She nodded sharply and looked down at the pocketbook in her hands. She was shaking.

"Tell me." He lowered his voice and strove to use a lighter tone.

"She was deported."

"Where to?"

"I don't know."

"You didn't care enough to ask?" His voice was gentle, but she still flinched.

"She lied to me!"

"How? How did she lie?"

"She didn't tell me she was Jewish."

"That's because you couldn't handle the truth. Clearly. Look what happened to Eva . . . to me, when you found out."

"She told me you were her brother." Another accusation that had nothing to do with Greta, but one she had undoubtedly used to rationalize what she'd done.

"I'm not her brother."

"So she told two lies."

"Your husband is a murdering bastard, and you are worried about lies told to preserve life?" He fought to keep his voice level.

"Are you even a priest?" she asked, her voice dripping with scorn.

"Yes."

"Not a very good one," she retorted fiercely.

"No. Not a very good one, though I've always done the best I could," he said honestly, and realized suddenly that it was true. He'd always done his best with the strength and resources he had.

"My husband said you were in love with Eva." Again, derision, as if his love were incredibly distasteful.

"I am in love with her. I have always loved her. And I'm going to find her." He held her gaze, unwavering, unapologetic.

"I knew there was someone. You are the boy from home. The one she wouldn't talk about."

He nodded once, and she deflated before his eyes. When she looked at him again there was no more defensiveness, no more contempt. There was only remorse.

"I didn't want to tell Wilhelm. I cared about Eva. But I knew if he discovered it some other way, if he found out I knew, he would hurt me. Frau Caruso knew, and it was only a matter of time before she talked to others. The secret was just too good. Too rich."

"I need to find out where Eva was taken. Can you find out?"

"I don't know," she whispered, shaking her head. She seemed to fall back to helplessness when she was scared, and he guessed Greta von Essen was scared most of the time.

"Find out where she was taken, and we will do our best to get you out of Rome if you need help doing so. You need to go home, Signora."

This brought her head up. "Why? Aren't the Germans winning? The Americans have been defeated at Anzio Beach . . . haven't they?"

Angelo shook his head. He knew it was only a matter of time. God would not be quiet forever. "They've been stalled. But America has the firepower, the manpower, and most important, they have the right on their side. The kind of evil I have seen has to be stopped. This war isn't about two equal but opposing forces who disagree. This war is about right and wrong, good and evil. And evil must be stopped. It *will* be stopped. And people like you will be caught in the cross fire when that happens."

"If I find out where she was sent, how will I get word to you?" she said quietly, not even arguing about good and evil, right and wrong. She had to know on some level. She had to.

"Tell Father Bartolo. He will tell me."

10 May, 1944

Confession: I don't know what to do.

Eva's been sent to Bergen-Belsen. I felt immediate relief that it wasn't Auschwitz, and then I realized I didn't even know where Bergen-Belsen was. Greta von Essen came through with the information. Father Bartolo said she was sure, that she'd seen the transport records. I don't know how she accomplished that, but I couldn't ask. A few days ago, Greta von Essen left Rome in the company of a group of nuns returning to Germany from an Easter pilgrimage to the Vatican. Monsignor O'Flaherty arranged it.

Northern Germany. Bergen-Belsen. I have a destination. But it might as well be the moon.

The German police in Rome are growing more vicious and desperate as the days go by. A surprise raid on a monastery in the San Lorenzo district of Rome has resulted in the arrest and seizure of three monks and a dozen foreign Jews. One boy tried to escape and was gunned down in front of his parents, who at that point threw themselves on his inert form and were shot as well. The monks were imprisoned, along with the rest of the captured refugees.

We were tipped off by a local Fascist official that a raid would be carried out at an abandoned villa south of Rome where fifty Jewish orphans had been hidden and watched over by an order of Capuchin monks. We beat the raid by an hour, scattering the children among village homes until the Germans left. When they did, we returned the children to the villa and to the care of the monks. We are all praying the Germans don't go back.

It is a game of cat and mouse, priest and prey, and it's a wonder more aren't breaking under the stress. But we have a purpose and none of us thinks beyond the moment, beyond the day. We scramble and pray and sleep when we can.

Temperatures are warming and people in the southernmost parts of the city, near the catacombs and the caves of Ardeatine, are starting to complain about a smell. The dead are making themselves known. The anger and fear in the city, the desperation of the occupying forces, and the ticktock of the end seem to permeate the air with the same stench of death. None of us will be able to hold on much longer. But for Eva's sake I will. And wherever she is, she just has to hold on too.

Angelo Bianco

CHAPTER 24
THE AMERICANS

When members of America's 5th Army finally captured Rome on June 4, 1944, there was very little fanfare. The Germans simply left. The long red banners and the Nazi flags were removed from the headquarters on Via Tasso. The homes they'd requisitioned were vacated. The political prisoners were abandoned. They simply retreated. Some said it was the Pope's influence, some said it was a strategic regrouping. A few said it was respect for Rome's considerable historic and artistic significance, but whatever the reason, when the time came, they left.

Then the people waited with breaths held, ears peeled. The American planes had dropped leaflets the day before, urging civilians to stay indoors, to stay out of the way in case the conflict grew heated. But there was no fighting. No bombing. Just the quiet fall of leaflets and the dawn of a clear June morning.

When the first American trucks and tanks rolled into town, people didn't stay inside. They danced in the streets. It was a strange sight, really. Italians, who had allied themselves with a ruthless dictator and fought and died beside Germany's sons, were welcoming the Americans into their capital city. When German tanks and troops had descended on Rome a mere nine months before, people had died trying to keep them out. It said a great deal about the feelings of the Italian people, about their resentment for being drafted into a war very few of them wanted, made to fight and die for preposterous goals and ridiculous men.

Angelo could only watch with bittersweet relief as the parade of military vehicles clattered along cobblestone roads and people wept with jubilation. Mario and his little family, the nuns of Santa Cecilia, and even Monsignor Luciano and his sister stood and greeted the American troops, who were smiling and waving like movie stars, as they rolled into the city. For Rome, the war was over. For the clergy, for the resistance, and for the Jews in hiding, this day was a staggering victory. They had survived.

Most of them.

But some had not. Some still would not. The war was not over for those who'd been taken. It was not over for Eva and for the numberless Jews still imprisoned in camps in the north and in the east. It was not over for the Allied soldiers who would fight on, pushing the Germans into further retreat.

Two days later, on June 6, Angelo and a small group of priests at the Vatican gathered around a radio as the BBC declared that "D-Day had come."

"Early this morning, the Allies began the assault on the northwestern face of Hitler's European Fortress," the announcer reported. "Under the command of General Eisenhower, Allied Naval Forces, supported by strong air forces, began landing Allied armies on the northern coast of France."

Throughout the following days, countries aligned against Hitler waited with nervous hearts and shaking hands, listening for updates and reports. The Germans only suffered a thousand casualties that first day.

The Allies suffered ten times that, but by June 12, all five of the beach-heads of Normandy were linked and in Allied control, giving them the foothold they needed to run Germany out of France.

From Normandy, Paris was a straight shot east, and when Paris was liberated in late August, Angelo implemented the only plan he'd been able to devise. A soldier with the 5th Army, a major who'd spent the last year in Italy, had given him some advice.

"The 5th is being split up. Some of us are being sent into France. The war in Italy is going nowhere, Father. We've been here for too damn long, fighting our way up one hill only to face another right behind it. We've taken Rome, but if things continue as they have for the last nine months, it's going to continue to be a slog, and we sure as hell won't be getting out of Italy until Germany surrenders, or we do. It's a battle of inches here. If you want to get to this girl, your best bet is to get into France and follow the Americans into Germany from that direction."

Angelo told Monsignor O'Flaherty his decision and was given his blessing, along with a reminder that he was "still a priest." He had not been laicized. He would not be given permission to marry. That kind of permission had to come from the Pope himself, and it was never granted. If he wanted to marry Eva, he would have to do so outside of the Catholic Church. But Monsignor O'Flaherty embraced him any-way and told him that when he found Eva, he should bring her back to Rome so he could see her again.

The American army had moved into the Hassler Hotel—known by locals as the Villa Medici—making the newly renovated site their headquarters for the duration of their stay. Angelo found himself there, dressed in his cassock, his cane tucked out of sight, waiting to speak with the commander of the 5th Army who had taken the city two months before. He had taken the major's advice. He was there to enlist in whatever capacity they needed him. His only goal was to get to Germany.

The hotel was filled with memories of Eva, even though, in its current state, it looked nothing like it had the night Eva played her violin for a room full of the enemy. He could see her so clearly, resplendent in her black gown, her slim neck bowed over her instrument, a sparkle at her ears and a gleam in her eyes as she looked at him. He'd held one of those earrings in the palm of his hand that night as he'd contemplated the future, leaning over the sink in her hotel room, warm from the bath and cold from the evening's events. His nerves had been shot from the raid, his emotions running high. He had felt the shift, the realignment of his priorities, and as he held the earring in his hand, Eva sleeping in the next room, he had been heartsick with love and soul weary with waiting.

"Father? What can I do for you?" A trim man in a neat uniform with slicked-back hair and a cigarette clenched in his teeth waved him forward from his office door. His "office" was the large coatroom where Eva had told Angelo about the suspected raid. Angelo stood and followed the commander inside, trying not to reveal his limp and probably making it more noticeable for his efforts. He decided to get right to the point, and after sitting down across from the commander, jumped right in.

"I've come to see if it would be possible to be of service to your men."

"We have chaplains, Father, but we could always use a few more. Is that what you mean?"

"I've lived in Italy since I was eleven years old, but I'm an American. I speak fluent German and Italian and passable French. I could be an interpreter as well as a chaplain."

"Why? The army doesn't pay well. And you don't have to do this."

"I *do* have to do this. Plus, the priesthood doesn't pay well either. That isn't why most of us do what we do, is it, Commander?"

"You got that right, Padre. But what are *your* reasons?"

"A Jewish girl, a girl who is very important to me, was deported and sent to a concentration camp in northern Germany almost five months ago. I intend to find her. I was told the best way to do that would be to follow the American army into Germany. I will serve in any capacity you wish, just as long as you'll send me where I have the best chance of getting to Germany the quickest."

"You'll have to stay for the duration. Even if you, by some miracle, find this girl. You'll have to see it through to the end. You won't be able to quit."

"I understand. My only goal is to find her and get her to safety. I will fulfill my commitments."

"Father O'Flaherty said you were determined."

Angelo started at the mention of the monsignor.

"He sent me a message, said you'd be coming to see me. He managed to hide several of our downed pilots from the Germans. We owe him. He told me I could repay him by helping you."

Angelo could only nod, humbled by the gesture. Leave it to O'Flaherty to do whatever he could.

"What's with the leg? You limp."

"It's a childhood ailment. I can outwalk everyone I know. I always carry my own weight, Commander. You won't need to worry about me."

The commander laughed and sat forward in his chair. "I believe you, Father. Sounds to me like you have a guardian angel on your shoulder. Monsignor O'Flaherty told me about the massacre at Ardeatine. That won't go unpunished. I promise you that."

"Many good men were murdered that day," Angelo said softly.

"Many good men have been lost in this damn war. It's what keeps me going. I'll do my best to help you find that girl. But I'm warning you, it's going to be a long, hard road yet. The Germans aren't done fighting. And as long as they're still kicking, we have to fight too."

"I don't know what else to do. I can't simply take a train into Germany and demand her release. But I can't sit here either. I have to go. The only thing keeping me standing is the belief that she is there. And if I can just get to her in time . . . if she can hold on until I get to her, then that's what I'm going to do."

The commander took a deep drag off his cigarette and released the smoke slowly as he eyed Angelo. Then he nodded, as if he'd made up his mind and was at ease with his decision. "We have an army transport leaving for France in three days. You'll be on it. We'll find enough work to keep you busy, and you'll probably wish you'd never signed on. The 20th Armored Division just arrived in the south of France. They'll be working their way up quickly to the border between France and Germany. That's the best I can do for you, Father. Godspeed."

◯◯◯

"I'm coming with you," Mario said firmly.

"Mario, no. No, you aren't." Angelo had walked down the steps of St. Peter's Basilica to see Mario waiting just beyond the gates, an army duffel bag on his back and determination in his eyes.

"I'm a doctor. They will take me. I don't speak very good English, but you do. You're an American, after all. Together, we can do this. I'm a doctor; you're a medic. A spiritual medic. God's medic." He smiled and shrugged.

"Ah, yes. I'm saving souls right and left," Angelo said with a self-deprecating smile. His duties the last few months had been of the temporal nature. Food, shelter, safety. He hadn't performed any of the more sacred rites because he felt unworthy to do so, committed as he was to leaving the priesthood behind if he found Eva.

"I'm coming with you," Mario repeated.

"Mario, you have a wife and three children who have been through hell. You are finally free to resume your lives. They need you. You have to think of them."

"Giulia agrees with me. She and the children will stay at the convent, and I will send them my stipend every month. They are safe, and Giulia has help. I'm not a soldier. I won't be fighting. I will be saving lives and getting paid to do it. And if that fails, I'll join the Red Cross. I have spent the war hiding while my people are being slaughtered. This is my way of making a difference, of fighting back. I don't have a job—"

"You could find one! If something happened to you, Mario, I would never forgive myself. The world can't afford to lose any more Jewish men. The world can't afford to lose a man like you, period. Don't make me carry that weight," Angelo interrupted.

"If I don't come with you, I won't ever forgive myself. Eva Rosselli sat with her back to my door, her legs braced against the wall, while the Gestapo shot through it. She single-handedly saved my entire family. And she has been taken. Signora Donati, my neighbor, faced down men with machine guns to inform them that my apartment was empty, that no one lived there anymore. She was taken too. I've watched you put yourself at risk over and over. I've watched you scramble and maneuver and work to keep hundreds of Jews safe. You were beaten and sent to die, and you could have talked. You could have exposed us. But you didn't.

"I have been forced to let all of you sacrifice for me and my family. I had to. But not anymore. It's my turn. I intend to be there when those camps are liberated. It's my turn to save lives. I'm coming with you, Angelo. And you can't stop me."

13 December, 1944

Confession: I couldn't part with Eva's violin.

I have walked through France with a violin case on my back. Everyone asks me to play, and when I tell them I can't, they look at me like I've lost my mind. Maybe I have. I left everything else, including the three remaining journals, with the nuns at Santa Cecilia. But I couldn't leave her violin. Eva will want to play it again when I find her.

The soldiers think I'm a strange one. My clerical collar is confusing enough. I wear it with a standard-issue uniform instead of a cassock. All the chaplains dress like soldiers, for the most part. I think Mario told a few of them my story in an effort to quiet speculation, because now they all seem to know that the violin I can't play belongs to the girl I'm looking for. But Mario doesn't speak very good English, so who knows what rumors he may have started.

Still, the teasing has lessened considerably and everyone now calls me Father Angelo. A few of the guys call me Angel Baby, but nicknames are pretty standard around here and seem to communicate a certain amount of affection. In some ways, it's like being in the seminary again—only with guns, less food, and frozen blisters. On the bright side, having only one leg means only one case of trench foot.

There is a hymn that talks about rescuing "a soul so rebellious and proud as mine." It's a Protestant hymn my mother sang a long time ago. I heard a soldier singing it last night in the non-denominational church service I organized for the division. I don't mean to be sacrilegious, but I am convinced my rebellious soul is the only thing keeping me from defeat, and I don't want to be rescued from it.

It's been almost four months since I left Rome. Close to nine months since I saw Eva last. Now, without explanation, instead of continuing north into Germany, we are being sent east to Luxembourg, and it's all I can do not to abandon my unit and set off on my own. I can only pray Eva's soul is as rebellious as mine.

Angelo Bianco

CHAPTER 25
BELGIUM

The cold was relentless, and the cotton candy comparison made by a soldier was apt, but if the fog was like being immersed in white spun sugar, the cold was like living in a vat of ice cream with none of the sweetness and none of the pleasure. Rumors of the coldest winter on record were being bandied about, and Angelo was convinced it must be true. He may have been born in New Jersey, but he was acclimated to Florence and Rome, and though both were cold in winter, neither were the Ardennes. He'd never been so cold or miserable in his whole life. He did his best not to think of Eva in a camp in Northern Germany or the temperatures and conditions she would be enduring. The thought made him grit his teeth and avoid a word of complaint. He was making deals with God right and left. Keep Eva alive. Keep her safe, and he would suffer whatever he had to suffer in exchange.

But God didn't work that way. He didn't deal and he didn't yell. He didn't always make himself known. In fact, he rarely did. Angelo had had to faithfully look to find evidence of his existence. God was still quiet. Impossibly quiet. Just like the snow and the fog and the skies. He'd been quiet as Angelo had wandered, following the 20th Armored Division up through France, to the outskirts of Metz, where France, Luxembourg, and Germany came together, hoping against hope that they would continue up into Germany, forcing a cessation to war and a chance to make his way to the camp where Eva was held. But though Metz had been a victory for the Allies, it had not been enough to punch through and deliver a deathblow to the Reich. He and Mario had waited, Mario needing to go home, Angelo needing to press forward. And God had been endlessly quiet.

The Ardennes Forest was quiet too. Eerily so. It was known as the Ghost Front for the cold white mist that clung to the ground and for the silence that hadn't been penetrated by war. The troops had been talking about going home. The Ardennes front was the place divisions were sent when they'd taken too many casualties or they needed to rest up. It was eighty-five miles of forest, and the Americans were taken completely by surprise.

Just before dawn, on December 16, all that changed, as the sky was illuminated with floodlights and the silence was decimated by an artillery barrage. Behind it, a massive force of German troops poured across the eighty-five-mile front into Belgium under the cover of fog and foul weather.

Angelo's detachment had passed through Luxembourg, believing they were to be quartered there. But instead of stopping, like they'd initially thought, they'd been sent on to a town called Noville, in Belgium, with no idea of what their orders truly were. Angelo had discovered that that was army life for the men in uniform—the chaplains, the medics, and the soldiers. Someone pointed, and you marched. Maybe it was better that way, not knowing what you were in for, not knowing what was around the bend. Maybe sometimes it was better when God was quiet.

In Noville, the company they were assigned to had been told to keep the German 2nd Panzer Division from progressing. Nobody knew they were outmanned ten to one and way outgunned. Maybe that was better too, fighting without knowing the odds. Every man who could fire a gun, did, and the town was caught in a small-arms fight that lasted until the Tiger tanks were breathing down their necks, and everyone was told to retreat to Bastogne, three miles down the road.

"Bastogne is where everything intersects, boys," their commander told them. "It's the hub of a wheel, seven main roads converge there, and the Germans know they've got to have it if they want to control the area and keep pushing on into Antwerp, the biggest supply base for the Allied troops on the Western Front."

It wasn't an easy three-mile march. Instead, they'd been pinned down in ditches, taking fire from behind and stemming blood on injured soldiers with bullets whizzing over their heads, until the 101st Airborne had arrived, parachuting in to save them all at the last minute, helping the team stumble into Bastogne, only to fight again.

"It's gonna be bloody," their commander said. "We can't get any air support with the weather. It's gonna be man to man. Or Tiger tank to pop gun. Son of a bitch! It's like fighting in a freezer."

"We just gotta slow 'em down. Just make life hell for them until the weather clears and our boys in the sky can blow 'em away," the commander from the 101st had encouraged, and everyone had nodded and hunkered down.

Thankfully, the people of Bastogne had run from the town as word of the approaching Panzer Divisions started to spread through the countryside. They abandoned their sleepy village, pushing hastily packed carts loaded with all they could gather, most likely wondering who would be in charge when they returned. Some of the residents had already rehung their Nazi flags above their doors, just to hedge their bets. The evacuation made it easier to establish an aid station of sorts, and the unit assembled a makeshift hospital in the basement of a three-story building on the Rue Neufchâteau. A store sat on the main level with living quarters above, which the medics commandeered, while their frazzled unit billeted in an apartment house a few buildings down and across the street.

Constant shelling accompanied their days. Angelo and Mario made their way among the injured, along with the two volunteer nurses from the area and Jack Prior, the American doctor assigned to the division. They did the best they could with almost nothing—a few bandages, very little morphine, some sulfa pills, and plasma. The aid station in some old Belgian barracks a ways down the road, organized by the 101st Airborne Division, didn't have it any better. Gangrene was the biggest problem, and Dr. Prior wasn't a surgeon. The best hope was keeping the wounded alive long enough to evacuate them, which hadn't happened yet, and wouldn't happen unless the enemy could be pushed back.

By December 21, the town of Bastogne was completely surrounded by the Germans with the 101st and much of the 20th trapped inside. The soldiers started joking, "They've got us surrounded, poor bastards. No matter where we shoot, we're bound to hit one." "Poor bastards" became a rallying cry in the days to come.

On December 22, a German commander sent a letter to General McAuliffe threatening annihilation if Bastogne was not surrendered, to which a terse "Nuts!" was the only answer he received. The soldiers were laughing about it, and Angelo puzzled about the response for all of ten minutes, then shook his head and laughed too, supposing it was simply slang he didn't understand. He'd discovered he liked Americans and was proud to be one, if only by birth.

Reports of a massacre of almost one hundred American soldiers near the village of Malmedy—soldiers who had only a few days before found themselves surrendering to a Panzer Division—probably made it easy to refuse the Germans when they urged surrender. Angelo figured "Nuts" meant "You're crazy." That . . . or "Go to hell." Either worked. With divisions biting at the German flanks and the 101st refusing to surrender, the battle in Bastogne had gone on for almost a week.

Angelo did his best to be another pair of hands and to aid the dying physically and spiritually. He had started to think that he might make a decent doctor if he lived to see the end of the war, if he found Eva, and if they ever made it home. If he couldn't be a priest, he had to do something.

It was after dark on December 24, a Christmas Eve like no other in his memory, when an old woman came into the field station, asking for help for a village woman who had gone into labor.

Mario was in the middle of stitching a wound and Dr. Prior was stemming a hemorrhage. Mario looked around wildly for someone to assist the adamant woman. She was pulling at his arm, urging him, and chattering about pain and length of contractions and the baby being stuck.

"Angelo!" he called across the space. "There is a woman in labor not far from here. She needs help."

"Why didn't they evacuate with the rest of the city?" Angelo finished helping a wounded soldier sip some water and then moved toward Mario and the old woman.

"The mother was afraid of going into labor. Looks like she was right," Mario answered. The old woman had backed up, away from the blood, and her eyes were weary and desperate.

"I will go with her. You can't leave," Angelo agreed, trying not to think about what he might find.

"If she can, have her get on her hands and knees, Angelo. If the baby is face-first but hasn't entered the birth canal, sometimes this position will help it turn on its own." The instructions had Angelo drawing up short and reconsidering.

"Mario, I can't do this," Angelo said softly. "I'm not a doctor. I don't know the first thing about delivering babies, especially if the mother or child is in trouble."

"I know. But go, see what can be done, and if you can, bring her here. We can better help everyone if they're all in one place. Take the cart."

∽

The old woman kissed her rosary beads even as she walked and tugged, reminding Angelo of his *nonna* back in Florence. He pulled the cart to a house only three buildings from the aid station, and the woman picked her way up the icy steps. He followed her, treading just as carefully as she opened the front door and removed the scarf from her head, calling out to whomever was in the house.

"I've brought a priest," she hollered in French. "He was the only one they could spare."

She turned to Angelo, who kicked the snow from his mismatched footwear—a consequence of having a prosthetic leg with a permanent black boot—and shut the door behind him.

"She's been trying to walk, thinking that would help. I don't know what else to do. She's so exhausted, and it's been going on so long." The old woman looked ashamed, as if she, being a woman, should be of more help.

Slow steps, measured as if there was pain with each footfall, sounded on the landing above them, and Angelo raised his eyes to the top of the stairs. The woman's hands were pressed to her back, as if holding herself together, and her hair was a dark cloud of curling disarray around her thin shoulders, but Angelo's eyes went immediately to her stomach, which was enormous and made even bigger by the size of the girl who wielded it. She wore a droopy pink sweater around her shoulders and a loose black frock that had seen too many washings but was obviously chosen to fit over her burgeoning belly. Her feet were slim and bare, despite the cold, and her toenails, miraculously, were as pink as her sweater. Angelo wondered for two seconds how she had accomplished such a feat before his eyes rose to her face, and his world teetered and turned upside down. The woman was staring down at him like he had risen from the dead, a modern-day Lazarus come to visit.

"Eva?" he gasped.

One hand left her back and stretched toward the wall, as if she felt them closing in. She didn't question his presence but only stared as if she expected him to disappear as soon as she blinked, and her legs buckled dangerously.

He would never recall how he traversed the stairs, or even if he did. He must have flown, because he found himself standing before her, the stairs at his back, Eva slumped against the wall, shaking her head in disbelief.

"Eva." He said her name again, and then she was falling into his arms. For several breaths they stood with their arms locked around each other, and then Angelo was pulling away just enough to look at her again and make sure she was real. Her hands framed his face as her incredulous eyes traced his features. She kept saying his name, the word *Angelo* opening her lips and melding them more completely against his when he kissed her, first on the mouth and then everywhere else—cheeks, chin, nose, forehead—before seeking her lips once more.

"Eva!" A startled cry rose from the bottom of the stairs, making them pull apart briefly. The poor woman was clearly beside herself as she watched a stranger—a priest!—kissing her pregnant charge.

"This is my Angelo, Bettina," Eva cried, laughing and weeping simultaneously, as she continued to touch his face in disbelief. "This is my Angelo."

"Angelo? *Le père du bébé?*" Bettina gasped, and she immediately crossed herself again, his cleric's collar obviously confusing her. Eva must not have shared everything. Then the woman's shocked words penetrated Angelo's euphoric disbelief.

"The child's father?" he repeated, suddenly remembering why he'd been summoned in the first place. His hands fell to Eva's swollen abdomen, and his eyes followed. Then he was looking at her again, at her beautiful, weary face and her tear-filled eyes.

"Yes. The child's father," she whispered, her eyes never leaving his, and her breath caught and her hands clutched, and she was in his arms again as he held her through the pain of a labor he was wholly unprepared for.

"The contractions are deep and strong," she panted. "I've been in labor since yesterday, and I don't think it's progressing like it should."

"You need to get on your hands and knees," he urged, walking back into the room she'd obviously vacated. A fire was roaring in the grate, and water and towels and a bed made up with clean sheets were at the ready. Clearly, Bettina had done all she knew to do. Angelo walked Eva to the bed and helped her ease into a crawling position on her hands and knees. Her arms and legs wobbled in fatigue. She seemed extremely weak, and he could see why Bettina had gone for help.

"I have to go get Mario. This may work, but you're going to need a doctor," he said urgently.

"Mario?" Her voice rose in amazement. "Mario is here too? How can this be? Where did you come from, Angelo? I thought you were dead. They told me you were dead." The shock weakened her further, and her arms wobbled wildly.

"Shh. We have time for that. We have so much to talk about, but you need a doctor."

"Don't leave," Eva entreated, her eyes pleading even as she attempted to reach out a hand and swayed dangerously. "Please, Angelo. Please stay with me."

He felt it too, the foreboding sense that if they parted now, the fissure that had opened up and allowed them to step through time and distance and find one another, would close forever. He hesitated, knowing he needed Mario but unwilling to let Eva out of his sight.

"*J'y retournerais,*" Bettina volunteered from the doorway. The poor woman had just climbed to the top of the stairs. "I will go again."

"Madame!" Angelo called after her. "Tell Dr. Sonnino I've found Eva. He will come."

∽

But Mario didn't come. Bettina never returned either. Instead, the Luftwaffe parted the clearing December skies with screaming fire, and all at once the night was as bright as noon in July from the magnesium flares. Seconds later, a hellish shrieking pierced the air, and Angelo draped himself over Eva as the first bombs found their targets and the earth shook with their impact. The apartment trembled, but it hadn't been hit. Angelo braced as the screaming, whirring, shrieking began again, signaling another bomb was hurtling toward them.

"I love you, Angelo," Eva said in his ear, and he could only return the words, sheltering her the best he could as the world exploded around them. And still the building stood. Then the strafing began, a German bomber dropping low to pepper the area with machine-gun fire. The sound of shattering glass and strafing was punctuated by the screams and shouts of the survivors outside, and Eva and Angelo waited breathlessly, delivered from one trauma by the arrival of another.

"Angelo," Eva panted. "It's coming. The pain is different. There's pressure now. The baby is coming." He had braced Eva for as long as she could maintain the position on her hands and knees, and then eased her down to her side, letting her rest between rounds before agony twisted her up again.

She smiled as if he'd performed a miracle, and he closed his eyes in grateful relief before he helped her to sit, pulling her legs back into her chest. He didn't know how he knew what to do, but somewhere in the recesses of his mind, he remembered a woman assisting his mother as she labored to bring his little sister into the world. His mother had won the battle but had lost her life. That would not happen now. He wouldn't let it.

"Bettina?" Eva panted, interrupting his terrified train of thought. Her eyes were wide and worried. "Mario?" The fact that neither had returned was an alarming indication that the bombing had wreaked death and destruction in the streets, but Angelo had one goal, and he would worry about Mario when Eva was no longer in danger.

"I don't know, Eva. But I'm here. Everything will be okay," he soothed. The fear inside his belly was so great it had congealed into a massive rock, but he would be calm. He had found her, and she was having his child. He would be calm.

Eva smiled, just the smallest wisp of a smile, and she nodded, believing in him like she always had. Then her eyes filled with tears as the pain built again, making her chin sink to her chest and her back bow in protest.

"Tell me . . . ," she panted. "Tell me how you found me."

"I heard you were sent to Bergen-Belsen. After the Americans liberated Rome and then Paris, I went to France and began following the army up through the country, trying to find a way to get into Germany and up to you. I have been so frustrated. There were days I almost set out on my own, but Camillo always held me back."

"My father? What do you mean?"

"Camillo went to Austria and never came home. I knew I would never see you again if I wasn't prudent. Every time I wanted to rush in, it was like he stood at my shoulder, directing my paths."

"He was with me too. If it hadn't been for him, I would be in Bergen-Belsen now. I dreamed about him, and he told me you were with me. Inside me. I didn't understand what that meant until I found out I was pregnant."

"How did you end up here? In Belgium?" he asked, trying to distract her from the building agony. He sat at her back, letting her lean into his chest, turning her face into his neck as she tried to escape the waves of pressure.

"I jumped." She groaned out the words, tucking her face into him as she began to shake. "I jumped, and then I walked." She stopped talking then, speech too great a task, and he could only marvel at her words. She jumped. And then she walked.

Her contractions seemed to grow until there was no relief, no brief moments to regroup and quietly rest, and Eva began bearing down helplessly, her body demanding that she push. It was an onslaught, a blitz, and one hour grew into another and then another as the world beyond the shattered windows continued to burn, and the woman he loved begged for deliverance. Angelo moved her bed beside the fire and nailed blankets over the windows to keep out the worst of the cold and to block the light in case the German bombers returned, but conditions were far from favorable. Bettina had brought in plenty of boiled water, and Angelo kept the area as clean as he could and Eva as comfortable as he was able, when finally, as midnight neared, she reached the end.

A surge of blood-tinged water soaked the sheet beneath her as she groaned in agonized protest. She bore down, pushing and crying with an endurance born of love and little else. Angelo, on his knees before her, begged the Madonna for intercession, and a little baby boy, conceived in love and tribulation, came into the world on Christmas Day. The baby's cry broke the sacred stillness of the moment, his little arms and legs kicking in outrage as his father greeted him for the first time.

"It's a boy, Eva. It's a little boy," Angelo cried, overcome. In a bombed-out village, in a foreign land, a tiny leaf had appeared on a new branch, a new sun dawning on a day when so many sons had slipped away. Shaking and afraid of his own emotion, Angelo carefully laid the baby across Eva's sweat-stained chest and cut the cord that connected mother and child. Eva's smile was weak, but her breathing was deep and her face serene. She covered her son with a clean towel and searched his tiny face with glorious eyes.

"He is here, my little Angelo Camillo Rosselli Bianco."

Her baby stopped crying almost immediately and stared up into his mother's face with curious wonder, making Eva laugh even as her tears continued to fall, unabated. And then she started to sing, more a whisper than a song, and Angelo bent his head near hers to listen to the carol she'd sung exactly a year earlier in the cab of a delivery truck, wedged between Angelo and Monsignor O'Flaherty.

"Oh, my divine baby
I see you trembling here,
Oh, blessed God
Ah, how much it costs you,
Your loving me.
Ah, how much it costs you,
Your loving me.

Dear chosen one, little infant
This dire poverty makes me love you more
Since love made you poor now.
Since love made you poor now."

Angelo kissed the tears from Eva's face and tasted them on her lips. Love had not made them poor. Love had made them wealthy. In that moment, they were royalty, a king of fortune and a queen of destiny, embracing a tiny prince of peace. Angelo still had no idea where Eva had been, how she had ended up in a town called Bastogne in the middle of a firefight, but he'd found her.

He'd found her.

And there was no man on earth or angel in heaven who could convince him that miracles did not exist. For once, God had not been quiet.

CHAPTER 26

BASTOGNE

In the early hours of morning, Angelo and Eva heard the door downstairs being forcibly opened and feet clattered into the house, accompanied by shouting. Angelo, who had been dozing in a chair near Eva's bedside, was up and out of his chair instantly and hurrying to the door. He flung it open and moved out onto the landing.

"Mario!" he called, the relief heavy in his voice. "Up here. We're up here!"

Eva pulled her baby deeper into the blankets Angelo had laid over them, listening as boots pounded up the stairs, and Angelo laughed in sheer gratitude.

The men began talking at once, clapping each other on the back and reassuring each other they were both okay. Then Mario Sonnino was standing in the door, his face black with filth, his uniform splattered in blood and looking like it had survived a direct hit from an enemy bomb.

"Bettina—the woman who told me where to find you? She's safe. We couldn't get to you because there was debris as high as my head piled in front of the door. The building next to you took a direct hit, right through the roof. We had to wait for a bit. All hell was breaking loose outside, and none of us could stand out in the opening, clearing rubble," he explained. He shook his head as if trying to clear his vision, and he rubbed at his eyes wearily. He looked as if he couldn't quite believe what he was seeing.

"Hello, Mario," Eva said softly, and smiled at his awestruck face. He walked slowly to her bedside and knelt beside her with humble deference. Angelo followed him, his eyes on Eva, his mouth trembling with emotion.

"Meet Angelo Camillo Rosselli Bianco," she murmured, revealing her son's sleeping face. "Born on Christmas Day."

Mario just stared, dumbstruck. "How?" he finally uttered, his voice cracking on the word.

"When two people love each other very much," she said teasingly, "sometimes they have children."

"How?" he said again, looking up at Angelo, who just shook his head as if words failed him too. Angelo pressed the exhausted doctor into the chair he'd vacated and brought a clean cloth, a bar of soap, and a bucket of water to his side.

"Wash, Mario. And Eva can tell us the story."

She told them about Pierre, the boy from Bastogne, whose mother had convinced him to jump from the train bound for Bergen-Belsen. She told them how it felt to fly through the air with bullets whizzing around her, and how it felt when she realized she had done it—she had jumped and lived. She recounted finding the sign and realizing they were in Germany. And then she told them how she and Pierre had hid in a church for two days and drank water from the outdoor pump and ate sacrament wafers until the pastor had found them and fed them a real meal before sending them to the next town, clean and more appropriately clothed, with instructions to "find Father Hirsch."

Father Hirsch sent them to Father Gunther in Gustavsburg. Father Gunther sent them to Father Ackermann in Bingen. Father Ackermann sent them to Father Kuntz in Bengel. They walked or were smuggled toward Belgium, town after small town, relying on the integrity of the Catholic Church, which wasn't always reliable. One priest had warned them to avoid the priest in the next town, who was a Nazi sympathizer with a brother who served in a high position with the Reich.

When they had reached the border, they were loaded into the back of a cart, covered loosely in a plastic tarp, and manure was spread over them, piled high to disguise their hiding place. A German farmer hitched the cart to his mule and walked sedately across the boundary between Germany and Belgium with nobody saying a word. He took them to the outskirts of St. Vith, and from there they'd gone south, sleeping in the forest one night because they were too tired to walk the final stretch to Bastogne. It took them three weeks to go one hundred and fifty miles, and when they'd arrived, Eva had been sick for two months. After she missed her second period, she realized that her exhaustion and nausea weren't due to extreme stress and overexertion, but to pregnancy.

"And I have been here ever since," Eva finished, "hiding. There were still Germans in the area for a while, though not in large numbers."

"Where is Pierre now?" Angelo asked.

"Bettina and I made him leave when the town was evacuated. He's among friends."

"It's better that he did. I didn't know what I'd find when I came through those doors," Mario said. "Bombs were falling like rain. The aid station took a direct hit too. I was in the kitchen in the back. We keep the plasma in the fridge. It was little more than a glassed-in greenhouse. I was blown outward, through the glass. I landed in a snowbank. I have a few scratches. That's all. But the station caught fire. We pulled a few of the wounded out. The rest were buried by the rubble."

"You lost your glasses," Angelo observed.

"But that was all. That was all I lost. One of the nurses—Renee—is dead. She kept going back inside for the wounded. The last time she didn't come out."

"Another hero, created by war," Eva whispered. "Thank you, Mario."

Mario met her gaze.

"Thank you for finding me. Thank you for your friendship."

"Angelo never gave up hope, Eva. He was determined to find you," Mario said.

"He is a man of great faith," she murmured, and smiled at Angelo, whose eyes hadn't left her face through the whole long retelling of her journey to Bastogne.

"A man of great faith," Mario agreed.

◈

The day after Christmas, Patton's 3rd Army rolled into town, relieving the beleaguered 101st Airborne, who claimed with considerable braggadocio that they hadn't really needed the help. And maybe they hadn't. They'd been surrounded on all sides—those poor German bastards— and given easily as good as they got. But whether it was needed or just welcome, the battle in Bastogne ended, and in the following days, the front moved out and away as the bulge the Germans had created in the Allied line righted itself and the smoke cleared, allowing wounded GIs to be moved, supplies to be dropped, and the remains of the dead to be uncovered.

Mario reassured Angelo, after giving Eva and baby Angelo a rudimentary checkup, that he'd done just fine. Better than fine.

"You are a doctor in the making, Angelo," he said seriously, wrapping the squalling infant, who hadn't much liked the inspection. Eva took him, cooing and laughing at his outrage, and left the room to feed him. Angelo watched them go. He still hadn't lost the wonder. He still couldn't believe what had transpired. He turned to Mario and addressed the compliment.

"I actually considered it. But I don't want to be a doctor. I don't want anything more to do with death, my friend. Camillo always said we are on earth to learn. I think I want to teach. I want to teach history so that the world doesn't have to repeat her mistakes. Eva's journey across Germany has me convinced that there are many good German people too. They are just as afraid and damaged as the rest of us. Italians have no room to judge. Italians fought for Hitler too. Maybe people had no choice, but I wonder sometimes what would have happened if everyone without a choice had made a choice anyway. If we *all* chose not to participate. Not to be bullied. Not to take up arms. Not to persecute. What would happen then?"

Mario nodded. "We've all been at Hitler's mercy. I'm sure it's the same for many of the Germans. He and his minions have lied to the world, and no one will know the whole truth, no one will even be able to believe the truth, until the conflict is truly over."

"Hopefully, it won't be much longer," Angelo mused. He didn't know if he could bear leaving Eva again, but his division was pulling out, and he was obligated to go with them.

"Dr. Prior told General McAuliffe your story, Angelo. You and Eva will be going back to Rome just as soon as she and the baby are fit to travel," Mario said, smiling. Angelo sagged in relief and brought his face to his hands.

"Thank God. Will you be coming too?"

"I hope it won't be long until I can join you, but they won't let me leave yet. They need doctors too badly, and I volunteered. When I signed up, I committed to seeing this through to the end. This war is going to end sooner than later," Mario said. "And I want to see the truth for myself. I have to."

As the rubble and debris were cleared away from the collapsed aid station, one of the soldiers found a violin case—horribly scratched, dented, and white with ash—and looked it over, trying for a moment to figure out what he'd discovered. He managed to open the bent clasp and found that the violin inside was completely unscathed.

"Hey, doesn't that belong to Father Angelo?" someone shouted from below. The soldier shrugged and shut the clasp before passing it down to the man who'd spoken up. The soldier loped off to the reassembled aid station, knowing exactly where to find the priest who had carried a violin on his back for the last five months.

The day waned and the fires were lit, and as the 10th Armored Division and the 101st Airborne prepared to roll out on the morrow, sweet music lilted through the destroyed thoroughfare and soldiers stopped, cocking their heads to listen. A melody, haunting and pure, was coaxed into existence by a woman who hadn't held a violin in nine months, not since she'd played for a room full of German police and been exposed as a Jew.

Eva stood in the middle of the street, bundled against the cold, and played unceasingly, one piece after another, and the war-torn town was liberated again, freed by music, soothed by her song. It was her gift to the men who'd brought Angelo to her, to the everyday heroes of a never-ending war. Christmas hymns and lullabies, sonatas and symphonies, warmed the frigid air. The whispers began as some of the men realized who she was and started gathering around, making a loose circle in the town square.

"She's the girl Father Angelo was looking for."

"She escaped the Germans."

"He found her, here in Bastogne."

"It was her violin he was carrying!"

"It's a miracle."

With one awed whisper after another, the story of Eva and her violin spread through the crowd and down the streets. It trickled into the fields and among the soldiers who were halted, listening to the sweet tendril of music that filtered through the icy mist, and the Ghost Front became a little piece of paradise, if only for a little while.

Angelo watched Eva playing from an upstairs window in the apartment that overlooked the street, his son in his arms, his ears peeled, not wanting to miss a note. It *was* a miracle. There had been many, and before the war was over, there would be more. He lit a candle and watched it flicker, its light reflected in the cross that hung on the wall. And he listened to Eva play.

EPILOGUE

3 August 1955

Confession: August makes me think of Maremma.

*We've never been back to Grosseto or the beaches of Maremma. Maybe some-
day we will take our children there and show them the tide pools and let
them watch the pink flamingos. We will swim in the clear waters and gather
pinecones from the maritime pines that line the white beaches and climb the
craggy cliffs. But I don't know if I can.*

*Now we go to Cape Cod every August, joking that it is just a smaller
boot. We stay in a cabin, and we eat pasta and lobster, and I play my violin.
Angelo's skin turns black and his eyes look bluer than the ocean, while I do
my best not to burn or dwell on faraway places that linger in my mind like
endless long notes in the wind.*

*We look for pearls and steal kisses and sneak away to make love as if
we're teenagers in the abandoned fish shack all over again. August at the
seashore hurts me a little, but it is a sweet kind of pain, a necessary agony.
It is the anguish of existing, of feeling joy, when so many cannot. Sometimes*

I smell Babbo's pipe, and I hear Chopin from somewhere in the distance, as if Felix is reminding me of who I am.

I still dream of the train, as if my subconscious knows I never arrived. I jumped, cheating death, and still I'm forced to keep jumping. I hate those dreams and always wake with the stench of blood, urine, and gunpowder in my nostrils. Angelo never asks about the details. He knows. He just gathers me in his arms, and I bury my nose in the hollow of his throat, breathing him in and breathing fear out, because August makes me think of Auschwitz too.

Babbo left me in August. According to records, which the Germans kept with meticulous care, he was gassed the day he arrived at the camp. Most men over forty were, and Babbo was fifty-two. Uncle Augusto and Aunt Bianca were gassed shortly after their arrival at Auschwitz too. Levi and Claudia made it through the initial selection but were given the option of riding in a truck to the camp, which they were told was ten kilometers away. This was a lie told to further weed out the "lazy." They were gassed alongside their parents. Of the roughly twelve hundred Jews deported from Rome in the October roundup that the Sonninos and I narrowly escaped, over eight hundred were immediately gassed. Of those who were admitted into the camp, one woman and forty-seven men survived. Forty-eight people out of twelve hundred.

Pierre's mother, Gabriele LaMont, didn't survive that final winter in Bergen-Belsen, though she held on for eight months, which was almost unheard of. My son and I would not have survived that long. I doubt my baby would have survived my womb. Sixty thousand prisoners were interned there by the end of the war, and typhus was rampant. Bergen-Belsen was liberated by the British in April 1945, giving the world its first real glimpse of the horrors that no one had believed possible. I made myself look at the photographs. I owed it to those who didn't have a white angel to hide them, those who hadn't found the strength or opportunity to jump, and those who hadn't been able to hold on.

Angelo and I didn't stay in Italy, though we went back to Florence for a time after the war. We were married in a small ceremony—non-denominational, though we added our own defiant touches. I am still a Jew and Angelo is still a priest. Those are things that cannot be undone, nor would we want them to be. But he is laicized—unable to perform holy ordinations—and our marriage is not recognized by the Catholic Church. But I think it is recognized by God, and that's good enough for me. No one calls him Father anymore . . . except our four children, and they usually call him Babbo. It is Italian for "Daddy," and we are italiani after all. We always will be.

Santino and Fabia wanted us to stay with them in Florence. They wanted to love our children and love us. They wanted to be a family again. After all, the villa was our home, a home they returned to me after the war. But there are some hurts and some memories that are better laid to rest, better left to the mellow patina of photographs and selective remembrance. We needed to make a life together beyond the shadow of war, beyond the dictates of our pasts, and beyond the whispers and speculation of those who thought they knew us.

We stayed in Florence until little Angelo was two and Felix Otto—our second son—was six months old. The twins were born in America, two little boys we named Fabio and Santino, a nod to their great-grandparents, who had decided if they couldn't convince us to stay in Italy, they would join us in America.

The years have been kind, and I am teaching my children to play the violin, insisting on long notes and scales, making them read the dots and count the lines, reminding them that music is something no one can take from them. They are undisciplined, much like I was, but when they play, I hear my life and the life of my family lifting off the strings, just like Uncle Felix said it would.

Angelo teaches history and theology at a small college in upstate New York. He is Professor Bianco now, and the title suits him. He knows more about religion than any man I know, yet he still has a million questions.

I just smile and shake my head when he gets tangled in dogma and disillusioned by doctrine.

"There are two things I know for sure, Angelo Bianco," I tell him, just like I've told him a dozen times before, and he always pretends not to know what I'm going to say.

"Tell me," he says. "What do you know?"

"No one knows the nature of God," I insist, holding up a finger.

"What else?" he asks, with a twinkle in his eyes. I point my finger toward him and shake it, as if I'm scolding him like a good Italian wife should. But my voice is tender.

"I love you. I have always loved you, and I will always love you."

"That is enough for me, my wise and devious wife," he whispers, and he wraps his arms around me so fiercely that I can barely breathe.

It is enough for me too.

      Batsheva Rosselli-Bianco

AUTHOR'S NOTE

I have long been fascinated with World War II, but I never thought I would be able to write a book set in the time period, simply because of the vastness of the topic and the enormity of the task. When I stumbled upon an article about Italy's Jews being hidden by members of the Catholic clergy, I was intrigued and dug deeper. And deeper. And I started to believe that there was a special story for me to tell. My prayer is that the people of today will know the past so they won't repeat it.

The historical setting and the events that Eva and Angelo find themselves immersed in are all factual. The gold that was extorted from the Jews in Rome—and then simply left at the Via Tasso when the Germans left Rome—the massacre at the Ardeatine Caves, the round-ups in cities throughout Italy, as well as the experiences of those hiding in convents and monasteries, were based on actual events. Many priests, monks, nuns, and so many regular Italian citizens risked everything for the sake of others, and I was truly awed and touched by the sacrifice and courage of so many. It was a terrible time, but the silver lining was the revelation of such goodness and heroism. For me, the horror was eclipsed by the stories of bravery and valor. Eighty percent of Italy's Jews survived the war, a marked contrast to the eighty percent of Europe's Jews who did not.

As with most historical fiction, Eva and Angelo were not real, but they interact with people who were. Jake Prior was an actual American doctor who worked the aid station in Bastogne during the Battle of the Bulge. I thought about changing his name, but then thought how lovely it is to give credit, even through the use of a name, when I can. Pietro Caruso, Rome's Chief of Police; Peter Koch, head of a violent Fascist squad in Rome; as well as Lieutenant Colonel Herbert Kappler, head of the Gestapo in Rome, were actual people. The Irish priest, Monsignor Hugh O'Flaherty, was a true hero, working from the Vatican to rescue and aid up to sixty-five hundred people in and around Rome during the war. Rabbi Nathan Cassuto was the spiritual leader of the Jews in Florence in 1943, when the Germans occupied Italy. His story both inspired and haunted me. He showed incredible leadership and courage and survived Auschwitz only to die in February of 1945 in a forced death march at the hands of his captors. He was thirty-six years old when he died, and showed more fortitude, grace, and strength in his young life than most will ever exhibit. I dedicated the book to him.

The world owes a debt of gratitude to people like Monsignor O'Flaherty and Rabbi Cassuto, but I owe them too, for inspiring me and guiding me through the telling of *From Sand and Ash*. I did my best to represent the Jewish and Catholic religions and people with love and respect. Any mistakes I've made or inaccuracies in practices or positions are my own and were done inadvertently.

In addition, I know history can be murky and accounts can be muddied. My wish was not to condemn or to vilify, nor was it to exaggerate, but I did not invent the atrocities in this book. Sadly, every atrocity cited and used was based on true events and actual accounts.

I want to extend special thanks to Father John Bartunek for helping me to fall in love with Florence, art, and Catholicism. I am grateful for his generous time and attention, for his passion for his calling, and for sharing Donatello's Saint George with me. I know I didn't quite capture the essence of being a worthy and committed priest, dedicated to the work and to the calling, but I believe Father John understands it full well, and I am grateful for his time and friendship.

Thank you, Karey White—my personal editor and friend. I am grateful for your honesty and integrity and for your belief in me and my books.

Tamara Bianco—the best personal assistant in the history of assistants. There is nothing you can't do, but this book needed you more than most. Thank you for your help with the language issues, and thanks to Simone Bianco as well, for use of his last name and for his help with all things Italian.

For Jane Dystel and the folks at Dystel and Goderich, I always feel like you have my back. Thank you for that. For the people at Lake Union Publishing, for loving my book and believing in this story. Thanks to Jodi Warshaw, Jenna Free, and so many others who worked to make this book a success.

And, finally, I'm so thankful for my husband, who never seems to doubt my abilities, and for my children, who have to put up with having a mother with her head in the clouds or immersed in history. My husband, children, parents, siblings, and family are the best parts of my life. Thank you for loving me and believing in me.

Like Angelo, I believe that God *is* quiet. But he is not blind or impartial in the affairs of man. I don't know his mysteries, and like Eva, I'm not convinced anyone does. But I am grateful to know him to the extent that I do, to feel his love and influence in my life, and to walk quietly with him as best I can.

ABOUT THE AUTHOR

Amy Harmon is a *New York Times, Wall Street Journal,* and *USA Today* bestselling author of ten novels, including the Whitney Award–winning *The Law of Moses.* Her historical novels, inspirational romances, and young adult books are now being published in twelve countries around the globe.